The Silver Trumpet

An Adventure

Simon Weir

ISBN-13: 978-1492969433

For Emily

Contents

Prologue

Dear Dad. Everything is fine in the new house. Today I saved the world.

Penelope Oaks sat in the living room, looked at the last words she'd typed and shook her head. That wasn't quite right.

Today I saved two worlds.

That didn't cover it either. And it would make her father think she was completely crazy when he got the email. How could she explain it? Her father was away at sea, the navigator on a cargo ship. Emails were the easiest way to communicate with him.

Today Frank and I saved two worlds.

No, that was even worse. Though Penny supposed he'd be pleased to learn that she was getting on with her step-brother at last. She deleted the sentence, sat back in her chair and glowered at the screen. Why wouldn't the right words come? Then her step-mother Maggie called from the kitchen – supper was ready. Sighing, Penny put the laptop on the coffee table and left the room, switching off the light as she went.

It was silent in the living room now, and dark – the only hint of light was the ghostly glow of the laptop's screen. Then something stirred in the shadows. Approached the computer. Before the screensaver could plunge the room into total blackness, something reached out of the shadows and slowly, carefully tapped the keys, signing the mail.

Dear Dad. Everything is fine in the new house. Penny

Something clicked on "send" and chuckled.

Nobody could know.

Book One
The Secret Letters

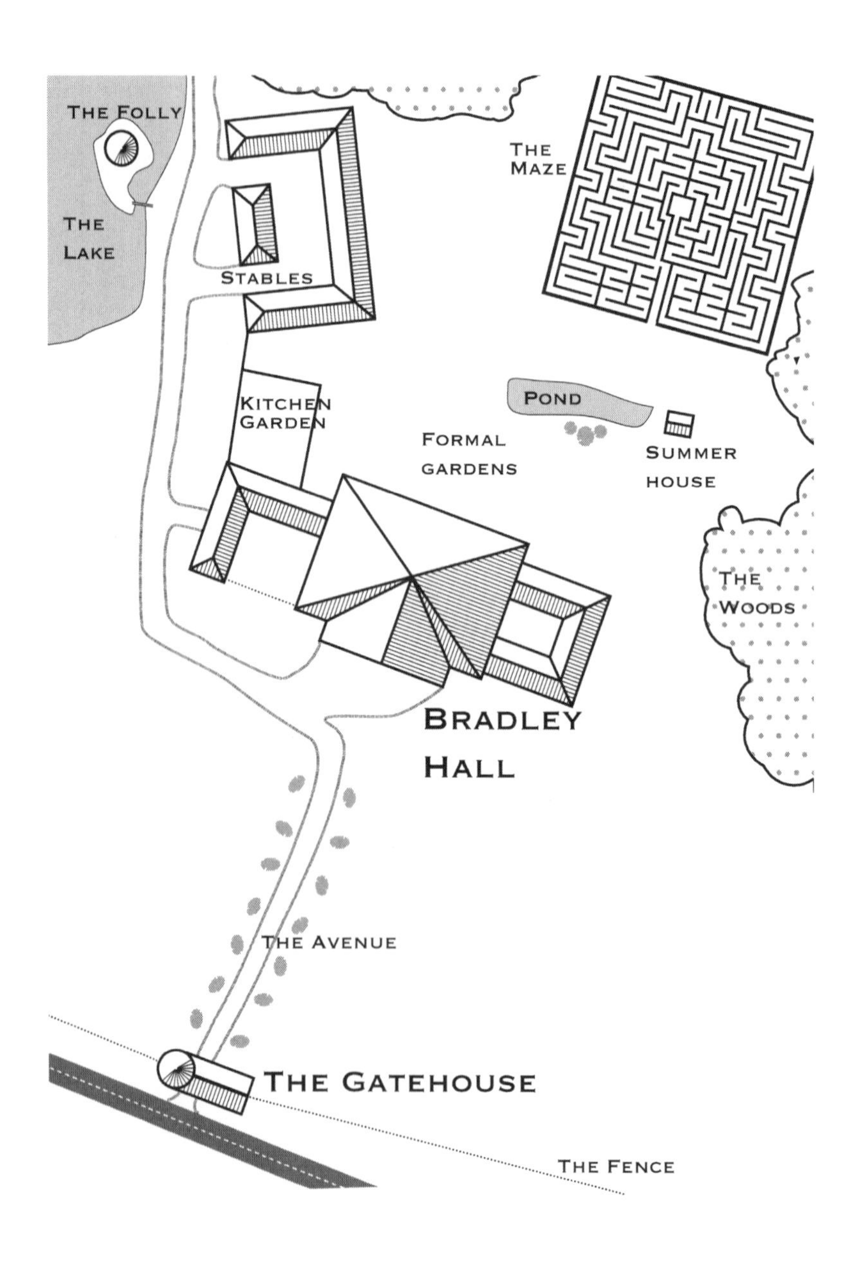
THE FOLLY
THE LAKE
STABLES
THE MAZE
KITCHEN GARDEN
POND
FORMAL GARDENS
SUMMER HOUSE
THE WOODS
BRADLEY HALL
THE AVENUE
THE GATEHOUSE
THE FENCE

Chapter One

The First Note

It all began with the letters. Penelope Oaks received the first one the day after her father went back to sea. It was there when she woke up in her new room in that strange old house, with its wood-panelled walls and its cold, musty smell. Waking up there for the first time was strange and a little bit scary. But even as she lay there, huddled under the covers for warmth, there was no way Penny could have guessed that life in the Little House was about to get a lot stranger and an awful lot scarier.

She shivered and stretched. Penny had tried going back to sleep, putting off the moment when she'd have to get up and face the first day of her new life in her new house. But it was no good. She was awake now and she was hungry, so she switched on her bedside light and got out of bed. And froze.

Her bags were by the door. Neatly packed. Her books were stacked up beside them. Everything she owned apart from the pyjamas she was wearing had been gathered up and packed away. It was as if she was ready to move out of the room – not as if she'd only just moved in the afternoon before. Balanced on top of the pile of her belongings was a sheet of yellowy paper.

Cautiously, Penny took two steps across the rug to get a better look. She reached out her hand then drew it back. The paper looked thick and very old, yellowish and slightly greasy. She didn't want to touch it. There were three words written on it. Like a threat. They were scrawled in thick black ink in large, old-fashioned handwriting:

GOODBYE LITTLE GIRL

For a whole minute Penny just stood there, staring. It felt like icy spiders were crawling all over her skin. Her mind was blank. This made no sense but something about it was scary. She felt…

she couldn't have put it into words. Just a sense of wrongness. Someone had been in her room while she was asleep. Touching her things. Packing her things. Telling her to leave.

Then Penny laughed. It was a short, bitter laugh that sounded more like a cough or a gun shot. It was a laugh that didn't have any humour in it. The Revolting Frank, she thought. It had to be his idea of a practical joke: welcome to your new home and let me see if I can scare you.

Grabbing the paper, she screwed it into a ball and threw it at the bin in the corner of the room. She briefly wondered where Frank had learnt to write like that, but then the thought fled as she got on with the job at hand. Bags opened, clothes unpacked, books back on the shelf: in three minutes everything was where it should be. She nodded to herself as she left the room. Maybe she could get a lock for her door.

"Funny joke," Penny said to the Revolting Frank when she walked into the kitchen. He was stuffing toast into his mouth and getting chocolate spread all over his pasty face.

"What? I haven't done anything," he said, spitting crumbs. He sounded so surprised that for a second Penny almost believed him. But then she shook her head. He's a liar, she thought. She gave him an angry stare, which he returned in silence.

"Now look," Maggie turned round from the sink, instantly picking up on the atmosphere. "We need to settle in without you two fighting all the time. It is going to be odd at first, not knowing anyone round here. But you both start the new school in two weeks. Until then, especially when I'm working at the Big House, it'll just be the two of you. So you'll have to get on. No nonsense – got it?"

The children glared at each other for a second longer, neither wanting to be the first to look away. "I said, have you got it?" demanded Maggie, with a real edge to her words. One thing they both knew – when Maggie used The Voice, they'd better listen. Sullenly, both nodded. Breakfast was eaten in silence.

Penny refused to think of Frank as her step-brother. He was

just Maggie's son as far as she was concerned. She didn't even regard Maggie as her step-mother, really – just as her dad's wife. Her real mother had died when Penny was a baby but she'd never thought it was sad: that was just the way things were. Which had been fine, when it was just her and her dad. But then he'd met Maggie and everything had changed. Marrying her had been bad enough – but now he'd gone away to sea and they'd come here.

The Little House wasn't like anywhere Penny had ever been before and she had to admit it was kind of cool, in a slightly creepy way. For more than ten years – which was almost her entire life – she'd lived in a one-room flat near the seafront with her dad. After the wedding, they'd all moved into Maggie's terraced house with two rooms upstairs and two downstairs and no front garden. For the past three awful months Penny had been made to share a bedroom with the Revolting Frank. Those had been little houses. This wasn't. It looked like a miniature castle.

"It's the gatehouse for Bradley Hall," Maggie had explained when they arrived. "Years ago the Big House – which is the hall – had a lot of staff. There were servants who stayed here just to open the gates for the carriages. I think it's nicer to call it the Little House, not the gatehouse. It's where we're going to live."

Penny had stared at the Little House, amazed. It was built of old, grey stone but there was no way to walk round it to get a better look, because tall iron railings were set into the walls on both sides. The left part of the gatehouse was a tower five floors high and topped with a pointed grey slate roof like an upturned ice-cream cone. Beside that was an archway almost as tall and wide as the whole of Maggie's old house, through which a yellow gravel drive passed, barred by ornate iron gates. On the right of the archway was the actual house part. It was square, three storeys tall, with battlements at the top and a straggly rosebush growing up the wall beside its green wooden door.

When Maggie had led the way in, the Revolting Frank tried to push past her even before she'd taken the key from the door. Penny had followed quietly into a dry, cool, dusty hall with black-

and-white tiles on the floor. For a moment, she'd thought she had seen some kind of animal scampering away up the wooden stairs that faced her, but when she'd blinked and looked again there was nothing. Must have been a trick of the light.

Maggie had gently squeezed the girl's shoulder. "Go on, Penny," she'd said. "Say something."

Without thinking, Penny had whispered, "I wish my dad could see it."

"He's seen it already, doofus," the Revolting Frank had sneered. "Richard came out here last week, remember?" The boy had grinned horribly at her, even though his mother had given him A Look.

Maggie had patted Penny's shoulder again. "Come on, Penny," she'd said. "Let's go and find your room."

"I want to be in the tower," the Revolting Frank had shouted. "Can I? Can I?" Just because he was ten months older, he thought he should get first choice of everything. And it seemed to Penny that just because he was Maggie's son, he got it most of the time.

"The tower's not really part of the Little House," Maggie had explained. "It's just store rooms. And I want to make it clear right now that it's out of bounds. Got it?" She'd said that in The Voice – which meant there was no arguing.

They'd climbed the stairs in silence. Maggie had already chosen one of the rooms on the middle floor, but there were three rooms at the top of the Little House – a bathroom and two bedrooms. Penny's room was opposite Frank's, though it wasn't as big. But she didn't mind – it was her room and she'd never have to share with Frank again. Besides, it was above the archway so it had a brilliant view of Bradley Hall. The gravel driveway emerged directly beneath her windows and from the back of the Little House it ran between two lines of tall trees, straight as an arrow, all the way to the distant hall. Which was huge and looked like something from a film.

But then, so did the Little House. There were grey-stone fireplaces in every room and the walls were all made of stone or panels of old, dark wood. Most of the wooden panels had strange carvings on them – each one looked like it could be a secret door, if only Penny could figure out how to open it. The windows were made of lots of small panes of glass and most of them let a draught in, so all the rooms were a little bit cold. The whole place was ever so slightly creepy, like the set of a horror movie. Even the brightly lit kitchen was more intimidating than inviting.

Penny wolfed down her cereal and quickly washed her bowl. The Revolting Frank was still eating – demolishing another piece of toast and chocolate spread. The girl hurried up the stairs to her room but when she went to open the door, it wouldn't budge. For a second she thought about calling Maggie, but no... Penny put her shoulder to the door and pushed. It moved an bit, then stuck again.

Kneeling down, Penny put her eye to the gap that had opened between the door and the frame. She couldn't see what was stopping the door moving. From below, she could hear the Revolting Frank starting to climb the wooden stairs. She didn't want him to find her here like this. Standing, she took a step back and threw herself at the door. It burst open halfway and she staggered into her room.

And wished she hadn't. All her things were packed up, piled behind the door. Penny went cold all over. What was going on?

Chapter Two

Packing

Goose-bumps rose on Penny's arms. Her mouth was dry and she felt sick as she stared at the pile of her belongings. Her head was spinning. Had some sort of ghost had been in her room? She stood up straight and brushed a strand of long blonde hair out of her eyes, tucking it behind her ear. She could hear the

Revolting Frank stomping up the stairs, getting closer, so she hurriedly shut the door before he could see into her room. She had to think about this.

She knew with icy certainty that the Revolting Frank couldn't have done this – he'd been in the kitchen the whole time. So had Maggie. Besides, nobody could have piled the stuff up behind the door and then left the room. It didn't make sense. Yet all her things had been packed up, just like before. Bags stuffed with clothes. Books stacked beside them. Well, she guessed that's where the books had been – they were scattered all over the floor now, after she'd forced the door open. She shivered.

For a long moment, Penny just stood there. She didn't know what to think. How had her things been packed again? It just didn't make any sense. After a minute in which she couldn't figure out what was happening she gave up and decided to focus on what she could do: which was tidy up. Taking a deep breath, trying to stay calm, Penny set about unpacking her few belongings. Again. The first job was to pick the books off the floor and put them back on the shelf.

That's when she found the second letter. It must have been balanced on top of the books, only to have gone flying when she knocked everything over by forcing her way into the room. When she picked up a hard-back about the Vikings, she found another sheet of the thick, slightly greasy, yellowish paper lying face down on the floor. Its surface was rough when she picked it up and it smelt faintly of cinnamon and wood bark. There was more of the thick, old-fashioned writing.

YOU HAVE TO GO AWAY. PLEASE. YOU AREN'T SAFE HERE!

Without meaning to, Penny sank to her knees on the floor as she read it. She was shaking. Why wouldn't she be safe in the Little House? Apart from the fact that someone was able to get into and out of her room, packing her things up?

Yet even as fear sank its claws into her stomach, a stubborn spark ignited in her chest. This was meant to be her new home. Her dad had come and picked it for her – why should she go away? If she left, how would he find her when he came back from sea? Never mind how she was supposed to do leave, anyway... Somewhere deep inside her, Penny's resolve stiffened. She wasn't going to let anything scare her away.

But she was scared. Terrified, in fact. No denying that. She dropped the piece of paper and stood unsteadily, feeling lightheaded. She waited while her heart slowly stopped racing. Even when she felt steadier on her feet and more in control she just stood in the middle of the room, not sure what to do – a tall blonde girl frozen like a statue.

Then she made a decision. She ran out of the room and dashed down the stairs, almost bumping into Maggie on the first-floor landing. Her step-mother was carrying an empty laundry basket. "Woah! Slow down Penny," she laughed – then she looked at the girl again. "Penny? Are you alright? You're as white as a sheet, love."

"You have to come, Maggie. Right now. Please. You have to come and see this," she grabbed hold of the woman's arm and started pulling her towards the stairs.

"Alright, alright!" Maggie was trying to smile. "Stop dragging me. I'm coming."

They hurried up to the top floor and Penny threw the door to her room open. "Look!" she said.

Maggie peered through the door, then walked in, looking slowly from side to side. "What am I looking at, exactly?" she asked. "I see you've done a good job of making your bed. Thank you. It's all very neat."

Penny stood in the doorway, jaw slack. Everything was wrong. Well, it wasn't wrong – everything was exactly right. Where it was supposed to be. Tidy. And that wasn't right. She'd left her bags on the floor still stuffed with clothes, half the books still scattered across the rug. And the letter. The mysterious yellow letter…

…Gone.

Not a trace of it. Frantically, she stared around the room, trying to will the note to appear, to reveal itself. It had been there just seconds ago. The room had been a mess just a few seconds ago. How had everything been put away so fast? Where had the letter disappeared to? Who could have done this?

Penny realised her step-mother was looking at her oddly. She shivered, then tried to conceal her panic. What could she say? Maggie would think she'd gone mad if she explained what had happened. Penny looked up and tried to smile. "I thought you'd like how I'd tidied up," she said weakly.

"Penelope." Uh-oh. This wasn't a good sign. Maggie only called her Penelope when she was cross. "I am delighted at how tidy your room is. But I don't think you needed to drag me up here as if it was on fire, do you?"

Penny shook her head and looked at the carpet. This was probably not the time to get defiant and argue. Especially if she was going to want her step-mother's help.

Maggie hesitated, then patted her on the sholder. "Look, it's alright," she said in a softer voice. "I know it's exciting getting your own room. I'm glad you're proud of it. But remember, I have a lot of jobs to do. We haven't even been here for a whole day yet and I still have lots to unpack and the rest of the house to get straight. I'm not asking you to pitch in today, but I would like you to let me get on with it – okay?"

Penny nodded. She looked up and tried a smile. "Right," said Maggie briskly, another problem sorted out to her satisfaction. "I'll go and get on with my jobs, then."

When she was alone again, the girl sat on her bed and tried to think. She knew she couldn't tell Maggie her room was haunted by a ghost that packed bags and wrote letters, then tidied up again. Her step-mother would just get cross with her for being silly and would probably assume Penny was making it up to be difficult or to get attention.

Besides, when she thought about it, Penny didn't really believe in ghosts – and even if they were real she didn't think they went round writing letters. If a ghost wanted to scare you, it would just come out and scare you. So if it wasn't a ghost, who could have done it? And where had they come from?

She got up and slowly checked every inch of her room, tapping the walls and looking for hidden doors. But as far as she could tell all the wooden panels were solid and none of them moved. The ceiling appeared to be totally solid and lacking in hatches. She even rolled back the rug and checked the floorboards – no trapdoor there. One of the windows did open, but only a few inches – nothing bigger than a sparrow or maybe a really skinny pigeon could have got through the gap. It didn't make sense. The only way in or out was through the door.

Penny got dressed quickly, swapping her pyjamas for her favourite jeans and hoodie. As she did, she made a decision. No matter what happened, she wasn't going to be scared away. She promised herself she'd be brave. She wasn't going to let herself be frightened by the mysterious letter writer.

No, she was going to catch them. She began to make a plan.

She stayed in her room for about two hours, trying to be quiet in the hope that whoever had packed her stuff might try to come back – though she knew it was a long shot. Penny gave up on hiding pretty quickly. For one thing, it was boring just sitting in the bottom of her wardrobe, but mostly she simply thought it didn't have much going for it as a plan. She decided that whoever had packed and then unpacked her stuff must have some way of knowing when she was in her room.

She needed to find some way to trap her mysterious visitor. The trouble was, she had nothing with which to make a trap. No spring-loaded nets, no cages – not even any string or a good sized box to drop on an unsuspecting head. And she didn't want to leave the room to get anything, giving them a chance to sneak in.

So Penny decided to be difficult. She got all the clothes

out of her wardrobe. Suddenly she wished she was more like the girls in her old school who had loads of trendy clothes. But she thought she had enough. Tying each garment together, she formed a long, rough rope. She took the quilt cover, sheet and pillow case off the bed and tied them up as well. Carefully she wound it all round the top corner of the wardrobe and the leg of the bed, tying it onto the back of her chair. She spread her books across the floor like slippery, papery tiles. Then Penny left the room with her bags, which she put in the bathroom.

Just as Penny's foot touched the bottom step the stairwell echoed with a slightly muffled bang from the top floor. That was it – her chair had fallen over. Her trap had worked! She turned and bounded up the stairs: time to see what she had caught.

Chapter Three

Ribaldane

Penny couldn't believe her eyes. She flung open the door to her room, panting heavily. As she'd run up the stairs, she'd known what she was expecting to see: some kind of stranger, struggling in a tangle of tied-together clothes and bedding, slipping about on a pile of loose books. Maybe trapped beneath the chair from her desk. She definitely wasn't expecting what she actually saw.

All her bags. Neatly packed and standing in the centre of the rug. All the books, neatly stacked in a pile beside them. The bed perfectly made. The chair tucked in tidily at the small desk in the corner of the room. The whole bedroom immaculate. And on top of the bags, another letter on the greasy yellow parchment.

PLEASE LET ME HELP YOU. GO NOW! HURRY!

Tucking her hair behind her ear, Penny smiled to herself. She knew she should have been frightened – not just be the escape of her sinister visitor, but also by the remarkable speed with which the tangle of clothes she'd spent an hour or more creating had been packed away. Yet for some reason she was actually starting to feel strangely reassured. This letter sounded almost friendly, but also a bit nervous. Compared with the terse threat of the first message, this one seemed almost desperate to do her some kind of favour.

Slowly, she unpacked again. All the clothes had been beautifully folded – you'd never have known that she'd screwed them up and tied them together. Stacking all books back on her shelf, she nodded to herself. Maybe a different approach was needed. If traps didn't work and confrontation wasn't possible (how can you confront someone who won't show themselves?) maybe she should try negotiation. Penny took one of her pencils and a piece of paper, then wrote a letter of her own.

Please don't pack my things again. Talk to me. Tell me who you are and why you think I should go.

She hesitated, then added:
Can we be friends?

She left her letter on top of the bag, slid it under the bed, then went downstairs. She decided to spend a while out of her room. Maggie was about to put a DVD on for the Revolting Frank to watch, because it had started to rain outside and he'd had to come in. It was a good movie, but Frank just made fun of it all the way through, trying to spoil it. When it was over, Penny rushed upstairs again. Her things weren't packed this time. But there was another letter – lying on her bed.

WE CANNOT TALK. YOU WOULDN'T BELIEVE IN ME. IT IS NOT SAFE TO STAY. PLEASE TRUST ME. I WOULD HAVE LIKED TO BE YOUR FRIEND.

This was the most curious message yet. What did that mean: "you wouldn't believe in me"? She couldn't make sense of it, but Penny definitely wasn't scared now – she was intrigued. It felt like she'd stumbled onto a mystery that only she could solve. If she could just figure out what was going on. She was quietly excited, fascinated by the identity of her mysterious visitor. She turned the letter over and grabbed a pencil to write another reply, trying really hard to make it sound friendly.

We could be friends. My name is Penelope but you can call me Penny. Please tell me your name. Don't be shy. I'd like to meet you. But you must tell me why you think it isn't safe here.

Whoever was leaving the notes clearly didn't like coming out when she was in the room, so she ran downstairs again. Maggie was making sandwiches for lunch, so Penny laid the table. After they'd eaten – Frank with his mouth open half the time – the children had to help tidy the kitchen before Penny could go back to her room. As she'd hoped, there was another letter.

IT IS NOT SHYNESS THAT KEEPS ME HIDDEN – I WOULD GET IN TROUBLE IF WE MET. IT IS FORBIDDEN. HUMANS MUST NOT SEE US. IT IS NOT SAFE FOR YOU HERE BECAUSE NOT ALL OF MY KIND ARE SO FRIENDLY TO YOUR KIND. IF THE OTHERS WERE TO LEARN OF YOU... BUT I HAVE SAID TOO MUCH. MY NAME IS RIBALDANE.
I WISH I COULD BE YOUR FRIEND, BUT I DARE NOT EXPOSE YOU TO MORE DANGER.

For a long time, Penny stared at this letter, reading it again and again. The whole situation was making less and less sense. What on earth did it mean? "My kind" and "your kind" and "Humans must not see us"? It was the babblings of a crazy person.

And what kind of name was Ribaldane, anyway? Penny looked at it hard, trying to find the best way to pronounce it. In the end she decided it was Rib-all-day-ne. She turned it round and round in her head, mouthing it silently. Ribaldane. Ribaldane! What kind of name was that, anyway?

Penny hesitated. She didn't know that she wanted to talk to this strange person now. But she didn't want to keep finding her things being packed up either. She didn't want them to keep coming into her room. Certainly not while she was asleep. But she wasn't sure she liked the sound of them. Except… Ribaldane said he wished he could be her friend.

Actually, was Ribaldane a "he"? Penny couldn't tell from the name. She didn't think a girl would sneak into someone's room and leave them notes – but she couldn't be sure. She didn't think she really wanted anything to do with him. She spent a long time thinking, then decided to leave another letter.

Dear Ribaldane. I'm sure you mean well but I have to stay here. I will be safe, I promise. Please don't keep don't keep coming into my room

Feeling a little sad, Penny left the note on top of her bed and wandered downstairs. It was raining outside, Frank was watching football in the living room and Maggie was arranging her collection of sprays, dusters and clothes pegs in the under-stairs cupboard. Penny looked at her watch. She'd been gone three minutes – which should have been plenty of time for Ribaldane to reply if he wanted. She went back to her room. Sure enough, there was another letter there, propped up against the light on the bedside table.

MY DEAR PENNY,

OF COURSE I SHALL RESPECT YOUR WISHES. IN FUTURE IF WE NEED TO PASS MESSAGES LET US POST

THEM THROUGH THE PANES.

I WISH I COULD PERSUADE YOU TO FLEE, BUT IF NOT THEN I MUST BEG YOU TO BE CAREFUL. I SHALL DO WHAT LITTLE I CAN TO PROTECT YOU, BUT THERE ARE THOSE AMONG MY KIND WHO WOULD SEEK TO TRICK YOU OR TRAP YOU OR USE YOU FOR THEIR OWN ENDS IF THEY KNEW YOU WERE HERE.

KNOW THAT I TRULY HAVE YOUR BEST INTERESTS AT HEART. IF EVER YOU NEED MY HELP, YOU HAVE ONLY TO ASK. IF THERE IS ANYTHING YOU WISH TO KNOW, YOU HAVE ONLY TO ENQUIRE.

YOUR FRIEND - RIBALDANE

PS. STAY AWAY FROM THE ISLAND!

Penny felt relieved. There was something curiously formal about this letter – it made her think of a kindly old uncle (not that she had any uncles, old or otherwise). And Ribaldane said he wouldn't come into her room again. Which was good.

But there was plenty there that made no sense to her. What was his "kind" and how or why would they want to trick or trap her if they knew she was in the Little House? Penny still had a slightly nervous feeling that the only unsafe person she'd encountered in her life was the mysterious Ribaldane.

And yet… he'd got her attention. Everything that had happened was so strange it was frightening – but it was also fascinating. And the warmth of this letter appealed to her. She liked the way Ribaldane had offered to help her and to tell her things. His offer to "protect" her was reassuring. She found that, in spite herself, she wanted to trust him. Maybe it was the rich scent of cinnamon on the paper, maybe it was the sad but friendly words. Even if they didn't make any sense.

Penny realised she'd gone from being scared of Ribaldane to being angry with him to, maybe, nearly liking him. Well, to being curious about him now, certainly. She was all alone apart from the Revolting Frank – but here was Ribaldane was offering to be her friend. Should she trust him? She took up her pencil to write him one more reply.

Dear Ribaldane. Thank you for your letter, though it doesn't really make much sense to me. Please tell me more about your kind. Help me understand why you're worried. Please can we meet. Your Friend - Penny

But what was she supposed to do with the letter? She'd told Ribaldane not to come into her room – but how was he supposed to get her message?

Tap. Tap-Tap-Tap. Tap. Penny nearly jumped out of her skin. She turned to the window that faced Bradley Hall. Standing on the ledge outside was a scruffy jackdaw, regarding her with a bright black eye. It was dark grey with a black mask around its eyes, like a robber. It seemed to wait until it was sure it had her attention, then it hit the window again with its beak. Tap. Then it nodded its head at the paper in Penny's hand, before [illegible] her straight in the eye again.

Slowly, nervously, Penny stood and took a step towards the bird. The jackdaw seemed to nod its black-hooded head. It was standing beside the one window that opened. Was this what Ribaldane had meant about posting messages through the panes? Penny walked over and, with a shaking hand, reached up to unfasten the window. The jackdaw didn't fly away. It just stared at her and nodded. Cautiously, she opened the window a crack.

As soon as the corner of the sheet of paper passed through the window, the jackdaw grabbed it in its beak. It tugged it free from Penny's fingers, pulling it through the window with a shake of the head. The bird sprang from the ledge and flapped its way into the wind, following the line of tall trees towards the Big House. The girl was stunned. As she watched the jackdaw disappear, she shivered.

So when he wasn't letting himself into her room, Ribaldane could get birds to carry messages for him. And he was somewhere in the direction of Bradley Hall. Despite the trickle of ice running down her spine, Penny was suddenly desperate to find out what he would tell her about "his kind".

Chapter Four

Bradley Hall

Penny woke with a start. Her first was that she'd caught him sneaking into her room again, Ribaldane. Despite his promise. But as she rubbed her eyes she realised the noise that had woken her was just the Revolting Frank, shouting from the landing outside Penny's bedroom door. She gave a little growl as she kicked off the covers, annoyed with Frank – but also annoyed with herself for doubting Ribaldane.

Bleary eyed and dopey with sleep, Penny put on her dressing gown and went to the bathroom, then shambled grumpily downstairs. It was chilly in the Little House. Maggie was fussing round the kitchen. Frank was already stuffing himself with toast and chocolate spread, getting it all over his face as usual. Penny sat down and tried to go unnoticed, though the way Maggie dropped a plate with a piece of toast in front of her showed she hadn't managed it.

"I need you to eat up and get dressed quickly," Penny's stepmother said as she returned to the sink, where she was washing up. "I know it's Saturday but I said I'd go up to the Big House this morning. Also, it'll mean I can introduce you to the professor. He'll tell you where you can go in the grounds."

Frank started babbling excitedly, though he didn't stop eating. He was a large boy for his age, pale and fleshy with blond hair that was just a shade lighter than Penny's. Strangers sometimes thought they were a proper brother and sister, which irritated both of them. Penny watched in horror as crumbs flew from his mouth, half-eaten toast churning up and down as he gabbled on. Watching Frank eat was something she never got used to. She shuddered and looked away, trying to ignore him while she ate her own toast in silence.

Penny waited until the Revolting Frank had left the table before she spoke. "Maggie, can I get the laptop out and email Dad?" she asked.

"Oh, sweetheart," Maggie said gently. "I haven't got it set up yet. The Little House has been empty for so long that there's no modern phone line. The engineers are coming next week to do it. Once they set it up, we can get in touch with Richard. Can you wait? Okay? Good girl – now, hurry along and get ready."

When she got upstairs, Penny's room was just as she'd left it, bed rumpled, clothes hanging on the back of the chair at the small desk. She sighed, but at least her things hadn't been packed. And for a second she doubted herself – had she imagined everything that had happened yesterday? It all seemed like a dream.

Then, as she shut the door, there was a tap on the window. The jackdaw was back. It was on the ledge outside the window, head cocked to one side, regarding her with beady, intelligent eyes. It was standing with one foot on the window sill, one foot on a roll of paper tied with a red ribbon. Something about it reminded Penny of a picture she'd seen in a museum: a proud Victorian hunter who'd posed for the camera with one foot on the body of a lion he'd just killed. She shivered.

When she didn't move, the jackdaw bobbed its head towards the paper, tapped on the window again with its beak and gestured with its beak: come over here. Penny shook her head and walked to the window. As she opened it, the jackdaw hopped back a few steps. Without the bird's foot in place, the paper wobbled, as if about to roll away. The jackdaw came back a pace, leaning forwards and pushing on one end of the paper with its beak to stop it moving. It regarded Penny with suspicion.

The window didn't open very far. Penny could just about get her hand through, but the paper was just out of reach. She puffed and strained, reaching for it. The jackdaw nudged the paper forwards. The girl's fingers grazed it, nearly knocking off the sill. The jackdaw gave a kind of strangled cough, then shoved the paper forwards again. This time Penny grasped it and drew it through the window. The bird straightened, shrugged its head to one side, then took off with a clatter of wings, flying back towards Bradley Hall.

The paper was the same rough, slightly greasy and yellow parchment Ribaldane had used before. The ribbon was a dusty, worn velvet band as wide as Penny's thumb. It was tied in an elegant, floppy bow. She untied it and unrolled the paper, standing beside the open window. The letter smelt of salt and cinnamon, strange scents besides the cold, leaf-fresh air blowing in from outside. Penny found her heart beating quickly as she looked to see what Ribaldane had to say for himself.

DEAR PENNY

THANK YOU FOR YOUR LETTER. YOU ALREADY KNOW MUCH ABOUT MY KIND, I AM SURE - YOUR FOLK HAVE A HUNDRED TALES OF US, THOUGH MUCH THAT IS TRUE WILL BE REGARDED AS MERE LEGEND. I AM SORRY I CANNOT COME TO TALK TO YOU ABOUT US YET. I AM STILL VERY MUCH AFRAID - AND I DO NOT WANT TO PUT YOU IN DANGER. THE QUEEN'S GUARDS MUST NOT FIND ME. OR YOU.

BUT I WOULD LIKE TO GIVE YOU A TOKEN OF MY FRIENDSHIP. GO TO THE ROOM OF LEAVES IN THE GRAND HOUSE AND SEEK THE VOLUME OF THE EARTH. BENEATH IT YOU WILL FIND A KNOT. PRESS IT AND PROOF OF MY FRIENDSHIP WILL BE REVEALED.

YOUR FRIEND, RIBALDANE.
PS. STAY AWAY FROM THE ISLAND!

Slowly, Penny went and sat on the bed. Her mind was racing as she read and reread the bizarre message. It made no sense at all to her. Volume of the Earth? Room of leaves? It was a puzzle. But before she could figure it out, she heard Maggie stomping up the stairs. Quickly, the girl jumped up and stuffed the letter under her pillow, smoothing out her duvet and hurrying over to the desk to get her clothes off the back of her chair. Maggie knocked once on the door and came in.

"Oh, Penny – come on!" she exclaimed. "I told you I was in a rush. What have you been doing? Hurry up and get dressed." Maggie paused in the doorway and looked back. "But thank you for making your bed. Now hurry, okay?"

It took only seconds for Penny to throw her clothes on. She hurried downstairs to find the Revolting Frank sprawled on the floor at the foot of the stairs, struggling with his laces. At his age… thought Penny, brushing past him. Maggie was back, shooing them out to the car, which she'd moved to the back of the house.

Getting to Bradley Hall couldn't have been easier. From where it emerged beneath Penny's room, the long gravel driveway ran in an arrow-straight line from the gatehouse all the way to the front of the hall. Tall, thin plane trees stood on each side of the drive like soldiers standing to attention, but whispering in the breeze. Gravel crunched under the wheels of Maggie's small car like a marching army as it advanced slowly towards the Big House.

If 'the Little House' was a poor way to describe the imposing gatehouse, then 'the Big House' totally failed to do justice to Bradley Hall. It was a simply monumental building. Tall and wide, with huge windows, the front was dominated by a door flanked by four massive columns. It looked a bit like Buckingham Palace, Penny thought, though not quite as big and built of grey stone.

Still, it was certainly grand enough – and as she thought that, part of Ribaldane's letter suddenly made sense. Bradley Hall was the 'grand house'. Of course!

But Maggie didn't stop in front of the wide, curving flight of steps that led up to the hall's front door. Instead she turned to the left and drove along in front of it, past a lower wing that stuck out with its grey stone walls half-covered with ivy. Then she turned right to go down the side of the Hall. Up ahead Penny saw a jumble of lower buildings that looked like barns, when Maggie turned right again, to go between the stables and the back of the servant's wing of the hall. Penny wasn't looking at the hall, but out of the back window. That's when she spotted the island.

A thin screen of trees ran alongside the drive as it went down the side of the house, towards the barns. On the other side of the trees there simmered a wide expanse of water – a huge ornamental lake. At the far end was an island that looked pretty big and overgrown, but it wasn't the trees that caught the eye. It was the dark stone tower that rose above the trees on the island. Penny shivered as she saw it, but then she turned and looked forward again as the car passed beneath an archway and into a cobbled courtyard at the side of Bradley Hall.

A tatty Land Rover was parked in the courtyard, beside another grand stone staircase that led up to a big door. But tucked away to the left of the imposing entrance were a few steps that went down to a smaller wooden door. Maggie sent the children down to knock on it while she locked the car. There was a laminated note pinned to the door.

Dear visitor. I am currently conducting an experiment. Please come in and wait in the kitchen. Have a biscuit. I shall be with you shortly. Peter Mitchell

Penny knocked and then they waited. "What kind of experiments does the professor do?" called Frank, turning back to look at

Maggie. "Does he make time machines or bring dead bodies back to life or…"

"Nothing so exciting, young man," said a voice from the doorway. Penny jumped and Frank froze. "It's all terribly dull stuff to do with algae. I won't bother boring you with the details. I'm having a break, but you can still come in and have a biscuit."

The professor was standing in the doorway. He was a surprisingly young man – he didn't look much older than Maggie, though he didn't have much hair. He was tall and skinny, with thick horn-rimmed glasses and a gentle smile. As he held the door open, Maggie bustled the children through it and along a short corridor into a gigantic and very warm kitchen.

It was messy – no wonder the professor had hired Maggie to clean up after him. There was a plate of biscuits on a table, surrounded by piles of books and magazines and papers. There were dirty plates in the sink and tea cups everywhere. Penny took a chocolate biscuit from the plate and sat on a stool while Maggie and the professor talked quietly by the sink. On the table was a magazine with a picture of a lion on the cover so Penny began to leaf through it, looking for pictures… and that's exactly what she thought to herself: 'I may as well have a leaf through this'.

That's when she got it. Penny remembered her old teacher talking about 'the leaves of a book' when she'd meant the pages. So the 'room of leaves' must be a library – and Bradley Hall was bound have a library. It all made sense. She smiled to herself, pleased to have worked out another part of Ribaldane's puzzle.

She was just wondering how to sneak into the house and find the library when Maggie came over with the professor and introduced them properly. Frank paused guiltily, his third biscuit halfway to his open mouth. The professor smiled and said the children could go anywhere in the grounds but not into the stables or the barns. There were sheep in the grounds, to keep the grass short, so gates had to be kept shut to stop them getting into the flower gardens at the back of the hall and other places they weren't meant to be. Behind the flower gardens was a maze that was out of bounds, as it was too easy to get lost in it.

"What about the lake?" Penny asked cautiously.

"I don't want you going down to the water," said Maggie swiftly. "Not on your own."

"Can we have a look around the house?" asked Frank.

"Of course," the professor smiled. "You're always welcome to come into the kitchen to warm up, avoid the rain or get a biscuit. Today, you can have a look around the rest of the house too. It's a marvellous building but many of the things in it are old and delicate. And the top floor is private. My room and my work rooms are up there."

"Do you have a library?" Penny asked, worried it could be with the work rooms.

"Yes. It's on the first floor. I have many books, Penny," he said. "Was there a particular volume you wished to borrow?"

"A volume of the earth," she said quickly. That's what Ribaldane's letter had said to look for – the volume of the earth.

"Ah yes. A good atlas on which to follow the progress of your father's big ship," said the professor, nodding wisely. "Of course. Come this way – I'll give you the tour."

Bradley Hall was massive. Far bigger even than Penny's old school. They had to go up a flight of stairs from the kitchen to enter the main part. There was a vast ballroom, a huge dining room, a spacious music room with a grand piano, a billiards room with a large snooker table and there were several grand sitting rooms, not to mention nine huge bedrooms, several bathrooms and a maze of pantries, boot rooms, storerooms and cupboards that surrounded the giant the kitchen. And that was just the main house. There were two wings, full of rooms where furniture was covered with sheets to protect it from dust. Penny couldn't imagine how many people could live in luxury in the house.

The professor lived in the main part of the house, but it still looked like living in a museum. There were paintings on all the walls and vases or ornaments on every surface. And of course there was the library. It was a large, high-ceilinged room with two big windows on one wall and bookcases from floor to ceiling on the other three. The professor went to a low shelf and pulled out an atlas, which he gave to Penny.

There were two sofas in the centre of the library so Penny sat on one, clutching the book, wondering nervously how she could sneak back to the shelf where the atlas had come from. She needed to look for a knot, which Ribaldane's message said she had to press, but she couldn't do anything with everyone else in the room.

Then Maggie smiled at her. "Will you be alright here for a minute? I want to go and check some things with the professor."

Penny nodded, looking at the Revolting Frank. He was fidgeting by the door. "Can I go back to the ballroom?" he asked.

"Okay," said Maggie. "Both of you come back to the kitchen in five minutes, okay?"

As soon as the others had left the room, Penny put the atlas down and went over to the shelf from which it had come. She knew a knot was a brown circle in a piece of wood, but she couldn't see anything like that on the shelf or even on the floorboards in front of it. She sighed, cross with herself. Maybe she'd got something wrong. Maybe she hadn't solved Ribaldane's riddle, after all.

Then she noticed something. Standing between the libraries two windows was a large globe: a big map of the world. A volume of the earth. How had she missed that when she walked in? It was as big as a beach ball, set in a polished dark-wood stand. She rushed over to it and looked on the floorboards. There it was: a large dark-brown knot, the size of a walnut.

Penny knelt down and pushed it as hard as she could with her thumb. At first nothing happened. Then, ever so slowly, the knot sank into the floor. She heard a click and looked up to see a section of bookcase had swung open. Ribaldane had guided Penny to a secret passage in Bradley Hall.

Chapter Five

The Secret Place

Penny got up from the floor, crept over to the library door and looked out. There was no sign of Maggie or the professor. Tucking her hair behind her ear, she went to the door that had swung open. Behind it was a narrow flight of stairs leading down. It was very dark and smelt unpleasant, like a wet dog. The stairs were dusty at the edges but not in the middle, as if someone had walked down them recently. She couldn't see more than four steps down before they vanished into the darkness.

For a long moment Penny hesitated. She was suddenly afraid – but she was also more intrigued than ever. She knew she was on the edge of something mysterious and exciting. But could it also be something dangerous? After all, what did she really know about Ribaldane? Nothing.

And yet... there was something about the letters. About the way they'd changed, becoming friendlier. That was because Penny had asked for Ribaldane's friendship. Penny wanted to trust him. Now here was the proof Ribaldane had promised – a token of his friendship. As she stood there, alone at the top of the darkened stairway, Penny realised she wanted it. She wanted Ribaldane to be her friend, no matter how strange or mysterious he was. It was exciting – nothing could be more exciting than a genuine secret passage.

Just inside the door was a little shelf on which stood a candle in an old-fashioned candlestick. Next to it was an ancient box of matches. Penny wasn't supposed to touch matches, but she needed light to get down the stairs. She really wanted to find out what Ribaldane had left her. She didn't have time to go and fetch a torch. She really, really wanted to light the candle and go down the secret stairs. Even though she knew she shouldn't.

Penny went back to the library door again. Still no sign of

the professor or Maggie. She returned to the secret door, bit her lip. Exciting secret friendships might required exciting, secret actions, she told herself, and slowly reached out for the matches. As long as Maggie never found out, it would be okay.

The box was old and dusty. She'd never lit one before, but the first match bust into flame with a hiss when Penny struck it on the rough edge of the box. It was hot and smelly and she was afraid of burning her fingers, so she lit the candle quickly then shook the match out and dropped it on the top step. She picked the candlestick up with a shaking hand and stepped through the secret door.

The door had a little brass handle in the middle so Penny stood on the broad top step and pulled it. She didn't mean to shut it completely, just pull it too so anyone walking into the library might not notice it, but the door closed with a quiet clunk. Despite the candle it was very, very dark inside. There was a rail on one side of the stairs, so Penny held on tight to that with one hand and carried the candlestick with the other. The rest of the stairs were narrow, steep and close together so she had to walk down slowly, one step at a time.

The stairs went down and down – Penny counted twenty-five of them. At the bottom was a narrow corridor and as she walked along, Penny counted her steps so she'd know how far she'd come. After ten steps there was a door on the left. In the flickering candlelight it looked dirty, made of coarse wood with dull brass studs on it. She tried the handle but it was locked, so she kept on walking. After another ten steps there was another door, this time on the right. It was also locked. After another ten steps the passage stopped in front of a third door.

Penny realised she was holding her breath. She tried to laugh as she breathed out, but that made the candle flame dance alarmingly. Quickly, Penny gripped the thick brass handle and it turned easily. The door opened on a cosy room lit by an old-fashioned oil lamp hanging from the ceiling. A fire crackled quietly in an open fireplace. There was a rug on the floor and a small table. There were three other doors, one in each wall, and between the doors were tall glass-fronted cupboards. Most of the things in the room were covered in a thick layer of dust.

What grabbed Penny's attention straight away was the table. In the middle was a small leather box. Beside it was a letter: yellow parchment, rolled and sealed with a dusty red ribbon.

DEAR PENNY

IF YOU ARE READING THIS, YOU HAVE FOUND THE SECRET PLACE, SO PLEASE LEAVE ME A MESSAGE. THE THING IN THE BOX IS FOR YOU. PLEASE KEEP IT SECRET AND SAFE, BECAUSE IT IS VERY PRECIOUS. IT IS ALSO VERY POWERFUL: IF EVER YOU NEED ME, THEN USE IT AND I WILL TRY TO FIND YOU. BUT IT IS NO TOY – I MUST STRESS THAT YOU SHOULD REGARD IT AS AN ORNAMENT AND USE IT ONLY AS A LAST RESORT, IF ALL SEEMS LOST.

YOUR FRIEND, RIBALDANE.

Putting the candlestick on the table, Penny opened the box. Inside lay a small silver tube – only about two centimetres long and not even half a centimetre wide. It was completely hollow and had a small hole in the top, near one of the open ends, and was attached to a fine silver chain. It was a tiny whistle.

But what was it for? She took it out of the box and had it halfway to her mouth to blow it ... but Ribaldane's message was clear: use it only as a last resort. That sounded serious. Penny hesitated, then slipped the chain over her head and tucked the whistle out of sight under her T-shirt.

Curious, she quickly went to the other doors. Two were bound with brass but one had thick black bands and an ornate black wrought-iron handle. All three were locked. She wondered if Ribaldane had come to this room from the library, or if he'd come through one of the other doors. What was on the other side of them? How many rooms were down here? Was this even on the same level as the kitchen, or was it even deeper?

She tried to peer through the dusty glass of one of the cabinets but couldn't see what was inside – it looked like lots of jars, but there was no way to tell what was in them. Penny tried to open the cabinet, but it was locked. She sighed, then went back to the table. There was a pencil on the edge, so she wrote Ribaldane a letter.

Dear Ribaldane. Thank you for showing me this secret place. I promise I won't tell anyone about it. Thank you for the whistle. I love it. But I won't blow it. Only as a last resort, like you said. I hope you will stop being shy and come to talk to me soon. Your friend, Penny.

It must have been five minutes since Penny had left the library, if not more. She realised she had to hurry before someone noticed she was missing or, worse, came back to the library to look for her and she wasn't there. That would only cause trouble. She put the little leather-covered box that had held the silver whistle in her pocket, picked up the candlestick and left, closing the brass-bound door behind her.

It seemed extra dark and cold and smelly in the passage, after the warm room. Penny hurried along – thirty steps – to the bottom of the steep stairs and climbed all twenty five of them as quickly as she could. At the top she grasped the brass handle on the back of the door... but it didn't turn. At all. Was it locked? How could she open the door and get back to the library?

Penny took two deep breaths, trying to keep calm. She was sure Ribaldane wouldn't have led her in there and given her the whistle if there was no way out. She thought about it for a couple of seconds and had another look at the back of the door by the flickering light of the candle. The handle was just like the knobs on the kitchen cupboards in the Little House – maybe it was just for pulling to shut the door, not for opening it. The door was just one big, smooth, shiny piece of wood, reflecting the flickering light of the candle. Penny couldn't see any way to unlock it.

Then she looked at the door frame and the wall next to it. They were made of wood too. And there, in the wall next to the frame, was a large round knot of dark-brown wood. Penny pushed it as hard as she could and after a second felt it move. With a quiet click, the door swung open a crack and a ray of daylight flooded into the secret stairway, hanging motes of dust in the stale air.

Penny didn't rush out into the library. She blew out the candle, put it on the shelf beside the ancient matchbox, then peeked through the tiny opening and listened hard. No sign of anyone – so she pushed the door open, slipped through quickly and shut it again with a quiet clunk. Hurrying down to the kitchen, she found Maggie and the professor in the pantry making a list. Maggie looked up as Penny entered, apparently surprised to see her.

"You didn't have to rush down, Penny," her step-mother said. "You could have had five minutes. Just wait quietly in the kitchen and when Frank comes down, we'll get going. I need to go and buy some things for the professor and I need to get you two some new school uniforms. Okay?"

Penny nodded, confused. She was certain she'd taken longer than five minutes to explore the secret room. Maybe time flew when you were exploring mysterious passages. She'd just sat down when the Revolting Frank came back into the kitchen, brushing dust off his knees. He glanced sullenly at Penny then made straight for the plate of biscuits and helped himself without saying a word.

They left Bradley Hall shortly after that. Maggie drove to the nearest town and they traipsed round unfamiliar streets, going into shops that were different to the ones in the town where Penny had grown up. Everyone spoke with a funny accent, only now there were only three of them, it sounded like Maggie, Frank and Penny were the ones speaking strangely. They had burgers for lunch, which was a bit of a treat but it was spoilt when Frank dropped his milkshake and made a scene, as that put Maggie in a bad mood. And all the time, Penny was itching to get back to the Little House, looking forward to the next message from Ribaldane. To see if his next letter would lead her somewhere even more mysterious.

Chapter Six

Another Puzzle

Penny didn't hear anything from Ribaldane when she got home. Nor the next day. She thought about writing him a note, but didn't know how she'd summon the jackdaw to collect it. She wanted to write to her father as well, but until the phone company came to replace the ancient telephone – it had a dial that had to be turned to select the numbers – there was no way to connect the laptop to the internet. Penny tried not to be upset about that, because she knew he'd be busy on the ship and it was a long way away. But Ribaldane was close. Even if she couldn't write to him, why wasn't he writing to her? Penny began to worry she'd somehow done something to upset him. She was quieter than usual, not that Maggie noticed. She was too busy at Bradley Hall.

At least the revolting Frank left Penny in peace – he was off exploring the grounds of the hall. Penny went out a lot too, though she didn't play with Frank. She explored on her own, particularly the flower gardens and the parkland in front of Bradley Hall. But she stayed away from the lake, with the island and its eerie tower.

After three days, Penny had almost given up on checking for letters. If it wasn't for the whistle necklace that she wore every day, she'd almost have thought she'd imagined everything. Then, when she least expected it, there was another. She was reading on her bed after breakfast when there was a sharp tap-tap-tap at the window. It was the jackdaw, with another roll of yellow paper on her pillow. Her heart leapt – she hadn't been forgotten, after all. He still liked her.

This letter was different to the others. It scruffy and the writing was a bit scribbly, as if Ribaldane had been in a rush when he wrote it. It had a dirty mark like mud on the outside and was tied with scratchy, hairy string not a nice neat ribbon. But Penny didn't mind. All that mattered was that he was writing again.

DEAR PENNY

I AM SORRY TO HAVE TAKEN SO LONG TO WRITE. I HAVE BEEN HIDING. THE QUEEN'S GUARDS ARE CHASING ME - I ONLY JUST ESCAPED. I HAD TO WAIT BEFORE COMING, AS I DARE NOT LEAD THEM TO YOU. I HAVE LEFT SOMETHING FOR YOU INSIDE THE MEASURE OF LIGHT, AT THE HEART OF THE LABYRINTH. UNWIND THE DART TO RELEASE IT. DO NOT REPLY TO ME NOW - THE BIRD CANNOT REJOIN ME. PUT YOUR WORDS IN THE MOUTH OF THE PORTAL GUARDIAN AND THEY WILL REACH MY EAR.

YOUR FRIEND, RIBALDANE.

It was another puzzle and Penny had no idea what it was about. 'Measure of light'? 'Heart of the labyrinth'? And what on earth was the 'portal guardian' and how was she supposed to put her words in its mouth? There were too many riddles. And why were the Queen's guards chasing Ribaldane? Wouldn't that have been on the news? She didn't know what to think.

If only Penny could have asked the Revolting Frank to help her figure it out, because he was really clever… but she knew Frank would only tease her or ask loads of questions about Ribaldane. Questions she didn't want to answer. Questions she couldn't answer. So she couldn't ask Frank. She almost went to ask the professor, but decided she couldn't involve an adult. Especially not the professor, in case the puzzle led to another secret place in Bradley Hall. She'd just have to work it out on her own.

She half remembered something from one of her history books – she had one about the Romans, one about the Greeks and one about the Vikings. She flicked slowly through them all and eventually found it in the Greek book: the labyrinth. It was a horrible dark maze with a monster in it. She didn't like the sound of that very much. Then she realised what the labyrinth in Ribaldane's letter had to be: the Bradley Hall Maze. It was out of bounds, but maybe there was a way to explore it without getting caught. Without getting lost, either.

Going downstairs, Penny found her step-mother in the kitchen. "Can we all go into maze today?" she asked. "I'll be ever so good if we can." Penny tried a smile.

"Oh, you will, will you?" Maggie said, smiling back. "Alright, after lunch. I'll ask the professor to show me the route and we can all go. It could be fun." While her step-mother was being so helpful, Penny decided to push her luck.

"Maggie," she asked sweetly. "What's a portal?"

"A portal? That's another word for a gateway," she replied. "Why do you want to know?" But she'd already turned her attention back to the washing up.

"No reason. Just heard it on the telly," Penny said as she walked off. She went straight outside. A portal was a gateway! Well, the Little House was built around the gates to Bradley Hall. You couldn't get more of a gateway than that.

The two gates were huge – twice as tall as Penny's father and made of thick black iron bars, topped with gold-painted points like spear tips, with curling cross-pieces making an intricate pattern like a rosebush. The gates rose to within a handspan of the roof of the archway. The only modern bits were the silvery metal arms for the motors that swung them slowly open – you had to know the combination for the keypads on each side of the gates. Penny didn't know it because Maggie said she didn't want the children letting themselves out onto the road.

Penny walked into the archway under the Little House. It was shady and dark, the gravel tightly packed beneath her feet. She'd never actually bothered going in there before, except in the car when Maggie took them to the shops. The gates were hung halfway along the tunnel and though the walls looked pretty plain when you were driving past, Penny realised they weren't. They were covered in all kinds of carvings.

There were animals and trees and all kinds of creatures – dragons and unicorns and other beasts Penny couldn't identify, one with the body of a lion, a man's head and scaly wings, another looked like a turkey with a woman's head and huge claws. Then she found, tucked away by the hinges on the tower side of the passageway, a funny old man carved onto the pattern on the wall. It was just his head and shoulders, rising out of an intricate rose bush, but his face was quite big. He had a pointy nose and pointy ears and a droopy, pointy hat. He had been carved so it looked like he was whistling. And his mouth was open, a dark little hole about two centimetres across....

This had to be it! He had to be the portal guardian – the place where the reply for Ribaldane was meant to be left. Penny looked furtively around to make sure nobody was watching her, but there was no sign of Maggie or the revolting Frank so she ran back into the house to write a letter of her own.

Dear Ribaldane.
I think I know where to look, but I am not sure what to do when I get there. I will do my best. Why are the Queen's guards chasing you? Are you alright? Can I help you? Please let me know. When will you come and talk to me?
Your friend, Penny.

Tearing off the spare paper at the bottom of the sheet, she rolled the note up into a tube. Penny went outside and snuck over to the carving of the little man, poking the rolled-up letter into his mouth until only a tiny bit was left sticking out. After that she went inside quickly and watched some telly. The Revolting Frank had come down to the kitchen and was building a model with Maggie's help, making sure he was the centre of attention as usual. They seemed to be taking ages to do it.

Lunch was late and just as they were all set to go to the maze, it started raining. So Maggie said the trip was off. Penny got a bit upset and shouted a bit – she knew she was making a scene, but she was so frustrated she couldn't help herself. Maggie got cross and sent Penny to her room to calm down. She stamped up the stairs and slammed the door, being made angrier by the sound of the Revolting Frank laughing in the kitchen. Probably at her. Penny stayed in her room until it was nearly time for tea. It was still raining. She knew there was no way she'd get to the maze that day.

But at least being in her room gave Penny time to work out what the 'measure of light' might be. She was looking through her book about the Romans, because she was supposed to be tidying her room and she'd left her books on the floor earlier. The thing that gave her a clue was a picture of a sundial. That's how the Romans used to tell the time. They'd line it up right, then use the shadow cast by the sun to tell the time. Penny knew it was the shadow they looked at, but it was measuring where the sun was. It was a measure of light!

So if Penny was right, she'd find a sundial in the middle of the maze. The only problem was, it looked like when she got to the middle of the maze Maggie and the Revolting Frank would be there with her – maybe even the professor as well. There was no way she'd be able to have a good poke at the sundial to find what Ribaldane had left for her – not with them all hanging around. And she still didn't understand what he could mean by 'unscrew the dart'. The sundial in the Roman book was a big pointy thing, like the fin on the back of a shark.

Penny decided not to worry about that for the time being. What she had to do first was work out how to get into the middle of the maze on her own. In the Greek legend about the labyrinth, Prince Theseus unwound a ball of wool as he walked through the maze and then followed it to get out. Would that work? Probably not. For one thing, Penny had no idea where to get a ball of wool and for another she couldn't imagine finding one that would be long enough. The maze was pretty big, after all. But as she put the rest of her books away, she had another idea. She was pretty sure it would work...

Chapter Seven

The Maze

Penny woke full of excitement. The sun was streaming through the windows of her room at the top of the Little House. There was no sign of the previous afternoon's rain and it was a beautiful day. She wondered what her dad would be doing on the ship, but when she got downstairs Maggie said there was still no email from him. So as she sat nervously fiddling with her toast, Penny ended up turning her plan over and over in her head. It seemed like it couldn't fail. This would be the day she conquered the Bradley Hall maze and solved Ribaldane's latest puzzle

As it was such a nice day, Maggie didn't drive to work – she walked up to the Big House and Penny went with her. The Revolting Frank stayed in the Little House, sitting in the kitchen and eating biscuits, reading a football comic and, Penny thought, picking his nose. The gravel of the drive crunched as Maggie walked on it, but Penny preferred to walk on the close-cropped grass along side it, softly springy underfoot. They didn't talk much, but it only took five minutes to reach the hall.

However, when went down the steps from the courtyard to the kitchen Penny turned left and walked through a cool, shady passage that led to the back of the house and the flower gardens. These were really big – there were gravel paths and low hedges around lots of small flowerbeds. To her right was the terrace that stuck out from the Big House, with its wide stone steps down to the gardens. Penny hurried up them and looked down at how the garden's low hedges made a pattern around the flower beds. It was one of the best things about the gardens of the Big House.

But Penny's destination was on the other side of the flower garden. There was more lawn with a few big trees dotted around, though nothing like the huge expanse of grass at the front of Bradley Hall. At the back of the lawn was a stone summer house beside a tall, dark green hedge. This was the outside of the maze.

Penny felt herself becoming more and more nervous as she walked across the grass. Partly because the thought of trying to find her way through the maze on her own was daunting, but it was also partly because as she left the flower garden she caught sight of the dark tower, rising up from the island like an accusing finger. It was a fair way off, beyond the stables and barns, but it still made goosebumps rise on Penny's arm. It was sinister and Penny couldn't shake the feeling that it was watching her, somehow. She hurried over to the summerhouse.

The entrance to the maze was a simple door-shaped hole cut into the hedge. There wasn't a gate or anything, just a gravel path disappearing beneath the tight green arch of leaves. To make sure she wouldn't get lost in the maze, Penny had borrowed the Revolting Frank's bag of marbles. She was going to do this just like Hansel and Gretel, leaving a trail of marbles so she could find her way home. It had seemed like such a good plan when she was in her bedroom – but standing nervously in front of the shady path that led off into the maze, her throat felt very dry.

When Penny stepped through the arch from the garden, it felt like she was entering another world. Inside the maze it was cool and quiet. All the sounds seemed to be coming from further away, from the hedge rustling gently in the breeze to the muted birdsong. There wasn't much light because the hedges were so high, keeping the path in shadow. The air smelt sweet, like a pine air-freshener but not so strong.

The first choice was simple: left or right. Penny went right, dropping a marble. Every ten paces, she dropped another one. It was a circular maze so the passage curved off so the next turn would be to the left, in towards the centre. That first turn to the left didn't last long, turning into a dead end after only a few paces. Penny turned round and went back to the first path, picking up the marbles as she went, carrying on past the entrance and leaving a fresh trail of marbles as she went.

For about twenty minutes Penny stumbled around the maze in near silence, turning this way and that. All the passageways looked the same. There was no way to tell where she'd been apart from the marbles dropped every ten paces. All the time, the eerie silence made her feel more and more nervous. When she finally reached the middle of the maze, Penny gave a long, loud sigh of relief. She knew mazes usually had a space in the centre with a bench for people to rest on, but the Bradley Hall maze was so big it had a space as large as Penny's bedroom in the middle. There were two benches and, in between them, a small metal statue on a low marble base.

At least, that's what she thought it was at first – a statue that looked kind of broken ball made of metal strips. Then she noticed that the metal strip going across the middle wasn't just a piece of shiny brown metal. It was an arrow. Penny hurried over to it for a closer look. It began to make sense to her. There was the arrow passing through the centre and one of the other strips of the ball had lots of marks that looked like this:

I II III IV V VI VII VIII IX X XI XII

Of course! Those were Roman numerals, the numbers from one to twelve. The arrow was casting its shadow on the line of Roman numerals – which meant the strange, ball-type statue was actually a sundial... the measure of light. So the arrow had to be the dart.

Now she understood what Ribaldane had meant – she just had to just unscrew the arrow to get what he'd left there for her.

But how could she do that? Penny looked closely at the sundial but it just looked like a solid bronze statue. The arrow wasn't really that big – maybe forty centimetres long and one centimetre thick – but there wasn't anything to suggest how to unscrew it. Or even that it could be unscrewed.

Sighing deeply, Penny took hold of the arrow head and tried to turn it one way and then the other. It was the right thing to do, though it didn't work how she'd expected. She'd thought the whole of the arrow might unscrew – but just the arrow head did. It was easy at first, nice and loose as if the mechanism was freshly greased. It didn't come all the way off, but it turned round twice and then seemed to stick. Penny twisted it a bit harder and there was a click, then it stopped moving.

For a minute she didn't know what to think. Nothing seemed to be happening. She was so frustrated that she felt like crying. She looked down at her shoes – and then she noticed. One of the panels in the sundial's low marble base had popped opened slightly, just like the secret door in the library. Penny knelt down and opened the door. It was only about fifteen centimetres tall and ten centimetres wide. Behind it was a shallow space, like a secret cupboard. What she found inside excited her.

It was a key. A small brass key, maybe three centimetres long. It was one of those old-fashioned types, with a fat circular shaft and a big tooth cut like a set of steps. And it was resting on a piece of paper. Penny took it all out of the secret place and sat on one of the benches to read the letter.

DEAR PENNY.

TAKE THIS KEY AND KEEP IT SAFE. IT WILL OPEN ONE OF THE DOORS IN THE ROOM I HAVE ALREADY SHOWN YOU. INSIDE ARE MANY THINGS - YOU MAY CHOOSE ONE FOR YOURSELF, THOUGH I WOULD ASK

ALSO THAT YOU FETCH ME ONE THING. I NEED THE SMALL SILVER TRUMPET. PLEASE BRING IT BACK AND PLACE IT WHERE YOU FOUND THIS NOTE - BUT WHATEVER YOU DO, NEVER SOUND IT! TELL THE GUARDIAN OF THE PORTAL WHEN IT IS DONE. YOU ARE A GOOD GIRL AND HAVE MY THANKS.

YOUR FRIEND - RIBALDANE

Penny slipped the key and the note into her pocket and shut the door on the little stone pedestal. It was stiff, but as it clicked shut the arrowhead span around to its original place. She was really eager to leave the maze and get back to the Big House and sneak into the library. She just had to get out of the maze.

There were two ways out of the central space of the maze, but Penny knew through which one she'd come. As she turned and started walking towards the exit, she thought she heard something behind her. Whipping round, out of the corner of her eye she thought she saw something flicker and dart out through the other arch in the hedge. Rubbing her eyes she stared again and listened carefully. Nothing. She must have been mistaken.

Trying to keep calm, Penny retraced her steps from marble to marble – every ten steps there was one. She had planned to pick them up as she left the maze, so she could sneak them back into the Revolting Frank's room without him noticing they'd gone. But as she'd have to come back here to leave the trumpet for Ribaldane – and especially because she really wanted to get out of the spooky maze as fast as possible – she decided to leave them. They would make getting back to the middle of the maze much quicker when she returned.

The Hansel and Gretel plan worked perfectly and Penny got back to the arch leading out of the maze in minutes. She looked right and left before stepping out into the garden – nobody in sight – and then ran across the lawn. She wanted to get away from the maze and out of sight of the tower on the island as quickly as she could.

Penny planned to get into the Big House and sneak off to the library straight away. But when she went across the courtyard, down the steps and let herself into the hall's large kitchen, the Revolting Frank was sitting at the big table. He gave her a strange look and asked where she'd been and what she'd been doing.

"None of your business!" Penny replied sharply.

"Tell me! Or I'll tell mum you were somewhere out of bounds," threatened Frank. "Like down by the lake, perhaps?" He was staring intently at her.

Penny scowled. "I was nowhere near the lake," she said. "I was exploring the woods behind the maze."

Frank gave her another long, strange look but as he opened his mouth, before he could ask any more questions, Maggie breezed into the kitchen and said it was time to go. Frank shut his mouth instantly, but Penny started to protest. Her step-mother held up her hand – and Penny knew better than to argue. Getting the trumpet for Ribaldane would have to wait another day.

Chapter Eight

The Silver Trumpet

Sometimes, Penny thought bitterly, Maggie was so unfair. All Penny wanted to do was go to the Big House, enter the secret room behind the bookcase in the library and use the key to get the silver trumpet for Ribaldane – but she wasn't allowed. Well, Maggie didn't know about the secret room, the key, the trumpet or Ribaldane. But the point was that Penny wasn't allowed to go to Bradley Hall. Instead she had to go shopping again and then she had to go to a stupid museum (it might have had good stuff in it but Penny was so cross she didn't really look at it). When they returned to the Little House, Penny ate her tea and just went up to her room, fuming at the wasted day. Even worse, with no internet yet there was still no word from her dad.

The next day was no better. There was another trip to the shops that took all day. Penny couldn't believe there was so much to buy – books and pencils and bags and stupid stuff for school. Maggie took them out for lunch at a pizza restaurant, which Penny grudgingly admitted was nice. Then she took the children to the cinema to see the new Pixar movie – she said it was a reward for them being so good, but Penny thought it was really to distract her from the fact that the phone engineer had put back the time of his visit, so the computer couldn't be set up.

The film was pretty good, even if the Revolting Frank snorted loudly at all the funny bits and stuffed his face with the popcorn – Penny hardly got any of it. But all the while that she sat in the darkened cinema, she was fidgety and didn't really concentrate on the film. All she wanted to do was go and get the trumpet for Ribaldane, but by the time they returned to the Little House it was so late there was no way Penny could have gone to the Big House. Not without it looking suspicious.

The next day really was very peculiar. As Penny was dressing before breakfast she heard the sharp tap-tap-tap at her window that signalled the arrival of the jackdaw. Sure enough, when she looked the scruffy bird was perched on the sill, staring at her with its bright black eye. It gestured sharply with its beak, pointing at the roll of paper it was holding under one raised foot. Penny hurried to collect it, undoing it quickly to see what Ribaldane had to say.

DEAR PENNY.

PLEASE HURRY. THE QUEEN'S GUARDS ARE AFTER ME. I MUST AWAY. PLEASE BRING THE TRUMPET. I NEED IT DESPERATELY.

YOUR FRIEND – RIBALDANE

Penny didn't know what to think about that. Didn't he trust her to get the trumpet as fast as she could? She was doing him a favour, after all – he should have been more polite, she thought. Anyway, there was nothing she could do. After breakfast, Maggie took them all to the supermarket. They were there for ages while she bought loads of stuff – much more than normal. Then she explained that she was doing the shopping for the professor as well. And when they drove back, they'd have to take his shopping up to the Big House.

That was brilliant news, as far as Penny was concerned. She pretended she didn't want to help, but she did really. Frank helped load the car and when they drove home, he suggested that Maggie kept driving up the long, tree-lined drive all the way to the Big House to drop the professor's stuff off first. As they drove round the side of the Hall, Penny looked nervously through her window at the island with its brooding tower, but then the car was passing beneath the arch and into the courtyard.

Penny helped unload the shopping, carrying bags down the steps and into the kitchen. Even the Revolting Frank helped. Then asked if they could go and play in the Big House. It was odd – they both asked at exactly the same time and Maggie just looked at them. "What, go and play together?" she asked. There was a bit of a pause.

"Don't be silly," Penny said. "I don't play with boys."

"And I definitely don't play with girls," said the Revolting Frank, looking at Penny and sticking his tongue out. He's revolting, she thought.

Maggie looked a bit disappointed. "Oh. Well. As long as you don't disturb the professor while he's working, or make a mess, or break anything, then I suppose it's alright," she said. "Go on, off you go."

Frank and Penny went to walk out of the kitchen and up the stairs into the main part of the house. Then they stopped. Then they both went to go again. They nearly got stuck in the doorway, trying to go through it at the same time. "Where are you going?" hissed Frank.

"I want to go and look at the atlas in the library," Penny told him. "I want to look at where my dad's sailing his ship."

"Oh. Okay. I'm going to the big room with all the portraits, to play on my Nintendo," he said. "Don't you come disturbing me, okay?"

There was definitely no way Penny was going to do that. As soon as they got up the stairs, the children went their separate ways. Penny rushed into the library. She'd planned ahead and brought a little rucksack with her – Maggie had thought it was cute that she'd got a handbag. Inside it Penny had put a small torch she'd taken from under the stairs in the Little House, so she wouldn't have to use the matches again.

She shut the library door behind her and went straight over to the globe between the windows, then pushed down hard on the knot on the floorboards beneath it. The secret door in the bookcase gave its quiet click and swung open slightly.

The secret staircase was still dark, still damp smelling. Still a bit scary. Penny switched on the torch, stepped through the door in the bookcase and pulled it shut. Then she went slowly and carefully down the steep, narrow stairs, holding on tight to the railing with her free hand. Her heart was pounding.

As she hurried along the dark, narrow corridor – thirty paces – Penny's breath seemed to echo loudly in the cold, dark space. Somehow the wavering circle of light from the torch didn't illuminate the passageway half as well as the flickering, gentle light from the candle had. But Penny knew where she was going and she went quickly so there wasn't time to get scared.

When she opened the door with the brass handle at the end of the corridor, the room inside was in darkness. The lantern and fire weren't lit and the room was cold. It smelt smoky and musty, like a bonfire on a rainy day. As she walked across it, Penny bumped into the corner of the table with her hip and made herself jump. She laughed, but the way her voice boomed in the dark, empty room made her even more scared. She decided she liked the room better when the fire was lit.

Penny tried shining the torch through the dusty glass of the cabinets that lined the walls, but still couldn't see what was inside them. She decided not to waste any more time, as it felt like spiders were climbing on her skin. She decided to leave.

There were three other doors in the room, but Penny didn't know which one the key would fit. Shining the torch on them, she saw that two doors had brass handles like the door from the passage, but the other one had a black handle. When she touched it, the metal was cold in her palm. Its keyhole was smaller than locks on the other two, so she tried that one first.

Ribaldane's small key fitted in the lock easily, but it didn't seem right. Nothing happened when Penny tried to turn it. She almost took it out, but then she turned it the other way – which should have been the wrong way. But it wasn't. It was stiff and hard to turn but slowly, with a faint rasping sound, the key turned in the lock.

Taking a deep breath, holding the torch awkwardly under her chin, Penny took the key out and cautiously turned the handle. The door swung open easily and silently, but it was dark on the other side. Taking the torch in her hand again, Penny shone it through the doorway and made out a long, narrow room with a high ceiling. She could just about see that there was a long, tall table on one side and a row of bookcases on the other. At the far end of the room – and it was a big room, as big as the kitchen in the Big House – there seemed to be another door, though the torch's beam barely shone that far. She wondered how many other rooms were down here, beneath Bradley Hall.

When she stepped through the door, something happened that nearly made Penny scream. Lights came on. Not electric lights, but candles. Hanging from the ceiling in lanterns. They just burst into flame. It was like magic – and if she'd read about it in a story Penny would probably have thought it was cool. Actually being there when it happened made it terrifying. Unnatural.

Wrong. She felt a flash of sickness, goosebumps stood up on her arms and she very nearly turned and ran at that point.

But she didn't – because she could see the silver trumpet. She could see lots of stuff. The long table at the side of the room had twelve glass boxes standing on it, spaced equally along its length. Each box had a thick black metal frame, but as the sides were glass it was easy to see what was inside. They were a bit like the display cases in the museum. The trumpet was in one of the middle boxes.

Slowly Penny walked all the way down the table, looking at each object in the boxes. Though all the glass cases were the same size, the things they contained were all different sizes. There was a big silver knife with a jewel in the handle, a small book with silver trim, an old-fashioned silver baby's rattle, something that looked like a silver feather, a skipping rope with silver handles, the trumpet (though Penny thought it was probably a bugle or a horn because it didn't have any buttons), a small silver ball, a silver bell, a black square like a roof tile but with silver edges, a mirror, a silver ring and a silver comb.

Ribaldane had said Penny could take one of the things, but she wasn't sure what she wanted. In fact, she wasn't sure she should take any of them. But they were so beautiful and it was very tempting. She quite liked the look of the ring and the mirror, but couldn't imagine what Maggie would say if she saw them. In the end, she opened the fifth case and took out the skipping rope. The silver handles were icy cold to the touch, so Penny put it in her rucksack quickly.

Then she opened the sixth box and took out the little trumpet. That was really cold too. Penny shivered. Suddenly she felt uncomfortable. She stood stock still for several seconds, wondering if she should put the things back. But then she reached a decision. She'd trust Ribaldane – he was her friend. Moving quickly, before she could change her mind, she went out and locked the door behind her. She hurried all the way down the dark passageway back to the library without looking back.

Chapter Nine

The Missing Boy

When Penny got back to the library with the silver trumpet and the skipping rope, she didn't rush straight out to the maze. Part of her knew it would be best to go and put the trumpet in the secret compartment in the pedestal beneath the sundial as quickly as she could... but another part of her was telling her that it was wrong. That she shouldn't have taken the things. The flash of certainty she'd felt as she stood in the spooky secret chamber had evaporated as she'd fled down the dark passageway. Now she was having second thoughts about taking the things. She wasn't going to put them back immediately, because she couldn't work out what she'd say to Ribaldane, so she decided to take a bit of time to think about it.

Besides, it was starting to rain outside. Not heavy rain – just a shower – but that was enough to make going outside look unappealing. So she went down to the kitchen and found the professor drinking a cup of tea and reading the paper.

"Ah, there you are my dear," he said, looking up. "We wondered where you two had gone – we went to find you and you weren't in the library."

"I went to the toilet," Penny said quickly, feeling uncomfortable. The professor looked at her with his big sad eyes. She didn't like lying to him. She looked away, pulling a stool out and climbing onto it. "I didn't think I was that long," she added.

"I suppose not," he sighed. "Still, as soon as Maggie's found Frank it'll be time for you three to go home." He picked up his newspaper again.

They sat there in silence for a few minutes, the professor sipping his tea and reading his paper, Penny brooding and feeling guilty about taking the things from the secret chamber. She was about to speak when Maggie came in, looking flustered.

"Well thank goodness one of you's here," she said. "Have you seen Frank, Penny? I've looked all over the house for him."

She shook her head. The professor put his paper down again and looked at Maggie. "Right, I'd better come and help look," he said. "Maggie, you take Penny with you – we can't have her getting stuck in another toilet. You two start down here, I'll go and start on the top floor and we'll check every room, including all the toilets, until we meet in the middle. Okay?"

So that's what they did. Penny got a better look at the lower floor of Bradley Hall than she'd had before – the scullery behind the giant kitchen, the three different pantries, the laundry, the drying room, the boot room, the boiler room with its hot clanking pipes. There must have been a dozen rooms down there, rooms that had been run by the servants when the Big House had lots of staff, where all the work was done. There was no sign of Frank anywhere. Maggie even led the way down the steps to the wine cellar – the only room that Penny thought could have been as deep down as the secret rooms Ribaldane had revealed.

Then they went up to the first floor, where the rooms are all a bit grander, with high ceilings and ornate chandeliers and pictures of horses or ladies hanging on the walls. They checked the ballroom, the dining room, the smoking room where the professor has his telly (Penny didn't know why it was called that because he didn't smoke), the billiards room, all the sitting rooms, the music room and even the toilets.

And of course they looked in the library too. Penny was tempted to press the knot and open the secret door, to show Maggie and check Frank wasn't down there – but how could she explain knowing about it? What would Maggie have said about her taking the trumpet and the skipping rope? Besides, Penny gone straight there and knew Frank had gone somewhere else and anyway, he didn't know about the secret door and the passage and the rooms. That was all secret between Penny and Ribaldane.

So where had Frank disappeared to? Penny didn't know if she was worried about him, cross that he was the centre of attention and making her traipse all over the house… or relieved that she had something else to thing about besides the growing feeling of guilt at taking the silver trumpet.

Maggie and Penny went up to the next floor and into the formal parlour, then met the professor on the landing. He'd checked all the bedrooms and bathrooms on the top two floors – including his study and his work room – and the rest of the rooms on the middle floor. He hadn't found Frank either.

Maggie was starting to look really worried now. The professor was trying to keep her calm. Penny didn't know what to do. She could see that her step-mother was upset. Maybe it was contagious, because Penny was also starting to get a little concerned and she really wanted to help.

"Did he go outside?" she asked. She didn't know why she said that – it was the first thing that popped into her head and she wanted to help.

"Of course not, don't be so stupid," snapped Maggie. She was only cross because she was a bit panicky about Frank, but that still hurt Penny's feelings.

"No, it's not a stupid question," said the professor soothingly, patting Penny's shoulder. "But the only door to the outside that's left unlocked is the one from the kitchen to the courtyard, Penny. Maggie was in the kitchen all the time unpacking the shopping."

"Are you sure?" Penny asked cautiously. "Because there's stuff that lives in the pantries. Could Frank have sneaked past when you were in a pantry?"

Maggie thought about that for a moment and shook her head slowly. "Okay. It is a good question Penny, but I still don't think Frank could have done that. There wasn't much stuff for the pantry today and I was never gone from the kitchen for very long." She shrugged. "But then again, it has to be worth thinking about. Where does he like playing outside?"

Penny looked at her feet. "I don't really know," she admitted. "We sort of… do our own things when we play out there. Just kind of go off in different directions."

Maggie sighed. "I wish you two would play together more.

Don't you have any idea where he likes to go?"

"Well, I like the summer house by the maze and the woods, or mostly out at the front of the house," Penny said. "So he might be in other places. Like the kitchen garden or woods by the lake – I always stay away from that. Or maybe he went to the woods or the maze because he knows I'm in the house."

"He could be anywhere!" said Maggie crossly. But she seemed a bit more relaxed. Then she looked at the professor. "The lake… you don't think he could have fallen in?"

"I'll go and check right away," he said reassuringly. "But Frank's a sensible boy. I'm sure he wouldn't go anywhere near the edge. Don't worry." He pointed at the window. "Besides, look at it. If he is outside, he's probably just taken shelter somewhere out of the rain. I'll check the sheds and summer houses and the follies too. It'll take a while, so you'd best settle down and wait. Maybe make us a spot to eat – we'll be hungry when we get back."

They all went back down to the kitchen. The professor put on his big waxed jacket and his hat and walking boots, then took a heavy, knobbly walking stick with a silver handle and went out to look for Frank. Maggie bustled around and kept Penny busy too, running out to the panty and stirring pots.

The longer they waited, the more tense Maggie seemed to get. She was a bit snappy and cross, but it was a surprise that she wasn't crosser, considering. The professor must have been gone for an hour and Penny was getting really hungry. She was a bit worried about her step-brother as well, but her stomach was rumbling so much it made her forget about Frank a bit.

Eventually the kitchen door flew open with a bang. The professor staggered into the kitchen – carrying Frank. Maggie screamed and ran over to him, knocking over the pot on the edge of the cooker.

"It's alright, it's alright," said the professor. "He's just had a fall and banged his head. He'll be alright."

Penny didn't know what to do, so she rushed over to the stove and stood the pot up again – the water had gone everywhere and there were potatoes on the floor and on top of the stove. The flame had gone out but the gas was still coming out, so she turned the ring off. She turned round to see that the professor was laying Frank down on the huge kitchen table, Maggie fussing at his shoulder.

Frank looked really pale. His skin was all white and looked damp and clammy, apart from a big red bump on the side of his forehead. His clothes were really dirty and it looked like he'd torn his jacket. He didn't seem very damp though – which was a bit surprising, because it was raining pretty heavily by then.

While Maggie stroked Frank and made little cooing noises, the professor came over to Penny and patted her shoulder. "Well done for sorting out the stove, Penny," he said. "And well done for working out that Frank had to be outside. Good job or I wouldn't have been able to find him."

Frank was sitting up by then, looking really confused. His mouth was going up and down but no words were coming out. The professor came and put his hand on Frank's shoulder.

"Don't worry, old boy," he said. "You're quite safe now. I came and found you and brought you back. You'd just tripped and banged your head. Nasty, but nothing to worry about now. Everything's back to normal – alright?"

Frank just looked at the professor, open mouthed. Then after several seconds he nodded. "I'm fine. I'd just like to go home."

Chapter Ten

Another Writer

Penny woke the next morning excited, as this was the day when the engineer was coming to fix the internet so she could finally email her father. The day swiftly became more exciting – and confusing – when she received not one but two letters. The first one was from Ribaldane. She'd barely got out of bed before the jackdaw was at the window, tap-tap-tapping urgently on the glass. Yawning, Penny read the note with growing frustration.

DEAR PENNY.

PLEASE DON'T LET ME DOWN. MY NEED FOR THE TRUMPET IS GREAT. PLEASE HURRY.

YOUR FRIEND – RIBALDANE

On the one hand, Penny knew she'd taken a long time to get the trumpet, but it wasn't her fault. She wasn't sure Ribaldane should be so pushy. She still hadn't decided whether she'd actually give the trumpet to him anyway. She thought she'd be better just putting it back. She sat in the end of her bed and got her bag, thinking she'd look at the trumpet while working out what to do… and that's when she found the other letter. It was tucked away in her rucksack, next to the trumpet.

Little Girl. Please put the trumpet back where you found it. We are lucky Ribaldane does not know you have it or it would have been taken in the night. Please believe me, Ribaldane must NEVER get the trumpet – A Friend

Now Penny really didn't know what to think. Who was this person? They'd snuck into her room, the way Ribaldane used to. How could Penny believe this new letter-writer was a friend? She thought Ribaldane was her friend. And why couldn't he have the trumpet? Penny was really confused. But she was also getting a bit angry at being bossed about by people who never showed themselves – and quite scared.

When she went downstairs, Maggie wasn't about but Frank

was in the kitchen. He had dark rings under his eyes, as if he hadn't slept much – which wasn't surprising after what had happened to him the day before. Penny said hello quietly... and that was when things began to get really confusing. Frank looked around, to make sure Maggie wasn't near, then he whispered, "Has he contacted you? Left you notes?"

Penny was surprised but tried not to show it. She pretended not to understand. "What are you talking about?" she asked.

"Don't be silly, Penny. This is important," he said. He still looked really pale and though the lump on his head had gone down, it looked worse now. It wasn't red any more – it was all dark, like the bruise on a banana. Penny kept staring at it.

"That's right," Frank said. "I got this because of him. I got lost because of his notes. I don't really know what happened or how I got back... I just... Look, you have to tell me honestly. Have you had any notes like this?"

And Frank took a note from his pocket. It made Penny's blood run cold.

DEAR FRANK.

YOU'RE THE ONLY ONE I CAN TRUST. THE FATE OF THE KINGDOM DEPENDS ON YOU. PLEASE HURRY AND FETCH ME THE KEY.

YOUR FRIEND - RIBALDANE

Just then Maggie came into the kitchen and Frank stuffed the note back into his pocket. He gave Penny a long, meaningful stare and nodded his head at the back door. She just stood there with her mouth open.

"Hungry, Penny?" Maggie asked. She made the girl sit down and have some cereal but Penny's mind was reeling. Frank had been getting notes from Ribaldane. Her Ribaldane. Her friend Ribaldane. Who said Frank was the only one he could trust. What did it all mean? Frank had nipped out of the back door. They couldn't talk to Maggie about it – none of it made sense, all the mysterious notes and secret passages.

Penny hurried through my breakfast as fast as she could, though she'd quite lost her appetite. Then she hurried out into the back garden of the Little House. Frank was kicking his football against the wooden fence. Maggie knocked on the window and shouted at him to stop it. He shrugged, put his hands in his pockets and walked over to Penny.

"When did you get the first note?" she asked him.

"On the first day we were here. I couldn't figure out where it came from," he said. "But I thought it was exciting."

"That's just what I thought," she agreed. "But I didn't think you'd be getting notes as well. I thought it was just me. It made me feel special."

"I think that's the idea," Frank said. "To trick you, so you think you're special – his friend. So you'll do what he wants."

They were quiet for a minute. There were so many questions Penny wanted to ask. "What did he want you to do?" They'd walked out of the garden and onto the drive leading to the Big House. There was no way Maggie could overhear them.

"Well, he wanted a key that was hanging up in the professor's study," said Frank. "I knew I shouldn't have taken it, but he said it was important because something he'd lost was locked up and he couldn't get it without the key."

Penny hesitated, then took the key from her pocket – the key Ribaldane had left in the centre of the maze. "Was it this key?"

If there'd been strong gust of wind at that moment, it could probably have knocked Frank over. He stopped walking and goggled at Penny in amazement. "Where did you get it?" he breathed. "That's the one I took."

"Ribaldane left it for me, with a note, in the middle of the maze," she said. "He told me he's being chased by the Queen's guards. He wanted me to get something for him and I had to use the key to get to it."

"What was it?" asked Frank.

"A silver trumpet," Penny said. "Has he given you anything?"

"No. Like what? What did he give you?"

Putting the key back in her pocket, Penny carefully pulled the tiny silver whistle on the chain from beneath her t-shirt, holding it out so Frank could see it. "He gave me this and told me that if I was in trouble, all I had to do was blow it and he would try to come and help me," she said.

"I could have done with that last night," muttered Frank bitterly. "Or then again, maybe not. I'm starting to think that maybe the last thing I'd want is for Ribaldane to come."

"How do you know that?" she asked. "How do you know it was Ribaldane that hurt you? Maybe it was the Queen's guards."

"I know how I got hurt," said Frank grimly. "But the more I think about things, the less I think Ribaldane's a friend. I wasn't sure – not until now. But if he's really our friend, why is he writing to both of us separately?"

"Well, that's because we don't really play together."

"Okay, fair enough," said Frank. "But why does he get me to steal a key and then get you to use it to steal a trumpet? Why not get me to do all of it? Because it is stealing. Come to that, why does he need us to steal things? And from Professor Mitchell. I like the professor. That just makes it worse."

"Stealing's stealing," Penny said. "That's the bit I'm not happy about. I don't know why he didn't get you to do all of it. Or me. Or why he didn't do it himself. Maybe it was so neither of us would be left out."

"So neither of us would escape him, more like," said Frank. "So neither of us would go to mum or the professor. He's got both of us where he wants us. We can't tell about him now – not now we've stolen things."

"But who would believe us, anyway? We've never seen him. All we get is the notes and I don't even know how they get delivered. Do you?"

"No. I tried staying awake to catch him sneaking into my room one night, but nothing. I must have fallen asleep eventually and the note was just there in the morning," said Frank.

"Is Ribaldane the only one writing to you?" Penny asked.

"Of course," said Frank. Then he grabbed her arm. "Hang on, you mean there are others? You've had other notes?"

She was just about to show him the other note when Maggie appeared on the drive and called to them. Talking more with Frank would have to wait until later.

Chapter Eleven

Frank's Story

It was really frustrating. For the first time ever, Penny wanted to talk more with Frank, but instead Maggie had them running around so there wasn't a chance. First they had to go to the doctors, so Frank could get a check-up because he'd banged his head and was still looking really pale. The doctor said he was fine, but Maggie was fussing. Then they had to go to the Post Office for the professor, then they had to go to the shops. Then it was time for lunch.

All of which meant that Frank and Penny didn't get any time alone until the afternoon, Maggie was heading up to the Big House to work. It was a sunny day, so the children told her they were going to play outside. She gave them a long look – she'd never heard them say that we'd play together before, but after a silent moment she just nodded and didn't say anything.

They all walked up to Bradley Hall then, after Maggie gave them strict instructions on where they could go and what they weren't allowed to do, Frank and Penny continued out across the flower gardens and the lawn. They sat opposite each other on the low, cold benches in the summer house next to the maze. Only then did they start talking.

"So who else is writing to you?" asked Frank.

"I don't know. I found the note this morning – it's the first one from someone else." She showed it to Frank.

"That's interesting," he said. "The writing's like Ribaldane's but not nearly so wobbly or fancy. I wonder who it's from."

"Me too. They said not to trust Ribaldane."

"I *don't* trust him. Not after the trouble I got into last night," said Frank. He looked sad.

"What happened, exactly?" Penny asked. "I mean, you don't have to tell me if you don't want to, but…"

"I can't exactly remember too clearly," admitted Frank. "I'd decided I should try to get the key back and return it to the professor's study. That was the start of it…

"Did you know there are secret passages in the Big House?" he asked. Penny nodded but didn't speak. She was waiting for him to say more.

"Well, there's one in the big room with all the portraits, the ballroom," he continued. "If you press a knot on one of the wooden panels on the wall, a door at the back of the fireplace opens – you know how big that fireplace is, it's massive.

"So I went through that door. There's a narrow passage that slopes up for ages. I think it takes you up to the floor where the professor's study is. It's really dusty inside and full of cobwebs – you'd probably hate it. Anyway, at the top of the slope it turns to the right and pretty soon there's a little door – and I mean really little. I have to duck to get through it.

"Behind the door is a room like a classroom. It has a table in front of eight little desks – really small ones, like the ones they use for the tiny kids in reception class.

"I'd found that room thanks to one of Ribaldane's notes. When I went there the first time, I found a big book on the table and another note. The book seemed to be a story about a group of brave knights fighting to free their kingdom from a wicked witch queen. It was full of pictures and was written in old-fashioned writing. I couldn't read a lot of it. The note said Ribaldane was the last of the knights – but he needed my help. I had to get the key and take it back to that room.

"So that's what I'd done. But now I was having second thoughts. I didn't like sneaking around and taking the professor's things. I mean, it had seemed like a game but I knew it was wrong. So I was going back to that little classroom to see if the key was still there – if it was, I'd return it to the key tin in the professor's study.

"But the key wasn't there. Instead there was… something. I don't know how to describe it," said Frank. He looked away. "If I tell you what I saw, you'll think I'm crazy."

"I won't, Frank," Penny said. She got up from her seat and sat on the bench beside him, putting her hand on his arm. "You can trust me." And she meant it. She knew she wouldn't tease him or make fun of him this time, no matter what he said.

"I saw… or I thought I saw…" Frank hesitated. Then he turned and looked Penny straight in the eye and said: "I saw a creature. I don't know what it was. But it was like something from a fairytale. A gnome or a goblin or something. It was an odd thing. And it was in that room, sitting at the table. You think I'm mad, don't you?"

"No I don't, Frank," she said gently. Penny was shivering and didn't know what to think. But she could see Frank really meant every word he said.

"It wasn't very big – I mean, it was taller than me but not much. Not as big as a grown-up. It had a fat body and long, skinny arms and legs. It was wearing clothes like servants in the olden days – a red velvet jacket with a lacy collar and funny sort of shorts with white stockings and black shoes with a shiny silver buckle. And its face…" Frank's voice tailed off. He looked like he might be about to cry.

"Its face, Frank – what did it look like?" she asked gently.

"Sort of like a monkey without fur. All lined and leathery. With a big mouth. A horrid, wide, ugly mouth full of dirty, jagged teeth." Frank shuddered. "Its breath stank. It was horrible. It looked like a cross between a real person and a chimpanzee."

"So what did you do?"

"I screamed and ran away. Or rather, I tried to," said Frank, staring at the floor. "But I told you, the door of the room was really low. I turned and went to run but I banged my head on the doorframe. That's how I got this," he touched his bruised head.

"I fell over and the thing grabbed me. It was incredibly strong. It held my arms by my sides and marched me out of the door and down the long sloping passage… and this is where it gets really weird." Frank looked at Penny again. "You really won't believe this bit. I'm still not sure I believe it and I was there."

"What happened, Frank?" she prompted. "Please tell me."

"When we went out through the secret door behind the fireplace, we weren't in the Big House anymore," he said. "Or we kind of were, but everything was different.

"We were in the ballroom – but all the pictures on the walls were different. They weren't of ladies and horses. They were pictures of creatures like the one that was marching me across the floor. And there were more of them in the room. At least five or six of them. They all looked really scared to see me.

"The one who'd captured me took me to the smoking room, with four of five of these things walking in a group behind us. They were chattering away in a language I couldn't understand." Words were pouring out of Frank. Penny had never seen him like this before. He wasn't trying to be clever or show off. He was just speaking honestly and simply, trying to tell her everything as fast as he could.

"There were two more creatures standing by the smoking-room door," he continued. "They were different. Big things. In armour. I couldn't see much of their faces, just dark eyes gleaming from the shadowy slots on the front of their helmets. They were at least as big as a really big grown-up – but they weren't human either. They had huge shoulders and really long arms so their hairy hands almost reached the floor. As soon as they saw me, one of them knocked on the smoking-room door.

"The door opened and another of the funny little creatures

looked out. He made a kind of screech when he saw me and chattered some noises at the one guarding me, then waved me into the smoking room. He seemed really cross or excited about me being there. I wasn't sure which. He was just really agitated.

"Once I was in the room, the first one let go of me. Well, I wasn't going to run anywhere now. I was too scared. Especially as, standing up from behind a desk, was a lady. A tall, skinny lady. I don't think she was really human, but she was beautiful all the same. She was dressed in white, with long blonde hair and green eyes. She was really graceful. She came up and stood in front of me, then she spoke. I can remember every word of it.

"She said: 'What is your name, little boy?' So I told her, trying not to sound too scared – even though I was terrified. She stroked my cheek and told me not to worry. She said something in the funny language and the one who'd opened the door – a particularly fat chap in a green jacket – replied to her and then went out of the room.

"She looked at me without speaking for a long time, which made me feel really uncomfortable. But somehow she didn't seem unfriendly so, even though I didn't understand what was going on, I was beginning to feel a bit less scared. Eventually she said to me, 'Frank, you should not have come here. You must promise to keep your visit to our palace a secret – will you do that?'

"Well, I nodded. She didn't seem cross or anything. Maybe a bit sad, but not angry. Then the fellow with the green jacket came back and she said: 'Marrowbash has brought you a drink. It will make you feel better.' And he was offering me a goblet with a bright blue liquid in it. So I drank it... and the next thing I knew, the professor was carrying me down the steps to the kitchen."

Chapter Twelve

Pickatina

Frank sat in silence, his tale told. Both children were silent for a long time. Penny felt dizzy - she didn't know what to make of his story. She didn't even know whether to believe it. It was so amazing, like something from a book, so magical.

But so was receiving mysterious notes from invisible people.

She wondered if Frank was just making it all up, as some kind of way of making fun of her. Not this time. Frank met her eyes. She could see he wasn't lying.

"You think I've gone mad, don't you?" he said quietly.

"No – and that's what scares me," she said. "If you're mad, then so am I. Nothing like that has happened to me. I just found a secret room, got the whistle, then got the trumpet. I haven't seen any creatures though."

They sat without speaking for another minutes. "So what do you think Ribaldane is?" Penny asked. "Do you think he's one of those creatures?"

"Could be, I suppose." Frank shrugged. "Could be a big one like the things in armour. Could be like the tall lady. Could be something else entirely. If you hadn't been getting notes as well, I'd have said he could be a figment of my imagination – and I had gone mad already." He laughed bitterly. "All I know is that he's real, somehow. But he's not what he pretends to be."

"That's what I think too," Penny said, then she laughed. Normally, if it looked like they were going to agree, one of the children would switch just so they didn't. Just so they could fight about it. For once, that didn't seem important.

Understanding that, Frank smiled too – but he couldn't laugh. "You haven't given him the trumpet, have you?" he asked.

Penny shook my head. "No. It's here in my bag. Do you think we should go and put it back where it came from?"

"Where was that?" asked Frank, so Penny explained. "We

could try it," the boy said cautiously, "But what if there are more of those creatures down there?"

"There haven't been, so far," Penny said. "Anyway they didn't actually hurt you, did they? You hurt your head when you banged into the door frame, but all they did was give you some kind of drink that made you fall asleep so they could… what, give you back to the professor?" A strange thought occurred to her. "You don't think he knows about them, do you?"

"No, not the professor," said Frank dismissively. "He's only interested in his experiments. He wouldn't go poking around looking for secret passages. Besides, he's too old. I bet grown-ups don't get notes. I bet Ribaldane wouldn't try to trick them."

Penny said nothing. She was beginning to suspect that the professor knew more than he was letting on, but she didn't want to argue – and anyway, Frank was still talking: "I reckon we should put that trumpet back and then I'll put the key back in the professor's study. If we're lucky, he won't have noticed it was ever gone."

So they walked back to the house. Maggie wasn't in the kitchen, so they carried on to the library… and that's where she was, duster in hand.

"What are you two doing in here?" she asked.

"I just wanted to show Frank where my dad's sailing," Penny said quickly. "The professor lets me look at the atlas."

"You know it'll be easier to see that by looking at the live-tracking of his ship on the company's website," Maggie said. "The engineer should come and set it up tomorrow, then I'll get the laptop out and we can check where Richard's ship is."

"But the atlas is so cool," Penny said. "The maps are all different scales and they're much more detailed than a rubbish outline on the computer. Besides, I like looking at the maps and imagining what the different places would be like to visit."

"Hmm. Well just treat it carefully and put it back when you've finished," said Maggie. She stared at the children for a moment, then left the room. Frank and Penny exchanged a look. He went and shut the library door while she went over to the globe, knelt down and pushed hard on the knot to open the secret door.

The torch was still in Penny's bag, so she led the way down the stairs. Frank was really close behind her. "It's really dark in here, isn't it," he said unnecessarily.

As they reached the first door on the passage way, Frank tried the handle. Penny kept walking because she knew it was locked, but Frank called her back. "Penny, give me that key for a minute, will you," he said. "I want to see if it will open this door."

"Why, Frank?" she hissed. It seemed extra spooky in the dark corridor and Penny didn't want to be there any longer than was necessary. She just wanted to put the trumpet back as quickly as possible and get out of there. She sighed. It was typical of Frank to try to take charge. She should have known.

"I'm curious, that's all," he said. Then Frank smiled at her. She'd never really seen him smile like that before. She wondered if he might be alright, if he just stopped trying to show off all the time. "Sorry – it won't take a second, though. The key probably won't fit anyway."

"Alright," Penny said. "But just a quick look." She gave him the key and he turned it in the lock. They exchanged a glance, then Frank opened the door a crack and Penny shone the torch through the gap.

Inside was a small room – smaller even than Penny's bedroom in the Little House. There was no other furniture inside, just a big pile of straw and rags on the floor in the corner of the room. Frank was about to go inside when Penny thought she saw the rags move. She put her hand on Frank's arm. "What is it?" he asked.

Penny shook her head. "We shouldn't go in there," she said. "I think there's something in there. Let's just go."

Frank looked like he was about to argue, when the bundle of rags moved again. A small head poked out. Penny nearly screamed. A little wrinkled face was smiling at her.

Now she understood what Frank had meant when he'd described the creatures as a cross between chimpanzees and people. This one had a leathery little face, all creases and wrinkles. Big dark eyes and a flat nose, a really wide mouth that was smiling and showing lots of uneven, pointy teeth. There wasn't much hair – just one tall tuft standing up on top of the head. Something about the way the creature was looking at them made Penny think it was friendly. And female.

"It's alright," Penny whispered. "We don't mean any harm. We'll just go. We're really sorry to have disturbed you."

The creature's mouth moved a couple of times but no sound came out. Then she spoke in a funny, rustling voice like leaves blowing in a strong wind. "Girl Pen, please do not leave me here. Let me come with you. I beg you," she raised her skinny arms and waved her hands slowly. "I beg you. Before the mistress finds out I left you a note of my own. Before she finds out I did not fetch the trumpet when you had it."

Penny stared at the creature for a second, unable to think. Luckily, Frank spoke. "You left Penny the second note?" he asked.

"Yes Boy Frank," she said. "I left also the notes for you from the mistress. For both of you. The mistress cannot be sneaking into your places. Her servant Grimshock sends me with them. I am small and I have the way of the shadows to sneak into your world, even in the day if needs be. Please forgive me. I did not want to trick you."

Her dark eyes looked all watery, as if she was about to cry. "We forgive you," Penny said. "What's your name? And, er, if you don't mind me asking, what are you?"

"My name is Pickatina and I am what your people call a goblin," she said.

Frank nudged Penny and whispered, "I told you…"

"Okay Pickatina," Penny said. "You can come with us, if you want to."

"I must escape, I must!" she said. Then a look of fear crossed her face. "You have not left the trumpet for the mistress?"

"No. We were on our way to put it back where I found it," Penny said. "Frank just wanted to see what was in here."

"We must hurry, then," said Pickatina. She stood up and came padding over towards the children. She wasn't a big goblin like the ones Frank had described – she wasn't even as tall as Penny, though she did have a round little body and long, skinny arms and legs a bit like a frog. Her clothes were really ragged and she had bare feet. The little goblin smiled again and this time Penny smelt her breath – Frank had been right about that as well; it was really stinky. Poor thing.

The three of them retreated to the corridor and Frank shut the door, locking it. He still looked a bit stunned. Pickatina hurried along the passageway, beckoning for the children to follow her. "We must hurry, before Grimshock comes," she said.

She bustled them through the door and into the room with the glass cabinets. This time the fire was lit and the room was warm – not nearly so scary as it was when it was dark. Or that's what Penny thought. But Pickatina was making little whimpering sounds as if something about the room scared her.

Penny put her torch in her pocket and went to the door to the room with the cabinets. She was holding her hand out to Frank, for him to hand over the key, when Pickatina give a little squeal. Penny turned round properly to see the door from the corridor opening again. A big creature was entering the room.

It was an ugly beast. Taller than a big grown-up, with wide shoulders and long arms almost reaching the floor. This one wasn't wearing armour, so we could see its face. It had a large pointy nose like a carrot and small pointy ears. It looked like the guardian carved on the gatepost. But much hairier. And much, much nastier. It had a vicious expression on its face.

It growled when it saw the children. "Now I have you. I'll grind your bones for this Pickatina – and yours, human brats," it roared.

Chapter Thirteen
Grimshock

For a second, Penny didn't dare move. She just froze in terror. Pickatina shook her elbow. "The whistle, Girl Pen. Blow the whistle quickly," she said.

The big creature was rushing towards them, but Frank was pushing Pickatina and Penny around the table away from it. It growled and lunged, trying to grab Frank. It had huge, dirty claws at the end of its fingers. The girl was fumbling at the silver chain around her neck, pulling the whistle free from her jumper.

She could see the big creature getting ready to leap across the table as she put the whistle to her lips. She blew on it as hard as she could... and nothing happened. It didn't make any noise.

Except, somehow, suddenly, the creature wasn't there any more. The three of them were still in the same room, but it was pitch black. The fire wasn't lit. The lantern wasn't lit. Pickatina was holding onto the girl's arm with one hand and gripping Frank's hand with the other. Penny took the torch from her pocket and shone it around the room – the big creature was definitely not there.

"Don't worry," said Pickatina. "Grimshock has not the shadow ways. He cannot be following us back to your world."

"What do you mean?" the children asked at the same time. Pickatina let go of them and sighed.

"I am not the best person to be explaining it to you," she said. "A wise man you need, like our Queen's chancellor Marrowbash or the great wizard Mitchellpete."

"Please try, Pickatina. We don't know those other people," Penny said gently. "You'll have to help us understand."

"Alright, I will be trying to explain it," she said. "It is like this. The human world and the faerie world lie side by side, all twisted together like two strands of wool rolled up in a single ball. In a few special places, crossing from one world to the other is possible – especially if you have the art of the shadows or certain devices like your whistle.

"Your Bradley Hall was built on one of those places. It was made with great magic and exists in both worlds at once. It is a very special place, like two buildings at once – one in each world. The secret ways were built to let humans move between the two worlds – so when you pass through the hidden doorway from the library, you are also passing from your world into ours."

"So now we're in the human-world version of the secret cellar? What's to stop that thing, that Grimshock, using the doorway to come after us?" asked Frank, looking nervous.

"It is daylight, for one thing," said Pickatina. "Most of my folk cannot cross between the worlds except at night. And the doorways between the worlds were made by your people. They work for humans. They do not work for faerie folk.

"Most of my people need to be using items of powerful magic to cross between the worlds. Only the shadow walkers can cross between the worlds easily. We do not need magic devices, just our art. And we can even come in the daytime, as long as we do not walk in the sun," Pickatina sounded proud, but then she added sadly: "But there are hardly any of us – that was why the mistress had captured me and forced me to do her bidding."

"So are you saying that every time we go through one of the secret doors, we'll move from one world to the other?" asked Frank. "Won't we end up in the faerie world again if we go through the library door? Grimshock could be waiting for us."

"Be calm, Boy Frank," said Pickatina. "Did I not just say that the doors would not change world for the faerie folk? If you are holding my hand, the doorway between the worlds will not work when you pass through it."

"That's what happened to you last night Frank," Penny said, understanding it. "If you'd gone through the door behind the fireplace on your own, you'd have come back to our ballroom. But because the goblin who caught you was holding your arms, you stayed in the faerie world and got to see their version of the hall and meet the queen."

"Okay," said Frank slowly. "I think I understand that bit. But how did we just escape that monster?"

"It was the whistle, silly," Penny said. "It's one of the devices of magic you were talking about, isn't it Pickatina?"

"That is right Girl Pen," the little goblin said happily. "The whistle will take the person blowing it from one world to the other – and because I was holding your arm and Boy Frank's hand as well, we were coming with you. It was lucky for Boy Frank that I am a shadow walker, because another goblin could not have crossed between the worlds in the daytime – so Boy Frank and goblin Pickatina would have been left behind with Grimshock!"

"Ribaldane said he would come if I blew the whistle," I said. "Is that true?"

"I do not think so, Girl Pen. She told you a lie – it is what she does. But there was a hint of truth in it, because if you blew the whistle you would come to the Aerthlyon, the faerie lands," said Pickatina. "And in the faerie lands, you would be able to meet her. As great as her art is, she cannot come to the human world without a device of great magic power. Even that whistle has not the power to move her between worlds."

"So, er, let's put the trumpet back and get out of here, shall we?" asked Frank.

And then Penny realised something. Something bad. She'd dropped her rucksack. It was still back in the faerie version of the cellar. With Grimshock. She felt lightheaded. Slowly, she told the others. Frank looked a bit disappointed but Pickatina started whimpering.

"What's the matter, Pickatina? Surely it's not that bad?" asked Frank. He patted her awkwardly on the shoulder.

"It is a disaster, Boy Frank," she cried. "If the mistress gets the trumpet, unstoppable she will be. It is a disaster. I must try to get it back. Stand away from me – I am going to walk the shadows back to my world." Pickatina began to mutter in the goblin language – a series of clicks and whistles and grunts – and moved her hands as if she was painting a picture with an invisible paint brush… and vanished.

"Wow. That's what she meant by shadow walking," said Frank. "She must have gone back to the other cellar. With that thing. That's really brave. Hang on – we can't let her do that. Blow the whistle, Penny."

"Frank, we can't – you saw that thing," Penny cried. "It'll tear us to pieces if we go back there."

"It'll tear Pickatina to pieces if we don't," he said. "We have two advantages: surprise; and the whistle. Grimshock won't expect us and he can't follow us. So we blow in there, grab the bag and grab Pickatina and get out again as quickly as we can. All we have to do is get hold of them and then you can blow the whistle again. You heard Pickatina – even if Grimshock grabs us, he can't travel into the human world because it's daytime. But we have to hurry or Pickatina's going to be dead meat."

He was right – but Penny was so scared she could barely move. Frank grabbed her hand and gave it a squeeze. She raised the whistle and blew it before she could change her mind.

Of course, she'd dropped the torch. The two children seemed to snap back into the same room, but it was darker now. Not quite as dark as the human cellar, because a fire still flickered in the fireplace, but the lantern had been smashed. It was really hard to see, but it was clear that fighting was going on. Grimshock had his back to the children and his huge arm was raised as if he was about to hit something – and he probably was. It must have been Pickatina.

Frank didn't hesitate. He jumped at Grimshock and grabbed his arm, pulling it down. At the same time he shouted, "Get the bag, Penny. Pickatina, go to her."

"I'll eat your heart, you human brat," growled Grimshock, spinning round and trying to shake Frank off. As he lifted his other hand to hit Frank, Pickatina grabbed it and bit him. Hard. The big monster threw back his head and roared. Penny couldn't watch, though – she was crawling across the floor trying to find her bag.

By the flickering firelight she spotted it on the floor by the table, surrounded by broken glass from the lantern. She grabbed it and jumped to her feet, running over to Grimshock. He had his back to her again, with Frank hanging onto one arm and Pickatina on the other one. Penny had the bag hanging from her wrist and the whistle between her lips as she reached for her friends. She grabbed a handful of Pickatina's rags and got Frank by the hair. It didn't matter. She blew the whistle as hard as she could.

The three of them snapped instantly back into the inky darkness of the cellar – the human-world cellar – and fell to the floor. Grimshock wasn't with them. Frank started laughing. "We did it! You're both so brave. Well done everyone," then he added, still chuckling, "That really hurt, Penny. I think I'm bald now."

Penny smiled, but didn't laugh. Something wasn't right. She felt her way across the dark floor and found the torch. Then she opened the bag, shone the light inside… and her heart sank. The trumpet wasn't there.

Chapter Fourteen

The Queen

It took Penny a minute to muster the courage to tell the others two that, even after all the danger of fighting Grimshock, they still didn't have the trumpet. When she did, Pickatina looked like she would cry.

"Back I must go again. I must. She must not get it," the little goblin said, but Frank put both his hands on her shoulders.

"You can't go back again, Pickatina," he told her. "We surprised Grimshock last time but that won't work again."

"But the mistress must not get the trumpet," cried Pickatina.

"Who is the mistress?" Penny asked.

"The mistress? The one you call Ribaldane," said the little goblin, looking confused.

"Ribaldane's a girl?" Frank and Penny said at the same time.

"Not a girl. A witch. A powerful witch. An ancient, clever witch," said Pickatina. "She is cunning and strong in the arts of magic. A witch. Once she was ruling our faerieland and a dark place it was with her as our queen. But brave knights, human knights, defeated her and she was driven away. Our good queen has ruled since and we have had peace.

"But the mistress was only defeated, not destroyed. She slowly got her strength back. She has waited and she has watched. Meanwhile our queen has become older, her kingdom weaker… and now the mistress is preparing to strike, to steal back the faerie kingdom. With the trumpet, she will be able to call the Black Legion to fight for her. They have never been defeated."

"Well, what can we do?" asked Frank. "We can't go back now. Can't we go and tell the queen or… or… Marrowbash or someone? The queen had some of those big things like Grimshock. Maybe they can go and get the trumpet from him."

"Yes, yes, the queen's hobgoblin guards might be able to fight Grimshock, if they can find him… but he is cunning as a fox," said Pickatina. "We must hurry."

"Good," said Penny. "I just want to get out of this creepy place. Come on." And she started leading the way down the passage towards the stairs to the library.

"Remember, Girl Pen," said Pickatina, "If into the faerie world you would go, we must not be holding hands as you pass through the doorway into the library. But if you want to go back to your world, take my hand and I will be accompanying you – then I will walk the shadows back to my world and confess to the queen all I have done."

"Don't be silly, Pickatina," said Frank. "Of course we'll come with you. We were there too – and if anything, it's our fault not yours. It was me and Penny who got the trumpet for Ribaldane."

Nobody spoke as they climbed the stairs. Penny was a bit afraid of having to meet the queen and admit she'd done, getting the trumpet. But she also knew she had to be brave about it. One thing she'd learnt since living with Maggie was that it was always better to own up fast after doing something wrong. Besides, it wouldn't be right to let Pickatina get the blame when it was Penny who'd taken the trumpet – and had left it with Grimshock when Frank had been brave enough to rescue Pickatina.

On the top step, Penny hesitated before pushing the knot to open the door. "Don't hold onto me, Pickatina," she said. "We're all in this together, the three of us."

The library the children entered was very different to the one in the Bradley Hall. The room was the same size and shape as the one they'd left, with windows in the same place. But the bookcases were very different. The professor's books were all neat, mostly the same size and most of them with black or dusty brown spines, but the bookcases in this library were crammed full of huge, colourful books of all different sizes. There were scrolls stacked on shelves, parchments scattered everywhere and, in the middle of the room was a desk covered in a huge pile of paper.

A little goblin with half-moon spectacles looked up from behind the desk – he could barely see over the top of the pile of paper – and he croaked in alarm. Pickatina came through the door after Penny and clicked and whistled at him as Frank came through and shut the door, looking nervously over his shoulder.

"Do not worry, Boy Frank," said Pickatina. "Grimshock will not dare come through that door into the palace. Another entrance to the tunnels he uses. And long gone he will be by now."

Meanwhile, the librarian goblin had opened the library and was beckoning for them all to go through it. "See the Queen you must," he hissed. Pickatina nodded, but she looked sad.

"Come," she said. "Latchbrook is right, we must not delay. We must go quickly to the queen. She is always upset when humans come to our world. It has been forbidden for many hundreds of your years."

"And I've been here twice in two days," said Frank.

"Yes, and about that she will be most unhappy," said Pickatina.

It was only a short walk down the corridor from the library to what in Bradley Hall was the smoking room. There were two big guards – hobgoblins, Pickatina had called them – standing outside. One of them knocked on the door and, just as Frank had said happened on his first visit, a fat little goblin in a green jacket opened the door and looked out.

"Majesty, the human boy is back," he squeaked. "But he is not alone. There is a girl child with him and... and... oh my! They are with Pickatina! Come in here, the three of you. Come in!"

They hurried into the room that, in the human world, was the smoking room. In the faerie palace it was a very different place. No big, comfy sofas and no television, for one thing. Just a big desk and a couple of chairs, plus a funny kind of couch thing in front of the fireplace. But Penny didn't spend long looking at the furnishings. She had eyes only for the lady who was walking towards her – the Queen of the Faeries.

She was very tall, just as Frank had said. And willowy and slender and very beautiful, with long blonde hair and piercing green eyes that seemed to see straight through Penny. At first glance she looked young – but the girl realised, looking at the queen's eyes, that she wasn't young at all. In fact, she must be incredibly old. But then the Faerie Queen looked away.

"Frank, you should not have come back," she said sadly. "And bringing Penny with you as well... that is not good. But we are delighted to see Pickatina again. If you have rescued her from the one we fear has held her, then we are grateful."

Pickatina bowed low and, without looking up, said: "I have failed you, majesty. The mistress made me her slave and I helped her. She brought the human children here – and it is my fault too."

"Hush, little one," said the Queen. "It does not matter. Now you are safely back with your family and all will be well."

"It cannot, majesty," wailed Pickatina. "The mistress will strike me down. Worse, she has the trumpet. Her creature Grimshock will be taking it to her. She is near. When she hears I have betrayed her, she will finish me. Send your guards to the island of the truce and they may yet catch Grimshock and save the trumpet."

The Queen nodded to Marrowbash, who ran to the door and clicked some orders to the hobgoblins outside. The children heard them rushing off, their armour clanking. Meanwhile the Queen bent down and held Pickatina's face in her hands.

"How will the witch strike you down, my child?" she asked.

Pickatina parted the rags at her neck to reveal a thick silver necklace. "The mistress fitted me with a throttle," she cried. "When she learns I have left her, she will choke me with it."

The Queen stood up quickly and looked flustered. "This is art beyond my power," she said. "We need Mitchellpete. Quickly, Marrowbash, fetch the wizard – we need him here. Hurry!"

The fat goblin rushed from the room. The Queen looked at the children and for a long time nobody spoke. Something about the way she stared made it hard to break the silence. Penny was just plucking up the courage to speak when Pickatina gasped, grabbed the chain at her neck and fell to her knees.

"Too late," the goblin cried. "The mistress knows I have betrayed her. She must have the trumpet. All is lost. My queen, farewell."

"Hold on little one," cried the Queen. She held Pickatina's face in her hands, closed her eyes and hummed. Pickatina cried out. "Hold on, Pickatina," said the Queen. "The wizard is coming. He will get the throttle off – just hold on."

And as she said that, there came the sound of footsteps running in the hall outside and the door burst open. "Thank goodness you're here, Mitchellpete," cried the Queen. "You have to save her."

And into the room rushed… the professor.

Chapter Fifteen

Mitchellpete

The children gaped as the professor rushed into the room. There wasn't time to speak to him – he didn't even look at them. He just went straight over to where the Queen was cradling Pickatina and knelt down beside them.

"A throttle!" he gasped. "This is dark magic indeed. I haven't seen one of these for years. Okay, stand back your Majesty. Penny, Frank – I need you two to come and assist me."

They hurried over but didn't speak. The professor was doing all the talking. "Penny, I need you to take Queen Celestia's place. Hold Pickatina's head and try to keep her from moving."

While Penny sat down and the Queen stepped away, Pickatina was coughing and gasping as the silver chain tightened around her neck. "Frank, I need you to help me now – be as strong as you can," said the professor. "Help me pull the chain. Use both hands now."

There wasn't much room as Frank and the professor tried to wiggle their fingers under the chain. Pickatina gave a gurgling squeak and a hideous choking noise, but then Frank was tugging and there was a tiny gap. The professor put his hand in his jacket pocket and pulled out a pair of gardening secateurs, like short-bladed scissors.

"Careful now," he whispered. "These can't touch Pickatina. They're steel. Hold the chain up Frank."

"I'm trying," panted Frank. He was sweating and red in the face with effort.

Pickatina squirmed but Penny gripped her head tighter. "You mustn't move, Pickatina," she said. "It'll be alright."

Carefully the professor slipped the silver chain of the throttle between the hooked blades of the secateurs. Then, squeezing hard on the handles, he snipped it in half just as if it was a thick stem on a rose bush.

The chain dropped to the floor – but it didn't lie still. It shook for a moment and then started to slither like a snake, as if it was trying to escape. The professor dived out and grabbed it. The horrid thing began to wrap itself his around hand, but it was clear that the professor was ready for it. In his other hand he had the secateurs and he carefully gripped it between their blades – not squeezing enough to chop it up, just using enough pressure to grip the chain. As soon as he did that, the throttle went limp.

"Frank," said the professor calmly. "In the other pocket of my coat is a metal box. Please put it on the floor with the lid open. Make sure no part of it touches Pickatina or anyone else, okay?"

Puffing and shaking, Frank did as he was told. It was a very small red box – one of those tiny strongboxes you see people keep the money in on stalls at school fairs, the kind with a lock. Frank turned the key and opened it.

Moving slowly, the professor lowered the secateurs towards the box, getting his other hand under the lid, ready to flip it shut. As soon as the end of the throttle touched the bottom of the box, it seemed to come to life again, twisting and turning. The professor forced it down with the secateurs and folded the lid of the box over. It wouldn't shut because the secateurs were in the way, but he pulled them out gradually, pressing down on the lid, until only the blades were inside. A stinky black smoke was escaping from the gap – then the professor snipped the secateurs shut and pulled them from the box, slamming the lid completely closed. He turned the key and sat back, breathing heavily.

"Well, that will be the end of that nasty thing," he said. He stood up and carefully put the box back in one big pocket of his waxed jacket and the secateurs in the other. He bowed to the Queen. "I'm glad I got here when I did, Majesty."

"Without you, Mitchellpete, we would have lost our precious Pickatina," said the Queen, hurrying over to kneel next to Penny and the little goblin. "And she has only just been returned to us."

The professor was looking at Penny and Frank with quite a stern expression on his face. Frank opened his mouth but the professor shook his head.

"Obviously, your Majesty, the children should not be here. Frank certainly should not have returned," he said. "But it seems they have done you a great service by rescuing this one, who we thought was lost."

The Queen stood up. She was taller than the professor. Penny thought she might be taller than any adult she'd ever seen. She looked stern. "When you persuaded me to restore the boy's memories and let him leave with you, I was happy to do that because he is of your household and you have long shown us your friendship," she said. "But you promised he would not return."

"I hadn't had a chance to talk with him," said the professor sadly. "If only I had, we could have avoided this."

"But it has happened, Mitchellpete," said the Queen. She looked cross. "It has happened and he has brought another child with him. And they have returned poor Pickatina to us – and you also have our thanks for saving her from the throttle – but you know it is forbidden for humans to come here."

"Majesty, please," said Pickatina. "Boy Frank may have returned anyway. Like Girl Pen, he was being led by the mistress. She tricked and tempted and led them here with her lies. Girl Pen would definitely have come – this I know. And if she had come on her own without Boy Frank, then in grave trouble we would be."

"We are in grave trouble, little one," said the Queen. She looked at the professor. "They have delivered the silver trumpet to Ribaldane. She can use the Black Legion against us."

After sitting politely by for so long, Penny felt she'd had just about enough of this. Everyone talking about her and Frank as if they weren't even there. All this talk about the trumpet and the Black Legion. She didn't know what was going on.

"Will someone please tell me what you're talking about," she snapped. "None of this makes any sense. I'm really scared and really confused and I just want to understand what's happening and what's going to happen next."

The Queen and the professor looked at each other in silence for a second, then the professor said, "Alright Penny. There's a lot to explain, but the most important thing for you to understand is that humans aren't supposed to come here, to the faerie world."

"I know. Pickatina explained about the two worlds," Penny said sulkily.

"Okay. Well did she explain that usually if a human is caught here, they get given a blue drink that makes them forget everything?" asked Uncle Peter.

"No, but I told Penny about that," said Frank. "I drank it."

"Yes, you did," said Uncle Peter. "But you don't remember how long you were here. It was a long time. You were even in prison, but I persuaded Queen Celestia here to let you come back with me and she returned some of your memories. That was a serious piece of magic because usually when a human drinks the blue juice of oblivion, it takes away all their memories. You'd have woken up not knowing who you were or where you were or even recognising your mother."

"But you're allowed to come here," Penny said accusingly. "They even sent for you when Pickatina was in trouble."

"Mitchellpete is the guardian," said the Queen. "There is always a human guardian, charged with protecting the cross-over point, where the two worlds become one. He alone is allowed to visit our world – because he protects it. And is supposed to prevent other humans from straying into the faerie lands." She gave the professor a stern look. He sighed.

"Majesty, forgive me. I have failed you," he admitted. "But this was not a case of curious children crossing over by chance. This was the work of an evil mind, an ancient mind. The children did not stray here – they were led here by Ribaldane."

"Yes – and they have helped her greatly," said Queen Celestia.

"Majesty, I beg you, do not punish them," said Pickatina. "They did not know. They could not know. If anyone is to be punished, it should be me. I helped the mistress trick them. I led them here. I made it all possible."

"Hush, Pickatina," said the Queen with a weary smile. "Nobody is to be punished. I know the children are not to blame – and neither are you."

"So... does that mean you won't make us drink the juice, lose our memories and go to prison?" Penny asked nervously.

"For the sake of Mitchellpete – and as a reward for rescuing our beloved Pickatina – I will not make you drink the juice," said the Queen. "Besides, I believe you will need your memories to help you in the task I intend to set the three of you."

"What task?" Frank and Pickatina and Penny asked together.

"Why, you must recover the trumpet," said the Queen.

Chapter Sixteen

How to Save the World

Queen Celestia had to joking. Recover the trumpet? From Grimshock and Ribaldane – Ribaldane who was not the children's friend but who was, in fact, a wicked witch? That had to be a joke. But one look at her face, and another look at the professor's, convinced Penny the Queen was deadly serious.

"How can we get the trumpet back?" the girl wailed.

Yet Frank didn't seem scared at all. "Of course we'll do our best, your Majesty," he said, bowing. "I don't know how we'll do it, but we'll do our best."

"Majesty, they're too young!" protested the professor.

"Not so, Mitchellpete," said the Queen. There was a steely edge to her voice. "I judge them to be just old enough to finish what they have started."

"We'll be fine," said Frank. Penny wanted to kick him. Fine? How could they be fine? Had he gone mad? What was he saying?

"Fine? Well, with Pickatina's art and Penny's brains and your bravery, I'm sure you'll manage it," said the professor. And for a second Penny thought perhaps he meant it. Until he added, "You'll manage it or die trying...

"Majesty, this is a very dangerous task – too dangerous for two children and a just-escaped goblin. Allow me to go instead, with a company of your hobgoblin guard."

But the Queen just shook her beautiful head. "No, Mitchellpete. These three were cunning and clever enough to defeat plans that have protected the trumpet for nearly five hundred of your years. Then they were bright enough and brave enough to escape our enemy's servant and warn us of the danger.

"They may not look like the heroes of old," the Queen continued, "But they have already performed feats any hero would be proud of – and their best is yet to come. I can feel it. This is their task. They will save our world and protect yours from the return of the dreadful tyrant Ribaldane."

And there was something about the way she said it that almost made Penny believe her. Almost.

"But you must let me accompany them," said the professor. "The children are too young and Pickatina is too young in the art to be trusted with this task."

"No, Mitchellpete. I am decided," said Queen Celestia. "Besides, you have your task – guarding the cross-over point. If their quest should fail, you will be your world's final defence. And besides, who will explain what is happening to the mother if you disappear as well? You cannot go with them."

"Then at least send Borrowgain or Broadwallow with them," said the professor. "Someone to swing a sword and protect them."

The Queen hesitated, then nodded. "Wise words, Mitchellpete. I will do as you request. Marrowbash, go fetch me Broadwallow. He will accompany our Pickatina and the children on their quest."

Penny looked at Pickatina. "Who is Broadwallow?"

"He is my cousin," she replied. "A great hobgoblin and

captain of the Queen's guards. A mighty warrior."

Penny suddenly felt like curling up into a ball and crying. Now she needed a mighty warrior for protection. Everything sounded far too scary and dangerous. She didn't understand what was happening. She wasn't alone.

"Excuse me," said Frank. "If it's not too much trouble, could someone explain what's happening, what you want us to do and how you think we can do it. I'm a bit confused and pretty scared – and I think Penny is too."

The professor sighed and looked at the Queen. "With your permission, Majesty, I'll explain." Queen Celestia nodded. "What do you want know?"

"Would you really have come and stolen us away?" Penny asked the Queen. "Ribaldane said you would."

Uncle Peter shook his head. "No – that was one of her lies. In the olden days, when Ribaldane was the queen, she did send hobgoblins into the human world at night to steal children away. But that has never happened under Celestia's rule."

"What was that thing on Pickatina's neck?" Frank asked. "Will we have to fight things like that?"

"That was a throttle," said Uncle Peter. "A piece of magical jewellery. The witch controls it and uses it to choke her victims. And yes, you might well have to fight things like that – maybe not throttles, but other things that will look to you like they've come from fairytales.

"But the big advantage you have is being human. That means you can touch iron and steel. None of the faerie folk can – it's deadly to them. They call it the death metal. That's why Bradley Hall has an iron fence all the way round – so that even if a goblin or some other creature from this world crosses over into our grounds, it won't be able to get out. It's part of the way we keep the two worlds apart.

"And iron and steel can defeat faerie magic as well. That's why I could cut the throttle with a set of steel secateurs. That's why putting it inside a steel box destroyed it. That's also why we had to be so careful to make sure the secateurs didn't touch Pickatina when we cut the throttle off her. Just touching her with the steel might have been enough to kill her – it would certainly have made her very sick. If I'd have cut her even slightly, she'd definitely have died. That's how dangerous iron and steel are for the people of the faerie world.

"That's also why Ribaldane had to use you to get the trumpet. The handle on the door to the room where it was kept was made of iron and the trumpet was inside an iron-framed cabinet. No faerie could touch them."

The professor put one hand on Penny's shoulder and one on Frank's. "I'd like to get you some useful items to help on your quest – a steel knife and maybe a bag of ball-bearings you could throw, but there isn't time. You can take my secateurs and my steel box. They've saved me many times and might help you in dangerous situations."

"Can't we just use Penny's magic whistle to escape dangerous situations?" asked Frank. The professor and the Queen stared at the girl, so she pulled out the whistle and showed them.

"The whistle!" gasped the Queen. "We thought that had been lost centuries ago. That is a powerful device indeed. But you must be cautious where you use it – when you are here at the cross-over point, the land is the same in both worlds. Even my palace is built exactly the same as your Bradley Hall. But the further you go from here, the less the two worlds are alike. You may be standing on solid ground in our world but blowing the whistle could transport you into a lake in the human world, or into a strange building or even into thin air above a cliff."

"Or into the middle of a busy road," said the professor. "So you can use the whistle only within the grounds of the Hall."

"But we're not going to stay within the grounds of the Hall – are we?" Penny asked. "Where are we going to have to go?"

"You will head north," said the Queen serenely. "Ribaldane has the trumpet so she will head to the North Pole to wake the Black Legion – mighty warriors who will obey whoever has the trumpet. If they fight for her, she will conquer my peaceful realm and then she will be ready to attack your world too.

"So your quest is simply this: find her, take back the trumpet and return it to its place in the cellars."

"Doesn't sound like too much," said Frank, sounding slightly hysterical. "Just chase the monsters, fight the monsters, save the world..."

"Don't be cheeky, Frank," said the professor sternly. "You both knew you shouldn't have taken things without asking. Now you have to face the consequences of your actions."

"But what's mum going to say when we don't come home?" asked Frank. "She'll panic like anything."

"Ah, well," said the professor. "For once, time will be on your side. Time works differently here. How long do you think you've been here so far today, with all your adventuring and rescuing and battling monsters and meeting the Queen?"

The children exchanged glances. "Dunno. Maybe two hours?" the girl guessed. "At least an hour and a half."

The professor shook his head. "So far as your mother's concerned, you've been gone less than five minutes – and almost all of that would have been the time when you were back in the human world, in the secret cellar in Bradley Hall.

"A year in fairy world is less than a day in the human world," he explained. "You could be here for a few months and your mother would think you'd been gone for a couple of hours. I'll tell Maggie the two of you have gone to play in the woods and you'll be back for supper. You should have plenty of time to complete your quest.

"But be careful. It will be dangerous. You must be brave and clever, but you must also be cautious. Stay safe – and if it looks like you could be hurt, come home."

"Yes, you must stay safe," said the Queen. "But you must also succeed. The fate of both our worlds is in your hands."

Chapter Seventeen

Broadwallow

Penny looked at Frank and Frank looked at Penny. The fate of the world in their hands? Frank looked like he was going to be sick. Penny definitely felt too small for this. Pickatina came over and slipped her hand into the girl's and gave it a squeeze.

"We will be alright, Girl Pen," she said. "My cousin Broadwallow is coming. He will help us. It will all be alright."

And sure enough, just then there was a knock on the door and in came Chancellor Marrowbash, the fat goblin in the green jacket. With him was the biggest hobgoblin they'd seen – even bigger than Grimshock. He was wearing a suit of shiny bronze armour but carrying his helmet.

This hobgoblin didn't look fierce, like Grimshock. He had lots of white hair, big sad eyes and a large pointy nose – he looked a bit like a glum snowman. But when he saw Pickatina, a huge grin spread across his face. Penny guessed this huge creature was Broadwallow. He bowed to the Queen.

"Majesty, I have come – but with bad news," he said in a very deep, whispery voice. "We did not catch the renegade Grimshock. If he has taken the trumpet to his mistress, they have already escaped."

"Very well, good Broadwallow," said the Queen. "Then it seems we must have a quest to recover the trumpet. It is to be led by these human children, Frank and Penny. Pickatina, who they rescued, will accompany them and so will you. Guide them, aid them and protect them. Whatever happens, you have one month to either find the trumpet or return the children here, unharmed. Is that clear, Captain Broadwallow?"

"Yes, Majesty," said Broadwallow. "When do we leave?"

"Straight away, man! Straight away!" chirped Marrowbash. "There is not a second to lose, is there Majesty?"

"My chancellor is right – there is need for great speed," said the Queen. "But we must allow the children time to say their farewells to Mitchellpete. Go and prepare what you need for the trip, Captain. You may have your pick of my stables for the journey. You leave in half an hour."

And with that, the Queen waved her hand and Penny realised they were expected to leave the room. Marrowbash fussed and clicked away in the goblin language, shooing them out of the Queen's presence and into the corridor.

"Mitchellpete, can you bring the children to the stables?" asked Marrowbash. "I would like to take my daughter to our rooms and get her some fresh clothes for the journey."

Daughter? Penny gasped. But it had to be true – Pickatina was holding the chancellor's hand and the two goblins were already heading off towards the corridor to the servants' wing of the house. Broadwallow had already gone somewhere. The professor led Frank and Penny back to the library. Latchbrook the librarian politely left the room so they could talk in private.

"Now look, you two," said the professor earnestly. "What you're about to do could be very dangerous indeed. But it is also very, very important. The good news is that you have Broadwallow with you. He's a good chap – not too bright, but honest and trustworthy and brave. He'll keep you safe, if anyone can. And of course you'll have Pickatina with you as well. She has some magic and that might come in handy."

"Are you really a wizard, professor?" Penny asked, getting off the point straight away.

"No, of course not!" he laughed. "I did learn a few tricks from Dropstipple – he was Marrowbash's grandfather – but not proper magic. For the faeriefolk 'wizard' is a term of respect, like professor. It's their version of that, I suppose. And it goes with the job. The guardian of the cross-over is supposed to be a wizard, though I don't think anyone has been for hundreds of years."

"Why do they call you Mitchellpete?" asked Frank.

"It's my name. When I first came here I was only a little bit older than you two are now. When I met Dropstipple, he asked me what my name was and I said, 'Mitchell, Pete Mitchell'. But I was so nervous I said it really fast and he thought I said my name was Mitchellpete Mitchell. And they've called me that ever since."

"What are we going to do?" Penny wailed suddenly, terror catching up with her. "I'm really, really scared. I don't want to go on a quest and fight Grimshock. I still don't completely understand what's happening."

"We'll be fine, Penny," interrupted Frank, looking smug. Penny took a deep breath and was about to tell him what she thought of that, when the professor spoke.

"Stop it," he snapped. "There isn't time for you two to argue. You'll only get through this if you stick together. That means you need to think before you speak, both of you. Frank, stop being so cocky. Penny, stop being so ready to pick a fight with him. You have the biggest fight of your lives on your hands as it is. The only way you'll get out of it is by helping each other.

"But you shouldn't be too afraid, Penny," he said. "If you trust Broadwallow, you'll be fine. I won't lie to you – what you're about to do is incredibly dangerous. I wish you didn't have to do it, but Celestia is right. There's nobody else. So you have to do it. You have to succeed. And you will. You're clever enough to trick or trap Ribaldane and Grimshock and get the trumpet back – I know you are."

"But what if we get lost or trapped out there?" Penny asked. "How will we get home?"

"Well, if you ever get really trapped, you can blow the whistle – but that will be dangerous the further you get from the palace," said the professor. "When you're near here, the land is similar to the countryside around Bradley Hall – but it changes pretty quickly. The faerie world isn't as big as our world and it's very different. It's... well, you'll see for yourselves.

"I'm glad you have your bag, Penny," he continued. "Here, put the steel box and the secateurs in there. They might help you if you get into a tight scrape – but for goodness sake don't let

Broadwallow or Pickatina touch them. Faeriefolk can't survive contact with iron or steel. So keep them in the bag, okay?"

Silently Penny took them and put them inside the rucksack. The skipping rope was still inside. Penny almost asked what the skipping rope was for… but she was still ashamed about having taken it, so kept quiet.

Frank looked at the professor. "Don't tell mum what we're doing, will you?" he asked quietly. "I don't want her to worry about us."

The older man just laughed and ruffled Frank's hair. "I won't tell your mum that you're going on a quest to steal a magical silver trumpet from a witch so you can save the land of the Fairie Queen," he said. "Not because I don't want her to worry – but because if I told her that she'd think I was stark-staring mad. Especially if I told her you'd be back by suppertime, having saved the world."

Everyone grinned at that. "Come on," said the professor. "We may as well go and wait for the others in the stables."

They walked slowly through the house. There was no rush. There were quite a few goblins in the corridors and they tagged along behind the humans. It made sense to go to the stables – the children had guessed there were no cars in Fairieland. They'd expecting to ride on unicorns or something – horses at the very least. But the stables were full of dogs. Giant dogs. Dogs the size of horses, with big slobbery tongues hanging out of their mouths.

Broadwallow was already there, putting a saddle on a huge black-and-white mastiff with a fierce expression. Pickatina was sitting astride a dog that looked like a large spaniel, with floppy ears and curly fur. There was fat yellow dog with lots of bags on its back, as well as two other dogs waiting with saddles – a pretty, skinny one with floppy reddish hair and a lean, muscular black-and-brown one with intelligent eyes.

"Ah, Penny, you had better ride the setter, I think," said the professor, pointing to the red dog. "Frank, take the Doberman."

He'd just helped the children into their saddles when the

Queen walked in, followed by several goblins in dresses who looked like ladies in waiting. The goblins and the professor all bowed when they saw her. The children quickly did the same.

"Noble friends," she said. "We are here to wish good luck and good hunting to Captain Broadwallow, Pickatina and the human children Penny and Frank. They are embarking on an important mission that will call for bravery, intelligence and daring. As tokens of our good wishes, I bring them these gifts."

And the Queen gestured to one of the goblins-in-waiting, who came and gave Penny a big cloak with a hood and small bowl, covered with a lid. Frank also got a cloak and he got a small bronze dagger with a leather sheath, which he slipped into a pocket. Pickatina got a cloak and a book and Broadwallow got a bow and a quiver full of arrows.

Then, before anyone else could speak, Broadwallow gave a whistle. The dogs pricked up their ears and, without another word, they were off – out of the stables and faerieland, into the unknown. On the quest for the Silver Trumpet.

Book Two
The Pursuit

Chapter Eighteen

Dogs and Ducks

Penelope Oaks had never ridden a horse. The closest she'd come was sitting on a donkey that had been led by someone walking next to it. Riding the dog turned out to be surprisingly hard: she was being shaken all over the place and could barely hang on. Her bottom hurt when it was banged up and down in the saddle. Her neck hurt from her head shaking backwards and forwards so much. And she'd barely left the stables – hadn't even left the stable yard. What was she going to do?

Luckily Pickatina saw her distress. She rode along side Penny and made her dog stop, clicking and whistling in the funny goblin language so Broadwallow heard and stopped his dog as well. "Have you never ridden a dog before, Girl Pen?" Pickatina asked.

"I've never ridden anything at all," she wailed, feeling tears welling up. This was no way to start a quest. Penny felt herself becoming hot. She had to do better than this.

"You are sitting all wrong for the riding," said Pickatina kindly, explaining the technique. After a second, they started again and Penny found it easier – but definitely not easy.

The stable yard of the Faerie Palace was just like the stable yard at Bradley Hall… but at the same time it was very different. Bradley Hall was built of a dull, grey stone. Not the Faerie Palace. It was carved from a strangely creamy stone that seems to glow faintly from within. And while Bradley Hall was built of huge blocks of mortared stone, the Faerie Palace appeared to be carved from one giant piece of stone.

The walls of Bradley Hall was smooth and grey with a grey slate roof, but the Faerie palace was decorated with carvings, trimmed with cheerful red-painted wood and topped with multi-coloured tiles on the roof. Bright flags fluttered from poles and there were flowers everywhere – in window boxes, on vines climbing up the sides of the buildings, bursting out in thick drifts of colour all along the path. The children had never seen anywhere so colourful.

They didn't ride very far to start with: from the stable yard, Broadwallow led them to the bridge leading to the island. The big hobgoblin dismounted, gesturing for the rest to do the same.

"You must be touching the dogs as you cross the bridge," Pickatina said. "It is another portal, so if you cross it on your own, return to the human world you will."

"That must be why Ribaldane told us to stay away from the island," Penny said to Frank. "And the professor. If we'd crossed the bridge, we'd have left our world and come here. We might have found her or Grimshock on the island."

Pickatina nodded. "Maybe. Or perhaps she wanted to keep you from crossing into our world because if you had been caught by Queen Celestia's guards, her scheme would have come to nothing. Though our people seldom come to the island, even though it is so close to the palace. It is a place of ill-omen."

In single file, holding tightly onto the placid giant dogs, the two humans crossed wooden bridge onto the island. It was, thought Penny, pretty big when you actually got there – slightly bigger than a football pitch, but shaped like a comma. The island was pretty thickly covered with shrubs and trees, all laden with flowers. But what took the children's eyes was the tower. It dominated the island – the professor had called it a folly, which is a building with no purpose apart from looking pretty.

Except there was nothing pretty about the folly. In the human world, it was built of the same grey stone as the hall, though it managed to look more dramatic and a bit sinister. The faerie version was carved from a single huge, glassy black rock. It was so dark it looked almost like a hole cut into the daylight to reveal a moonless night beyond. The tower was three floors high, slender like a finger, topped with a fluttering black flag. The narrow windows were hard to spot, winking from the black walls like the dark eyes of ravens.

Three hobgoblin guards waited outside the tower. They saluted Broadwallow as he drew closer. "They were here, Captain," said the biggest of the other hobgoblins. "We nearly caught them as they were loading a duck, but the traitor Grimshock put up a good fight. He injured one of our lads and held us off long enough to escape."

Loading a duck? The girl looked at Pickatina and she gestured to the lake. Out on the water floated biggest duck she'd ever seen – it was the size of a mini-bus.

"I have seen your little ducks, but ours are bigger," Pickatina explained. "They can carry us from place to place, but only land on water and they can't fly far with a heavy load – and Grimshock and the mistress will be heavy for the poor bird carrying them."

Broadwallow was gesturing impatiently. "We should be checking the tower," he said. "We must be finding clues to where they are going. Will you help?"

Pickatina smiled up at him. "Of course we will, cousin," she said. "We little people will be looking for the clues."

Broadwallow looked relieved. He bent down so his face was at the same height as Penny and Frank. "I am good at the fighting," he admitted quietly, "But for finding clues we will be needing your cleverness and Lady Pickatina's too."

Pickatina led the way into the tower, where it was dark and cool, but it smelt vile. The room the entered was dark and empty but the walls looked strangely shiny – Penny realised they were covered in slime. "Grimshock is a messy eater," muttered Pickatina. "Look, he has thrown his juice everywhere."

It was a small room and Penny began to feel claustrophobic – especially when Broadwallow squeezed in and shut the door. Frank hurried straight to the stairs that curled up the wall to the next floor and the rest followed. There was no banister but the girl didn't want to put her hand on the slimy wall, especially as it was the slime that smelt so bad.

The room on the next floor was smaller still, but at least had dry walls. It was full of rags and straw – a thick layer of mess all across the floor. There was so much of it that it came up nearly to Frank's waist. The rags were all of a stripy blue-and-lavender material and Pickatina cried excitedly when she saw it.

"Do you see, Broadwallow? This is a mighty clue!" she cried.

"Yes. Of course. I see," said the huge hobgoblin, though it sounded like he didn't see at all.

"This cloth comes only from one village," Pickatina said. "It is from Honeypatch, on the bank of the great river. It is not far. A duck would be able to carry the mistress and Grimshock. I think they came from there and brought their bedding with them."

"This is their bed?" Frank asked.

"Well, how do you little humans nest?" asked Broadwallow, who stood on the stairs with just his head poking into the room.

"We lie on mattresses, with a cover and a pillow," said Frank.

"Huh. Doesn't sound very comfortable to me," said Broadwallow.

"Well it is," said Frank. "And it's a lot less messy than this. Look, what's all this stuff down here?" And he bent down, as if he was going to pick something up from the floor. But suddenly he threw his arms up and disappeared under the straw and cloth.

Pickatina cried out and dived into the mess after him. Broadwallow rushed up the stairs into the room, nearly squashing Penny against the wall. He was trying to pull out the big sword he carried on his back, but the girl yelled for him to stop.

"Don't use the sword – you might hit Frank or Pickatina!"

Just then Pickatina popped up on the other side of the room... though that was still within the reach of Broadwallow's long arms. "He is here, cousin – quickly, pick him up," she said.

Broadwallow leant forward and lifted Frank clear of the mess of cloth and straw. The boy had both hands raised and was defending himself from... a strip of cloth. It had wrapped itself around both his legs and one end was raised, waving menacingly like a snake and darting at Frank's face, as if trying to hit him.

"Grab it, Frank," Penny shouted, reaching into her bag.

"It's not that easy," he shouted back, sounding scared.

"Anyway, it's grabbed me!"

"Put him down next to me, Broadwallow," Penny said as her hand closed around the handle of the secateurs. "Now you and Pickatina must stand well back."

Frank managed to get both hands around the top of the cloth. It was fighting him but couldn't escape. Penny pulled the secatuers out of the bag and starting cutting it by Frank's ankles. Wherever the secateurs touched it, the cloth turned black, smoked and then crumbled to dust. So she stopped cutting and just rubbed the secateurs on it. The piece Frank held thrashed about madly, but couldn't escape. In minutes it was reduced to smoky dust.

"Was that another throttle?" Penny panted.

"Much worse," said Pickatina. "That was a spite. It is like a throttle, but a little bit intelligent. A spite can hunt and attack on its own, unlike a throttle – which the witch must be operating."

"I'm fine, thanks for asking," said Frank as he got up. He seemed a bit grumpy about being rescued, but Broadwallow rested one of his massive hands on Frank's shoulders.

"It was brave of you to try catching that thing, Boy Frank," he said. "You were not to know it was a spite. It is lucky Girl Pen has Mitchellpete's death metal – the spite could have killed you."

"I just feel stupid for letting it catch me," he said. "But thanks, Penny."

"You're welcome," she replied, putting the secateurs safely back in her bag. "Um. You don't think there are any more of those horrid things in here, do you?"

"I am sure there will not be," said Pickatina. "To be making a spite is difficult. It takes a lot of time and will be tiring, so the Mistress will surely have had time to make only one. Still, we must proceed with care while we search the top room."

She led the way to the stairs, followed by Frank and Penny. The top floor was so small Broadwallow probably wouldn't have fitted in there unless the rest of them came out first.

At least it was tidier than the one below. In fact, it was

almost empty, apart from a cauldron hanging over the ashes of a fire and a three-legged stool. Pickatina went to look in the cauldron, but she reeled back and banged into Frank, who banged into Penny – and if Broadwallow hadn't been standing behind her, she'd have fallen down the stairs.

With a nasty, growling croak, something the size of a loaf of bread hopped out of the cauldron. It flicked a long, red tongue at Pickatina, who dodged and rolled across the floor.

"A guard frog!" gasped Broadwallow. "Do not let the tongue hit you, children – it will be poisoned!"

The frog had turned to follow Pickatina, so it had its back to the two children. Frank drew the dagger Queen Celestia had given him and dived at the guard frog. He hit it so hard his blade went right through it and stuck in the floorboards beneath. Frank rolled away, leaving the guard frog stuck there with a startled expression on its ugly face. It didn't even croak.

"Thank you, Boy Frank," said Pickatina, standing up. "That was bravely done."

"Hmmm. I am not the only mighty warrior here, it seems," chuckled Broadwallow, with a noise like a great tree creaking in a high wind. "Are there any clues here, do you think Pickatina?"

The little goblin was brushing herself down as she looked around. "No – I am not thinking so, cousin," she said. "But luckily I think there will be no more traps either. Still, we should be following the clue we have. Let us ride to Honeypatch!"

Chapter Nineteen

Goblin Food

They trooped downstairs behind Broadwallow, the huge hobgoblin taking his time on steps that were much smaller than his feet. Outside they climbed onto their dogs – Penny's was all wet, as if it had been swimming in the lake, maybe chasing ducks. Then Broadwallow led the way across the bridge and out on the road away from the palace. It went exactly the same way as the drive at Bradley Hall. There were even the trees planted in the same places on either side of the drive.

But there was no mistaking the grounds of the Fairie Palace for the grounds of Bradley Hall. The trees were strange, tall and colourful – wispy branches covered with flowers swayed in the wind as if dancing slowly to unheard music. The lawn on either side was thick with poppies and buttercups and daisies. The children saw big fluffy sheep chomping happily on the grass and flowers, just as there was at home – but there was something odd about these sheep.

"Look at the sheep, Frank," Penny called. "They have two heads!" One was at each end of their bodies. While one head was bent down, eating, the other head was up, looking around.

"Very hard sheep to catch," said Broadwallow sadly. "You can never sneak up on fairie sheep. Makes it difficult to get the wool." As if they had heard and understood him, the nearest sheep tossed their heads and strutted off.

They rode straight for the fairie version of the gatehouse – it looked just like the Little House, only carved from a single giant orange stone and decorated with green woodwork, with multi-coloured tiles on the roof. Penny had a sudden yearning to go inside and blow the whistle, to return to the human world and her own bedroom, where she could climb into bed and pull the covers over her head. But the urge lasted only an instant, because she knew it wasn't an option. She couldn't leave Frank on his own. He's a boy, Penny thought – she had no idea what trouble he'd get himself into if she wasn't there to keep him sensible.

One thing was different about the faerie version of the gatehouse: there were no gates. And Penny suddenly realised there were no fences stretching away on either side. There was nothing to mark the boundary of the palace grounds. But of course, that wasn't necessary. She understood now that the iron fence around the Bradley Hall estate was there for one very specific purpose: to keep any faerie folk who managed to cross over to the human world trapped within the grounds. So the little party just rode beneath the unbarred archway of the gatehouse and out across wide, open plains of flowers that stretched away before us for as far as the eye could see.

The children already knew the geography of Fairieland was different to the geography of the human world, but the first few miles on the dogs really showed them just how different. At home, when Maggie drove away from Bradley Hall the nearest village was less than a mile away. The dogs weren't running as fast as a car, perhaps, but they were going far quicker than a person could run. Penny was being shaken back and forth (though she did think she was getting better at riding the dog already) but even after half an hour in the saddle, there was no sign of a village. Or a town. Or… well… anything at all. Just more gently rolling plains, covered with flowers.

Far away in the distance the children could see the faint shapes of mountains, the tallest topped with snow. There had been no mountains near Bradley Hall, not even on the far horizon. Though she was getting hot, Penny shivered as she really understood why the Queen and the Professor had told her not to blow the whistle outside the palace grounds – there was nothing in the landscape around her to suggest where she'd end up if she transported herself back to the human world now.

They rode for hours. It was devastatingly tiring, holding onto the dog and trying to bounce along a bit with him. The sun was slowly setting, painting the scattered clouds with pink and orange light. Penny was almost falling out of the saddle with exhaustion by the time Broadwallow finally gave a whistle that made all the dogs slow to a walk and then stop.

"Here we will nest for the night," he said, dismounting. He walked around and lifted each of his companions down from the saddles – Frank looked just as tired as Penny and even Pickatina looked worn out. The burly hobgoblin whistled and clicked something the dogs seemed to understand. It must have been the command for 'lie down' because that's what they all did, spaced out to form a circle around the travellers.

The children helped Pickatina unload the bags from the yellow pack-dog, which was lying placidly and panting, a tongue like a pink hall rug hanging out the corner of its mouth. Meanwhile, Broadwallow had taken out his big sword and was cutting big armfuls of grass and flowers. He brought them over and made a big mound in the centre of the ring of dogs. Pickatina opened a bag and pulled out seven or eight big silky blankets, which she and Broadwallow stirred into the pile of grass.

They stood back, smiling broadly. "Is that not a homely looking nest?" asked Broadwallow.

Frank and Penny exchanged a look. Neither knew how to say it politely, but the girl thought she'd better try. "Erm, we don't sleep in nests, remember," she said gently. "We need beds."

"But we do not have your human beds, Girl Pen," said Pickatina. "Can you try to sleep in a nest like us goblin folk?"

"Well, we can try," said Frank. "It'll be a bit like camping. Besides, I'm so tired I could probably sleep standing up."

"What are we going to have to eat?" Penny asked.

Pickatina looked nervous. "About human food I do not know much," she admitted. "I do know it is different to goblin food. But did not the queen give you a gift, Girl Pen?"

Penny took the bowl with the lid out of her bag. Sitting cross-legged on the floor, she took the lid off and the bowl began to fill before her eyes... with a lumpy pale-grey mixture. She dipped a finger in and sniffed it – it didn't smell of anything. Cautiously, she put a little on her tongue. Yuk! It was lukewarm, sticky like cold porridge but with a worse flavour, like oats that had been strained through sweaty socks. Coughing, the girl managed to swallow it down. She guessed they wouldn't starve if they ate it, but you'd have to be desperate to eat it because it tasted so bad.

She looked across to see what Broadwallow and Pickatina were eating. They were tucking into big, long black things that looked a bit like… no, it couldn't be… yes, it really was… They were eating slimy giant slugs – and they smelled awful.

"I don't want to eat what they're eating," said Frank quietly. "What's the porridge like, Penny?"

"You're welcome to it," she said, handing him the bowl. "I'm not feeling too hungry."

Broadwallow was chomping and slurping away, licking his lips and burping. Pickatina was more ladylike, but even she was burping and slurping as she gobbled up her slug. Frank tried a mouthful of the porridge, but grimaced and gave the bowl back without a word.

The sun was setting fast. The dogs, lying in a circle around the big nest the goblins had built, were snoring quietly.

"Don't we need to feed the dogs?" Penny asked.

"Feed the dogs?" asked Broadwallow. "Why would we do that? What do they eat in your world?"

"Erm, dog food – it's like meat in a can," said Frank.

"Oh. Much better organised are our dogs," said the big hobgoblin, burping. "They are catching flies as they are running through the fields. That is all they need to eat. Now they will sleep all night without moving, until I wake them."

Penny looked at her red setter. It had long front legs, sticking out straight in front of it, covered in thick soft fur. One of its floppy, furry ears was covering them.

"If you don't mind, I'll sleep with my dog," she said. "By the way, what is it called?"

"We do not give names to animals, just numbers," said Pickatina. "Yours is 748. Frank's is 888. Mine is 996 and Broadwallow's is 998. The pack-dog is 620. But they answer to their numbers only if you call them in our goblin tongue. We will try to teach you tomorrow, if you like."

Yawning, Penny lay down on her dog's legs, pulling the new cloak the Queen had given her tightly around herself, then draping the dog's ear over the top. It was all warm, though everything smelt of dog. She noticed Frank was curling up under the floppy ears of Pickatina's spaniel.

It was getting really dark now and, looking out across the rolling fields of flowers, Penny saw lots of small glowing lights emerging. She called to Frank: "Look at all the fireflies."

Pickatina came and stood by her. "Those are not fireflies, Girl Pen," she said. "Those are fairies. Each one is the size of a tooth, with delicate wings and tiny sharp teeth. They tend the flowers in the dark, singing their songs through the night."

So Penny lay back and tried to listen to the fairies singing. They were so quiet, they were almost impossible to detect. But as exhaustion slid the young girl down beneath a blanket of sleep, she thought – just for a moment – that she could hear their song. But then she was lost in a peaceful, dreamless slumber.

Chapter Twenty

Honey Bears

Penny woke with a start. For a fraction of a second she thought she might be back in my bed in the Little House – but almost instantly she knew that wasn't right. For one thing, she was far too uncomfortable to be in her own bed. For another, everything smelt of dog and she had fur in her mouth and eyes. She spluttered and sat up, remembering.

It was dawn on the fairie flower plains. A hazy mist rose above the ground and the sun was rising, so the tiny lights of the fairies seemed fainter as they hovered above the flowers. Penny looked around and saw that Frank was still asleep, poking out from beneath the ear of the giant spaniel. He was snoring quietly, mouth open. So was the dog. There was no sign of Pickatina or Broadwallow, hidden in their nest of rags and fresh-cut flowers.

Penny got up quietly and stretched. She ached all over. The air was chilly without being really cold. Pulling her cloak tight around her body, the girl tiptoed past the dogs and walked up to the top of the slight hill they were camped on. She looked out across the plains… and froze in terror.

There, written in giant black letters on the green-and-gold slope of the next gently rolling hill, was a message:

TURN BACK OR DIE. YOU HAVE BEEN WARNED.

It could have come from only one person – Ribaldane. Penny had no idea how it could have been written, but that wasn't why it scared her. The message meant not only that the witch knew she was being chased, but also it suggested that she probably knew Penny and Frank were following her.

Penny turned and ran back to the camp, calling for Pickatina and Broadwallow. They emerged sleepily from their funny nest. "What is the matter, Girl Pen?" asked Pickatina, yawning mightily.

"You have to hurry," the girl cried. "Come and see."

Moving like clumsy robots, the two goblins hurried over and the human girl led them up the slope. They stopped at the top and looked across to the next hill with the words carved into it. "That's from Ribaldane, isn't it?" Penny asked quietly.

"You are right, small human girl," said Broadwallow. "She knows we follow her. That is a bad thing, I think."

"Do not be panicking yet, cousin," said Pickatina thoughtfully. "Not so sure am I that the mistress knows we are following. Your guards nearly caught her and her creature Grimshock fleeing from the island of the truce, so certain it would be that pursuit would follow her. I am thinking she may have been leaving this message to scare any who were following her – it is not certain she would be knowing the human children and I would be leading the chase."

Frank wandered sleepily up to join the others. "Blimey," he said. "You don't see that every day. How'd Ribaldane do that?"

"It is a minor magic, Boy Frank," said Pickatina. "The mistress would have written the words on the air as she few past on her duck. As the letters fell, they would have swelled. When they touched the flowers on the hill, they would have been burning them up, leaving nothing but black ashes – which is what makes the big words we can be reading from a long way away."

"Well, I'm not impressed," Frank said, with a grim note of determination in his voice. "She can threaten us all she likes, but Ribaldane's the one who's running away. Not us. Right, I'm hungry – let's have some breakfast."

Slowly they walked back down to the camp. Penny was subdued, still a bit frightened by the message, but she didn't want to show it. The others were all acting as if everything was normal – even Frank. He didn't even seem to be missing home.

"Well, Professor Mitchell said time isn't really passing at home while we're here. Mum's not going to miss us, so we might as well make the most of it," he said when Penny asked him. "Let's be honest – it's not very often that I do anything adventurous. I'm a bit chubby and I spent too much time indoors being a smarty-pants for the kids at the old school to let me join in with the exciting stuff. I daresay the new school won't be much different. So the way I see it, this is my chance to do something brave and have an adventure."

Penny looked at him, open mouthed. Had she misjudged him? She'd always thought Frank was really popular and liked things at school. Though it was true that he could be a bit of a smarty-pants sometimes. But she realised Frank was right – this was a chance to do something really adventurous.

If they'd have the energy to do it, that was. Penny got out the magic porridge bowl but, even though both children were hungry, the grey gloop tasted so horrid that neither could have more than a few mouthfuls each. While the two goblins were slobbering over their giant slugs, the humans found the blankets from the nest and packed them into the satchels carried by 620 the pack-dog.

Penny decided to try to learn how to say "748" in goblin, to could call the dog by its name – but she just couldn't make the right kind of clicks. After a few goes Pickatina asked her to stop, because every time the girl tried to do it she said a rude word in goblin instead. Pickatina wouldn't say what it was, though.

"How far do we have to ride today?" Penny asked as Broadwallow went round waking up the statue-like dogs. As the animals shook and stretched, the girl rubbed her sore thighs. She wasn't looking forward another ache-inducing day in the saddle.

"Not far, Girl Pen," said Broadwallow. "We are as much as halfway to Honeypatch. We will be there in time for lunch."

"Great… if you fancy eating slugs," muttered Frank.

They all climbed back into the saddles and set off, riding past the letters Ribaldane had burnt into the next hill – and on and on across the huge plain of flowers. Penny kept trying to look, but she didn't see any of the tiny fairies that had come out the night before. Maybe they only came out when it was dark.

They rode for several hours, the landscape barely changing. It was just one gentle slope of thick flowers after another. Penny hadn't seen many insects – which she thought was just because that's what the dogs were eating, sucking as many flies out of the air as they could while they were running. But at one point she thought she heard a faint buzzing, like distant bees. She was just about to ask if anyone else heard it, when Broadwallow held up his hand and the dogs all stopped. The huge hobgoblin cupped a hand to his ear and seemed to listen, then he turned to Pickatina with a look of horror on his face.

"Ride fast, cousin," he cried. "Take the children – there are honey bears coming. I hear them."

Surely, Penny thought, he meant honey bees? That's what buzzes… but Pickatina wasn't arguing. The little goblin whistled and clicked a few commands and all the dogs apart from Broadwallow's 998 bounced forwards and started running faster than they'd travelled before.

Looking over her shoulder, Penny saw Broadwallow turn to

face back the way they'd come, drawing the enormous sword he carried on his back. The girl was being shaken about so much by her huge dog that it was hard to see exactly what was happening further away – but it did look like something was coming towards Broadwallow through the long grass and flowers.

Then she was at the top of the gentle hill, her dog galloping down the other side as fast as it could go. Penny had to look forwards and concentrate on not being shaken out of the saddle. On and on they rode, but still the buzzing kept getting closer, getting louder. Sounding angrier. As they started climbing the next low hill, Penny took another look over her shoulder.

It looked like someone was mowing the flower plains. Or rather, that five people were. Five strips were being cut through the tall flowers and long grass – and they were aiming straight towards the humans and their goblin guide. There were two strips off to Penny's left and three off to the right. Broadwallow was riding down the first strip to the left. As the girl watched, he stood up in the stirrups of his saddle and swung his massive sword at something down on the ground in front of him.

A huge bear-like creature seemed to rear up as Broadwallow rode past it. The thing had a big hairy head and body, with short arms it waved in the air. Clearly, it had been hurt by Broadwallow's sword. The big hobgoblin made his dog turn in a tight circle and he rode past the creature and hacked at it again. This time it fell down, out of sight.

But that wasn't what made her cry out in terror. It was the way the four remaining strips being cut into the flower meadow changed course that terrified her. There were no gaps between them now. And they were all coming straight towards her.

Penny looked away again and urged 748 forwards. The things in the grass were catching slowly but steadily gaining on her. She'd reached the top of the gentle hill and still there was no change in the scenery ahead – nowhere she could see that could offer any protection from the honey bears.

On they rode, Frank calling back to his step-sister and

urging her to speed up. Penny glanced back again in time to see Broadwallow hit another honey bear. He didn't stop to fight this one – just kept riding forward, into the grass that hadn't yet been eaten, trying to catch up with his cousin and the children.

Broadwallow's dog was running quickly, but leaving an injured honey bear behind him had been a mistake. Penny realised that as soon as she saw it take to the air. A pair of large, clear wings seemed to unfold from its back and the buzzing noise increased. The body of the bear seemed to hang from the wings like a sock filled with stones swinging on a washing line.

"Behind you, Broadwallow," she screamed. "It's behind you."

But there was no way he could hear. He was too far away. Penny really thought the honey bear was going to catch him, but something must have alerted the hobgoblin – maybe it dripped blood on him – because as the flying bear swooped towards him, Broadwallow rolled to one side until he was hanging right out of the saddle beside his dog. As he did so, he swung the huge sword in a tight arc. He only dealt the honey bear a glancing blow, but it was enough to make it tumble from the sky.

"Keep riding," he bellowed. "Don't slow down!"

But Penny didn't have much choice in the matter: 748 was flagging. His tongue was hanging out and he was panting heavily. Pickatina and Frank were quite a way ahead, almost out of sight over the top of the next hill.

The girl flicked the reins and called to 748 to go faster, trying to keep the panic out of her voice. She even tried to click and whistle his name to encourage him.

"You can say that again," shouted Broadwallow. He was riding alongside her now. "Girl Pen, I will grab you. My dog can carry both of us, but yours is too tired."

"I can't leave him for those things," Penny cried, but really she was desperate enough to do anything to escape.

"He will run faster without having to carry you," grunted Broadwallow – and with that he grabbed the back of her cloak in his massive hand and plucked Penny from the saddle of 748. For a second the young girl thought she was going to be dropped, but then she was sitting in the hobgoblin's lap, clinging onto him while he breathed his stinky slug-breath all over her. She looked behind them. The three remaining honey bears were really close.

Now she could see them more clearly, they didn't really look like bears. More like gigantic ants with fur and wings – though they did have only four legs, not six like ants. But the way they moved their heads, big jaws clicking as they mowed through the flowers and grass, that was very ant-like. And also very, very scary. Especially as the creatures were moving extremely fast. Penny stifled a cry of fear – but she didn't think it would be long before they were caught.

She looked forward again and saw that, just as they reached the top of the hill, there was a neat, low hedge ahead. Beyond it was a collection of low buildings with white walls and thatched roofs. Then 998 was jumping up and over the hedge, landing with a bump on the other side.

Penny hoped that perhaps the honey bears wouldn't follow through the hedge… but they did, munching rapidly through it. But a crowd of goblins was rushing out from the houses – some with pitchforks, others with scythes, a couple with spades or big gardening forks. They fell on the honey bears as they came through the hedge, bellowing with rage and chopping them up in an instant, before they could fly away.

Broadwallow skidded 998 to a halt and jumped down, almost dropping Penny to the floor. Before the hobgoblin could rush off to join in the slaughter of the honeybees, a short goblin in a black leather waistcoat came over and grinned. "You choose an exciting way to arrive, I am thinking. Thank you for slowing the honey bears," he said. "Welcome to Honeypatch. You will be safe here."

Chapter Twenty One

The Naga

Penny patted the sweaty side of 998 – too shaken to do anything more than stand and pant and stare speechlessly around her. She saw that 748 had escaped the honey bears, the pretty red setter standing with 620 and Frank's dog 888. To her, 748 was looking a bit embarrassed, as if it knew it should have been able to carry its new mistress to safety. Meanwhile, Frank and Pickatina were rushing towards her – even Frank looked worried.

"Are you alright?" he asked. "I thought those things were going to catch you. Don't know what I'd have told mum and your dad if you'd been eaten. Good job Broadwallow's so good with a sword. He's not a bad rider, either."

Penny found she was shaking and, now the chase was over, she was frightened. She didn't understand why she hadn't been scared when she was fleeing from the honey bees – but now she was safe, she was almost paralysed with terror.

"You have had a scare, Girl Pen," said Pickatina gently, putting an arm around the girl. "But you are alright now. Come, we will walk into the village and find you something to drink – you will feel better. You are safe."

Penny was beginning to feel rather foolish, like she was making an unnecessary fuss and everyone was looking at her, but she couldn't help it. She still couldn't say anything, so she just nodded and let Pickatina lead her away. "Boy Frank, please be helping my cousin look after the dogs," the goblin said over her shoulder. "Tell him to come to the Naga's home when everything is settled. We will be there."

The two of them walked into the village. The little white-walled houses were close together, but all still had neat little gardens with well-trimmed lawns and pretty window boxes full of flowers. The paths between the houses were dry, dusty dirt tracks. A few cheerful-looking goblins in brightly coloured clothes waved as they passed, but Pickatina kept them moving and soon they reached the village square. This was a wide cobbled space about as big as the playground at the old school. It was full of market stalls, brightly coloured affairs like a jumble of half-built tents, striped sides bulging in the gentle breeze that stopped the day being too hot.

There were stalls selling bundles of wool, bolts of cloth, apples and pears and funny-looking vegetables. A fat goblin in a stripy apron had a huge stall selling slugs and snails and nasty slimy things on sticks. There were stalls selling hats and cloaks, gloves and scarve, and boots and sandals that ranged in size from as small as Penny's thumb to as big as her body. I wouldn't like to meet the person who needed a boot that big, she thought. But still she couldn't make her jaws work to say that to Pickatina.

The little goblin didn't pause to buy anything in the market – she just hurried the human straight over to the biggest building in the village, the only one that seemed to have two storeys. The ground floor was open on three sides, ringed with sturdy pillars and full of solid-looking tables and chairs. Inside it was cool and shadowy. Goblins sat in groups of two or three at most tables, with big tankards of smelly, foaming drink in front of them. But the two didn't stay downstairs.

Pickatina carried on to the back of the huge room and up a small staircase to the first floor. There was a long, gloomy passage lined with doors and, at the very end, Pickatina knocked on the smallest door.

"Who's there? Go away," came a voice from inside.

"It is Pickatina," Penny's friend called. "I need your help. Please let me come in, wise one."

There was a muttering, grumbling sound from the other side of the door, then noises of someone shuffling across the room. When the door opened Penny saw dirtiest, scruffiest, smelliest, oldest goblin she'd seen so far. The ancient one looked the human girl up and down.

"Ah, a girl-child. So nice, so sweet, so tasty! She seems to be in shock, Pickatina. What have you done?" this stranger asked.

"I have done nothing, Naga, but we were chased by honey bears and this little one was nearly caught," said Pickatina. That's cheeky – Penny said to herself – Pickatina shouldn't call me a little one when I'm taller than her. Why can't I say that out loud?

"It is because you are in a state of shock, little one," said the venerable goblin, as if she was reading Penny's mind. "Well, come in – I'll see what I can do for you. I should have something here."

The wrinkled creature turned and shuffled off, leaving the door open. Pickatina followed, leading Penny into the messiest room imaginable. There were no windows and only a single candle flickered on a shelf in the corner. In another dark corner was a big nest of straw and rags, smelling abominable. In fact, there was straw almost everywhere. The two walls Penny could dimly see were lined with bookcases crammed with colourful books of all shapes and sizes and a tattered assortment of rolled-up scrolls. In the middle of the room was a vast table, cluttered with bottles and flasks and tiny pots like miniature cauldrons.

The old goblin was poking through the bottles, holding some up to get a better view of their labels in the candle light, shaking some, uncorking others and sniffing them – often recoiling from a bad smell – tapping some with a dirty fingernail. Eventually she found one that seemed to satisfy her. She looked about, then scurried over to her nest and reached inside to pull out a cup. She hobbled rapidly over until she was standing in front of Penny, pouring some of the liquid into the dirty old cup.

"Drink this, human girl," said the crone, smiling like a dog that was about to be sick. "It will do you good, I promise." She waved the cup under Penny's nose – and the girl turned pale. Whatever was in there smelt revolting, like cheesy feet that had trodden in something awful. "Drink up, drink up – it will make you better," the old goblin cackled.

Penny twisted and turned her head, trying to get away from the smell of the stuff. Pickatina still had her arm around the girl's shoulders and wasn't letting her escape. "If the Naga says it will do you good, then drink it you must, Girl Pen," she insisted.

The dirty old goblin waved the potion under Penny's nose again. The human thought she was going to be sick, it smelt so bad. "Take it away!" she cried. "Take it away! I can't drink that. Please, get it away from me."

The Naga laughed like a fire spitting in a grate and suddenly span away on her heel. She threw the liquid from the cup on the floor, where it seemed to sizzle.

"It is alright, Pickatina," she said. "It has done its job. That is the drink-we-do-not-drink. The fumes do half the magic, the threat of having to drink it does the rest. I never met anyone it could not fix." She turned back and fixed Penny with her bright, beady eyes and grinned. "Smelly, isn't it?"

Penny nodded. "Thank you – I do feel better," she said softly. And it was true – she did feel much better, somehow. But also self-conscious and a little ashamed of having caused such a fuss.

The Naga patted her on the shoulder with a dirty hand. "Don't be silly. A terrible scare you had, nearly being caught by the honey bears. Enough to rattle anyone that would be," she said kindly. "Now, Pickatina, what are you doing here? And with a human child as well. Strange days indeed. Tell me all."

"Wise one, there is much to tell," said Pickatina. "We are on a mission for Queen Celestia. The mistress of lies has obtained the silver trumpet and is going to raise the Black Legion. We have been sent to stop her and bring the trumpet back."

"Just you and a human girl?" asked the Naga. "The child gave Ribaldane the trumpet, I assume."

"Yes, I did," Penny admitted, looking at her feet. "It's all my fault, though I don't really understand much of what's happening."

"There is much to understand – too much to explain in one go, I think," chuckled the Naga. There was something a bit menacing about the way she laughed. "I can see that the Queen would need to send a human – if you are to defeat the mistress there will be tasks ahead no faeriefolk can do – but I am surprised she sent you with Pickatina. No offence my dear, but you are not the usual sort that is chosen for questing."

"I also helped deliver the trumpet to the mistress," admitted Pickatina. "I must make amends. But we are not alone. We have another human child with us, a boy child. And we also have..."

At that moment, the door to the little room was flung open and Broadwallow stepped through.

"My son," gasped the Naga.

"Mother," replied Broadwallow. They stared sternly at each other and for a moment Penny thought they might start fighting, they looked so fierce. But instead they both suddenly started laughing and the Naga hobbled across the room and hugged the huge hobgoblin.

"My, how you've grown," she said. She barely came up to his waist. "Now I am thinking this quest has a chance. Show me your other human? Hmmm. Very good. A boy child."

"A very hungry boy child," said Frank. "Isn't there anything to eat around here that isn't slimy?"

"Lucky you are to have met me, young man," said the Naga with a twinkle in her eye. "I know much that is hidden from the ignorant, the young and the type of person who is more interested in physical activity than in reading books. For instance, who here knew that the slugs and snails we goblins are loving to eat will make a human sick?"

"I might have guessed it," muttered Frank.

"But who knew that this – which we cannot eat," and from beneath the table she picked up a huge, dead centipede the size of a big stick of French bread, "Is fine for a human to eat? I know it does not look nice to you, but I'm told it tastes just like something you call... chocolate."

Chapter Twenty Two
Magic

Broadwallow's mother was a very peculiar old goblin. The children never did find out her actual name – everyone called her the Naga, which Penny eventually decided was a title, like the Doctor, but for a nice witch. And the Naga had to be a witch of some sort because she definitely did magic. All the time.

The Naga had claimed the big centipedes tasted like chocolate, but the looks on Penny and Frank's faces clearly showed that they doubted it. And that was when the children got their first glimpse of the Naga's magic.

"Now, watch me carefully, humans," she said with a sly grin. A flick of her fingers and a flame was conjured beneath a metal pan. She took a big knife from the table and started to cut up the centipede, throwing bits of it into the pan, where it sizzled like bacon. But she was right – the smell was like a cup of hot chocolate. Penny's stomach rumbled loudly.

"Soon it will be ready," laughed the Naga. "Have a seat." And she waved another hand and a pair of stools came skittering across the floor out of the shadows, stopping directly behind Penny and Frank so they could sit down. Broadwallow slapped his thigh and laughed at their startled expressions.

Soon the Naga was handing out plates of centipede – which didn't look very nice, though they smelt delicious. Penny stared at hers, wondering whether she could actually eat it. She glanced at Frank, who had a doubtful expression on his face as well, but he'd already picked up a leg of centipede and was sniffing it.

"Well, it definitely smells good," he sighed. Then he took a small, cautious bite. Brown juice dribbled down his chin. As Penny watched him, a big smile slowly spread across his face. He took a bigger bite, and another. "It's lovely, Penny," he said with his mouth full. He could still be revolting sometimes.

The girl had a little bite – Frank was right. The centipede was delicious, rich and tasty like a chocolate mousse, only warm. She gobbled as much as she could. In no time, the children had both cleared their plates, had second helpings and eaten that as well. Meanwhile, Broadwallow and Pickatina were sitting on a nearby bench eating crunchy snails, shells and all.

When everyone had finished eating, the Naga cleared the plates away with a wave of her hand – they danced across the room and hopped into a bowl of soapy water. A brush started cleaning them on its own, before the plates floated over to a towel that dried them and stacked them on a corner of a shelf.

"How do you do that?" asked Frank. "Don't you need a magic wand to do stuff like that?"

"Not at all, Frank," said the Naga. "Humans may be achieving small feats of the art by using a wand. Faeriefolk who lack the gift may use them as well, but those of us born with the true talent are needing no such things. I am the magic, the magic is as I am."

"So are you a witch like Ribaldane?" Penny asked timidly.

The Naga just laughed. "I can see you have not yet met the mistress of lies," she said. "Much bigger than me, she is. And a very different kind of creature. I am light and she is dark. I am feeding you something nice, she would feed you… well, she would be feeding you *to* something nasty I suppose. I like humans and she does not, I use my magic for good and she does not. We are very different, she and I."

"Can't you use magic to get the trumpet back?" asked Frank.

"It does not work like that, Frank," said Pickatina. "Magic can let us be moving things or changing things. Sometimes it lets us see or hear things. But to move a thing from one place to another, you must be able to see it – like moving the plates from here to there. And for all magic there is a cost. To move a small thing like a plate is negligible, but to move something as mighty as the trumpet – which is heavy with its own sorcery– would take a terrible cost. More than one life could pay or the mistress would have moved it with magic herself."

"Pickatina is wise, human children," said the Naga with a twinkle in her eyes. "Though I have not taught her all my secrets yet. There is much magic about which she does not yet know. But even I could not do this for you. I do not know where the trumpet is, for one thing. But more importantly, this is your task – your quest. It is not a task that will be solved by magic, but by bravery and cunning and a true friendship between our worlds. Only by working together can you defeat the mistress of lies."

"So you can't help us?" Pickatina sounded slightly sad.

"Oh, hush!" said the Naga. "Did I say that? Of course not! But I cannot do this task for you. I cannot accompany you. I will help you today, but tomorrow you must be on your way, before those you chase get too far away from you. You are in a race as much as a chase – surely you understand that, Pickatina? For even if you are getting the trumpet away from the mistress, you must be getting to the North Pole before her."

"Why?" asked Broadwallow. "My orders are to get the trumpet and be returning it to the palace. Why keep going to the North Pole if we get it before then?"

"Because, my son, the trumpet has returned," said the Naga. "While it was gone, the Black Legion slept. If it has returned the soldiers will wake. Slower than if it is sounded, to be sure, but wake they will. And if there is nobody there to lead them with the power of the trumpet, they will be seeking a leader of their own. Still it could be Ribaldane, or it could be her creature Grimshock – it could be anyone. Unless you are using the trumpet's power to command them to return to their slumber, they will stalk our world causing havoc wherever they go."

"We can't just catch Ribaldane, grab the trumpet and go home quickly?" Penny asked.

"No, Penny, I'm afraid not," said the Naga with a wicked smile. "And even catching the mistress will not be easy."

"Where will she be going?" asked Frank, in a no-nonsense tone of voice. "You seem to know a lot about it. Can you tell us?"

"Which way she will go, I do not know," said the Naga. "But

I can make a good guess. She may sail down the great river for a way, but then she will probably go through the wild wood – thinking nobody would follow her there. From there she will cross the Dragon Mountains, heading for the Last Citadel. Only there can she get a boat across the Sea of Dreams, to the Great Ice Sheet. Once she gets there, it is but a short journey to the Silent Palace at the North Pole."

"Sounds like a long way to me," said Frank. "And we have to get the trumpet, do the journey ourselves, then get back to the palace all within a month. Can we do that?"

"With my son and Pickatina to help you, of course you can," said the Naga. "Now, let us be making preparations for your journey." She waved a hand and there was a loud knocking, just as if she'd banged on the floor with a stick. The children looked around to see what magic was going to appear, but for a moment, nothing happened. Then there was a knock on the door. A little goblin lady looked in and the Naga whistled and clicked at her a few times, then she was gone.

Pretty soon there were goblins coming and going so fast the children's heads were spinning. Big goblins, small goblins, skinny ones and fat ones. Penny thought she recognised some of them from fighting the honey bears, or from when she'd walked through the village. But they were all talking in the goblin language, telling the Naga things while Broadwallow and Pickatina listened – but the children couldn't understand any of it. So they just sat and waited silently, feeling powerless.

Eventually, the door opened and in came the short goblin with the leather waistcoat who'd welcomed the children to Honeypatch. He was leading an old, scruffy goblin in much-patched clothes. When he saw the children, the short goblin smiled. "Ah, the humans! How good to see you," he said. "I am Stockturn, mayor of Honeypatch. You should be hearing the tale this one has to tell, I am thinking."

The old goblin told his story in the goblin language, which Pickatina translated. "This old one is Swallowfart the boatman," she explained. "He says that last night a duck landed, carrying the traitor Grimshock and the mistress. The duck was exhausted, so they bought his boat from him and set sail down the great river."

"The Naga was right!" exclaimed Frank. "That's great!"

"Not great is what Swallowfart also heard," Pickatina said. "He is saying he heard Grimshock ask the mistress how she planned to stop the humans following them down the river."

"They know we're following them!" Penny gasped.

"Yes, though maybe that was just a guess," said Pickatina. "Anyway, that is not the bad bit. The bad bit is what the mistress was saying in reply. She said she would stir up the pike."

Penny thought for a minute. She knew that pike were fish with sharp teeth and they could get pretty big, like a cricket bat. That's in the human world. But when faerie dogs were as big as horses, she couldn't help but wonder... "Just how big are your pike?" she asked nervously.

"The small ones are twice as big as Broadwallow, faster than hawks, with teeth like knives," said Stockturn cheerfully. "We have the toughest pike on the river. They will be eating anything."

"So how can we escape them?" Frank asked.

"Simple," said Broadwallow. "We do not sail on the river. We will be keeping on the dogs and riding along the banks."

"No, my son. Too slow that will be," said the Naga. "You need to fly. Tomorrow you will resume your chase. And you will travel along the great river – by duck."

Chapter Twenty Three

Flying

Penny had trouble sleeping that night. Pickatina, the Naga and Broadwallow were all curled up inside the Naga's messy nest. The children could hear them snoring, like three drains gurgling in the dark. The Naga had used magic to make some bits of rag all thick and fluffy, like mattresses for the humans and they were sleeping under the cloaks the queen had given them.

Frank burped in the dark. "Excuse me," he said. "Those centipedes might taste nice, but they do repeat on a fellow."

"I can't sleep either," Penny said. "I'm worried about flying."

"Can't be anything to worry about, can it?" said Frank. "Or the Naga wouldn't have suggested it."

"But Frank, I'm afraid of heights," Penny said. "I get scared when I have to climb up ladders and things – you know that. You teased me often enough about being afraid. Remember when I got stuck in the tree house in the park?"

"Oh. Yeah. Sorry about that," said Frank quietly. And he did sound sorry. "Look, this won't be like that, I'm sure," he continued. "You'll see. It'll be like a fairground ride, but with feathers. Just like riding the dogs was fun, not scary." He yawned.

"And that's another thing," Penny said. "What's going to happen to the dogs? I like 748. I don't want to leave him behind. Frank? Frank?"

But Frank had fallen asleep. Penny lay there for a bit, worrying, but in the end must have fallen asleep too.

She woke to the smell of frying centipede – except of course it smelled like hot chocolate, so actually it was quite a nice smell. Frank was already up, sitting on a stool and tucking into his breakfast. Penny scrambled out of bed, eager to get some food.

Nobody really talked while they had breakfast, apart from the Naga. She fussed around, chattering all the time. Everyone else was quite subdued, as if they were feeling as nervous as Penny but didn't want to admit it.

It was quiet when they left the Naga's room after breakfast. The big open hall on the ground floor was empty and the market square was deserted. They passed one or two silent goblins hurrying along the narrow streets. It must have been early as it was quite cold, a hint of mist thickening the air as the Naga led the way downhill between rows of neat, white goblin houses.

Soon Penny could see the river ahead. It was steel-grey and wide, the far side lost in the fog that seemed to thicken as the travellers approached the banks. Stockturn was waiting for them, with the dogs. Two ducks were bobbing patiently in the water. The mayor smiled broadly when he saw the humans coming.

"Ah, my human friends – so good to see you this morning," he said heartily. "All rested? All set for your trip? Good, good. I have picked out two of our finest ducks. They will be carrying you downriver for a whole day – but if you could let them rest overnight and then fly back to us tomorrow, I would be grateful."

"Of course, Mayor Stockturn," said Pickatina. "You are most kind to lend us your ducks."

"But how will we travel once the ducks have gone back?" Penny asked.

"Why, by dog of course," said Pickatina. But she could see that the children didn't understand how they'd take the dogs with them. The ducks were big – but not big enough to carry a dog. Not if anyone was going to ride the ducks as well.

"I am understanding your confusion," said the Naga, smiling kindly. "Let me be showing you a little faerie trick."

She waved her hands over 998, Broadwallow's giant dog – and it began to shrink. Frank and Penny gasped. The huge dog lay down while it was shrinking, seeming to go to sleep. In less than a minute the enormous mastiff was no bigger than an orange.

Broadwallow stooped and picked the tiny 998 up. "Thanks mum," he said. "You are the best at this."

The Naga just shrugged and said nothing, but Penny thought she looked a little bit proud. The old goblin walked round shrinking all the dogs – 748 the setter, Frank's 888, Pickatina's 996 and 620 the baggage dog. Broadwallow picked them all up one at a time and stowed them carefully in his bag.

"This is how faerie folk take animals to market," said Pickatina. "The animal sleeps through the journey and you can get lots of them in one bag."

"I've never seen anything like it," said Frank. Penny was too surprised to know what to say. "Can you do people too?"

Pickatina and the Naga exchanged a look. "It is possible – but very difficult," said the Naga. "It is the kind of dark art used by the mistress of lies. No good goblin would do such a thing. Besides, I like you both far too much for that."

She reached into her grubby robes. "I have bought you a present, to say goodbye," she said, pulling out a huge centipede in each hand. "These will keep you going for a few days at least."

"Now, it is time for you to be going," said Stockturn. "You want to be making a good start. Come, I have arranged the transport for you. Pickatina and Frank, you take this duck. Broadwallow and Penny, please take the drake – he is a strong bird and should be coping with Broadwallow's weight."

Penny swallowed nervously. The ducks were floating right next to the bank, with quaint leather saddles on their backs and reins just like a horse. But the way the drake fixed her with its expressionless black eye made a squadron of butterflies take off in her stomach. It didn't look the least bit friendly.

"It's okay Penny," said Frank, who had already clambered onto his duck with Pickatina without hesitating. "It's really comfy and safe, you'll see."

The Naga patted the girl on the shoulder. "You will be alright," the old goblin said. "My son will look after you, because he knows otherwise he will have to answer to me. Just take a deep breath and trust Broadwallow."

The big hobgoblin kissed the Naga goodbye then picked Penny up and lifted her onto the duck's back. It didn't seem too bad – no worse than sitting on the dog. At least, until Broadwallow climbed on in front of her. Then the drake rocked backwards and forwards in the water and for a second the girl thought she was going to fall off or perhaps the bird would sink.

"Have no fear, Girl Pen," said Broadwallow. "I will take care of you." That reassured her. A bit. She managed a brave smile as she waved goodbye to Stockturn and the Naga while the ducks swam slowly away from the shore.

132

Soon the ducks were in the fast main current, a football-field's length from the bank, when they began quacking quietly. Broadwallow stiffened, then drew his huge sword.

"What is it?" Penny asked. But with a sinking feeling in the pit of her stomach, she knew what the answer would be.

"Pike," Broadwallow said. "The ducks sense them. The mistress has somehow roused them – normally they would never go near a duck, or even this close to the village. But we must be careful. I am wanting the ducks in the air as quickly as they can."

That's when Penny saw the pike. It broke water alongside the drake, swimming beside her for a moment. Its head was as long as the girl's body, with a big mouth clearly full of razor-sharp teeth. Its body was almost as long as a lorry. It stared at Penny with a dead, cold eye, then vanished under the water again.

"Make haste, cousin!" shouted Broadwallow. Pickatina didn't answer, but she cracked the reins of her duck. It seemed to spring into action, swimming forwards faster and faster, flapping its wing and seeming to run on the water until it took off.

Then a pike jumped out of the river and fastened itself onto their duck's foot.

The drake was right behind them, running and flapping too. The huge fish hanging on the other duck slowed it down and for a second it seemed the birds were going to crash into each other. Then Broadwallow jumped up so he was standing on the on the saddle and, leaning forward so far Penny was convinced he had to fall, he grunted and swung his sword. It hit the pike behind the back of its ugly head with a noise like a car door slamming.

Black blood fountained from the sword cut. The huge fish opened its mouth and dropped back into the river. The splash was colossal. Waves of icy water were thrown into the air, splashing over Penny. Pickatina's duck shot into the sky. As Broadwallow sat down, dripping with water, the drake seemed to tip back like a horse rearing – then it took off, wingtips splashing softly on the surface of the water. Penny looked down as the grey river and its terrible pike fell away into the mist beneath her – she was flying!

133

Chapter Twenty Four
Pike

The ducks climbed lazily into the air. Every now and then one of them would quack and the other would answer, but it was quiet up in the sky. Actually, that's not true. All Penny could hear was the rushing of the wind. It was like a gentle but overpowering shhhhhh. Broadwallow turned in the saddle to speak to her, but she couldn't hear him until he shouted.

"How do you like flying, Girl Pen?" he asked, a hopeful grin on his big sad face.

"It's good!" she said. And she was surprised to find that she meant it. There was nothing scary about this – now she was safe from the huge pike in the river.

The ducks were flying high now, with Faerieland spread out beneath them. Mist lay across much of the land – a perfect circle of it like an enormous drop of milk that had been spilt on a map. Honeypatch was right on the edge of it, a cluster of little buildings like a model village rising from the mist as if on an island rather than a hilltop. Behind it the tops of the hills of the rolling flower plains stretched away into the distance. There was no sign of the faerie palace, so it must have been a long way away.

Looking forwards Penny could see nothing but the bizarrely perfect circle of mist for miles and miles. It rose in a high dome before spreading out. Just visible beyond it was a lake like a shiny silver coin dropped on a grey-green carpet. On the other side of that was a dark green mark, like a stain, which she guessed must be the Wild Wood. Because on the other side of that was a fine line of grey and white which had to be snow-capped mountains. They still looked tiny, so they still had to be a long way away.

"How far is it to the mountains, Broadwallow?" she shouted.

"It is two days by duck, if you follow the river," the hobgoblin bellowed. "But I think we will be landing at the town on the lake. We may hear a rumour of the mistress there."

Town on the lake? Penny squinted, but couldn't see anything. Though the lake was still a long way ahead. She settled back to enjoy the journey. Even though she hadn't been awake for long, she felt strangely sleepy. Soon she nodded off.

Penny woke with a stiff neck, shivering. It was cold and grey and she couldn't see much at all. The other duck, the one with Frank and Pickatina, was just a grey blur a dozen metres away.

"What's happening, Broadwallow?" she called.

"Awake, are you, Girl Pen? We are coming to land on the great river," he replied. "The fog is on us – we will be losing our way if we cannot see through it. So come down we must and wait until it passes. Then we can continue."

"But what about the pike?" Penny looked anxiously down.

"We must hope our ducks can get to the bank before any notices us," he said grimly. "I am sure they can. Do not be afraid."

That was easy for him to say, thought Penny. He'd hit a pike with his sword. He was big. The girl didn't have a sword and she reckoned one of those monster fish could eat her up in a single mouthful. Before she could say anything, there was a bump and a splash and a shushing sound as the drake touched down. Then they were sailing smoothly across the water.

Frank and Pickatina's duck landed a moment later. They were just faint shadows in the nearby fog. The river was so wide and the mist was so thick Penny couldn't even see the shore. Broadwallow seemed to know where it was, though. He flicked the reins of the drake and it began swimming silently in what the petrified human really hoped was the direction of the bank.

Then Penny heard a noise – a gentle *ber-loop-ahh* kind of noise. She looked in the direction it had come from in time to see, not five metres from the duck, a large fin disappearing beneath the surface of the water.

She nudged Broadwallow and pointed, but of course there was nothing there by then. He raised an eyebrow, then raised a finger to his lips, urging silence.

Then Penny heard it again. *Ber-loop-ahh*... and this time Broadwallow heard it. His head swivelled round and they looked at the water between their drake and the duck carrying Frank and Pickatina. And there it was, just disappearing... a grey-green fin the size of a car door, fan-shaped with sharp, webbed points.

Broadwallow silently mouthed one word: pike.

Panic gripped Penny. She felt as hot as a pan suddenly boiling over on the stove, but at the same time as frozen as a leaf trapped in an icy pond. She didn't know what to do with herself. Her skin was itching madly but she couldn't move her hands to scratch. Only her eyes moved – all she could do was look about, desperate for some sign of the river bank. But there was nothing. Nothing but more pike...

It was so misty it was hard to see far, but she counted three other fins breaking the surface on the left, plus one between the drake and the duck. Penny couldn't see if there were more pike on the other side of Frank's bird but, from the way he was looking about and pointing, his step-sister guessed there were.

She was drawing air raggedly in, barely breathing out, as if she might scream at any second when she heard another sound – unexpected and beautiful. It was someone singing in a high and clear voice, almost like the song of a nightingale – though Penny couldn't understand any words. As she breathed out, she realised the voice really was whistling like a bird between the words.

It was Pickatina. Standing up on the saddle of her duck, singing in this strange but enchanting voice. Penny wondered what the little goblin was doing, but Broadwallow nudged her and pointed. The pike between the drake and Pickatina's duck had rolled on its side and was half out of the water. It was swimming listlessly along on the surface as if it was listening to Pickatina.

Penny looked to the other side of the drake and there was one pike also rolling on its side. Pickatina had to be doing some kind of magic with the song, making the giant killer fish dopey.

It was just a pity the spell wasn't working on all the fish. The other ones on the far side of the drake weren't looking dopey at all. In fact, they were looking brutal. Worse, they were looking hungry. They were swimming along even faster than the drake, cutting savage curves through the water with their jagged fins.

Then one of them jumped. It flew clean out of the water, a huge thing with a solid, muscular body and a huge mouth that it opened wide. Penny had never seen anything with so many teeth. For a second it hung in the air and fixed her with its evil, flat eye and then it vanished smoothly into the water with barely a splash.

Penny couldn't help herself. She gave a little shriek. It was only a small one and it escaped without warning. But of course, crying out only made things worse.

The dopey looking fish nearest to her and the one between the drake and Pickatina's duck both shook their heads, as if they'd been distracted from the song. The one between the two ducks settled instantly back into its odd lying-on-its-side-to-listen swim. But the other one, the one furthest from Pickatina, didn't settle down… it seemed to wink at Penny. As if it was thanking her for waking it up. Then it rolled over in the water and disappeared beneath the surface.

A second later, the pike reappeared. It leapt from the water in a high, curving arc – it soared through the air as high above the surface of the river as the drake's head, then splashed back down. It didn't spear its way into the water like the other pike that had jumped. It landed flat, throwing up huge sheets of water that fell on Penny like a dozen punches. The wind was knocked from her, she was drenched and chilled to the bone.

Broadwallow roared, drew his big sword and stood up on the saddle. "Keep down, Girl Pen," he barked harshly.

Another fish jumped. And another. Each time they landed, they showered the drake and its passengers with more water. Penny was shivering uncontrollably, hunched over and clinging onto the drake's feathers. Broadwallow was swinging his sword every time a fish jumped, but they were always too far away for him to hit. Then the drake quacked in alarm… and the girl saw the fish in between the ducks wake up too. Both ducks were swimming really quickly.

The drake went to flap his wings, but suddenly shook and twitched to one side. Penny saw a pike was hanging onto the tip of its wing. With a massive shrug that almost made Broadwallow fall into the river, the bird shook his wing free. He flapped both wings together and seemed to hop forward, lifting slightly.

Then a pike jumped directly at the drake. It hurtled out of the water and soared through the air above the drake's back. It went no more than ten centimetres above Penny's head, dripping water that smelled cold as death. Broadwallow dropped flat on his belly, hanging almost off the drake's neck – his passenger was sure the fish was going to bite him. But instead he rolled to one side and held up his sword. It cut a deep, bloody line along the pike's belly. Black blood spurted over the hobgoblin.

Another pike jumped and the drake had to dip his head to avoid being bitten by its massive, wide-open jaws. Penny looked to the side and saw a V-shaped wave heading straight towards her – a pike swimming fast, just below the surface. When it was about three meters away it leapt high into the air. It might have sailed right over the drake but Broadwallow sprang up, swinging his sword, and cut its huge head clean off. Blood rained down on the human child and the drake.

Then the drake shook and Penny was thrown backwards out of the saddle. She slid down slick feathers, just catching hold one of the saddle's straps with her left hand. Broadwallow gave a high-pitched yelp and fell off the side. The girl drew a breath, unsure whether to scream or concentrate on pulling herself back towards the saddle, when she heard the hobgoblin's crackling laughter. The duck shuffled a little forwards and stopped. It was on the bank. Pickatina and Frank were already there, ahead of her. Penny dropped to the ground, dripping and bloody. But they were safe.

Chapter Twenty Five

Ambushed

"Are you alright?" called Frank. He had climbed down from his duck and was standing on the river bank a few metres away, a ghostly figure in the mist. It took Penny a moment to answer. She still couldn't quite believe she'd escaped the pike.

Broadwallow stood up and sheathed his sword. "We are fine, Boy Frank," he said. "I have a small bump on my head where I fell as our drake climbed the bank, but Girl Pen is unhurt."

"But I'm cold and filthy," she said. "I'm covered in fish blood and… urgh… it stinks! And anyway, what do we do now?" Penny looked around, but there was nothing to see. No trees or bushes, hedges or villages, not even any hills that she could see – nothing but white mist over grassy bank and glassy river, limiting the view to a hundred meters in every direction. It was like being trapped inside a boring snow globe.

"Well, we could wait for the mist to lift," said Pickatina. "Then we could ask our ducks to fly again."

"But what about the pike?" Frank asked. "Won't they be waiting for us?"

"It is possible," admitted Pickatina. "The mistress has stirred them up and made them angry indeed."

"Couldn't you do your magic again?" asked Penny.

"I could, but there are too many fish," she said. "You saw that, Girl Pen. We were safe, but I could not calm the pike further away and so Broadwallow and you were attacked. Besides, I am not liking this fog. It is too thick for this time of year. I fear the hand of the mistress – but wary that makes me, for weather magic is unusually difficult. But if this mist was conjured up by the mistress then pointless it would be to wait for it to lift. Another way to continue we should find, I think."

"Well, we could just ride the dogs," Penny said. They all looked at her. "I thought you didn't liked being shaken about on the dog's back," said Frank.

"Well, I don't," she confessed. "But I don't like being eaten by giant fish either. I can't see fish attacking us on the land."

"No, but what about the honey bears?" asked Frank.

"Honey bears are very rare, Boy Frank," said Pickatina. "We were unlucky to be chased by them. They love the flowers around Honeypatch so that is where you are likely to be finding them."

"Besides," Penny added. "I feel sorry for the dogs being all shrunk up and shaken around in Broadwallow's bag."

In the end, the goblins agreed that it was the only thing to do. First, Pickatina got some rags that she dipped – carefully – in the river and wiped the worst of the fish blood from Penny's clothes. Then Broadwallow took the dogs out of his bag and carefully set them on the ground. With all the jumping about that he'd done, fighting the pike and falling off the drake when it landed, Penny half-expected the dogs to be a bit bent or broken, but they all seemed to be fine. They just looked like little models of the dogs. Except when the children touched them, they were warm.

Pickatina walked around from dog to dog, carefully stroking each one and clicking to it in goblin… and as she did so, each dog grew rapidly back to its original size. They all seemed pleased to see the children: 748 tried to lick Penny with a tongue as long as her arm.

With the dogs saddled up, the travellers set off down the river bank. The fog seemed to get thicker as they rode along. Soon Penny could see Frank in front of her and, if she turned in the saddle, Pickatina behind her. But she couldn't see Broadwallow at the front or 620, the baggage dog, at the back of their little column. The mist was cold and damp and muffled sound. They rode and rode and rode. Both children were getting really bored – especially as they couldn't even talk to each other – but at last Penny felt she was getting into a rhythm, riding better.

She mentioned that when they stopped for lunch – a bit of the chocolate centipede for the children; slugs for the goblins. Pickatina smiled and nodded wisely. "Faerie beasts, our dogs are," she explained. "Far faster they are than any of the creatures from your world at learning how to serve their riders. The more you ride your dog, the more it will understand you. The more it will tune in to your needs. Soon its senses will be focused on protecting you as much as protecting itself." The goblin gave a nervous laugh. "Not that you should need protecting now."

They fell silent at that. In the gloomy, oppressive fog it was quite easy to believe that they would need protecting. The damp, dull clouds looked perfect for some menace to lurk in, just out of sight. Yet when they set out for the afternoon's ride, everything seemed quiet and an uneventful few hours passed boringly by. The first warning that anything was wrong came from the dogs. It was 748 that whined, then he became a bit skittish – he kept tossing his head and trying to pull towards the river, as though he didn't want to go forwards. Penny patted his neck and whispered to encourage him, but he seemed very reluctant to move.

Then she saw Frank's dog was also starting to get nervous. Pickatina's dog bumped into Penny's. "Why have you stopped, Girl Pen?" asked the goblin, resting her hand on the girl's arm.

"I don't know," she replied. "Something's spooked the dogs. They don't want to go anywhere. Look." She flapped the reins and 748 suddenly leapt forward with a yelp, nearly throwing Penny from the saddle.

Frank was riding beside her, trying to grab her reins. Penny couldn't even see Broadwallow or Pickatina – but she was concentrating on staying on her dog.

Dull shapes appeared in the mist off to the left, running alongside the fleeing dogs. They were still about 30 metres away, lost in the gauzy white gloom of the fog, so Penny couldn't see what they were exactly, but they looked like animals with riders. But they didn't look like dogs or even horses. The children couldn't quite work out what kind of animals they were… or what kind of riders. But there seemed to be quite a lot of them.

Suddenly there was a whooshing noise, followed by a kind

of rapid pitter-patter. Penny felt something thud into the saddle in front of her... it was an arrow! A thin one no more than 15 centimetres long, with fine green feathers at the end of the shaft. Whatever was chasing them was shooting at them.

Luckily, none of the arrows had hit 748 – it was just the one stuck in the saddle. Penny didn't have time to worry about it, because more of them were coming. Another faint whoosh warned her of another incoming salvo. The girl flung herself flat against the galloping dog's neck, getting jolted viciously from side to side, her riding rhythm ruined. She heard the arrows fly over her head, splashing into the river with a noise like a handful of gravel being thrown into a pond.

Was the mist finally starting to thin a little? It was getting easier to see the attackers. No – the mist was just as thick but Penny realised the animals and their hostile riders were actually much closer than she'd thought – and much smaller. As she hauled herself back into a proper riding position she got a decent look at a couple as they swooped close to her. The animals weren't the size of the goblin dogs, they were the size of big normal dogs, but broader and shorter in the leg. They were black and white, with pointy noses – they were badgers!

And riding on the badgers were bizarre stick men with spiky armour and pointy noses. They looked very fierce.

Suddenly Broadwallow was galloping alongside her, swinging his sword at the funny creatures and shouting loudly in the goblin language, sounding the world's largest woodpecker. The badger-riders dodged nimbly out of his way, falling back into the mist. No more arrows came, but Penny kept her head down and kept riding.

For several minutes, they didn't see any more sign of the badger riders. Penny was starting to think they may have escaped. Just as 748 was beginning to tire, Pickatina turned to the right and rode away from the river. The rest of the dogs followed as the small goblin's dog climbed a gentle hill. They all stopped at the top, dogs panting. Even Penny was panting.

"We should be safe here," Pickatina called. "Everyone can climb down and be resting while I try to work out what to do."

"What were those things, Pickatina?" Frank asked, stepping down from the saddle.

"Pixies," she replied. "We entered their territory without asking and they are not liking that. Very proud, they are. So they sent a war party out to drive us off."

"They were only little," said Frank. "Can't we fight them?"

"No, young warrior," rumbled Broadwallow with a grin. "There are too many of them and they move too fast. They would tire us out, trick us, trap us, then probably eat us."

"Broadwallow!" said Pickatina crossly. "You know pixies do not eat people. You must not be scaring the children like that. No, Girl Pen, Boy Frank – ignore Broadwallow. The pixies would not eat us. They would just cut off our heads to decorate their camp."

"What?" they both cried. "Cut off our heads?"

"That's even worse," said Frank. "Come on – surely we have to be able to do something. We must be able to fight them or make them let us pass."

"We will have to be making a parley with them," Pickatina said seriously. "They are a proud and independent people. If we can apologise and be giving them a gift, then maybe they will let us cross their lands."

"Don't they have to let us pass?" Penny asked. "I mean, we're on a mission for the queen. Shouldn't they listen to that and be trying help us, not trying to stop us going where we want to go and shooting arrows at us?"

"Pixies are a wild bunch," said Broadwallow. "They do not live in villages like civilised goblins. They are living in tents, in camps that move from day to day, from week to week. They follow the mighty herds of beetles that roam the plains. They say they serve Queen Celestia, but really they are just wanting to be left alone. We have had many wars with the pixies because they are not good servants of the queen."

"So how do we arrange a truce or a parley with them?"

Penny asked nervously.

"We will have to send them a messenger, who can persuade them to listen to us," said Pickatina. "To try to make them hear reason, I shall go to them."

"I don't think you need to," said Frank quietly. "Look."

The rest of them looked up and there, looming out of the mist, came pixies on their badgers. There must have been at least 50 of them. They were all around the travellers. They were completely surrounded.

Chapter Twenty Six

The Brown Raiders

Pickatina stepped forwards to face the pixies. One had dismounted and was walking forward. Penny was going to follow her friend, but Broadwallow put his hand on her shoulder.

It was easier to see the pixie clearly as he came closer. He was very short – he would barely have come up to Penny's waist – and very, very thin. His arms and legs were no thicker than bits of rope. His body wasn't much stouter. But his head was much bigger – as long as his body and a bit thicker, with a pointy nose, sharp cheekbones and a small, cruel-looking mouth. His eyes were black and he had a mass of dark spiky hair. His clothes were rough, rumpled and brown, so he looked as if he was made of twigs.

Pickatina stopped a few metres from the pixie and raised her right hand. "Greetings, wind of the plains. I am Pickatina, daughter of Marrowbash, chancellor to the great Queen Celestia. May I know to whom I have the honour of speaking?"

Penny had expected the pixie to have a high voice, maybe a squeaky one. But he didn't. It was low and deep, like huge metal drum being rolled across the floor of a barn. "I am Paisley, hetman of the Brown Raiders. What brings you to our lands uninvited, daughter of the palace household?"

Broadwallow made a rumbling growl, but Pickatina held her hand up before he could speak. She replied to the pixie: "We are on a mission for the magnificent Queen who is mother to us all, great Paisley. A vital and important mission."

"Hmmm. It can not be such a vital mission I think," said the pixie. "Or I would know of it. How can it be so important if the great Queen has not told her greatest allies? How can it be so important if she sends the daughters of her house?"

"You would do well to mind your tongue, pixie," said Broadwallow. "You speak to a shadow walker and enchantress, the foremost apprentice of the mighty Naga."

"What the mighty Captain Broadwallow, chief of the Queen's hobgoblin guard, means to say," rushed in Pickatina, "Is that we were on our way to inform you of our mission and to seek your assistance. Of course we will need the aid of the Brown Raiders – how could it be otherwise?"

The pixie was staring hard at Broadwallow. "Captain Broadwallow would also do well to remember his manners," he said. "He doesn't have his hobgoblin legion with him now. Just two human children and a lady – and a lady, no matter how distinguished, could not save him if he insults our dignity again."

Broadwallow's grip on the girl's shoulder tightened and he grunted, but he didn't speak. Penny looked up at him and he was scowling angrily.

"My cousin meant no offence, mighty Paisley," said Pickatina. "He merely wanted you to understand my position in the royal household. I am no chambermaid. I am the royal spell-maker. By sending me to you, with human escorts and with the chief of her hobgoblins, Queen Celestia does you great honour."

The pixie hesitated before speaking again, looking a bit less sure of himself. "Very well, my lady. I see. I thank you Captain Broadwallow. Please forgive my harsh words." He paused for a moment. "My rudeness is unforgivable. Your forgiveness would be a gift, Captain. What would you ask of the Brown Raiders?"

"We need a guide, oh great Paisley," said Pickatina. "Safe passage across your huge homelands, with an introduction to your neighbouring tribe – if such unworthy neighbours can assist us. We have to reach the Town on the Lake as soon as we might."

"This we can do," Paisley said. "If Captain Broadwallow can forgive my words and extend the hand of friendship."

There was an awkward pause and for a moment the children thought Broadwallow might refuse, but as Pickatina turned to give him a hard stare, the big hobgoblin finally spoke. "Of course I forgive you, worthy Paisley. A harsh word between warriors is like a warm greeting between farmers, is it not?"

Broadwallow took two steps forward and bowed, then shook hands with the pixie. Or rather, held out a massive finger that the pixie gripped with both hands. They shook hands very seriously.

Suddenly the air was thick with clapping and the sound of deep, clanging, booming noises. For a second Penny wondered what it could be – then she realised it was the pixies talking and laughing. Their language sounded like water going down a well or large metal drums being tapped with hammers. The tiny creatures hurried forward, patting the dogs and chattering in deep, booming voices. They were uncanny beings and something about the way they moved made the hairs rise on the back of the children's necks. The pixies took high steps, swaying slightly from side to side, arms held high. Like evil puppets, without strings.

Paisley had stepped forward to stand in front of Frank and Penny, but he wasn't saying anything. Pickatina rushed up.

"Great Paisley, allow me to introduce Penelope and Francis, who are kin to Mitchellpete the mighty wizard and guardian of the human palace," she said. "They have been sent to assist us in our mission for the queen."

"I have never met humans before," he said. "You are not as… tall as I was expecting. However, it is a great honour to meet you both. I hope you will speak well of us when our journey together comes to an end."

Penny realised a reply was expected. She nudged Frank,

but he was just staring down at the pixie in astonishment, so she spoke. "Thank you, er, mighty Paisley. You are the first pixie we have met. We feel honoured too."

The pixie nodded with great dignity, then turned to Pickatina. "We should be riding, before the mist burns away. With luck we should reach our village in a few hours," he said. "From there it is but a short trip to the great lake and the town you seek. My braves can take you all the way there."

The ride to the pixie village was a strange one. Paisley rode at the front on his badger, followed by the children. Behind them came Pickatina and Broadwallow. Then, strung out in a long line, came all the other pixies. Penny didn't know how many there were – she thought there were about fifty but because of the way the mist stopped sound, and because the procession seemed so serious nobody spoke, the journey was absolutely silent.

Penny was definitely getting the hang of riding her dog – at least, riding slowly. Actually, she was quite enjoying it, which she wouldn't have thought possible after her first go at it. But she decided that riding is definitely more enjoyable when you're at the head of a procession, as a guest of honour, than it is when you're being chased by angry honey bears.

They did seem to be riding for a long time, but they weren't going very fast. At least the mist was gradually thinning, but as the sun was sinking it was getting darker and hard to see anyway.

All around them as they rode, the tiny fairies were emerging and hovering above their flowers, like tiny Christmas tree lights. They buzzed faintly and swirled out of the path of Paisley's badger as he rode forwards. The girl turned to look behind her, using one hand to stop her hair getting in her eyes – the long line of pixies was riding through a sea of multicoloured lights and leaving dark lines behind them where the fairies had fled, like a fleet of ships cutting dark wakes across a moonlit sea.

Just as it was getting properly dark, as hunger and exhaustion were beginning to make the children feel dizzy, the strange faerie procession came to the top of a hill – easily the biggest hill they'd climbed since they first started riding across the flower plains. The river was a long way to their left now and far below them.

At the top of the hill was a camp that could only be the pixie village. Dozens of dark tents were scattered across the top of the hill. Penny had been expecting to find a settlement of pointey teepees, but the pixie tents had rounded sides and looked more like inverted tulips, their dark sides glinting in the light of the flower faeries and the numerous small campfires that burned through the encampment. Paisley stood up in the stirrups and gave a long, wavering call like treacle glugging down a drain.

Suddenly dozens of little pixies – some of them no bigger than Penny's foot – rushed out from among the huts and started running alongside the dogs and the badgers. In the fading light, they looked almost like a swarm of rats. But they were calling excitedly in voices that were low and echoing. These had to be the pixie children!

The procession stopped in the centre of the village, where there was a small crowd of pixies waiting. They didn't have spiky hair, but long plaits – Penny realised they were the female pixies, though only the hair showed them to be different from the men. Paisley stood up in his saddle and clanged out a short speech in the pixie language, after which all the lady pixies scurried off, taking the children with them.

"They will prepare a feast," said Paisley, speaking the human tongue. "They will gather nest materials for our goblin guests. Our human guests may sleep in a lodge. Legend has it that they like beds. Be welcome here, friends. You are guests of the Brown Raiders, kings of the plains. Tonight, you will sleep in comfort."

Chapter Twenty Seven

Beetles

The pixie feast seemed very strange to the children. Everyone sat in big circle around a huge bonfire that had been built up in the centre of the camp – a fire so wide and high Penny couldn't see past it to see the pixies on the other side. It was completely dark, the stars were out and the moon was low in the sky, while beyond the pixie village the fairies danced above their flowers like millions of candle flames being reflected in gently bobbing water.

Frank and Penny sat with Pickatina, Broadwallow and Paisley, treated as honoured guests. The girl found she was a little afraid of the pixie chief when he was up close. The way his head was so much bigger than his body, the jerky way he moved, his hard black eyes… Penny was glad he had sat next to Pickatina.

The food was alright, though. The pixies had stew of a strange, black meat that smelled a bit like old tea bags, but the children didn't eat any of it. They had their centipede cooked with rice and flowers. It was almost like chicken nuggets, only it tasted of chocolate. It was like a proper meal – the first they'd had since coming to Faerieland. It was only as they ate it that they realised how hungry they were.

While the travellers were eating, the some of the smaller and – Penny guessed – younger pixie warriors put on a show, dancing round the outside of the huge bonfire and singing. Their deep voices filled the night air with unusual melodies, slow and sad. It was beautiful but at the same time the girl felt a chill creeping down her back. The pixies were such odd creatures, especially when they moved – their dancing was nearly graceful, but not quite. The overall effect was somehow menacing.

Given how exhausted the children were, it was fortunate that it wasn't long before they were shown to the place they were to sleep. Paisley led them through the darkened camp to a pixie lodge. Most of the smaller fires had died down so the only real light came from the flickering fire in the camp's centre, which was some way away. The lodge seemed quite small – as high as Broadwallow in the middle, perhaps, but the sides sloped down quite quickly. At the base it wasn't very wide at all – slightly bigger than Frank, but not much.

As she went to bend down and pass through the small door, formed where two panels of the sides met, Penny rested her hand on the lodge. And was amazed at how solid it felt – not like a normal tent at all. She paused in the doorway and tapped the lodge wall – it was as hard as wood. With so little light it was difficult to get a proper look at the structure. It was so dark it was like a black hole cut out of the starry sky. "What is the lodge made of?" she asked Paisley nervously.

"The wing cases of the great plains beetle," he said in his eerie deep voice. "We pixies live in harmony with the beetles. We track them, we hunt them, we eat them – but not a piece is wasted. Their hide makes our clothes and the saddles for our badgers, their wing cases make our lodges. Yes, we use every bit of the beetle."

Frank looked up at the dark lodge, impressed. "Those must be some big beetles," he said.

"They are the finest beasts in nature," said Paisley proudly. "In the morning, if luck is with us, you will see a herd before you leave our lands. There is one nearby that we are tracking. Now, please, make yourselves at home. I will see you in the morning."

And with that, he turned and stalked back towards the central fire. Frank and Penny crawled through the small door – it was so small that Frank nearly got stuck – and went inside. It was pitch dark inside and the children had to feel their way around. There was just enough room for the two of them – and the pixies had made beds for them. They were a bit small, but they were proper beds. The children crawled into them fully clothed and pulled the blankets over. Within moments they were asleep.

Penny woke, disorientated. It was still dark and for a second she wondered where she was. Her first thought was that she was back in the flat that she'd shared with her dad, but then she remembered. His marrying Maggie, moving, him going to sea and them moving again – to the Little House. Ribaldane. And, of course, the mess she was in now – on a perilous mission to save the world. For a moment she considered trying to sleep again, in case she'd wake up back in her own bed and find it had all been an elaborate dream. But her feet, sticking out from beneath the blanket, were too cold for that. She knew she wouldn't sleep again. More to the point, she knew it wasn't a dream.

Sighing, she crawled out of the bed. Frank was sleeping with his mouth open, one arm thrown wildly above his head and resting on the wall of the lodge. Penny crept past him and out into the pixie camp. Out of the lodge, it was a misty morning, a pale sun hovering over low over the eastern horizon in a grey sky. There were no birds singing, but the girl could hear the occasional low rumble – pixies chattering to each other.

In the middle of the camp she found the two goblins in earnest conversation with Paisley. As they greeted her, she wondered if any of them had even gone to bed. She sat quietly beside Pickatina and a female pixie hurried over to give her a bowl of soft rice in a milk that Penny really hoped hadn't come from a beetle. Frank arrived soon afterwards. Everyone was quite subdued and before too long they'd finished their breakfast and got on the dogs. With Paisley and a handful of pixies accompanying them on badgers, their little party set out. Tiny, twiggy pixie children ran alongside them, singing in their deep voices, until they were at the bottom of the hill.

The Brown Raiders' territory seemed much hillier than the gently rolling plains they'd ridden across between the palace and Honeypatch. As the sun rose and burnt away the last of the mist, the land soon more rugged than the plains they'd crossed between the river and the pixie camp too, with more grass and fewer flowers. Most slopes were still gentle, but they were longer

– hills were higher and valleys deeper. Every now and then they came to the top of one hill to find the slope down was far steeper.

They rode in silence, stopping for lunch after crossing two or three wide valleys. Just as Penny had clambered up into 748's saddle to start the afternoon's ride, she saw Paisley was holding his hand up. He was standing up on the stirrups of his saddle, head cocked at an angle as if he was listening to something.

"The beetles!" he intoned in his deep voice. "They come."

Penny couldn't hear anything. She looked over at Frank and was about to speak when she saw him grin. "Oh yeah, listen Penny," he said. "Well, you don't even listen. You more sort of... feel the noise."

Feel the noise? Come on... But then she got it. There was a tingly, itchy feel at the back of her neck, a funny shaking in the pit of her stomach. She looked at Pickatina. "Is that the beetles?"

"It is indeed," she said. "Mighty Paisley, which way are the beetles running? It sounds like a large herd. Should we not take care to stay out of their path?"

"You are right, of course, great lady," he said. "They are coming from the east, heading towards the Great Lake. Our path will run alongside theirs, I think. We shall let them stay in the valley. Come, let us climb to the ridge."

But at that moment the other pixies in the group began clanging in alarm. Penny looked to the right and saw a tall plume of dust rising above the valley. It was moving towards them. Fast.

Frank looked at her, a slightly frightened expression on his face. "Come on Penny," he shouted. "Let's get out of here."

She didn't need telling twice. Especially when she knew 748 would get tired quickly. She flicked the reins and called to him, setting off towards the top of the next hill at a gallop. The others were all doing the same. The neat, ordered procession broke up as the big, strong goblin dogs began to pull clear of the pixies' shorter-legged, slower badgers.

But they still weren't going fast enough. The cloud of dust above the advancing herd of beetles was gaining rapidly. Penny couldn't see the creatures yet, but from the broad dust cloud it was clear that they were strung out in a wide line all the way to the top of the hill. And she was riding right across their path.

The beetles were getting closer and closer with every second. Now Penny could hear proper sounds – the thud and thump of their feet hammering into the plain. Glancing to the side, she saw her first beetle – and it was huge. Almost as big as the ducks we'd flown on – which meant they were slightly bigger than the Professor's Land Rover back at the Big House.

And there were thousands of them. The first rank of them was visible in a line below the cloud of dust. All black, with tiny little heads down near the ground where big, wicked-looking jaws stuck out. Their bodies rose steeply backwards, swelling up like glossy black aubergines. Their six legs were short but fat, stamping hard into the ground as they ran, swaying wildly.

And they were running fast, getting closer and closer all the time. With an icy chill Penny realised there was no way she was going to get to the top of the hill before they reached her… and then it was too late. She was in among them.

Even sitting on 748, she couldn't see over the top of the beetles. They were everywhere, passing on both sides. They were between Penny and Pickatina and Broadwallow. She couldn't even see what had happened to Frank.

Worse, 748 was slowing down, twisting and turning, trying to dodge out of the way of the beetles. He was running off at any angle, as long as it kept him out of the way of the giant insects. Penny quickly lost all track of which way they were meant to be going. At one point she saw a pixie's badger run in front of one of the big black insects – it knocked the badger over and threw it over its shoulder with a toss of its tiny head. The pixie vanished into the sky with a deep, clanging cry that could only just be heard over the din of the charging beetles.

The air was full of dust. It got into Penny nostrils and was making her cough. It was hard to see and she kept blinking. She was being shaken from side to side, barely able to hold on to her terrified dog. She didn't know how much longer she could stay in the saddle - though she didn't even have time to think about what would happen if she fell.

And then something strange happened. A swirling current of wind seemed to throw up more dust and as the girl blinked again, the beetles seemed to vanish.

Or rather, they vanished from the ground. The whole herd seemed to have unfolded huge grey wings and taken off in the same instant. They almost blotted out the sun. But even though they were flying, the beetles weren't far above the ground and they were still stirring up huge billowing clouds of dust.

"Girl Pen – hurry," shouted Broadwallow. He was with the others, only about 50 meters away further up the hill and over to the left. "They will land soon. Hurry!"

Penny could tell that 748 was desperately tired, but she hauled on the reins to turn him so faced the others. Digging her heels into the dog's sides, she urged him forward, up the hill. The poor setter was dragging his feet and panting hoarsely, spitting out dust.

The air was thick with the sound of the beetles' buzzing wings and little gusts of wind hit Penny like slaps as they flapped. Then there was a loud bang – and another. And another. They were landing! But not delicately. Beetles were just thumping down to the left and to the right, throwing up clouds of dust like bombs going off. If one of them landed on her…

She felt 748 make one last, almighty effort – and then she was there with Frank, Pickatina, Broadwallow and Paisley, slowly taking the last few steps to the top of the hill. She was safe – as right behind her a sea of giant beetles fell back to earth with a resounding crash.

Penny stopped and turned to look back. The entire valley – as far as the eye could see – was full of huge black beetles. They weren't running now, or even moving about much. Just lying there, like resting cows. They looked almost peaceful.

Chapter Twenty Eight
The Town on the Lake

Dust hung in the air above where the beetles. Gradually, three more pixies emerged from among the huge creatures. The last one to appear was carrying the body of another pixie. When the others saw it, they all began clanging in loud distress. Penny was really upset – it must have been the pixie she'd seen getting thrown off his badger by a beetle. She thought he must be dead.

Paisley and the other pixies ran over to help carry the last of their fellows. Their voices dropped, low mutterings like metal bins rolling over distant cobbles. The children stood silently with Pickatina and Broadwallow – nobody said anything. Nobody knew what to say. They just waited awkwardly.

Then Paisley stood up and came back to join them. "Kinloss is badly injured," he said, simply.

"He's alive?" Penny gasped. "I saw him get tossed into the air by a beetle. I thought he must be dead."

"We are hard to kill, we pixies," said Paisley, with a hint of a smile. "Leven, Gorbals and Minch will take him back to the village. With time, he will heal. But I have a debt of honour to pay to Captain Broadwallow – he saved me from certain death as two bull beetles collided. If he hadn't pulled me out from between their crashing bodies, I would have been less lucky than Kinloss. So my quest is now your quest, at least until I have repaid my life-debt to Captain Broadwallow."

Penny wasn't sure what to think of that. She was still a bit scared of Paisley, with his odd way of moving and his fierce, oversized head. Luckily Pickatina was ready with a polite answer.

"We would be honoured to have a mighty pixie chief join us, great Paisley," she said. "But are you sure you can leave your people? Should you not return to your village with your fallen warrior? Who will lead your people when you're gone?"

"Minch will lead the Brown Raiders while I ride with you," said Paisley firmly. "It is decided. No more need be said. Come, let us carry on – we can still reach the lake before nightfall."

The other pixies were strapping their injured friend to the back of one of their remaining badgers. Only three had survived the beetle stampede. Paisley had taken one, so the four other pixies were sharing the other two. The pixie hetman saluted his warriors, then turned away and set off up the hill. Frank reached over in his saddle and patted his step-sister on the arm.

"I reckon it'll be alright having Paisley along," he said. "Those pixies seem tough. I'm glad to have him on our side – and the more people we have helping us, the better our chances are."

He was probably right, so Penny just smiled and said, "Of course. Come on – we can't let the others get away from us!"

Poor 748 was very tired, as he tried to keep up with the others. He had always been much slower than the other dogs and they had to keep waiting for us. Even the badger seemed to be quicker than the exhausted setter. At one point, as if he was bored, Paisley stood up on the back of his badger and started singing a strange song in the deep, mournful language of the pixies. Penny didn't know if it was meant to be a sad song or a happy song, but it echoed across the rolling flower plains, louder and stranger than any birdsong she'd ever heard.

The pixie was right, though. They did reach the lake town before it was dark – but not by much. The sky was pinking in the west and the flower fairies were starting to emerge, dancing above their blooms, when the friends came to the top of another imposing hill. Spread out beneath it was the great lake, burning with the orange and purple reflections of the setting sun.

It was certainly a huge lake. The professor had said the faerie world was smaller than the human world, but it didn't look like it from here. Penny couldn't see across the lake and it reached as far to the left and the right almost as far as she could see. It was like standing on a hill above the sea. She could just faintly make out some mountains in the distance on the right – but they looked tiny, like little sharp teeth rising straight out of the lake. She guessed these were the Dragon Mountains. But how far away were they?

But even from the high vantage point of the hill, Penny couldn't see the town. Where was it? The goblins set off down the final, steep slope to the water's edge and the children followed cautiously, all the time scanning the shore for some sign of a settlement. They even looked out on the water, in case it was one of those villages built on stilts over the lake. But they still couldn't see it.

There was a track, though. It was almost fully dark when they reached the shore, but Penny could see they were joining a well-used trail along the edge of the water. It just didn't seem to lead anywhere. There was nothing up ahead – no dark shapes of buildings or welcoming lights. Nothing to show where this town might be.

Penny was beginning to think she would have to sleep on the dog again when Pickatina turned in her saddle and said: "Now you will be seeing a wonder that few humans have ever seen."

Paisley had stopped at the waters' edge and climbed down from his badger. There didn't seem to be anything exceptional about this piece of the lakeside, unless perhaps it was that the track seemed to go into the water at this point. The pixie turned to face out into the lake, raised his hands above his head and clanged loudly in his language, then slowly lowered his arms. Nothing happened, so he did it again... and this time...

Penny blinked and rubbed her eyes. She couldn't believe what she was seeing. The water in front of Paisley was rising. It buckled and bowed upwards, like a fold in a rug. It seemed to be gently ebbing back and forth still – but it wasn't level, the way water in a lake should be. It had definitely lifted itself up to form a tunnel, with a grand arch facing the shore.

"This is the way into the Town on the Lake," said Pickatina. "We may teach you how to call the opening, if there is time. But now is not the time. Come, we must hurry as the way does not stay open for long."

The tunnel was tall, thin and very dark. It sloped gently downwards with the watery walls arching over the travellers, twice as high even as Broadwallow sitting on 998, but it was so narrow they had to go in single file. Paisley led the way, with Frank in front of Penny, then 620 the baggage dog, with Pickatina and Broadwallow at the back. The tunnel floor was smooth cobblestones and the walls were deep, polished black like marble. Penny reached out a hand and touched one – and her hand went straight into it, just as if she'd dipped her fingers into a bath. The water was icy cold.

"When it is light, you can see the fish of the lake swimming on either side," Pickatina called. Penny shivered, thinking of pike.

It was hard to see where they were going, because it was so dark. At first Penny could only just make out the back of Frank's dog. But then, gradually, she began to see light ahead – faint at first, but getting stronger.

"Hurry please," called Broadwallow from the back of the group, his voice echoing down the tunnel. Penny thought she heard a faint hushing sound. Looked over her shoulder she saw the tunnel was collapsing behind them. They'd have to get a move on or they'd be washed away across the bottom of the lake.

Frank and Paisley began trotting on ahead more briskly – but poor 748 was too exhausted to pick up the pace. What with a full day's ride and the terror of the beetle stampede, the delicate setter was panting heavily, staggering slightly with every step. Penny called to him to go faster, patted his neck, tried to urge him on. And he tried – he lumbered on a bit quicker, trying to keep up with Frank's 888 for a few steps before slowing down again. He was too tired to go any faster.

There was no way Broadwallow could pick Penny out of the saddle, the way he had when they'd been chased by the honey bears – the tunnel was far to narrow for him to get alongside her. The girl looked behind again. The top of the tunnel was curving down very low now. It was almost touching Broadwallow's head.

"Come on, 748!" she screamed and banged her heels on his sides. The dog seemed to understand that it was really important and made one last effort, springing forwards and galloping for a few strides. It was just enough – they burst into a wide, well-lit space with Pickatina and Broadwallow hard on Penny's heels.

They were only just in time. There was a sucking, splashing noise and, as Penny turned to watch, the tunnel vanished – with 998 still half inside. Broadwallow's huge dog gave a might leap and jumped out, but he was soaking wet on his back legs and his tail. He stopped and shook, making the big hobgoblin wobble from side to side. Broadwallow just laughed.

Penny looked around. They had ridden into a cobbled square, lined on three sides by tall walls and on the other the chilly black wall of the lake. It was lit by two flickering torches, on either side of a massive wooden gate with shiny brass hinges that was set in the middle of the wall directly in front of where the tunnel had been.

Broadwallow clambered down from 998 and strode up to the gate, banging on it with his huge fist. "Open, in the name of the Queen," he bellowed. He turned and smiled at us. "We will be welcome in the town," he said. "The people are my friends."

But they waited a long time. Broadwallow knocked again, several times – but there was no answer. He looked worried. Penny realised something was very wrong.

Chapter Twenty Nine

Harrow

Pickatina and Broadwallow looked anxious. Penny couldn't fathom anything from Paisley's expression. The goblins had a hasty conversation in their whistling, clicking language.

"What is it?" said Frank. "You have to tell us. What's wrong? What are you saying?"

"My cousin is concerned – and I am too, Boy Frank," said Picaktina slowly. "The people of the lake are friendly and never leave visitors standing before their gates. Never. So something must be wrong. We fear the mistress may have been here and wrought some foul mischief."

"I too am worried," intoned Paisley. "There is a strange smell to this place. I have never smelt it before. It makes me nervous."

Pickatina cocked her head to one side and sniffed. "I smell nothing, mighty Paisley – but your senses are sharper by far than mine," she said. "But perhaps… perhaps I can be guessing what has been done. Tell me, if Broadwallow was to stand on his dog's saddle and lift you up, would you be able to climb over the gate and open it for us?"

"I am a pixie hetman and warrior!" exclaimed Paisley. "I am no sneak thief, Lady Pickatina."

"Good Paisley, I do not ask you to steal – nor even to sneak," said Pickatina. "But I am certain the people of the lake need our help. I am sure the mistress has placed them under a foul magic and we can be breaking it – but not from outside the town. We must be getting in and neither Broadwallow nor I can fit through the gap above the gate. Nor can the humans. If we are to be saving these people, it will be because you are opening the gate."

Paisley was quiet for a moment. "Very well, lady. I shall do it."Then he sighed, "I fear that travelling with you strange folk will lead me to do many things a pixie of good standing would not normally consider. No doubt being handled by a hobgoblin will turn out to be the least of them. Come, Captain Braodwallow. Lift me like a parcel and post through the gap above the gate."

Broadwallow got 998 to stand in front of the gates, then the big hobgoblin picked up the little pixie and clambered up onto the dog, lifting the stick-like warrior until he could climb through the small gap between the top of the wooden gate and the arch of the wall. He vanished from sight, but there was the sound of a small thump from the other side of the gate.

"I'm alright," called Paisley. "I'm alright. Just a small fall."

A moment later there was a grating, scraping sound and the gates parted, just a fraction in the middle. Broadwallow moved 998 out of the way and gave them a shove. They swung wide open, with a faint 'oooff' noise. Everyone hurried over and looked behind the left-hand gate. Paisley was squashed against the wall. He didn't look impressed.

"Next time, mighty Captain," he gasped. "Please wait until I say 'push'."

"This is no time for clowning," whispered Pickatina. "I will need you, Paisley, and you, Broadwallow, to be on your guard. The mistress has been here. She has placed the town under a sleeping spell – I can smell it now. I have the trick of it so we can enter without being sent to sleep… but we must be careful. She may have left a guardian. Something to prevent the spell from being broken."

"What kind of guardian?" asked Frank. "Another guard frog? Or something like the spite and the throttle?"

"I do not know, Boy Frank," admitted Pickatina, looking nervous. "A living guard would take less magic, but the mistress is always preferring a magical guardian – one that will neither tire nor sleep. But she has been clever indeed. This is more than just a spell on this place – this enchantment is a trap as well. If bold Paisley had not smelt it and warned us, even I would have walked into the town unawares and fallen under the spell."

"Sounds like a big job," said Frank. "How long would it have taken her to cast this spell, then?"

"That is what I am worrying about," said Pickatina thoughtfully. "This is not quick magic. It can be said in a second, but much preparation is needed for it to work. I am thinking the mistress has been planning this for a long time. She may have prepared a guardian of most formidable magic. I fear… well, never mind – I could be wrong. Let us be sure to take great care."

With that, she scampered off to the placid baggage dog and fetched some rags from the bundle used for making the sleeping nest she and Broadwallow shared, tearing them into strips. She took a small bottle from a bag at her waist and dripped a few drops of liquid into the centre of the rags, whistling quietly as she did so. She tied one over her nose and mouth, so she looked like a robber or a cowboy, then passed a rag to each of her companions.

"Wear this over on your face, you must," she said. "It will stop you falling under the spell on this place. Do not take it off – even for a moment. You would be feeling dopey straight away and within a minute you would fall into an endless sleep."

"Before we go in, Pickatina," Penny asked. "What are we looking for? How do we break the spell? Frank doesn't have to kiss a sleeping princess, does he?"

"No!" cried Frank. "I won't do it, even to break the spell."

"There need be no kissing," said Pickatina. "At the heart of the spell will be a floating sphere – a ball of light. Inside it will be all the seconds stolen from the sleeping town. Once we break the ball, the seconds will be released and the people will be waking up and time will start to pass once again."

"That doesn't sound too difficult," said Frank. "Find the ball, break the ball. Piece of cake."

"It is no simple matter, Boy Frank," corrected Pickatina. "The ball of light will be hard to find and it will be hard even for a warrior as mighty as Broadwallow to break. And it may be protected. That is what I fear most. There are worse things than a spite."

Penny lifted the rag to her face – it smelt revolting. Much worse than the slugs the goblins usually ate. It reeked of rotten rubbish and pig farms. It made her feel queasy and she could see Frank didn't like it either. Paisley looked about ready to fall over from the smell of it – after all, it was his sensitive nose that had sniffed out the smell of the spell in the first place. But the pixie grimly fastened the rag over his face. He blinked, then seemed fine.

"Don't you mind the smell, Paisley?" Penny asked him.

"It feels like my face is melting," he replied, a note of

suppressed pain in his calm, deep voice. "The pong is dreadful. But a warrior must face such trials without complaint."

Frank shut his mouth suddenly and tied the cloth around his face without another word. Penny realised he wanted to be a warrior too.

Leaving the dogs behind, the little group walked through the passage behind the gate. It was dark and cool, but not very long. It opened out onto a wide street and there were plenty of people – well, goblins – but they were all frozen like statues. Some looked as if they were walking along, others looked like they were standing and talking, but they were all eerily still and silent.

The place seemed utterly deserted, apart from the statues. Yet when we'd gone a dozen steps Paisley stopped and stiffened, gesturing for everyone to stand still. As they did, the little pixie cocked his head to one side, as if listening to something too faint for the rest of to hear.

The group started moving again, but slower this time. Paisley made everyone stop after a few paces while he listened again. This time he turned and led the way down a side street. There were more goblins here – all stiff and still. Penny touched one as she passed. He was stone cold, like a frozen chicken.

At the end of the street, Paisley paused again. This time, the human thought she heard something – a faint scraping sound. But she couldn't tell what it was or where it might be coming from. She saw Broadwallow nod to Paisley, then unsheathe his huge sword. Paisley drew his bow and fitted an arrow to it.

They carried on down the street. Ahead was a market square – large and open, with only a few stalls arranged around the edge. But still Penny couldn't see what was making the noise.

Then it appeared from behind one of the stalls – two big gold hoops like wheels, with a wire ball somehow suspended between them. It was pretty big, almost as tall as the market stall. As the hoops rolled across the cobbles, they threw up sparks and made the faint scraping noise. Penny felt Frank tug at her sleeve.

"Oh no," said Picaktina, sounding scared. "It is a harrow."

"No it isn't," said Frank, pointing behind them. "It's two."
They were trapped between them.

Chapter Thirty

Fighting

The harrow in the market square hadn't noticed them. The one behind them had, though. It began rolling towards the little group at deadly speed, kicking up sparks on the cobbles. Pickatina grabbed Penny's shoulder and pushed her towards the nearest building.

"Inside!" she cried. "We must get inside, everyone. Hurry!"

There was no mistaking the urgency in her voice. Broadwallow was the first one to the door and he flung it open, ushering Penny, Frank and Pickatina through. Paisley dived through between Broadwallow's legs and as the big hobgoblin shut the door, there was a loud bang. A brass point like a dagger appeared through the wood, missing Broadwallow's hand by a couple of centimetres.

They were in a shop – a cramped space between a counter and the window. Bolts of coloured cloth sat on shelves behind the counter, but Penny was looking out of the dusty window. The harrow was right outside, standing up. It didn't look like two hoops and a ball of wire anymore, but like a giant metal stick figure without a head. The skinny body was a fine mesh of wires. Where the head should have been, there was something that looked like a clockwork motor from Frank's Meccano set. The harrow's arms and legs were curved brass with sharp edges, the hands and feet just wicked blades. It was struggling to pull free the 'hand' that was sticking through the door.

As Penny watched, the other harrow came rolling out of the market place. As it got close to the shop, it seemed to unfold, the hoops becoming the limbs as it turned itself into another tall, menacing golden stick figure. It stalked past the window but didn't seem to look inside.

"Quick, Penny," said Frank. "Get the secateurs out. If that thing tries to poke another pointy bit through the door, we can cut it off. That might slow it down."

While she hurried to get the Professor's deadly steel secatuers, Frank kept talking. "Pickatina, how do we fight these things? Do they have any weak spots?"

The little goblin had a pained expression on her face. "Please be quite, Boy Frank," she whispered. "Blind, the harrows are – they have no eyes. But they hear every noise and can tell what has made it… and usually they will attack it."

As she spoke, the door thudded again and shook in the frame. Another brass spike was sticking through it. Pulling her hand from the bag, Penny quickly clamped the blade of the secatuers around it, as close to the wood of the door as she could. Instantly, it started trying to pull away, but as it moved backwards a thin shaving of brass was taken off each edge, dissolving into thick black smoke. With a grunt of effort, she snipped the secateurs shut before all the brass limb could disappear. The tip of the harrow's arm fell to the floor with a clang.

Straight away another spike was rammed through the bottom of the door, right by where the piece had fallen. Again, Penny rushed to cut it off with the secatuers. In seconds there were two pieces going up in smoke on the stone floor.

She was feeling pretty pleased with myself – until another spike came through the door and scratched her arm. Before she could stop herself, Penny cried out in pain and surprise – and dropped the secatuers. As soon as the cry had left her throat, another brass spike was slammed through the door – at head height. If she'd been any closer to the door, it would have hit her.

Frank had picked up the secatuers and he dived at the door, cutting this spike off too. Penny backed away from the door, raising her cut arm to her mouth and sucking it – partly to see if it would stop it hurting and partly to make sure she didn't make any more noises. She knew she was lucky – the cut was hardly big or very deep and it was barely bleeding.

Paisley was standing by the window. "Each time you cut a point off, it reshapes its arm," he whispered. "But each time it gets shorter. I don't know that we will defeat it this way though."

Penny was also worrying whether cutting the harrow up in to small bits every time it attacked was the best way to beat it. But at least it was on the outside the door.

Or rather, it had been.

Paisley hadn't whispered quietly enough and the second harrow – the one that hadn't had any bits cut off – attacked the sound of his voice. It lashed out a long, thin arm and broke the window. Paisley jerked his head back just in time to avoid it.

All the noise as the glass fell out of the window seemed to confuse the harrows for a moment. They froze, their tiny clockwork heads moving from side to side, trying to work out what to do.

That's when Penny had her idea.

She took the Professor's lethal metal box out of her bag and held it up in front of her with one hand. Then, as quietly as she could, she reached into the bag with the other hand and grabbed the first thing she touched, which was the silver-handled skipping rope taken from the same room as the trumpet. Her heart was in her mouth, but she was sure this would work. Taking a deep breath, she used the handle of the skipping rope to tap on the back of the box.

The harrow that had broken the window leapt forwards, jumping through the jagged window frame and landing among the broken glass. It was practically on top of Paisley and within an arm's length of Pickatina, who was cowering silently against the shop counter. However, jumping on the glass and made a loud crunching noise. The other harrow came away from the door and stabbed a long, sharp arm through the window, catching the harrow on the inside a glancing blow. It wobbled, but straightened, its clockwork head tilting slowly from side to side.

Then it lashed out at Penny.

Or rather, it attacked the steel box. Penny felt it strike almost before she saw it move, it was that fast. The force of its blow was so fierce she nearly dropped the box. But somehow she managed to tighten her grip, dropping the skipping rope and holding the box with both hands. A thick pillar of black smoke started to rise on the other side of the box, where the harrow was stabbing its arm against the deadly steel.

The girl pushed against the harrow, against the force that was thrusting its arm into the box, trying to get to her. She could feel it pouring itself against her, cold and implacable and bent on killing her. But she could see and smell the smoke that meant she was hurting it, so she didn't panic – she just pushed harder.

And in that moment the harrow jerked itself backwards. Penny staggered forwards and lost her balance – but somehow Paisley had moved soundlessly in front of me. Hands raised above his head, he caught her and stopped her falling. Stopped her even putting a foot down. The girl was aware that, at the same time, there was a whooshing sound that ended in a clang. The harrow had nearly hit her with its other arm – it would have got sliced her open, but Broadwallow had whipped his sword out and blocked the blow. He'd saved Penny's life.

The harrow took a step backwards, sketching short, sharp arcs in the air with its arms. It seemed to be waiting, listening. Penny looked at Pickatina and silently mouthed the words "make some noise" to her. The little goblin looked blankly at the girl, so the human nodded and mouthed the words again. This time Pickatina's face lit up as she understood what was being said, though a second later her brow furrowed.

For a moment, nothing moved in the shop. Frank and Penny were holding their breath, too scared to risk the harrow hearing it. The girl was watching Pickatina intently. Her friend took something from her pocket and threw it at the broken glass heaped up next to the harrow's feet.

The metal beast whipped round and stabbed at the thing Pickatina had thrown. In that instant Penny leant forwards and bashed it with the steel box. She hit it as hard as she could on its tiny clockwork head – and felt it crumble. She kept the pressure on as the brass monster collapsed, smoke pouring from around the sides of the box. The girl was pretty sure she'd finished it off.

Unfortunately, hitting the harrow made a pretty loud sound. The other one responded straight away by leaping through the broken window and diving towards the source of the noise – and this time it did hit Penny. She was lucky that it misjudged where to strike. The point of its deadly arm speared the smoking head of its fellow, but it still clipped the girl with the flat edge of its elbow. It was enough to knock her sideways and she staggered into the shop counter with a bang, crunching broken glass beneath her feet.

A second of panic consumed Penny as she was certain the harrow would get her… when it fell over.

It took her a moment to understand what had happened. Paisley and Broadwallow had each taken up an end of the skipping rope, which had been lying where she'd dropped it. When the harrow bounded into the room, they hauled on the rope, caught its feet and tripped it over.

Quick as a flash, Frank leapt onto the monster and thrust the secatuers hard into the clockwork head. As soon as he snipped the blades shut, the harrow shook, went limp and black smoke billowed from the head. He'd killed it.

"Careful, everyone," said Frank as he stood up. He was holding the secateurs above his head. "This and the box Penny's holding are made of the death metal, remember. Stand back until they're safely in Penny's bag again."

Penny was shaking – she couldn't figure out how his voice could be so calm. She didn't trust herself to speak at that moment. But it was good advice. The girl picked up her bag with trembling hands and the children stowed the death metal away.

"Could I have my skipping rope, please," she said.

She put that away as well while Pickatina came over and picked up something from the floor – it looked like a brass padlock that she'd thrown into the glass to distract the harrow. The little goblin was looking at Penny thoughtfully, but it was the pixie who spoke.

"You humans fight well," said Paisley. "With great courage and ingenuity. I salute you. And your death metal was certainly the advantage in this battle – both harrows are no more."

Penny felt proud, but tried not to show it. "Everyone did their bit. We beat them by working together," Frank said. "But now it's safe, I think we should hurry up and get out of here. We need to break the spell and free the town."

Chapter Thirty One

The Heart of the Spell

The group stepped out into the street, leaving the remains of the two defeated harrows smoking behind them. Penny's heart wasn't beating so fast now and, with Ribaldane's mechanical monsters defeated, she was feeling optimistic. All they had to do was find the floating ball of light that was the heart of the spell putting the town under the lake to sleep.

"I think we should start in the market square," said Frank, who must have been thinking the same thing. "That's what the harrows seemed to be guarding. I'm sure that's where the centre of the magic will be. If we find it, we can break the spell – right?"

"I hope so, Boy Frank," said Pickatina. "But it is mighty magic. I do not know that I have the skill to undo it. But this is not the time to be having such doubts. First we must find the ball of time that the mistress will have set to catch the seconds of this town's life. Look carefully, for it may be difficult to spot."

The five of them spent five minutes poking around the

market square, but they couldn't find anything looking remotely like a ball of floating light. "Just how big is this thing going to be, Pickatina?" Penny asked.

"I do not know, Girl Pen," she admitted. "I have been reading about time catchers, but never have I seen one. I always imagined one to be the size of a melon, but it could be bigger or smaller."

"Maybe we should split up to search for it," suggested Frank.

"Nervous about that, I would be," said Broadwallow. "What if the mistress has left other traps to guard this enchantment?"

"Much magic goes into the making of a harrow, cousin," said Pickatina. "And they are very tough – I am not sure we could have defeated them without the death metal. It is clear to me the mistress spent a long time in the planning of this trick to throw off pursuit. Surely she would have thought two harrows would be sufficient protection for her spell."

"Well, let's just go in two groups, then," said Frank. "I'll go with Pickatina and Paisley, Penny can go with Broadwallow. How does that sound?"

Broadwallow nodded slowly. "We will search for an hour. Then be meeting here again. If you find the ball, give a loud whistle – I will hear," he said. "If we find it, we will call to you.

"And if you are finding the ball, cousin," he added, wagging a finger at Pickatina, "Do not try to counter the spell until we are all together again. Is that clear?"

"Yes, great captain," said Pickatina, saluting and rolling her eyes. Penny giggled.

"It pays to be clear on these matters," said Broadwallow. He sounded like his feelings were a bit hurt, so the girl slipped her hand into his – it was like a giant, warm, leathery glove.

"Come on, let's start looking," she said, smiling at him. "I bet we find it first."

Broadwallow and Penny headed back towards the gate. They passed dozens of goblins, all frozen as if they were playing musical statues – big ones, small ones, fat ones and thin ones. They all wore colourful clothes, mostly purples and blues and greens. And they looked a bit different to the other goblins and hobgoblins the children had met so far – their skin was a bit greener and their eyes seemed to bulge a bit, but she couldn't tell whether that was how they normally looked or if the greenish tinge was a side-effect of the spell Ribaldane had cast on them.

Broadwallow decided to look in the buildings, in case the heart of the spell was hidden inside one. It didn't feel right to Penny, just opening doors and letting themselves into other people's houses and into shops. But they didn't take anything-they just kept walking and looking, not even really talking much.

They must have been searching the town for almost the whole hour before they finally found the ball of light – and they nearly missed it completely. Penny's feet were getting sore and she was tired when she followed Broadwallow into a broad courtyard on the outskirts of town. There were four or five large dogs tethered to a hitching rail and several more leaning out of stable boxes around the edge of the yard, all frozen still.

Penny was waiting in the middle of the yard while Broadwallow searched all the dog boxes. Because she was so tired, she yawned and stretched, glancing up as she did so. And that's when something odd caught her eye. She looked up again, scrunching up her eyes. At first she couldn't really see anything – thought perhaps her imagination was playing tricks on her.

Then it came into sight again, whizzing round as though running laps of the courtyard – but as high as the rooftops surrounding it. It was, Penny decided, stretching things to call it a ball of light. It didn't really look much like a ball. It certainly wasn't a big, bright sphere like a miniature sun. It was just a circle, like a lens through which the background seemed to be more brightly illuminated – the way a magnifying glass makes the ground beneath it look brighter if you're studying ants in the garden. Only there was no white hot spot, just the strange circle of brightness orbiting the stable yard.

"Broadwallow," she called. "I've found it. Broadwallow? Broadwallow? Where are you?"

She turned around just in time to see the big hobgoblin fall backwards into the yard. He hit the floor and didn't move.

Don't scream, Penny told herself. Stepping over Broadwallow, coming menacingly towards her, was a tall, thin harrow.

Penny stood absolutely still, determined not to make another sound. If only she hadn't called out to Broadwallow... She really hoped he was okay – but just then all she could really think about was the harrow stalking slowly towards her.

The harrow's long, sharp metal arms were swaying in front of it, as if it was searching like a blind person. It edged forward, one small step at a time. It can't see you, Penny told herself. You'll be fine as long as you don't make a noise it can hear. She wondered if it would be able to hear her breathing. Her heart was thumping deafeningly in her ears. Surely it wouldn't hear that.

Just as it was getting to within a meter or two of Penny, Broadwallow stirred. The girl almost hooted with joy, but managed to keep quiet. The captain rolled onto his side, then pulled himself up onto his knees, groaning. The harrow stopped coming towards the human, turning its clockwork head in the hobgoblin's direction.

Broadwallow struggled to his feet. He was bleeding from a cut on his forehead. Blood streaked his face, running onto the cloth tied over his nose and mouth. He was shaking his head as if trying to clear it. Then he saw the harrow and seemed to wake up instantly, sinking into a fighting crouch and drawing his sword.

This was a mistake. The blade rasped from its scabbard and instantly the harrow pounced, leaping across the courtyard in four big bounds and slashing at Broadwallow.

As soon as the horrid clockwork thing was moving away from her, Penny reached into her bag for the secateurs. She was shaking so badly she could hardly hold them, but she pulled them free and gripped them with both hands, letting the bag drop. Then she ran towards the harrow.

Broadwallow had blocked its first attack with his sword, the harrow's sharp arms throwing up sparks as they slid along the blade. It changed the angle of its next attack, but Broadwallow blocked it again. The noise of the blows echoed around the courtyard – and that's what Penny was counting on.

She was only a meter or two from the harrow when it tried stabbing Broadwallow. Her friend was blinking as blood ran from the cut on his head into his eyes. At the last moment he saw the sharp point of the harrow's arm racing towards him and he hopped to one side, escaping the deadly thrust. But he puffed loudly as he jumped and straight away the harrow stabbed its other arm towards his head. Broadwallow staggered backwards.

The harrow was about to leap after him when Penny struck. She was so scared she nearly cried. She could barely see what she was doing and her arms felt weak with terror. But she knew she had to act to save Broadwallow.

Penny jumped and stabbed all in one motion, accidentally letting out a great roar. That helped – because in that instant the harrow hesitated before attacking Broadwallow. Then the secatuers were forcing their way into its tiny clockwork head, doing their deadly work. The force of the girl's jump knocked it down and she fell with it, but she kept the lethal steel blades jammed into the thing. She couldn't risk just hurting it – she had to destroy it now or it would probably kill her and Broadwallow.

For a long moment, Penny lay there, the angular brass harrow trapped uncomfortably beneath her. She realised she was crying, with Broadwallow stroking her shoulder and rumbling softly to her, kind words to make her feel better. "Saved my life a second time, you have, Girl Pen," he was saying. "Such bravery in one so small. The mistress does not know what she faces – and I am glad. For we shall surely beat her. Come now, Girl Pen, be standing up. The harrow is defeated. You have triumphed."

Slowly she got to her feet, wiping her tears away. She pulled the secatuers out of the smoking ruin of the harrow's head and put them safely back in her bag. She smiled up at Broadwallow, then pointed up. "Better call Pickatina," she said. "It's time to break this spell."

Chapter Thirty Two

Magic v Steel

Broadwallow let out a loud whistle – long and piercing. Pickatina and Paisley would definitely have heard it. The big hobgoblin sat down and rubbed at his forehead, where the harrow had cut him.

"Are you alright?" Penny asked, sitting next to him. "Is there anything I can do?"

"Ah, Girl Pen, you have done it already," he said. "Never did I think a human child could be so brave – or so deadly."

Brave? She'd been terrified the whole time. But she couldn't have let the harrow hurt him. She was about to tell Broadwallow that when she realised he'd taken off the cloth that had been tied across his nose and mouth, using it to wipe the blood off his face.

But the cloth had been soaked in the secret, stinky potion Pickatina had provided to protect them from Ribaldane's sneaky sleeping spell. The hobgoblin had barely lowered the blood-stained cloth from his face before he yawned. Penny could see from his eyes that he realised his mistake… but by then it was too late. He was fast asleep before the girl could even speak his name.

Suddenly she felt really alone and very scared. Not the way she had facing the harrow, a quick and panicky fear, but filled with dread. She didn't dare call out to Pickatina, Paisley and Frank. What if there was another harrow out there? It could be attracted to her call and then she'd be in real trouble. All she could do was sit and wait.

After about five minutes she heard a high, scratchy whistle. It had to be Pickatina calling to Broadwallow – and she sounded a bit cross. Penny tried whistling back to her, but she didn't know what she might have said in the goblin language.

A minute later, her three other companions rushed into the courtyard. They looked flustered, but none of them looked hurt.

"Girl Pen, thank goodness," cried Pickatina. "Where did you learn language like that? Not from my cousin I hope… oh no!"

She came and stood in front of Broadwallow. "The big dummy forgot to keep his nose and mouth covered," she said, but she didn't sound too cross.

"There was another harrow?" asked Paisley, pointing at the smouldering remains of the nasty clockwork beast. "How was it defeated, Penny?"

"I stabbed it with the secateurs, the way Frank did the other one," she said. "Broadwallow was distracting it. He saved my life."

"Blimey, Penny – that was brave of you," said Frank, sounding frankly envious. Why was that? Penny had been terrified. There was nothing to envy in what she'd done.

"I think you saved the Captain, young lady," said the pixie with deep seriousness. "But now he has fallen under this enchantment. Will we ever break it, Lady Pickatina? We have lost a brave comrade. We must find the heart of this spell."

"We can break it," Penny cried. "That's why we were calling you. We found the heart of the spell. The ball of light is up there… I think…" Now it came to it, she wasn't quite so certain. What if she was wrong?

But Pickatina saw the disc of light and gave a little clap. "Where would we be without you, Girl Pen?" she said. "I have never seen a time catcher before. Though it is not looking much like a ball of light, really. Now, to see if I can call it down…"

Everyone backed away from Pickatina while the little goblin crouched down on the floor, arms spread wide, and began to sing. Her voice was high and clear and beautiful – just as it had been when she charmed the pike on the river. Gradually she rose to her feet, turning slowly round and round as she did so. Soon she was spinning around, faster and faster, arms thrown out wide.

Then she began to rise slowly into the air. Not much at first… but gradually she rose and rose until she was high in above the cobbled yard. She was turning round at the same speed as the disc of light. As Penny watched, Pickatina began to turn more slowly. And ever so slowly, the disc of light drifted towards her, slowing down at the same time. In moments Pickatina was holding it in her hands, she had stopped spinning and she was drifting slowly to the ground.

Frank and Penny looked at each other, but neither of them could think of anything to say – they'd never seen anything like it.

"Now, Paisley," said Pickatina. "I had expected my cousin would be able to use his great strength to shatter the time catcher – but as he is not able to help, we shall be seeing if the might of the pixies is as great as your fame says. Take up your weapon and see if you can smash the ball – but please, take care not to cut off my hands while I hold it here."

The small pixie nodded, his eyes hard and black above the face cloth. He had put his bow and arrow away and drawn a small hatchet from his belt. "The sword would be too crude," he said. "Let me hew this spell as if it was wood. We shall break this enchantment."

He took a step forward, hatchet held high above his head, then brought it down in a sharp whistling chop – hitting the strange disc squarely on the top. There was a loud clang, which was actually Paisley grunting with effort... but the axe rebounded off the spell. Paisley lost his grip on the handle and it went whistling back over his head, landing with a clatter on the cobbles behind him.

"Let me try this," he grunted, drawing an arrow from the quiver on his shoulder. "If force does not work, maybe pressure will burst this accursed bubble."

He carefully rested the point of the arrow against the strangely light sphere and began pushing it, leaning on it with all his might. But again, he didn't seem to be harming it at all – he pushed Pickatina backwards, but the spell seemed unharmed. Then the arrow slipped and Paisley lunged forwards, almost stabbing the goblin with its sharp point. He stood up straight, shaking his head and puffing out his cheeks.

"I am sorry, Lady Pickatina – this is beyond my strength," he said. "I do not know if any living being would have the might to break this sphere, not even the great Captain Broadwallow,"

"We must find a way," whispered Pickatina. She was dripping with sweat. "And we must hurry. I cannot hold it much longer."

"Look, why doesn't Penny just stab it with her secateurs?" asked Frank. "They've destroyed the other magical things we've encountered. Even the harrows. Surely they can break the spell."

"That is a good idea, Boy Frank," said Paisley. "Hurry, young mistress – use your death metal and pierce the circle while the Lady Pickatina still holds it."

Pickatina nodded. "Hurry, Penny. I do not have the strength to hold it much longer. You must be quick."

But Penny was rooted to the spot in shock. So it was Frank who reached into the bag and grabbed the secatuers. He rushed over to Pickatina and poked at the circle of light, taking great care to make sure he didn't touch the goblin with the steel.

As soon as the secateurs touched the disc, a network of jagged golden lines spread out across its surface – now it looked more like a sphere. Black smoke billowed around inside it like an evil snow globe. Gradually the golden lines expanded, the sphere getting fatter until Pickatina seemed to be holding a golden football. Then suddenly everything seemed to go cold and there was a quiet sucking sound, as if all the air was being pumped out of the town. Then there was a kind of silent bang and Penny's ears popped, the way they do when you drive up a mountain in a car.

Frank put the secateurs back in the bag, then tore off the foul-smelling cloth tied across his face, then gently removed the one across Penny's. Paisley was taking his off too, but trying not to look relieved about it.

All around them, the sleeping creatures began to stir. Broadwallow was the first to wake – he must have been less deeply enchanted than the rest. He rose slowly to his feet and came and put his hands on the child's shoulders. "Girl Pen, please forgive me – leaving you alone like that. Falling under the spell, it was a terrible error," he said. "I failed in my duty to protect you."

"Yes, cousin," said Pickatina – she sounded severe but had an affectionate smile on her face. "But luckily no harm was done. Penny defeated the harrow and Frank pierced the time catcher with the death metal, breaking the spell. All will be well."

Penny didn't say anything. She was simply too exhausted – it had been such a long day. She'd ridden miles, survived the beetle stampede, discovered an enchanted town beneath a lake, fought three magic harrows and broken a terrible spell. It was all too much for her. She sat down in a corner and fell as deeply asleep as any spell-struck goblin had been.

Chapter Thirty Three

Sticklebee

Penny woke up feeling disorientated. But by now she was beginning to get used to the feeling: as if her brain knew she was still in Faerieland but her body seemed to expect to be at home, so everything felt wrong. This time, though, she had absolutely no idea where she was. She sat up and looked around nervously.

The room she was in was quite dark. A soft golden light spilled through a gap between the curtains on a window in the corner. It gave just enough illumination to see things faintly. She had been sleeping beneath her cloak on a big bundle of rags that had been arranged into something like a mattress. There was another similar pile of rags in the far corner, which suggested Frank may have been sleeping there – but there was no sign of him now.

So Penny got up and picked up her bag, which was lying beside the bed, then went to the small wooden door and out into a narrow corridor. She hesitated, unsure which way to go, until she heard a faint ringing boom from the left and guessed Paisley must be down there. Cautiously, she set off in that direction.

At the end of the corridor was a long room with a low ceiling and huge windows all down one side. Outside was the market square. The room was dominated by a long table with about twenty chairs on either side of it. Pickatina, Frank and Broadwallow were sitting there, talking with a goblin in flowing blue-and-green robes. Penny kew Paisley had to be there as well, but he was hidden from view behind Broadwallow.

As the girl came into the room, Pickatina jumped to her feet. "There you are, Girl Pen," she cried. "Come and meet the mayor of the Town on the Lake. He is very keen to meet you."

She came up and took the girl's hand, lowered her voice and whispered, "He's a bit deaf so you'll have to shout." They joined the rest of them at the table.

"Mayor Sticklebee, this is Penelope Oaks," Pickatina yelled.

The mayor bowed. He was truly ancient – far older even than the Naga. "Delighted to meet you, my child. Delighted!" His voice sounded like the pages of an old book being flipped. "I was here the last time humans visited, you know."

"Humans have been here before?" Frank asked.

"Oh yes, master Francis. Many, many years ago," grinned Sticklebee. "They were knights bold and fair, strong and stern. They helped our new queen overthrow the wicked old queen – the one you call Ribaldane. The humans had armour and weapons of death metal. They led Celestia's army and defeated Ribaldane's champions, driving her into exile in wastelands of the north. When the knights visited our town I was just a goblin lad. I held the reins for one of their strange beasts – a horse, I think it was called. Only time those monsters were ever in Faerieland..."

"Tell us more about the old queen, Sticklebee," Penny said. "What was she like? Did you ever see her?"

"Oh, I saw her alright," said the mayor, cackling. "She was as big as Captain Broadwallow and as warty as a toad. Her teeth were as sharp as knives and her nails like hooked daggers. Her eyes would tear the skin off you as soon as look at you. Of course, she wasn't like that in the old days."

"Eh? 'She wasn't like that in the old days.' So that's what she looks like now – but how do you know?" asked Frank.

"She was here, master Francis," chortled Sticklebee. "She came back through the gates with her servant Grimshock proclaiming her return. Soon she would rule again, he said. I rushed down to see at once, of course, and she was rude to me. Very rude. Just like an old-fashioned goblin queen. They knew how to lord it over peasants in the old days. Anyway, I hurried back here to send a message to good Queen Celestia.... And then you were all here and she was gone and I hear there were harrows in my streets. That's not good, you know. I don't like harrows."

"Neither do we, worthy Sticklebee," said Broadwallow. "But tell us, did the traitor Grimshock or his mistress tell you were they were going next?"

"What? Speak up Captain," said Sticklebee.

"Where are they going next?" bellowed Broadwallow.

"No need to shout," muttered Sticklebee. "They didn't tell me where they were going, but I guessed. They wanted four dogs and provisions. And I overheard them talking about the Hydra's Pass – they thought I was deaf, you know."

Penny looked at Frank. "What can you tell us about the Hydra's Pass?" she asked the mayor. "It sounds dangerous."

"Oh, it's the most fearsome route through the Dragon Mountains," chuckled Sticklebee. "But it is the most direct route to the north. Not many travellers go there on account of the snakes, but the old queen would be fine. They probably serve her, being creatures of darkness and all."

"How big are these snakes?" Frank asked.

"Oh, the small ones are no longer than this table. The big ones can be as tall as a beetle and hundreds of times longer."

Penny quickly worked that out: as big as one of the great plains beetles in the stampede would make the snakes two or three meters tall and two or three hundred meters long.

"Of course, hardly any travellers actually reach the Hydra's Pass," Sticklebee continued serenely. "Because to get there you have to go through the Wild Wood. Very dangerous place. Dark. Smelly. Full of all sorts of rough creatures. I never liked it one little bit. Every trip through it was horrible."

"But you have been through the Wild Wood, Sticklebee?" asked Pickatina, sounding amazed.

"I wasn't always this old, you know," he said, raising one eyebrow and winking. "There used to be trade between the lake and the wood. When I was a young goblin, I would be sent two or three times a year. Once I went all the way to the Last Citadel."

"Did you go by the Hydra's Pass, old one?" asked Paisley.

"Of course I did," Sticklebee said. "I wasn't going the long way round. Takes ages."

"How did you get past the snakes?" Penny asked.

"What? Snakes? Where?" he jumped up and looked around.

"No, I said, 'how did you get past the snakes'?" She repeated, a little louder.

"Why does everyone keep shouting? I'm not deaf, you know," said Sticklebee. "What was I saying? Oh yes. The snakes. I gave them mice to eat. Then ran very fast."

Frank had obviously had the same thought as his step-sister. "Exactly how big are your mice?"

"About this big," said Sticklebee, holding up his thumb. "Not very filling for such big snakes. That's why I had to run very fast."

"Mayor Sticklebee, can you make us a map showing the way through the Wild Wood?" asked Paisley. "One that will show how to get to the Hydra's Pass and all the way to the Last Citadel?"

"I can't make anything as complicated as that," said the old goblin. "I'm far too old." He paused. "Of course, you could borrow the old map I used to use, I suppose."

Frank clapped his hands. "Thank you, sir, that would be wonderful," he said. The old goblin nodded and shuffled off to fetch the map from another room.

"A long way ahead, the mistress is," Pickatina said solemnly. "To catch her now will be hard. However, I think the great scale of this magic means she thought it would trap any who pursued her – especially as it was protected by three harrows. She will not expect us still to be following and that will be our advantage."

"So when do we leave?" Penny asked.

"As soon as Sticklebee returns with the map," said Paisley.

"Not before breakfast, surely?" asked Frank and they all laughed. But Penny was with Frank: she was starving.

"No, Boy Frank, not before you have had breakfast," said Broadwallow. "An army marches on its stomach. We will eat well and get fresh supplies for the next stage of our journey. But once we are fed and watered, we must be away on our quest."

Chapter Thirty Four

The Wild Wood

They left the town on the lake later that morning. Mayor Sticklebee had given Broadwallow his faded, crumpled map and the people of the town had loaded 620 the baggage dog up with fresh supplies – slugs for the goblins, centipedes for the humans, some beetle meat for Paisley. They felt ready and confident to carry on the pursuit of Ribaldane – and this time they thought we might be able to surprise her.

This would be their advantage. Paisley said it was like hunting one of the giant beetles of the flower plains: if the beetle knows you're stalking it, it's very dangerous; if the beetle thinks it's given you the slip, a clever hunter can catch it unawares.

The only problem was that they were at least three days behind Ribaldane and Grimshock now. They'd have to make really good progress to catch their quarry. The goblins thought Ribaldane might slow down now she thought they'd given any pursuers the slip. The children only hoped they were right.

Especially as Broadwallow set a pretty leisurely pace as they rode away from the town beneath the lake. The afternoon sun was low in the sky, the scent of the flowers was rich and sweet in the air, the hills rolling gently up, higher and higher as the lake was left behind them. As dusk fell the travellers came to the top of a tall hill with a broad stone table on it, surrounded by carved stone mushrooms that seemed to be seats.

"This must be Highview, the point marked on old Sticklebee's map," commented Frank. It was certainly a great place to see the country – the view was stunning. Below the folded hills behind them, the great lake glinted like massive jewel in the sunlight. The gently rolling flower plains were spread out on the right, with the mountains to the left and straight ahead rising like a grey wall, topped in places with glistening white. And at the foot of the mountains was a broad belt of dark green – the Wild Wood.

"I think this would be a good place for us to stop," suggested Pickatina. "Even with our gentle ride, the dogs are still not fully recovered from yesterday's ride – and neither am I. Sure I am that the children could use a little rest as well."

"Yes, that is a good suggestion, Lady Pickatina," said Paisley. "While you make camp I will scout ahead and see if I can read some trace of our quarry. I have seen little so far, but perhaps when your great dogs are not stirring up the grass so much, the land will tell me more."

"Oh, if you insist," grumbled Broadwallow. "But I suppose the view is nice here. We'll stop here for tonight. Mighty Paisley, please learn what you can of the mistress and her companion."

Paisley was gone for a long time. The others had made camp, cooked and eaten a meal before he returned. The children were inclined to worry, but Pickatina reassured them the pixie would be fine – a hunter was best when out alone in the wild.

The stars were coming out in the velvety sky and the fairies were emerging to dance above their flowers when he finally returned. He rode silently up to the camp, a midnight silhouette on a badger. When he dismounted and came closer to the campfire, the sinister little pixie looked tired and grim.

"I have good tidings, friends," he said. "There is a river to cross at the bottom of the valley ahead of us. Fast and deep it flows. There is only one point I could find where it can be forded and there, in the mud, I found prints. It is clear to me that those we seek did pass this way – and barely two days ago. We were not so far behind as we had feared. And judging by the trail, they are travelling slowly. We should catch them inside of four days, if we make good progress."

"Good tidings indeed, brave Paisley," said Broadwallow. "We should reach the Wild Wood tomorrow."

"About the Wood, great Captain," said Paisley slowly. "Is there no way to reach the mountains but through the trees?"

"None at all," said Pickatina. "Does that bother you?"

"To be honest, Lady, yes it does," said Paisley. For a long moment he was silent, then he sighed. "My people do not venture into the Wood. The creatures that live there... Let us just say they have no love for the pixies."

"But you're on a mission for the Queen!" exclaimed Frank. "What do you think they'll do? They'll have to leave you alone."

"Wild is not the name of the Wood for no reason, Boy Frank," said Broadwallow slowly. "All manner of beasts live there. Few have even heard of Queen Celestia, let alone understood her rule. Wild and lawless are the peoples of the Wood. We must all travel carefully there, not just friend Paisley."

"What kind of creatures live in the Wood?" I asked.

"With luck we will not meet any," said Pickatina. "There are dryads and fauns, who are usually friendly. Harts and giant spiders dwell there too – animals best left alone. And to be avoided if we can are the centaurs. Fierce and fell, they are."

"But do not be afraid!" clanged Paisley heartily. "Enemies do not lurk behind every bush and bough of the Wood. I am sure we will pass through without seeing so much as a squirrel."

"I should hope not," said Pickatina. "They are as big as our dogs and twice as dangerous."

"Always go for your nuts, they do," added Broadwallow.

Penny wasn't so sure she liked the sound of the Wild Wood, but she knew they had to go through it – it was clear from the map that it was impossible to go round it. She looked out across the starlit land, trying to see it. In the deep dark of the night she thought she could make out an inky patch at the foot of the darkling mountains. It looked deep and mysterious. The girl shivered, drawing the cloak Queen Celestia had given her tight around herself.

Despite her worries, Penny slept like a log and woke early next morning feeling refreshed and excited. For the first time since coming to faerieland she didn't wake up feeling confused and disorientated. Maybe she was getting used to being here. After a hurried breakfast at the great stone table they were on their way again. The trail down to the river was steep, the grasses longer and there were fewer flowers among them. Sadly, the girl realised they were leaving the flower plains with their delicate dancing fairies.

Nobody spoke much as they rode. As hours slowly passed, they trotted across the broken, dusty land with the Wood looming ahead of them. It seemed to be getting bigger, growing taller on the horizon until it even threatened to block the view of the mountains behind it. The big trees were massive – as tall as a church, at least. Behind them, in the deep wood, enormous trees towered over the rest, as big as skyscrapers.

All the while Paisley and his badger (did it have a name? They never did find out) were ranging far and wide ahead of the party, scouting along their path and to both sides. The goblins were following a faint but still clear trail, while the pixie used all his skills to check for any sign that Ribaldane and Grimshock had taken a different path. He didn't find anything, though.

As dusk was settling over the land like a drab grey net the dusty, tired travellers reached the edge of the Wild Wood. It was as abrupt as fence – a solid line of trees, all the trunks close together, the branches low. It looked dark and cool inside, but not welcoming. A light breeze ruffled the leaves, giving a gentle hushing sound. The trail disappeared smoothly into a slight gap between two huge trees.

They were about to ride in when two spears hurtled out of the shadows beneath the trees, landing in front of Broadwallow's dog and forming a rough X shape blocking the path. The huge hobgoblin struggled to hang on as 998 reared, barking. A great voice roared from somewhere in the trees: "You shall not enter the sacred wood, pixie-lovers."

Paisley looked up at Penny, his dark face crumpled with fear. "Oh no," he cried. "It is the centaurs!"

Chapter Thirty Five

New Friends

Penny waited for Pickatina to speak, to talk to the centaurs and persuade them that their party should be allowed to pass because of their mission for the Queen. But that notion lasted only until the first centaur charged out of the forest.

Of course, the children knew what a centaur was – half-man, half-horse. They'd heard the stories. But they hadn't expected them to look like this. The first one rushed out of the trees. There was the normal horse body, glossy black but a bit unkempt, a long matted tail flowing out behind it. But where the horse's neck should have been there was a human chest, with a pair of muscular arms. The head on the top was human-ish – but more like a caveman, with a flat nose and one thick, low eyebrow shading both eyes. His mouth was drawn wide in a mighty roar, revealing dirty teeth with several gaps. He was waving a crude stone axe over his head.

Broadwallow whipped out his massive sword and deflected the blow of the axe, knocking the centaur sideways with a blow from the side of the blade. "Run, friends!" the hobgoblin shouted. "I will hold them off! Run!"

A swarm of centaurs was pouring out of the forest now. Five, ten, twenty... Penny froze. She had no idea how many were coming or where she should go. Paisley grabbed the reins of 748 and took off at a gallop, riding along the edge of the forest. Penny snapped out of it, looking over her shoulder to see Pickatina and Frank riding desperately after them, with the centaurs hard on their heels. Broadwallow was already surrounded.

But that was just a glance. Penny had to look forward and concentrate on staying in the saddle. She sensed that 748 was running as he never had before – not even when trying to get away from the beetle stampede or the honey bears. A primal fear of the centaurs was giving him extra reserves of speed – his rider only worried about how long he could keep this pace up. Ahead of her, Paisley's badger had its head down and was running for all it was worth, while the little pixie stood in the stirrups and leant forward, head down like a jockey. He still had hold of 748's reins.

There was a despairing cry of "Penny!" from somewhere behind her. It sounded like Frank. But she couldn't turn round to see – Paisley had led her under the trees now, ducking and leaning as slender branches whipped at her, trying to avoid being smacked by any bigger boughs.

It was like jumping into a swimming pool. The deep, dark cool of the Wild Wood closed over Penny's head. The sounds of fighting and pursuit vanished, as did the warmth of the sun on her shoulders. There was no time to dwell on it, though – the pixie kept up his frantic pace between bushes and trees, dragging the human behind him.

Their path was twisting and turning through the trees. Left, right, never straight for more than four of 748's large strides. In no time at all the girl had completely lost all her bearings. She had no idea which way they'd come, where the edge of the forest lay or in which direction the mountains were. Worse, she had absolutely no idea where Frank and the two goblins might be. All she knew was that they were falling further and further behind. Paisley kept them running for at least half an hour. When they stopped, Penny was so physically and mentally drained she could barely speak. She sagged in 748's saddle, exhausted.

"Are we safe now?" she asked Paisley after a few silent moments, when she had caught her breath. The little pixie looked up at her, shaking his head sadly.

"Brave comrades we have lost today, I fear Miss Penny," he said. "The centaurs are fierce foes and have no love of pixies – nor anyone the people of the flower plains count as friends. I fear I have done you all a grave harm by coming on your quest."

"You don't think they… they're dead, do you?" she asked. Her voice was just a squeak. She felt light-headed.

"In truth, I do not know," said Paisley slowly. "I know that the centaurs would not have hesitated to kill me. I would think they would not harm our goblin friends – but if Captain Broadwallow fought as fiercely as his reputation suggests, they may have had to kill him to save themselves. I do not think they would harm Francis except by mistake. But in battles, mistakes can happen. So I fear the worst and hope to be proved wrong.

"However, alive or dead, they are lost to us now," continued Paisley briskly. "Lady Pickatina had Mayor Sticklebee's map, though little use it would be to the two of us – lost as we are. I suggest we find somewhere we can lie up for the night and tomorrow we set out to return to the town on the lake."

"No." Penny was surprised to hear her own voice. But she realised it was the right thing to say. "No, we can't leave our friends. We have to rescue them from the centaurs. And if we find that they are… dead… well, you and I will have to continue with the quest. We have to get the trumpet back. If Pickatina and Broadwallow can't help, it'll be even more important for you to help me, Paisley. Can you see that? Will you help me?"

For a moment, the menacing little pixie stood gazing silently at her. She couldn't read the expression in his dark eyes, though they glinted in the dim light of the forest. Then he shook his head and let out a low, ringing sigh like the wind whistling across the neck of an empty bottle.

"Miss Penny… no, Lady Penny, you amaze me," he said. "There you stand, lost in a strange world, your companions captured or killed, alone but for a strange pixie. I see you shaking to your core with terror and sadness – and yet you still find the courage to carry on with your quest. Even to seek to save your friends.

"Yes, I will help. I shall be at your side every step of the way. Your bravery humbles me. Whatever you ask, I shall do, my lady. Let us look for somewhere safe to rest, then in the morning we shall try to find what has become of our friends and – if it is within our power – we shall rescue them from the centaurs."

There was a moment of silence, in which Penny grinned at Paisley. He was right – she was terrified. But she remembered what Frank had said: kids didn't get many chances to be heroic, so they had take whatever chances they got. Just thinking about that made her feel braver. But only for a second. Because suddenly a strange voice rang out. "Maybe we can help you."

"Who's there?" cried Paisley, drawing his short sword and his hatchet, looking around. The girl shrank back into 748's saddle.

"Do not be afraid. We mean you no harm."The voice was high and clear, tinkling like a small metal wind-chime.

"Show yourselves," clanged Paisley, like a grandfather clock striking the hour.

"We are here, noble pixie," said the voice. "Just look up."

For a second, Penny couldn't see anything. Then she spotted them, clinging to the tree trunks all around, slightly higher than her head would have been if she stood on 748's saddle. Six small creatures, rather like Paisley but greenish, with mossy hair and soft, kind-looking faces.

"Dryads," rumbled Paisley, lowering his weapons. "I had

thought the people of the wood were just a legend. In all my days I never thought to meet you."

The creatures scampered down the trunks like squirrels, standing up as they reached the ground and walking forward, smiling. They were almost exactly the same size as Paisley, with the same thin bodies and limbs, the same large heads. But where the pixie was all sharp edges and jerky movements, the dryads were gentle curves and graceful, fluid motion. The swayed as they walked, like trees blowing in a strong wind.

"I am Caro Elora," said the one that seemed to be the leader. The girl realised the dryads were all female. "Your names are Paisley and Penny. The centaurs have taken your friends. We will help you find them – for the sake of the friendship that used to reign between the Wood and the Plain. And the hope that it can be forged anew."

Paisley bowed deeply. "Fair Lady Caro Elora, I thank you. We would gladly accept any assistance you can give us."

"Come, then – we must hurry," said the dryad in her tinkling, musical voice. "The centaurs are still searching for you. We must lead you to our hidden village – there you can be safe."

She made a few gestures and tinkled away in her own language, two of the dryads running off in response. Paisley started in surprise, then clanged out a question in his bell-like pixie language. Caro Elora answered and for a few moments the two of them spoke, voices blending musically. It was beautiful to hear, though Penny had no idea what they said.

Then Paisley sighed and turned to her. "It seems the dryads and pixies are more closely related than either of us suspected," he said. "Come, Lady Penny. We shall follow the dryads. Lady Caro Elora has sent scouts to learn what they can of our friends. But now we must hurry from here."

They rode off into the dark wood with the dryads.

Chapter Thirty Seven

The Village in the Trees

It didn't take long to reach the dryad village, though Penny later worked out that they must have ridden for at least two hours because the sun was setting when they got there. As they rode along Paisley had talked with Caro Elora and the sound of their two strange voices blending in a spellbinding, bell-like duet under the fragrant canopy of the forest lulled her so she nearly slept. She almost forgot her sadness at being separated from Frank, Picaktina and Broadwallow.

They weren't riding fast – only as fast as the dryads could move through the trees, which was about as fast as Penny could have jogged. Their route took them through different areas of the forest. At first it passed through dark stands of pines, with thick trunks beneath a dense, distant ceiling of branches. There were groves of oaks, low branches heavy with acorns; tall beeches with bronze leaves hushing as a gentle wind stirred them and silver birches with white trunks and shimmering clouds of leaves.

The dryad village was reached through a narrow gulley, steep rocky sides covered with moss and flowering climbers towering above us. It was so narrow the slender girl had to get off 748 and lead him through. The lean setter only just fitted through – if they'd been there, the other dogs would never have got through, as they were all much broader.

"The passage is too narrow for the centaurs to come down," explained Caro Elora, smiling. "It keeps us safe. Now, you will be the first human ever to visit our home, Penny. I hope you like it."

She certainly did. The gulley opened up into a wide valley surrounded by high cliffs. A shining stream flow across well-tended grass dotted with gigantic, stately trees. But what took Penny's breath away was the village. Small round houses of polished wood with jewelled windows and golden roofs clung to the trunks of the trees, connected by ladders and silver walkways as delicate as spiderwebs. Lanterns twinkled like stars all over the valley. The girl had never seen any place so beautiful.

"We will go and see my father," said Caro Elora. "He is our chief and he will be eager to meet you. But first, the squirrels!"

She led the way to a pen by the side of the valley – a pen filled with squirrels. There must have been at least a dozen in there, all bushy red tails, feathery ears, sleek fur and bright eyes. They were packed in close together, climbing over each other so it was hard to see where one squirrel finished and the next one began. They were big – far bigger than Paisley's badger and maybe as big as 748.

Caro Elora opened the pen carefully. A single squirrel scampered out, belly low to the ground and tail waving in the air. Its tail was taller than Penny, waving like a great red flag.

"This is my squirrel," said Caro Elora as the giant rodent sniffed 748. "He has been with me since he was no bigger than my hand. He will not harm your dog."

And sure enough, dog and squirrel looked at each other and sniffed each other, but neither seemed inclined to fight. Eventually 748 licked the squirrel – the big setter's ultimate gesture of friendship – which made a kind of chirping, chuckling noise and scampered beneath 748's chin, dragging the long fluffy fur of its tail across the dog's face.

"I think they are friends now," giggled Caro Elora. "I will put my squirrel back in the pen and then the others will get used to the scent of the dog – after this dog and squirrels will work together, I think."

Penny got 748 to lie down, while Paisley tethered his badger to the outside of the squirrel corral, then they followed Caro Elora to the biggest tree, in the middle of the valley. The little dryad was almost exactly the same size as Paisley – to Penny, they looked like a matched set of giant dolls.

When they reached the enormous, red-trunked tree, Caro Elora swarmed up the trunk to the first little house, which was about five meters up in the air. Penny couldn't see how, because the bark looked so smooth there couldn't be any hand-holds. Once she was up, the dryad lowered a fine silvery ladder down. It seemed to be made of rope no thicker than one of the human child's fingers. She looked at the pixie. "I don't know if I can do this, Paisley," she admitted. "I'm scared of heights."

The pixie nodded earnestly. "I share your concerns, Lady Penny. However, I would not appear rude to our hosts – especially as we need their help to find our companions." Then his face softened into a rare smile. "Come, milady – you have defeated two mighty harrows. I do not believe a little thing like climbing this ladder will be beyond you."

That made Penny feel a bit better – but her heart was booming in her ears as she put her foot on the bottom rung of the ladder. It swung alarmingly. The girl squealed in surprise – then Paisley was there, holding the bottom of the ladder to stop it swinging. He may have been small, but he was very strong.

Quickly, Penny climbed the ladder – though Caro Elora helped her onto the small wooden platform outside the house. She had barely stood up, one hand resting on the wall of the house for comfort, when Paisley was standing beside her, running a hand nervously through his spiky hair. The girl was reassured to see the odd, brave little pixie was just as uncomfortable as her at being this far from the ground.

Caro Elora smiled reassuringly. "You are quite safe on the Moot Tree," she said. "There are railings everywhere to aid our visitors. Indeed, my father requires them as well sometimes. Come, let us hurry to see him."

She led the way around the platform and across narrow silver bridge that spanned the gap between this tree and the next. It swayed alarmingly as the girl walked across it, but she gripped the railings and concentrated on looking ahead. The only problem was, while the railing would have been chest-high rail for a dryad or pixie, it was barely higher than Penny's knee. She had to stoop to grip it and didn't think it would do much to stop her falling off the bridge – it was easier to imagine tripping over it.

And that first gossamer bridge turned out to be the least of it. The dryad chief's grand hall was built on a high platform at the very top of the tree. Penny and Paisley followed their dryad guide up and up – sometimes using ladders on the outside of trees, sometimes narrow, curling stairways carved inside the massive trunks that were almost too small for the human to get through. Twice they crossed to another tree on slender, swaying bridges with the ground a dizzying distance below.

Finally, they reached the top. The grand hall was only grand compared with the tree houses of dryad village – which all seemed to be about the size of a small caravan. But then, the dryads were so small they probably didn't need more space to live in. This made the grand hall, which was as big as the large kitchen in the Big House, relatively massive and imposing – especially since it was so high in the air.

Penny had to duck to get through the grand hall's door and, inside, she could only just stand up without banging into the ceiling. Flickering lamps sent eerie shadows dancing across the walls and filled the warm air with a scent of flowers. There were a dozen dryads sitting at a long, low table at the far end of the room.

But the figure that rose as the friends entered was different. He looked like a silver-edged version of Paisley. The pixie and the girl stopped when they saw him, mouths dropping open.

"Welcome," said this strange person, in the deeply ringing tones of a pixie. "I am Cullen, dryad chief. Though once I was of the Plain, I led the people of the Wood in war – and I have been here ever since. I can see you have many questions mighty Paisley, but before I answer them please eat. And you, Lady Penny. Please take refreshments – while you eat I will tell my tale."

Penny looked to Paisley and, followed his lead, silently took a seat while dryads rushed forward with bowls of food – very similar to the pixies' food. As the guests ate, Cullen began to talk.

"The dryads are not like the pixies," he explained. "They have no men – they are all women. This is not a problem in their society, except they need a male leader, a chief, to lead their war with the centaurs. Many years ago, about the time the dark queen was overthrown, I came here from the plains to be the war chief.

"For years we have fought – and we have won many great battles. We built this safe village, we have driven the centaurs from this side of the Wood, our clan has prospered. We even thought to re-establish links with the Plain. And now you are here, mighty Paisley – I can see you are a great hetman of your people. Brown Raiders, by your signs. A noble tribe.

"My scouts have already sent messages. They tell me that your friends are alive. The centaurs have them prisoners, but we think they have sent a messenger to the dark Queen – she passed through the Wood some days ago.

"I know what you have come here to ask. And we dryads will do it. We will free your friends – but if we do, there is something you must do for us in return. Something only you can do, mighty Paisley. When the battle is done, I will return at last to the Plain and there at last I will end my days beneath the open skies.

"But the Wood must have a chief dryad. And that must be you, Paisley. You must agree to take my place."

Chapter Thirty Seven

Paisley's Choice

For a long, silent moment, Paisley stared hard at Cullen. The two of them looked very similar – but Cullen was clearly much, much older. Where Paisley was dark and sharp, Cullen was silvery-grey and worn with age, all his edges rounded.

"If you are of the Plains, great Cullen," Paisley said slowly, his deep voice ringing with seriousness. "You will understand why I cannot take your place. First, I am here only because I owe a life-debt to Captain Broadwallow. Second, I have sworn to accompany Lady Penny step-for-step on her quest. Third, once I have discharged the first two duties, I have a tribe to lead."

Cullen smiled amicably. "Noble Paisley, everything you say is fair and true. A hetman of the Brown Raiders lives for his duties – I would expect no less. However, if you agree to our terms, you will have discharged your life-debt to Captain Broadwallow when we free him. As to leading your tribe – hetmen come, hetmen go. It is the way of the Plains. One of your clan must lead in your place while you are on the quest. And if you do not return in a year and a day, the tribe will elect a new hetman. We both know that. So the only problem is your pledge to the Lady Penny."

They both looked at her. She didn't know what to say – but she could see they expected some kind of judgement from her. "Well, we have to get the others back," she said. She wanted to say more, but didn't want to say something stupid either. Before she could work out what she should say, Cullen spoke again.

"We shall rescue your friends. You cannot do it without the aid of the dryads. And the price for that aid is Paisley taking my place as the chief dryad. He will not be able to continue on your quest once the rescue is done."

"What do you want, Paisley?" Penny asked slowly. "Would you like to stay here with the dryads?"

The little pixie hesitated, looked at Caro Elora, then looked back to his human companion. "I would like nothing more," he admitted. "But just hours ago I pledged to stay by your side for every step of your journey. What honour would I have if I threw that pledge aside? And so soon? What kind of hetman or chief would I be if my word could be so lightly set aside?"

He looked sadly at Caro Elora and again at Cullen. "I could not sacrifice my honour and still be fit to lead the dryads."

Cullen chuckled like a great cracked bell being hit with a mallet. "Very well, great Paisley. Your words are wise. Will you instead pledge to return to the Wood when your quest is done? To take my place then, as the war chief of the dryads?"

"That I can do, noble Cullen. By Plain and Wood, I do."

"Then it is settled," said Caro Elora. "Tomorrow we make

war on the centaurs to free your friends. Then we will continue on your quest."

"We?" Paisley and Penny spoke together, looking at the friendly, dainty dryad.

"Why yes – if our leader-elect is going on a quest, I shall accompany him," she said, very matter of fact. "To keep him safe, to teach him of the ways of the Wood so he will be ready to lead our people when he returns – and to get to know him better."

Paisley's eyes glinted inscrutably in the flickering lamp light, but Penny thought he looked pleased to hear this. She certainly was – she'd already decided she liked Caro Elora, with her tinkling voice and ready smile.

"It is settled!" growled Cullen, slapping the table. "Now, Lady Penny needs to rest and Paisley and I must plan tomorrow's raid. Clear the hall, my people! Caro Elora, take care of our guest and find her somewhere suitable to sleep."

That turned out to be a small house halfway up the gigantic tree – a cosy room no larger than a potting shed, all woody and sweet smelling. The furniture inside was far to small for Penny, but Caro Elora and four or five other dryads scampered across the tree and returned with arms full of soft quilts and blankets. The girl spread them on the floor, bade her new friends good night, then lay down and fell quickly asleep.

Next morning, Caro Elora woke her early. The dryads were ready for war and they wanted to get on with it. They gathered on the grass at the foot of the giant tree while Cullen addressed them. Paisley had come up with the plan and he stepped forward to explain it but he talked to the dryads and answered their questions in their bell-like language, clanging and tinkling musically, so Penny couldn't understand what they were saying. She had no idea what was going on and felt, frankly, a bit left out.

Eventually, the dryads jumped up, cheering and clapping. Caro Elora patted Penny's arm and smiled at her. "Now we will be going – the plan is a good one and we should be both successful and safe," she said. The dryads had painted their faces with black and white stripes of war paint. Caro Elora had helped the girl put some on as well – a solid white stripe across her face, from ear to ear across the bridge of her nose. But the dryad still didn't explain what was going on.

The war party left the dryad village in single file and rode silently through the forest. Most were mounted on squirrels, with Penny on 748 and Paisley on his badger, though scouts ran ahead, swarming through the treetops. Birds were singing, dew was beaded on spiders' webs like jewelled nets, the air smelt fresh and, where a ray of morning sun poked through the trees, it was warm on the girl's skin. It all very beautiful.

It was hard to believe they were going to war.

But it was war. By lunchtime, the warriors had spread out. Now Penny was riding with only Caro Elora, Paisley and another dryad called Caro Anessa. The rest had disappeared among the trees. The girl's stomach rumbled, but there was no way she could have eaten. Besides, they didn't have time to stop for food.

The beautiful, fragrant part of the forest was well behind them now. They had entered an area where trees were large and dark, hard and spiky. A thick layer of pine needles lay on the floor and the air smelt wet and rotten. It was very gloomy and there were thick brambles with huge thorns growing everywhere.

"The centaur camp is just ahead," said Caro Anessa, finally giving Penny the explanation she'd been too shy to request. "Mighty Paisley has persuaded our warriors to try a new plan. They will taunt the centaurs and draw them out of the camp, while you three sneak in at the back to rescue your friends."

The four of them dismounted and lay on the cold, damp pine needles for what seemed like ages. Penny watched a line of ants marching past in front of her, carrying huge leaves and sticks far bigger than they were. Then Caro Elora nudged her, "It is time, Penny," she said. "I hear the signal."

Leaving 748, Paisley's badger and Caro Elora's squirrel with Caro Anessa, the three friends crept slowly forwards.

They tiptoed through the trees as quietly as they could.

Small and light as she was, Penny saw her companions stiffen when she stepped on a twig and it cracked. She winced, hoping centaurs didn't have such good hearing as the pixies and dryads.

The centaur camp was a dirty, smelly place. It could be smelt before it was seen– a sour, sweaty stink of unwashed horses. There were no huts or houses or tents, just rough screens of woven branches hung between trees to make roofs. Penny couldn't see any centaurs, but she could hear them – away ahead of her, roaring and whinnying, crashing through the undergrowth as they chased the dryads Paisley had sent to distract them.

Paisley found Pickatina first. She was hanging upside-down from a tree branch, her arms tied behind her back, looking very uncomfortable and sad. Caro Elora rushed up the tree and cut the rope that held her up, lowering her carefully to the floor. Paisley quickly freed her arms and legs, while Penny looked around nervously. Still no sign of centaurs. Pickatina stood up and hugged each of rescuers, but nobody spoke. They all knew they had to keep quiet.

They found Broadwallow next. He was on the other side of the camp, nearer the sounds of fighting. He was tied to a vast tree trunk, his arms stretched back around it and held fast with a chain. His face was quite bruised – he must have put up a fight. His great sword was driven deep into the trunk of a tree right in front of him. The centaurs must have put it there to taunt him – leaving it in sight but out of his reach, so he'd know he was beaten and couldn't fight them.

Well, now he might be able to. Paisley took out his hatchet and hacked at the chain that held Broadwallow's hands together. The blow threw up a shower of sparks and made a loud noise but hardly dented it. Pickatina pushed the pixie aside.

"This may get hot, cousin," she hissed to Broadwallow. She took a deep breath, chanting quietly as she sucked the air into her lungs. Then she bent forwards and blew on the chain, a constant stream of air all aimed at one point. One of the links of the chain began to glow – dull red at first, then bright orange, then white.

"Now, Paisley," Pickatina said. "Hit the hot link."

The little pixie stepped forward again, delivering a two-handed whack to the chain and it split apart in a shower of molten metal. Broadwallow staggered forwards, regaining his balance as he grabbed his sword. Standing up straight, he took the hilt with both hands and heaved… but the sword didn't budge. It was firmly stuck in the tree.

Penny heard galloping. Getting closer. Fast. Centaurs were coming towards them. Broadwollow put one foot against the trunk, then both so he was standing on it, tugging on the sword for all it was worth. And still it didn't move. Then Pickatina was there, blowing on the sword blade. A thin plume of smoke rose from the wood and then the sword came out of the tree so quickly that Broadwallow fell flat on his back.

"Quick! Let's get Frank before the centaurs get here," Penny said to Pickatina. The goblin looked sick and exhausted, but she turned huge sad eyes to her friend and her expression became even more miserable.

"Boy Frank is not here, Girl Pen," she said. "The centaurs have taken him. Taken him to the mistress. He is not here."

But the centaurs were. Before Penny could say a word, three of the huge horse-caveman beasts rode into view at the edge of their camp. They took one look at the human and her friends, roared… and charged.

Chapter Thirty Eight

The Skipping Rope

Broadwallow leapt towards the galloping centaurs, swinging his sword in a lethal arc at the leader. That's all Penny saw. Paisley and Pickatina grabbed her arms and they were running. She had no idea where Caro Elora was. She was just running. Not running *to* anywhere, just running. Away from the centaurs.

Paisley suddenly shoved her. She staggered to the left, knocking into Pickatina. A centaur galloped past, brushing Penny's flying hair. If the strong little pixie hadn't pushed her, the horse-man would have galloped straight into the girl.

Pickatina dragged her beneath a low branch, through a narrow gap between two trees, then they were out of the centaur camp. There were shouts and cries behind them. Glancing over her shoulder, Penny saw centaurs heading towards her.

"The skipping rope," panted Pickatina. "Do you still have the skipping rope, Girl Pen?"

Why was she worrying about that now? "Yes."

"Use it. Start skipping," the goblin gasped. "I can make myself safe if I know you are alright. Use the skipping rope."

"What? Are you crazy?" Penny huffed. There wasn't time for this. She jumped over a fallen tree trunk, then they ducked round a big bramble bush and kept running.

"It is a magic device," Pickatina panted. "It will make you safe as long as you are skipping."

A centaur burst through a small clump of bushes ahead of Penny. She screamed and swerved to run behind the beast, but Pickatina dived straight under it, making it rear. The goblin rolled to safety. The girl had got away from the centaur, but now she was completely alone. She had no idea where her friends were, where the dryads were. All she could do was run hither-and-thither through the forest, trying to avoid centaurs.

"Over here, Penny!" called a tinkling, familiar voice: Caro Elora. The girl turned and ran in her direction, but then saw a centaur had swerved towards her, so she changed course. She ducked down behind a fallen tree, the massive roots sticking up from the earth and shielding her from the monster for a moment.

Penny thought frantically. She knew she couldn't keep running from the centaurs – they'd catch her sooner or later. Then they'd send her to Ribaldane, the way they'd sent Frank to her. Or worse. What could she do? Trust Pickatina, that's what...

Reaching into her bag, Penny took the silver-handled skipping rope, then put the rucksack on her back again. Would this really work? Could this possibly work? What was going to happen? She heard a gallop, a pause, a thud… a centaur had just leapt the fallen tree behind her. All it had to do was come round to where the roots were sticking up and he'd see the girl, crouching in the little muddy hollow at its foot. If she was going to try the skipping rope, it was now or never.

At her old school, the best skipper had been Melissa Braithwaite. Penny wasn't that good, but she was okay. As the rope whirled over head, under foot, over head, Penny prayed it wouldn't catch on any sticks or on her feet. She concentrated really hard on skipping as well as she could – she didn't pay much attention to where she was going. The rope whistled musically through the air and it took the girl a second to notice what was happening. The rope had generated a kind of faint milky blue bubble around her – like a force field in a space film. She was so surprised that she stopped skipping.

And fell to the floor. Not far – only as high as from the second step. But that was enough to make her fall over. She heard a centaur roared in triumph somewhere nearby, but Penny didn't even waste time looking for it. She scrambled to her feet and started skipping again.

This time she did look where she was going. And all she saw was a centaur – a huge horse-creature charging straight at her. Penny didn't stop. Just kept skipping. The milky bubble was around her and she was rising slowly from the floor.

The centaur slammed into the bubble and bounced straight off. It staggered sideways, legs tangling and tripping as it fell. Penny didn't even feel any impact. She just kept skipping forward at her own pace, slowly climbing higher and higher into the air. She tried to steer to avoid a tree but didn't quite manage it. As she looked at it, the branches just brushed the bubble and bent… then the trunk of the massive tree swayed and it tipped to the side ever so slightly, getting out of the way of the flying bubble.

Penny laughed. It was really fun – and funny. She was flying. Flying inside a skipping rope. And nothing could get in her way. But the funny bit was how natural it felt. For a second she almost forgot her friends as she delighted in the new sensation.

But of course her friends were still down there, battling for their lives. Desperately Penny looked around, trying to work out how to steer the bubble. Again, she nearly stopped skipping but realised just in time that if she did, she'd just fall back to earth again. Only now she was a long way above the ground. At least two metres above it. If not more.

How was she going to get down?

She very nearly panicked. But somehow Penny managed to keep calm and keep skipping. As worried as she was about Pickatina, Broadwallow, Paisley and the dryads, just at that moment she didn't have time to think about them. The only thing she was thinking about was how to get down without hurting herself.

As she looked down she saw one thing that might help her friends – a great mob of centaurs following her, throwing rocks and spears at her bubble. Everything bounced off, barely making a sound. But it meant that even if Penny did find a way to go down, she couldn't actually land. The centaurs would get her as soon as she stopped skipping.

But now she *was* going down. Not much. Not quickly. But a little. What had she done differently? How had she made the bubble descend? Of course! She'd been looking down. She looked to her right and skipped in that direction, looking and thinking about descending. And the bubble swung to the right and down. Penny looked straight up. The bubble began to climb. She looked down again. The bubble went down. Quite quickly this time.

Penny kept looking down. Looking at the centaurs. Looking *right* at the centaurs. Especially at the biggest, meanest, shoutiest centaur at the front. She realised they weren't very clever creatures, because they just kept running around beneath her, shaking their fists and shouting. And then their leader hit the bubble.

As Penny knew he would, the ugly centaur bounced off the

bubble. He knocked into one of the others and both animals fell over. Penny kept looking at them, skipping for all she was worth. The bubble followed where she looked and she banged into the centaurs again, knocking them back down as they tried to get up.

Suddenly, the girl was crying. She was raging. She was shouting with anger. Her arms were shaking and blood was pounding in her ears. What did these horrid, evil creatures think they were doing, tying up her friends and hurting them? Kidnapping Frank and sending him off to Ribaldane? Penny had suddenly had enough of being pushed about and scared by the evil creatures and the magic Ribaldane had unleashed. She was so angry she wasn't even thinking.

She rolled her bubble into the centaurs again and again, knocking them flying every time. They roared and raged and hurled themselves against it – and they never got anywhere. Gradually they began to understand that they couldn't get to the girl. They couldn't capture her or hurt her. They couldn't defeat her or even scare her now. They didn't have any power. She did. She had all the power.

And then they started to run. One or two of the smaller ones fled first, then a couple of the larger ones. Then suddenly they all seemed to be turning and running. Penny followed and knocked them down as many times as she could, to make it hard for them to escape. She couldn't chase them all. Eventually only the biggest, meanest-looking centaur remained – so battered and bruised he could barely stand but still spoiling for a fight.

Penny lowered the bubble until she was a few metres from the centaur. She stopped skipping and dropped a centimetre to the floor. The beast stood sullenly as the girl looked into his angry, hate-filled eyes. She could see he was beaten, but she didn't relax her grip on the skipping rope.

"Who are you, human?" the centaur growled.

"I am Penelope Oaks," she said proudly. "What have you done with my brother?" She'd never called Frank her brother before.

"He has been sent over the mountain, to the mistress," the creature sneered. "Your rat friends will not rescue him now."

"Which way did they go?" she asked. Demanded. Commanded.

"North, to the mountains," the centaur replied, gesturing with a shake of his head. "Soon the great snakes will have him. You won't beat them with your magic ball."

"What is your name, centaur?" Penny asked quietly.

"I am Charos, chief of the centaurs," he said. And at that moment, he leapt at Penny, both fists raised.

The skipping rope span twice. The centaur bounced off the bubble and fell to the floor, landing heavily. Penny landed again. "Don't bet I can't beat the snakes," she said firmly. "I've beaten you, Charos. And I'll beat them too."

Then the girl turned away and began to skip towards the mountains. She didn't know where the rest of her friends were, but she couldn't wait for them. All alone, Penelope Oaks set off into Faerieland to rescue Frank.

Book Three

Snakes & Dragons

Chapter Thirty Nine

Alone

Alone. Totally, utterly, completely alone. Lost in the Wild Wood. Penny tried not to think of it like that, but that's exactly how things stood. She was on her own, in the wildest corner of Faerieland. Her friends were somewhere in the Wood, but she wasn't looking for them. There were hostile centaurs down there too, but she wasn't looking for them either. She was looking for Frank. She had to rescue him.

There was a nasty metal taste in Penny's mouth, like she'd bitten on an old coin. She was shivering. Her arms and legs were heavy and aching. She'd been skipping for at least half an hour, so the centaur village was a long way behind her now. She didn't think any of the centaurs would have been able to chase her, even if they'd wanted to. The girl was skipping through the air above the trees, protected by the invulnerable bubble created by her magical skipping rope.

Normally Penny was a bit scared of heights. She didn't like getting up too high on things like climbing frames or trees. But she found she liked being in the big, safe bubble, floating through the air above the trees. And from up there, she could see the mountains easily enough. They rose behind the Wild Wood like a giant garden wall towering over an untidy flower bed. They were majestic, the tallest capped with snow even though it was warm.

Penny could even see what had to be the Hydra's Pass – a deep cleft between the jagged peaks. She had been skipping in that direction, brushing the tips of the tallest trees and startling starlings as she went, ever since leaving the centaur village. Ribaldane and Grimshock were heading for the Hydra's Pass. That was where centaurs had sent Frank – so she had to go there too.

Penny was completely out of breath, worried she'd lose her rhythm, trip on the rope and stop skipping. If that happened, the bubble would disappear and she would fall. And she was a long way up. So she began to descend, looking down and skipping gently until she was brushing her way through the trees. Where the bubble rubbed up against them, they bent out of its way – no matter how big they were.

Then Penny spotted a tree that looked like it could be ideal for her – a giant oak that must have been hit by lightning at some point. The trunk rose up, thick and strong, until it was nearly as tall as a house. But then it stopped abruptly, with a ring of raised, ancient bark around the edge of a wide, flat space from which four huge branches fanned out, turning upwards and growing towards the sky.

Holding the corner of her lower lip between her teeth and breathing intently, Penny skipped forwards until she was hovering just above the flat crown of the tree. She was stared intently at it and the bubble sank lower and lower until, when she was barely a rope's width above it, she stopped skipping. The drop onto the top of the tree was abrupt but short.

Penny savoured a huge rush of elation – she had rescued Pickatina and Broadwallow from the centaur camp, escaped, beaten all the horrid horse-men that had chased her, set off to rescue Frank and now she'd found a secure place to rest. She felt like dancing. Only she was too tired.

Seconds later a huge wave of sadness almost overwhelmed her. After all, she was separated from her companions – and she didn't actually know if they were safe. She didn't really know where she was, exactly where she was going, or how she was going to save Frank when she got there. She was exhausted, hungry and very, very thirsty. In the space of a moment, Penny went from feeling on top of the world to feeling ready to cry.

Instead, she just lay down on top of the huge tree, curled up inside her cloak and, even though it wasn't even dark, closed her eyes as if she really was ready to sleep. Even though the tree was uneven and hard, she was so worn out that's just what happened: in the fragrant hush of the treetop, Penny fell asleep.

There was a small sound, like a buzzing in her ear. She couldn't work out what it was, though it sounded familiar. Penny opened here eyes and it was properly dark, the strange stars of Faerieland painting the sky with spectacular patterns. She sat up and looked around. Night time on the flower plains was beautiful, with tiny flickering lights of dancing fairies hovering above the flowers. The Wild Wood was much, much darker… but there were still lights. Small, soft, lights shining among the trees. They weren't multi-coloured, like the flower-faerie lights – they were all shimmering shades of silver. And one of them was very near.

In fact, it was in Penny's tree. She realised this light was bigger than the flower faerie lights. Much bigger. Crawling carefully across the broad wooden top of the tree until she was very close, the girl leaned forward for a closer look…

It was a faerie! A proper, tiny, wings-on-her-back faerie. She didn't seem to have a little ballet dress like the pictures in the books at home – in fact, she didn't seem to have any clothes at all – but there she was. A perfect, beautiful, miniature lady with pointy ears and shimmering gossamer wings. She was no taller than a fifty-pence piece. Penny realised it was only her wings that shone, not her whole body. The faster her wings beat, the more brightly her light glowed.

"Excuse me, but what are you?" the faerie asked in a teeny, high voice. The human could only just make out the words.

"You can speak?" Penny was so surprised she almost fell over.

"Of course I can – I'm a faerie. What are you? How do you know how to speak?" the tiny creature replied. She sounded a bit like the cheeky kids in the reception class.

"I'm a human. My name is Penelope Oaks, but you can call me Penny. What's your name?"

"Name? Name? I don't… I don't think I have a name," the faerie sounded sad. "How do you get one?"

Penny thought about it. "Well, my parents gave me my name, when I was born."

"Oh. Faeries don't work like that," the tiny creature said.

"We grow with our plants. So I suppose this tree is my parent, but it's never talked to me in all the years we've been together. Never said a word, let alone taken the time to name me."

"Well, if you like, I could give you a name," Penny offered.

"Would you?" she giggled. "That would be so kind. But where do I keep it?"

"Keep it?" Penny was puzzled. "You don't keep a name in a box or a bag or a pocket. A name isn't a thing like that. It's just... it's just a word, a special word that means who you are. If you keep it anywhere, you keep it in your head. Or in the heads of people who care about you. Yes, that's where names are really kept – in the hearts and heads of those who love you."

"Oh. So who loves you?" the faerie asked. "I hope they talk about you more than my tree talks about me."

"Well there's my dad, though he's at sea sailing his ship," Penny replied. "And I suppose Maggie, who's my step-mother. I had friends, back before we moved. I don't know if I'll ever see them again. Maybe the Professor – but that's back in the human world. Here in Faerieland there's Frank – he's my sort-of-brother. I used to think he was revolting, until we came here. And there's Pickatina and Broadwallow. They're goblins, but really good ones. I don't know if they love me, but they are my friends. And there's Paisley, who's a pixie, and I think Caro Elora's nice – she's a dryad."

"And all those people keep your name for you?" asked the faerie. "Yours must be a really good name. Can I have one like yours please?"

"Okay," the girl smiled. "I give you the name of Faerie Oaks. You're the faerie for an oak tree and my name's Oaks, so your name is like mine."

The little faerie giggled and clapped her hands – it sounded no louder than two bits of straw banging together. "I understand! I can keep the name in my head!" she laughed. "If anyone asks for my name, I can give it to them – Faerie Oaks – and they can keep it in their head too!

"But, oh..." she sounded sad. "You're the only person I've met. How will anyone else ever get my name and be able to keep it for me? What have you been doing to meet all these people?"

"It's a long story," Penny said. "I was tricked by a witch – she's called Ribaldane. Have you heard of her?" The little creature looked solemn and shook her head.

"Well, Ribaldane pretended to be my friend, so I fetched her a silver trumpet. But it's a terrible thing that she can use to wake up the soldiers of an army called the Black Legion," Penny explained. "If she blows the trumpet, they'll obey her – then she'll be able to take over Faerieland. And then she'll be able to break through to the human world at Bradley Hall – that's where I live, in the gatehouse. So I was sent to stop her, with my friends to help me."

"So, where are your name-keepers?" the faerie asked, looking around.

Penny sniffed. "There was a battle, with the centaurs of the Wild Wood. Paisley and the dryads rescued my friends, who'd been captured. I was fighting the centaurs so they should have been able to escape. Except Frank wasn't there when we freed Pickatina and Broadwallow. He'd already been sent away to the mountains. To Ribaldane and Grimshock – he's the witch's servant. So I'm going to find Frank and rescue him as well."

"He has your name with him?" asked Fairie Oaks.

"Yes, but I don't know what good it will do," the girl said.

"Oh, I do," the faerie replied, clapping with happiness. "I can see that this keeping names makes one bigger and stronger. You have given me all their names and your own, so already I feel bigger and stronger. I could face any danger, now – even an owl." And she puffed up her chest and waved her fists, grinning bravely.

The girl laughed. "Thank you, little Fairie Oaks," she said.

"I mean it, Penelope Oaks," she said. "I feel it. It is true. Anyone carrying your name with them will feel stronger. Now rest. You will be safe here tonight. I will watch over you. Tomorrow you can rescue your sort-of-brother Frank."

The girl nodded. She was feeling sleepy again, so she crawled back to the middle of the treetop without saying another word, curled up inside her cloak again and lay down. Moments later, she was asleep. When Penny woke in the morning, Faerie Oaks was nowhere to be seen. The girl got up and headed towards the mountains again. Towards Frank… and the witch…

Chapter Forty

Buddy

Penny set off for the mountains, flying again, using the magic bubble generated by the skipping rope. As she flew she wondered about the other objects in the metal cases, locked in the secret cellar beneath Bradley Hall – the cellar reached only by passing into Faerieland. They had to be magical devices too.

The skipping rope had its unburstable flying bubble. The silver trumpet would, apparently, give whoever blew it power over the mysterious Black Legion. What did the other things do? There had been a comb, a bell, a mirror, a silver feather, a ring… Penny had heard about magic rings before. And there'd been a knife – a magic knife. If only she had it now… she was sure it would help. If only Frank had it. He needed the help most, wherever he was.

She was getting hungry – and tired from skipping – so she landed the bubble on a hill. She was still definitely in the Wild Wood, but as the land rose towards the Dragon Mountains, the trees grew thinner. The tops of the hills poked through, little grassy islands in the sea of trees. Penny poked around in the grass beneath the trees and found some nuts, but then worried that it wouldn't be safe to eat them. She pulled out the magic bowl Queen Celestia had given her and forced herself to eat a bit of the horrid porrige it produced. It filled her up, but made her feel ill.

She set off down the hill, walking between the trees. She seemed to be on the edge of a valley, on the far side of which the mountains sat, tall and menacing. Penny didn't want to do any more skipping for the time being – partly because it was tiring, but also because she was getting worried that if Grimshock and Ribaldane were somewhere ahead in the mountains – and if they had Frank, so were on the look-out for people coming to rescue him – they might spot her as she skipped through the air. She decided to walk for a bit, only skipping up every now and then to check that she was still going the right way.

It was a hot day, but it felt cool in the shade under the trees. It was quiet like a library, the only sound the hush of the wind in the treetops and the occasional call of a bird. Penny really wished she had someone to talk to – but she was all alone. She couldn't even see any tree faeries, though they probably only came out at night, like the flower faeries.

So Penny began to sing as she walked along. At first she sang pop songs, then she sang nursery rhymes – as many as she could remember – and soon she was just singing any old nonsense. She sang about what she could see and what she could hear and where she'd been and what she'd seen and what she'd done. She quite liked the way her voice echoed in the empty forest. So she nearly jumped out of her skin when someone started singing along.

"Who's there?" she asked, reaching into her bag and gripping the deadly steel secateurs. They were made of steel which was lethal to faeriefolk.

"Who's there?" came the reply.

"Is that just an echo?"

"Who are you calling 'just' an echo?" came the reply. Penny laughed nervously. There was a giggle from somewhere nearby. But it sounded friendly.

"My name's Penny," she said. "Who are you?"

"Who am I? Who am I? Can't you see me? I wonder why?"

"I met a tree faerie. She didn't have a name until I gave her one," she said. "Do you need a name too?"

"Need a name too?" said the voice. "I don't think I do."

"Can you show yourself?"

"How did you guess," came the voice. "I am an elf!"

And a little creature swung down out of a tree, dropped to the floor and came running towards the girl. It was like a small person – smaller than the pixies and dryads she'd already met. The elf didn't even come up to her knee. But where the pixies and dryads were a little unsettling, with big heads balanced atop thin bodies, the elf was perfectly proportioned, like a tiny human.

Carefully, Penny knelt down to get a better look. She saw a handsome little man dressed in green, with blonde hair, a smiling face and pointy ears. He bowed, then stood up again and smiled.

"A charming human you must be," he said, "To take the time to talk to me."

"What's your name?" she asked.

"My name? Tradition says to learn it we must play a game," he replied, laughing.

"What kind of game?" Penny tried to keep her voice polite, but she was beginning to get annoyed with the way he was talking. "Why do you keep trying to talk in rhymes? You're not very good at it, you know."

"Oh. Okay. Sorry. I didn't mean to make you cross," he said, sounding a bit cross himself. "I thought that's what you humans liked. You know, for the stories and such. Elves who talk in rhymes, laugh a lot, are faintly mysterious – that kind of thing. My name's Bud, by the way."

"We don't have to play a game?"

"Well, not if we're dispensing with the whole talking in rhymes thing," he said. "I mean, why bother?"

Penny realised she might have hurt his feeling. "I'm sorry Bud," she said. "You aren't really bad at talking in rhymes. I just wanted to know your name. I'm not very patient at the moment. I'm kind of in a rush."

"On a quest, are you?" he asked, looking interested.

"Yes! How did you guess?" she gasped.

"Well, we don't get many humans in these parts. Last lot came through – oh, must be a couple of hundred years ago, when they were here to get rid of the old queen. Wicked one, she was. And now you're here, also in a rush, so you must be on a quest as well. Stands to reason," he explained.

"I have to save my step-brother, Frank," she said.

"Away with the fairies, is he?"

"No, the centaurs," she explained. "They've sent him to catch up with Ribaldane – the old queen. She's going towards the Hydra's Pass. Am I going the right way to catch up with them?"

"Oh, you're going the right way – though it's not a nice place," said Bud. "I wouldn't be going there. Big snakes live up there. Huge. Eat anything that isn't nasty enough to eat them."

"I'm not scared of the snakes," she said firmly. "I have a way of dealing with them. What I'm worried about is Ribaldane. I know she knows a lot of magic – I don't know if I can beat that."

Bud looked serious. "If you'll give me a lift home, I'll have a think," he said. "We elves are pretty magical, you know. We're kind of related to the faerie queens – sort of cousins, you might say. Maybe I can come up with something that'll help you."

"You'll come on my quest?" she asked.

"Not likely!" he laughed – then stopped. "Cor, you're serious, aren't you? Sorry, I didn't mean to laugh. I suppose it's the reputation, isn't it? Fearless elves, fair and brave. Well let me tell you, we may be brave and we may be fair and we may even be a bit fearless. But there's one thing we're not – and that's stupid. We elves can't go getting mixed up in the affairs of the big folks! I mean, just look at the size of me. It'd be far too dangerous. Besides, Mrs Bud wouldn't like it.

"But if I can sit on your shoulder and you can give me a walk home, I'll see if I can think of a charm I can lay on you that'll help you if the old queen catches sight of you. That'll be my contribution to the quest." He smiled at me. "Best I can do."

"That'll have to do, I suppose," Penny sighed. "Thank you."

She picked the little man up and he perched on her

shoulder. As they walked through the wood, he pointed to various landmarks and different trees, telling her about their history. He'd known some of the trees since they were acorns – and now they were huge. Though she was too polite to ask, Penny wondered how old Bud was.

Then, suddenly, he tugged on Penny's ear. "Don't move," he whispered. So the girl froze. She tried not to breath loudly, straining her ears, but she couldn't hear anything. "Very slowly, kneel down," Bud whispered. "We need to hide somewhere – and we need to get there very quietly. Now."

Then she heard it too. Not close… but not far off, either. It was a quiet, muted whinny – but not quite like a proper horse would make. There was only one creature in these woods that would make a sound like that: a centaur.

Chapter Forty One

Frank

Bud got Penny to hide behind a broad sycamore tree. When she thought he wasn't watching her, she peeked round the trunk and saw, a little way off, a centaur. It was trudging along looking grumpy, tugging on a rope. Behind it, hands tied together, being pulled along, was Frank. He looked sore and dirty and absolutely exhausted. His head was down, his hair was lank and his clothes were torn.

Penny's blood boiled. She'd always thought that was a silly expression… but now it made sense. She was hot, flushed, she could feel her anger bubbling in her temples like a pan boiling over on the stove. This ugly centaur – this rude, crude, nasty thing – was pulling Frank along like a bad dog. As she watched, it yanked on the rope, making Frank stumble and stagger. Checking that she wasn't going to squash Bud, she put her bag on the floor, reached into it and took out the skipping rope. Then she reached in and took out the secateurs.

"Stay away from my bag, Bud," she whispered. "And away from these. They're made of the death metal. I don't want you to get hurt." She tucked them into the back pocket of her jeans.

"What are you doing?" the elf hissed, alarmed. "That's a centaur down there. It's already got one human prisoner."

"It won't have in a minute," she muttered grimly. She was going to sort this out. Right now.

Penny started skipping. Straight away the centaur turned and looked in her direction, but she was only about 20 metres from it. She rolled her skipping-rope bubble straight at it. Their eyes met: the girl's burning with fury; the animal's cloudy with surprise and puzzlement.

Then she hit it. Just like all the other centaurs she'd fought, this one was thrown backwards as if it was made of feathers as soon as the bubble touched it. The horse-man threw its hands up and whineyed in surprise, flying through the air to land in a heap. Luckily, it had dropped the rope that was tied to Frank's hands.

Penny kept going at it. The centaur had barely shaken its head and got its two front legs onto their knees when she hit it again. This time when it was sent flying it bounced into a tree, cracking its head. It fell to the floor and didn't move. The girl stopped skipping and, reaching into her back pocket, she advanced towards it with the secateurs in her hand.

"Don't, Penny!" shouted Frank. "It's a horrible creature, but don't kill it. Don't do that."

She stopped. Was that really what she had been about to do? She hadn't thought of it like that. She knew the steel secateurs were deadly – but at the same time, she hadn't thought of touching the centaur with the steel secateurs as killing it. Just... stopping it. Like she'd stopped the harrows. But of course it wasn't the same at all. The harrows had been magical machines; the centaur was alive.

Penny turned and ran to Frank, hugging him. "Thank you,"

she said. "Thank you. Thank you." She was almost crying.

"What are you thanking me for, you nut?" he laughed. "I should be thanking you for rescuing me."

"No, it's not that," she said. "I don't want to kill anything. I don't even like hurting things – even the centaurs. But I had to get you free. Are you alright? Can I cut the rope with the secateurs, do you think?"

"Slow down, Penny," Frank laughed. "I'm really tired and my wrists hurt where the ropes have rubbed them raw, but I'm alright. Really I am. I don't think you'll be able to cut the rope with those, but if you get the bag that centaur had slung round his waist, my knife should be in there. That'll cut the rope."

So she went over to the centaur. It did have a little satchel thing round its waist, where the caveman bit joined the horse bit. She hadn't noticed that before. Opening it, Penny found Frank's knife, then used it to cut the rope and set him free.

He stood up, rubbing his wrists, then hugged me. "That's brilliant, Penny," he said. "I never knew you could be so brave. Thank you. I promise never to be horrid to you ever, ever again."

"Don't make promises you can't keep," she teased.

"Alright, I won't be horrid while we're in Faerieland – is that a deal?" Frank grinned.

"Deal." They shook hands, then both laughed. "Come on," Penny said. "Let's get out of here. Before the centaur wakes up." She led Frank back to where Bud was hiding behind the sycamore tree. The little elf bowed low to Frank and held out a tiny hand to shake. Frank held out a finger in return.

"So you are Penny's step-brother," Bud said. "Pleased to meet you. I'm Bud – Buddy Greenleaf if you want to be formal."

"Pleased to meet you Mr Greenleaf," said Frank. "Did you teach Penny how to do that with the skipping rope?"

"It was Pickatina," the girl answered. "She realised what it was and told me how to use it. I don't know where the others are." She started to explain what had happened, but Bud was tugging on the leg of her jeans.

"Sorry, Penny, but can the story wait?" he asked. "Or can you tell it while we walk? Because as good as your skipping rope trick is, I don't want to be around here when horsey-boy over there wakes up – know what I mean? Let's make tracks. Or rather, let's get out of here without actually leaving any tracks, if you can."

So that's what they did – though poor old Frank couldn't walk very fast at all. Still, they set off with Buddy sitting on Penny's shoulder again, giving directions. While they walked, she told Frank everything that had happened since they'd been split up by the centaur attack.

"So what are we going to do now?" Frank asked. "Do you want to try to go back and find the others?"

"I don't think we can," she said. "Remember what the Naga told us: we're in a race. We have to get the trumpet from Ribaldane and get to the North Pole before the Black Legion wakes up. And I think we have to do that with or without Pickatina and Broadwallow. We can't spare the time to go back and try to find them. Besides, I reckon we're more likely to run into more centaurs if we go back. Especially if that one wakes up and goes to get his friends. We have to carry on. Just the two of us."

Frank nodded and sighed. "I know you're right, just I miss my dog. I miss Broadwallow and Paisley too. I'm so tired."

"Well, cheer up young Frank," called Bud. "There's not much further to go today. We're nearly at the elf-holme. Then you can have a nice long rest. My people will look after you, alright."

Bud's idea of not much further wasn't the same as the childrens'. They walked for several hours, angling along the shoulder of the valley and heading more or less towards the mountains. They were passing into a scrubby part of the Wild Wood now, with lots of hawthorn trees and elder bushes covered in frothy white flowers. It was tough walking, the land rising and falling. For every long slope they climbed, there would be a small slope down on the other side. It was hard for Frank, but he stopped talking and grimly carried on.

Finally, they emerged from a particularly dense clump of

trees and there were the mountains, snow-capped grey slopes rising majestically towards the sky. Penny had seen them when she'd been skipping above the Wild Wood, but they seemed much closer now. It was the first time Frank had seen them and he gasped – though Penny wasn't sure if he was gasping at the mountains or the huge gorge that was right in front of them.

The children were only a metre from the edge. It was really deep – and for Penny, who didn't like heights, it felt really high. She felt ill just looking across it. The sides dropped away and far, far below was a river rushing between giant boulders. It was so far down the children couldn't even hear it, though they could see where it was churning white against the rocks. The cliffs on the edge of the gorge were rough and cracked, with vines growing in places. Penny couldn't see any way to cross the gorge.

"Where's the elf-holme where you live, Bud?" She asked. She'd been picturing it in her head while they walked – imagining a nice village of pretty coloured mushroom-shaped huts, a bit like the dryad village but not built in the trees. Full of friendly, welcoming, singing little elves.

"Why, we're here!" he exclaimed. "You're right on top of it."

"What?" the children exclaimed, looking around us. No nice little houses. No crowds of smiling, singing elves. "Where?"

"No, silly," said Bud. "Put me down and I'll show you. Look, it's down there." And the little elf walked up to the very edge of the cliff… and pointed down.

That's when Penny realised, some of those cracks in the cliff face weren't cracks at all. They were little cave entrances.

"How can we get down there?" asked Frank. "We're too big."

"There is a special entrance, a passage to our great space, that's big enough for guests. I can show you," said Bud cheerfully. "Come along. It's just up here." And he led the way along the edge of the terrible drop for a few hundred metres, then pointed down to a broad ledge by a large, dark cave.

"It's easy," he said. "Just climb down here and you'll be safe."

Chapter Forty Two

Elf-holme

Frank could see that Penny was scared. The thought of climbing down the cliff face to the elf-holme entrance was simply too much for her – she was rooted to the spot. The boy patted her arm awkwardly, trying to be comforting. "It's alright, Penny," he said. "I'll go first and you can watch. You'll see it's alright. Look – there are lots of vines to hold onto."

And he knelt on the edge of the cliff, then began to lower himself down over the edge. He kept looking up at the girl the whole time, smiling. Then his head was gone and he was lower down. Bud was standing on the edge. Penny still couldn't move, so the little elf told her how Frank was doing.

"He's down, Penny. Safe and sound. Nothing to it," he said cheerfully. "Frank, shout up and tell her you're okay."

"I'm okay, Penny," Frank bellowed. "It was really easy. There are steps cut into the rock for you to use for climbing down."

But still she couldn't move. When she looked down, all she could see was that enormous drop. It made her feel dizzy.

"I don't want to rush you, Penny," said Bud in a low, urgent whisper, "But I hear something blundering about in the bushes further down the hill. Could be that centaur. Maybe with some of his mates. You don't want to be here when they arrive, know what I mean? Have a go at getting down now, there's a good girl."

That got her attention, though probably not in the way Bud expected. She wasn't scared of the centaurs because she knew they couldn't defeat her bubble... and that's when she realised: she could use the skipping rope to get down. All she had to do was fly over the edge, steer to where Frank was waiting and land beside him. If she could land on the top of a tree, getting it into the mouth of a cave should be easy.

"Jump on, Bud," she said, bending down to lift the little man onto her shoulder. "We're going for a ride."

Penny skipped out over the edge of the cliff and down into the gorge. She flew out and down and round in a big, slow circle so she came back to face where she'd just been standing. From there, ten metres from the cliff and hundreds of metres above the raging river, she could see the elf-holme.

And it was beautiful, in its own way. The whole front of the cliff was cleverly carved and polished. You couldn't see it from the top – it was skilfully camouflaged – but from here it looked like a glittering little city, with doors and windows cut into the rock, linked by little paths like ribbons cut into the cliff. Though they'd be too small for a human to walk on.

The big door was large enough, though. It would have been big enough for Broadwallow. It was about three metres below the top of the cliff, a tall pointed arch, the posts carved like a pair of trees. Frank was standing on the wide ledge before it, mouth agape. Buddy waved to him as Penny flew straight to the cave and landed the bubble, stepping down onto the firm stone beside Frank. He just stood there, open-mouthed.

"Blimey, Penny," he gasped. Then he shook his head. "How come you can fly above the terrible drop but you can't do the easy climb down the cliff? Are you mental?" But he grinned to show he meant it as a joke.

Before the girl could answer, there was a sound of running feet and the children turned to see a whole army of elves appearing in the gloomy passage beyond the arch. Most were dressed like Bud, though a couple were in armour and carrying spears the size of the canes Maggie used for growing tomatoes up.

"It's alright, friends," called Bud, standing up on the girl's shoulder. "Quick, put me down, Penny," he hissed into her ear.

"It's alright, everyone," he repeated, once he was on the floor. "These are my friends, seeking safe-haven in the elf-holme. Step aside and let them come in. There's a couple of bigguns at the top and we don't want them looking down and spotting us, do we?"

There was a murmuring among the throng of elves, then a stout one in a glittering suit of chainmail waved a hand. "Come in, then – and be quick about it," he said. "We'll work out what's to be done later. Let's get you to the hall, away from prying eyes."

They stepped into the cool dark of the tunnel, the crowd of tiny elves parting to stay out from under foot. It reminded Penny of the magic underwater tunnel that led to the town under the lake, so she pointed that out to Frank. The elf in the chainmail – who was slightly bigger than Bud – heard her and called out: "These guests have been to the ancient water-holme. They recognise the craft of our tunnels." There was a gentle murmur from the elves. Bud smiled at Penny and gave her a thumbs up.

They emerged from the dim tunnel into a grand chamber. It was as big as the ballroom in Bradley Hall, brightly lit by a couple of chandeliers hanging from the roof. The walls of the massive cavern were carved with balconies and galleries, They were lined with elves, all staring curiously at the two humans. There must have been at least a thousand of the little people there, the hubbub of their quiet voices like the gentle humming of bees.

In the centre of the huge room was a raised platform – about the size of a big coffee table. And in the centre of the platform was a large silver chair, with a very finely dressed elf with a long white beard sitting on it. As they approached, Bud beckoned for Penny to bend down so he could speak to her.

"That's Alistor, king of the elves," he said. "Best let me do the speaking. I'll know what to say."

But Bud didn't get a chance. A bigger elf, dressed in armour, climbed a flight of little stairs onto the platform and bowed to the king. "Buddy Greenleaf has brought us these humans, Lord," he said. "They have visited the ancient water-holme."

The king looked them up and down. "Tell me," he said. "What are your names? How did you come to visit our lost realm under the lake? What are you doing here? And are humans getting smaller? You seem much less… tall than the last ones I met."

Frank and Penny exchanged a look. "That's a lot of questions, your majesty," Frank said. "I'm Frank and this is Penny. We might be smaller than the last humans you met because we're children. But we're on a mission for Queen Celestia. That's why we're here. That's why we visited the Town under the Lake. It had been put under an enchantment and we broke it, freeing it."

"We're going to the North Pole," Penny added. "We have to catch the person who cast the spell on the Town under the Lake: Ribaldane."

There was a huge gasp from the crowd of elves – a sound like a train rushing through a tunnel. Then King Alistor sat forwards in his chair. "I would ask you not to utter that name again. But tell us, what has the mistress of lies to do with you?"

"She's going to wake the Black Legion," said Frank. "We've been sent to stop her. We were with Captain Broadwallow of the Queen's guard and Pickatina, who's learnt magic from the Naga. But we got split up by the centaurs. Now it's just me and Penny. But we have to stop Rib... er, I mean, her. The mistress of lies."

"Then you shall have the help of the elves," said King Alistor. "We will shelter you and feed you tonight, then tomorrow we shall give you provisions and help you on your way."

"Can help us find our friends?" Penny asked. "We were being helped by the dryads and the pixies as well as the two goblins."

"We shall send out scouts in the morning," said the king. "If your friends can be found, we shall put them on the same path as you – so they may find you. However, it seems to us that you should not delay your mission.

"Now, while food is prepared, please be seated and tell us more of your journey," the king continued. "Tell us about our lost realm under the lake. What was the enchantment that had been put on it – and how did you break it?"

So the children sat on the floor of the elves' grand hall and told the king – and the audience of hundreds of small elves – about everything they'd done since coming to Faerieland. While they were talking, elves brought out little buns the size of sweets – which were probably big loaves of bread for them – which the children tucked into hungrily. Whether they were tired from all the walking they'd done, or the food and the warmth in the hall, or both, but soon both Frank and Penny were feeling really sleepy.

But something didn't seem quite right. All the elves had gone quiet. Something was definitely wrong. Frank had finally shut his eyes and was starting to snore. Then Penny realised, someone else was coming into the great hall. Someone big. She tried to move, to stand up, but she couldn't. She tried to shout but she couldn't. Oh no... she though. They must have drugged the bread. She was passing out...

The last thing she heard was the new arrival speaking. "You have done well, little folk. Perhaps I won't destroy you quite yet."

And that's when she knew they were in trouble. Because she recognised the speaker. It was Grimshock.

Chapter Forty Three

Prison

Penny came to slowly. Her cheek was pressed against a cold stone floor. Her head ached. Her neck ached. In fact, every bit of her ached. She sat up, feeling dizzy and sick. She was in a small, dark room. Frank was lying beside her, breathing heavily, still asleep. He'd eaten more of the elves' bread than Penny – he must have been more heavily drugged. Frantically, she looked around for her bag, but it wasn't there. Grimshock must have taken it.

She realised she was really, really frightened. The fierce creature was Ribaldane's right-hand hobgoblin. He was as big as Broadwallow and much nastier. She didn't know if the elves who'd tricked them were really wicked, or whether Grimshock had forced them to help him. It didn't matter. What worried Penny most was that he seemed to know they were coming after Ribaldane – and had been able to lay a trap to catch them.

"Are you awake, Penny? Are you feeling alright?" It was Bud. The girl couldn't see him, but his voice coming from the corner.

"Over here – near the floor," he said. Penny crawled over. There was a tiny door – so small even Bud would have had to crouch to get through it. The children couldn't escape through it.

"I'm really sorry, Penny," Buddy said. "I didn't want to give you to Grimshock – none of us did. But he said he'd kill everyone in the elf-holme if we didn't find you and bring you to him."

"How did he know we were coming?"

"I dunno," Bud said miserably. "Something about the spell on the water-holme – the Mistress knew when it ended."

Penny sighed. Her friends had thought defeating that cunning trap would have given them an advantage, that Ribaldane wouldn't have expected anyone to get past that. Clearly, they'd underestimated how cunning she was. When she realised her spell had been broken, she must have been even more worried about who was chasing her. No wonder the centaurs had been waiting at the edge of the Wild Wood. No wonder Grimshock had bullied the elves into working for him.

"So where is Ri… I mean, the Mistress of Lies?" Penny asked. "Do you know?"

"We don't know," Bud said. "We never saw her. I think she's carried on into the mountains. Grimshock's supposed to take you to her. He said he'll be taking you away in the morning."

"I'm not going to let that happen, Bud," Penny tried to put as much steel into her voice as she could. "He's not taking me and he's not taking Frank. We have to get away."

"But how? And if you escape from here, the monster will slaughter everyone in the elf-holme. What are you going to do?" Bud hesitated, then added, "What do you want me to do?"

The girl thought about it. "Can you get me my bag, Bud? If I have my skipping rope, I can get away from Grimshock. In fact, if I have the bag I can make sure he doesn't hurt anyone."

"I don't know, Penny," said Bud. "Grimshock took it. But I'll try to get it – really I will. None of the elves likes this. We're just too afraid of him. Can you really deal with him?"

"Absolutely," she said. "No doubt about it. I'll fix him so he can't hurt you or Mrs Bud or any of the elves ever again."

Bud didn't say anything else, but she heard him scurry away. Moments later, Penny heard footsteps outside. The tiny door was opened and a tray filled with water was pushed through – it was probably a tin bath for the elves. Realising she was thirsty, Penny took it and drank the water straight away, then pushed it back out of the door. "More, please," she said.

"Penny?" Frank was stirring. He sounded sick and confused. His step-sister hurried over and helped him sit up, explaining what had happened.

"That's really, really bad," he said. "Why does Grimshock want to take us to Ribaldane, anyway? That's what worries me. In a way, I'd be less frightened if they just wanted to lock us up or kill us. The thought that she might want us for some reason scares me. I mean, it wouldn't be for anything nice, would it?"

"Maybe she's just a gloater," Penny said. "Wants us to witness her beating us so she can gloat about it."

"Nah – that only happens in films and in stories," said Frank. "If Ribaldane wants us, you can bet she has a reason."

They sat in silence for a while, just thinking. Worrying. Penny was trying to work out how long they'd been in Fairieland. It seemed like forever, but it was only a week – of faerie time. How long was that in the real world? Maybe fifteen minutes.

Then Penny remembered. She put her hand to her neck – yes, it was still there. Hanging from the chain around her neck was the silver whistle. The whistle that would transport her and Frank out of Faerieland and back to the human world.

"Grimshock didn't search me," she whispered to Frank. "I still have the whistle. I can get us home."

She could just make out Frank shaking his head in the darkness. "That's no good Penny," he said. "Remember what the professor said. If we use it outside the grounds of Bradley Hall, there's no telling where we'd end up. Could be in the middle of a road, the middle of a prison, the middle of the North Sea – it could even be in midair above a cliff. No, it's just too risky.

"Besides," he added. "I wasn't searched, either. I have the knife the Queen gave me. The one you got back from the centaur."

"There's no way you can fight Grimshock," she said. "Not even with that knife. And if he has a sword like Broadwallow's..."

"Yeah, you're right," sighed Frank. "But I'd like to teach that big bully a lesson. Imagine threatening to destroy a whole colony of elves, just to make them betray us. Anyway, I don't like Grimshock after how he treated Pickatina."

Just then there was a tapping at the little door and Penny heard Bud whispering again. "It's no good," he said. "I can't get near your bag. That monster has it round his neck."

The girl put her hand through the door. "Okay, Bud. Don't worry – and thank you for trying," She said. The little elf took her hand and hugged it. It felt like he was crying on it.

"I'm so sorry, Penny," he sobbed. "I really am. If only I could do something – anything. Just ask."

"Pickatina," hissed Frank. "Ask him to find her."

"Yes, that's what you can do to help us, Bud," I said. "Get out of the elf-holme. Get away. Go find the dryads, if you can. Find our friends Broadwallow, Pickatina and Paisley. Tell them where we are or which way Grimshock is taking us. Help them find us."

"I'll do it, Penny," he cried. "I promise, I'll find them for you." And with that, the little man was gone.

"Do you think he'll do it?" asked Frank.

"Yes, I do," she replied slowly. "He may have tricked us, but he didn't want to and he is sorry. And this is something he can do that shouldn't expose him or the other elves to danger."

After that, it wasn't long before Grimshock came to get them. Frank had been wondering how they'd been placed into this little room – and how they'd get out again, as the door was so small. It turned out to be a trapdoor in the ceiling. It was so dark the children hadn't seen it – not until it was thrown back and bright light from a flickering torch flooded into the dungeon.

"Stand up, human children," said Grimshock with a voice as rough as sandpaper. "Raise your hands above your heads and I shall lift you out."

They did as they were told. Frank was lifted out first, then Penny. They found themselves in a small galleried chamber, like a miniature version of the great hall where they'd met King Alistor.

"If the mistress were here, she'd fit the two of you with throttles, to make sure you followed orders," Grimshock sneered. "I don't have any throttles. But I do have collars. You'll wear them and behave like good little human doggies. Or else – got it?"

The children just nodded silently. Grimshock took a pair of stout leather collars with brass clasps and fitted them round their necks, hooking a length of rope through each clasp. Penny stared at her bag, hanging round his neck.

"And don't get any clever ideas," he snarled. "We're going to walk and we're going to walk quickly. And the two of you are going to be walking ahead of me. You won't escape me, you'll see. We're going to see the mistress. Come on, get walking!"

Chapter Forty Four

The Long March

Grimshock shoved the children through the passages of the elf-holme. Everywhere they heard wailing and crying. Some of the elves called out to us, urging us to be brave, many of them cried out, "We're sorry" or, "Forgive us". Frank and Penny said nothing. The collars were tight on their necks and neither wanted to make the monster angry. He just growled at the elves.

When they emerged into the bright sunlight on the ledge on the edge of the gorge, Grimshock turned and wagged his finger. "I'm climbing up first," he hissed. "You'll follow. No funny business, or I'll throw you over the edge. Got it?"

They both nodded wordlessly and watched as the huge hobgoblin swarmed up the cliff face like a giant spider. Frank turned to the girl. "Can you do this, Penny? Will you be alright?"

She didn't know. She'd always been terrible at climbing and Frank knew it. "Look," he said. "There are good steps here – see? If you go first, I'll follow and help. Just climb from one step to the next and don't look down. You'll be fine. It's not far."

"Come on, humans," snarled Grimshock from the cliff top. He tugged on the ropes attached to the collars, jerking the children painfully forwards.

Frank patted her arm. "You'll be fine, Penny," he said. She wasn't so sure. But she took hold of one of the vines growing up the cliff, put her foot in the first carved step and began. At first it even seemed easy. She quickly climbed higher than the top of the arch that led into the elf-holme. She was doing really well.

Then she looked down. Luckily, all she saw was Frank, right beneath her. He smiled. Penny went to carry on… and that's when she slipped.

Grimshock saved her. Well, him and Frank. Penny gave a scream as her toes slipped. But she didn't fall more than a couple of centimetres – because of the collar. She was aware of a great pain in her neck, but then Frank had reached up and grabbed her feet, putting them safely back onto the solid steps again. Penny grabbed the vines and held on tight, pushing her tummy into the cliff.

"What's going on?" shouted Grimshock.

"It's Penny. She nearly fell off," Frank shouted back.

"So? What are you doing now, Human Girl?" the hobgoblin called. "Get climbing again."

"I don't think I can," she whispered.

"She doesn't think she can," Frank hollered.

"Humph," Grimshock snorted. He peered over the top of the cliff, then his head disappeared. Next thing, he rapidly climbed down until he could reach Penny, grabbing her arm and swinging her roughly over his shoulder. It really hurt and the wind was knocked out of her. Even worse, her head was pointing down over the dreadful drop – but she didn't have time to shut her eyes before Grimshock had climbed quickly back to the top. He dumped her roughly down on the grass.

Frank climbed up over the top of the cliff. "Are you alright, Penny?" he asked. "How's your neck?"

Penny was gasping, sick and winded. "It's okay, I think," she said. That wasn't true and Frank could tell, but he could also see that she didn't want to admit how much it hurt. If she did, she might cry – and she didn't want to cry in front of Grimshock.

The hobgoblin harrumphed again. "Let's check you out," he said roughly. "Can't deliver damaged goods to the great queen."

Ah-ha! Penny thought. For all his nasty talk and his threats, Ribaldane must have told Grimshock he wasn't really allowed to hurt the children. That was a bit worrying because, as Frank had said, she probably wouldn't have any nice plans for them. But maybe it might help them trick Grimshock. Maybe they could even find a way to get away from him.

But as the next two days unfolded, Penny couldn't see how that would happen. Being in Faerieland wasn't any fun now they were with Grimshock. The brutish hobgoblin quickly gave up on making the children run ahead of him: they went too slowly for him. So he went in front, dragging them along behind him and setting a ferocious pace. At times they were practically running to keep up with him. If they went too slowly, he'd jerk on the ropes leading up to their collars. He didn't say much, just snarled and growled. Soon Penny was so tired she could barely see straight, stumbling along. It was all she could do just to put one foot in front of another without tripping.

If Grimshock made them march quickly, at least he stopped fairly often. The only problem was that he made the children eat every time they stopped – and all he had was a huge loaf of stale bread. He tore chunks off and threw it to them. It tasted awful but it was filling and gave them the energy to carry on. The trouble was, it also gave them belly aches.

Penny tried to persuade Grimshock to let her get the porrige pot from her bag, hanging around his neck, thinking she might be able to get the skipping or even the secateurs out of it, but the hobgoblin was having none of it. He just laughed and told the children to be grateful for the bread. It was a miserable time.

Neither of the children wanted to show any weakness in front of Grimshock, but as dusk was falling on the second day of the march Frank panted, "You must slow down. We can't keep up." Penny was glad he'd said it

"Stop whining, miserable humans! I will slow down when we have crossed the bridge," snarled Grimshock.

"What bridge?" Frank asked. Penny was too tired to ask.

"That bridge," their tormentor replied, pointing. All the bone-shattering marching seemed to have taken them on a long loop, emerged from the trees beside the huge gorge again. At first Penny thought they had just gone round in circles, until she realised they had to be higher up, because the gorge was neither so wide nor so deep as it had been by the elf-holme. And it was spanned, some way ahead, by a thin and spidery bridge.

As they got closer, the bridge looked terrifying. It was a rope bridge that had to be at least two-hundred metres from end to end, but the wooden slats were hardly as wide as Penny's feet and she saw there were big gaps between them. If she looked down, she could see the dizzying drop to the river below.

Grimshock shoved the children ahead of him again, onto the bridge. Frank went first, smiling bravely over his shoulder at Penny. She followed, trying not to be too scared. She couldn't avoid looking down, though – if she didn't watch where she put her feet, they'd have gone straight through the gaps between the boards. So instead she concentrated on staring the boards and stepping on them. Ignoring the yawning drop beyond them. Ignoring the way the bridge swung and creaked as the wind hit it. Ignored Grimshock, snarling behind her. And before she knew it, she was across – she looked up at Frank and smiled. She didn't think he'd expected her to cross it without making a fuss.

But then Grimshock was stepping off the bridge, urging them forward again. From now on they did have to walk ahead of him – but at least it was just walking, not running. They picked their way between large, rough boulders fringed with rough grasses and thorny bushes, following a faint track as the light faded. There seemed to be far fewer trees on this side of the gorge, just a desolate and stony land rising steeply towards the mountains that towered above.

When they finally stopped for the night, Penny was staggering with exhaustion. Frank had fallen over several times. Both were dusty and sweaty and so tired they felt sick. Grimshock made them sit and eat more of the dry, grey, chewy bread, then he told them to lie down and sleep. He never slept – they already knew that. He'd just sit, still as a statue, with a predatory look on his face and a knife in his hand, watching them. When the children woke, he'd be in the same position, ready to snarl at them as soon as they moved a muscle.

Frank and Penny curled up miserably on the floor, wrapping their cloaks tight around themselves. Even though the ground was lumpy, they were both so tired they fell asleep quickly.

It felt as though they'd hardly shut their eyes when Grimshock was shaking them away, snarling cheerfully. The early morning sun was shining brightly, dew beaded the scratchy grass around them and a few brave birds were calling across the mountain slopes. The mean-looking hobgoblin gave both children a drink and made them eat more of his awful bread – it was as though the loaf never ended. Ignoring their complaints, he forced them to their feet and got them walking again. Climbing steep and dusty trails towards the mountain pass.

Penny's legs were jelly. She was so tired it was hard to find the strength to put one foot in front of the other. On the steeper slopes, she could barely shuffle up at all. At one point she thought they must have come all the way across the mountains – because they'd reached a high point and the land dropped away. But then she lifted her chin, looked further ahead and realised that it was just a broad highland valley. More peaks rose steeply on the other side – with a notch between the two mountains opposite.

"Over there, little humans, is the Hydra's Pass," said Grimshock. "That's where you'll finally have the honour of meeting the great Queen, if you are good. So let's get going. Or I'll feed you to the snakes instead when we get there."

They staggered down the hill and stumbled across the valley. At one point they had to stop because Penny thought she was going to be sick. It made their captor angry. "You humans are moving too slowly," he hissed. "I have been kind, letting you stop, feeding you – and this is how you repay me? With slowness? We will be late. No more stops now. No more food. Keep walking."

It seemed to take forever. On and on they went, all morning, all afternoon, trudging painfully onwards. Finally, as the sun was beginning to set, Grimshock told them to stop. Again he fished out his revolting loaf and made the children eat. Then he gestured at the floor – he didn't need to say anything now. His prisoners just lay down, exhausted, and fell straight to sleep.

But when Grimshock shook them awake this time, it was still dark. "Come on," he muttered. "We have to move. We have to get to higher ground. The snakes are coming…"

Chapter Forty Five

Zigorath and Zanorth

The children looked around nervously, but there was no sign of any snakes. It was so dark it was hard to see, but nothing seemed to be slithering. They couldn't hear anything, either. How did Grimshock know they were coming? Penny assumed they'd have to run for cover, but their captor was sauntering casually towards a small rise nearby, leading the children by the ropes tied to the collars around their necks. He didn't seem worried.

The night was chilly and silent, the land around them painted in shades of deepest greys with faint silver edges marking a contrast with all the deep black shadows. The moonlight made everything seem uncanny. Distances were impossible to judge. The children found it hard enough just to work out where to put their feet to avoid tripping. They could see where rocks and bushes began but not where they ended. They stumbled through the darkness, tripping over roots and staggering as their feet found unexpected dips in the ground.

Soon they reached the small rise Grimshock had been aiming for. It was crowned with boulders – some rounded, others flattened. They had to climb them on the shadowed side, away from the light of the moon, so Penny couldn't see anything at all. Her hands traced rough stone covered with scratchy lichen, trying to find hand holds and foot holds.

"Come on, humans," growled Grimshock from the top of the rocks. "What is taking you so long?"

"We can't see, that's what," muttered Frank, rebelliously. "It's pitch black. We're not bats."

"Argh, you humans – pathetic," spat Grimshock dismissively. The great beast leaped down and gathered the boy up under one long, strong arm and climbed up in an instant, returning to scoop Penny up and carry her up as well.

"Now we are all here, we can wait for the arrival of the snakes," he said. "Listen – even now they are drawing near."

Penny cocked her head to one side and listened as hard as she could, but still she couldn't hear anything except the wind blowing gently across the barren valley. And then she realised – that wasn't wind. It was a hissing, but there was no wind. That sound had to be the snakes. It still wasn't close, but it getting closer and getting louder all the time.

They were peering out into the darkness, straining their eyes when Frank gasped and grabbed his step-sister's hand. "Over there, Penny," he panted. "Look at the size of it."

At first the girl couldn't see it – but then she realised that was because she was looking for the wrong kind of thing. She was looking for a snake – something like a hose or maybe one of those large draught-excluders that old people have by their front doors. She wasn't looking in the right place to see a faerie-snake. It was bigger – much bigger. In fact, it was huge.

Looking downhill, the moonlight was painting a silver line on the valley floor – which Penny had assumed was the edge of a stream. But it wasn't. It was moving. It was the back of a snake. A huge snake, hundreds of metres long. And it wasn't alone. There were at least two more behind it, sliding slowly along – and heading straight for the children and their hobgoblin guard.

And then Grimshock did something unexpected. He called to them. "Over here! We're here, on the rocks," he shouted. And he actually waved to them. Was he mad?

"I don't think we're high enough," Penny said, panic creeping into her voice. "Those snakes will still be able to get us."

"Get us?" Grimshock laughed, with a sound like glass being ground underfoot. "They will not 'get' us. But they will be able to get *to* us. And we shall be able to get to them. They are some of the oldest and most honoured friends of the mistress and we will not be scrabbling up their flanks as if they were dogs."

The first of the snakes was really close, hissing like a steam train, its scales rasping across the ground. Penny could just make out the shape of its massive head, low to the floor, flattened and wider than the body. Every few seconds a huge forked tongue would flick out.

"Do you mean," asked Frank slowly, "We're going to ride one of those monsters?"

"Do not be so rude, pup," Grimshock cuffed Frank roughly on the ear. "These are ancient and noble reptiles. Not monsters."

The big hobgoblin leant down until the tip of his nose was level with Frank's, dark eyes glinting with menace in the moonlight. "If you are looking for a monster, I'm right here," he whispered. Then he straightened up and turned back to address the arriving snake.

"Hail, Lord Zigorath," he shouted. "It is Grimshock, loyal servant of the glorious Queen Ribaldane."

"I know your sssscent," came a hissing voice from the darkness. A giant snake head loomed up in front of the rocks, an inky outline rising against the night sky until it blotted out the stars. Though the moonlight still shone on one side of the huge creature, it was barely lit – the light seemed to be absorbed by its scales without illuminating them. It towered over the children, its body as thick as a tube-train, its head the size of a caravan.

"What are thesssse other creaturesss I can ssssmell?" it hissed, its voice like gravel pouring into a metal wheelbarrow.

"These are the humans I was sent to bring to the Great Queen," replied Grimshock. "Both are to reach her. Alive."

"Sssssss… It is many yearssss sssince lassst I tasssted a human," hissed the snake.

"You are forbidden to feast on these two," said Grimshock firmly. "The Great Queen has plans for them. Besides, they are children. No meat on their bones."

"Isss there more on yoursss?" hissed the snake menacingly.

"I serve the Great Queen. I am her captain. I too am under her protection," the hobgoblin said confidently. "Curb your appetite for now, Lord Zigorath. When the Great Queen rules again, you will have your fill – yes, of humans too when we conquer their world. You will eat your humans soon enough."

"What do you mean?" exclaimed Frank. "You're not going to conquer our world."

Grimshock smacked Frank across the face with the back of his hand, sending the boy flying. He would have fallen from the rock, but the rope attached to his collar went taut and Grimshock pulled him back. "Save your insolence, boy," he snarled. "The Great Queen has promised. I will ride at the head of the Black Legion, through the gates of her palace and out into your human world. There will be glory and slaughter like you have never imagined. But unless you learn to keep hold your tongue, you will never live to see it – understand?"

Frank nodded. He was holding his hands to his mouth and Penny could tell he was trying not to cry. He sniffed, but didn't makee a sound. He wouldn't give Grimshock the satisfaction.

"You can't kill him," Penny said. "You have to take us to Ribaldane."

He span towards her, looking huge as he loomed over her. "I do not necessarily have to deliver you in one piece," he snarled. "If you like having your fingers, you will keep quiet."

He did scare Penny – even though she was sure he was bluffing. She realised he was trying to look fierce and important because the snake was watching. But the girl didn't dare defy him: he really was a monster. So she hung her head and pretended to cower. After a second, the hobgoblin turned back to Zigorath. "Can you carry us to the Great Queen, Lord Zigorath?" he asked.

"Ssssss... You forget yourssself, Grimssshock," hissed the snake. "I will carry the Great Queen, but no other. Definitely not thessse humansss. My son Zanorth will carry the three of you."

The gigantic snake lowered its head and hissed like an enormous pressure cooker. There was a crunching of stones and Zigorath slithered away, while another snake came closer. It was almost as huge, raising its enormous head and flicking out its forked tongue so it nearly slapped Grimshock like a giant whip.

"Sssso I am to carry you again, Grimssshock," it hissed menacingly. "And your rat cargo too."

"I am honoured Lord Zanorth," the hobgoblin said, bowing.

"Shhhhut up and climb on," Zanorth hissed. "Let'sss get thisss demeaning journey over with."

The great head dipped out of sight and Grimshock gestured to the children. They stepped to the edge of the rock and looked down. The body of the snake was directly beneath them, only a meter or so below, dimly seen in the moonlight. Frank jumped down first, then held up his hand and helped Penny down.

The snake was dry and cool to the touch, covered in scales the size of dinner plates. It was almost two metres wide, though the children could stand only on the central strip that was about forty centimetres wide, because its body sloped downwards on either side. Grimshock jumped down behind the children.

Placing one hand on each of their shoulders, he drew their heads together, bending down to hiss at them.

"Do not sit, or you will be trapped by the overlapping scales as the snake moves," he whispered. "Crouch, with your hands in the middle of a scale – not near the edge of a scale or you may lose a finger. If you lose your balance and fall, I will pull you back up by the collar around the neck. It will hurt. I will like that."

And then the snake moved and they were away, slithering into the darkness. Towards the mountains. Towards Ribaldane.

Chapter Forty Six

The Tent

Afterwards, Penny could never work out how fast the snakes moved. Both children agreed that the giant reptiles went quicker than they could have gone on the steep slopes – especially in the dark. Some places were so steep, it was all Penny could do to stay on Zanorth's back. She'd always thought snakes were slippery or slimy but this one was dry – which was good, because otherwise both children would have slid down his back like a slide as he climbed the inky-black, slopes of the Hydra's Pass.

The moon had gone behind a cloud and it was so dark they could see almost nothing, but they could hear loose stones cascading downhill behind us, rattling like marbles in a tin. Sometimes stones loosened by Zigorath would come cascading down and bounce off Zanorth's sides, but the huge snake ignored them. Penny wondered just how thick the snake's plate-sized scales were – it had to be like having a massive suit of armour.

Grimshock stood behind them, feet wide apart, like a man on a surfboard. He held the ropes attached to his captives' collars in one hands and every now and then, as he swayed slightly, he'd tug on them. Not enough to hurt or make anyone lose their balance, but enough to remind the children that he was still there.

But there was no way to escape. Not now. Not from the snakes. Even if they'd been brave enough to jump off Zanorth's back, it was pitch black, the mountain was steeper than a set of stairs and – most worryingly – there was a third snake following behind Zanorth. Penny thought the snakes could see in the dark and, no matter what Grimshock said about Ribaldane's orders, she was fairly sure they'd gobble her up she tried to run for it.

They rode on the snake's back for hours. Crouched, uncomfortable hours, until aches became pain that became agony. Eventually the ground levelled out and Zanorth began to slow down. It was really cold now. And blacker than ever. The clouds had blown away, but the mountains towering darkly on either side blanked out the stars, sometimes even hiding the moon from view. And still the snakes slithered on into the darkness.

Penny guessed they were in the heart of the Hydra's Pass now. She hadn't really thought about what it would be. A doorway, perhaps – a point where the two sides of the mountain met and with one step you went from clambering up from the woods to climbing down towards the sea. And maybe they would reach a point like that – but as the sky began to lighten with the dawn, she realised the meat of the pass was a long, narrow valley that picked its way between not just two mountains, but between two massive groups of mountains.

The world was changing as the sun rose. The colours shifted from blacks and grainy dark greys with hints of silver, to pale shades of brown or green edged with white or gold. The snowy tips of the high peaks sparkled with white fire as rays of light caught them. A gentle orange light melted the shadows slowly away on one side of the valley, but they seemed to pool even deeper at the foot of the slope still shielded from the sun.

At least the dawn gave the children a better look at the snakes. They were truly huge, coloured in dull browns and sandy yellows, with diamond patterns picked out in darker shades. And their eyes were terrifying – flat, dead grey. And the snakes looked even bigger now than they'd seemed in the night, when so much of their size had been lost in the shadows. When they'd arrived, Penny had assumed that Zanorth and Zigorath were similar sizes, but that wasn't true. Their heads were more or less equally massive, but the older snake was probably two meters wider and a meter taller than his son and at least twice as long. Zigorath must have been more than two-hundred meters long – long enough to wrap all the way round the Little House twice and still poke his head out through the gates.

The third snake travelling with them smaller than Zanorth, barely as long as a football pitch, with a smaller head and a body that was only as round as Penny was tall. It wasn't much beside the two massive snakes, but it was still pretty huge. And as they slithered slowly along the Hydra Pass, they saw more like him.

There were snakes everywhere. Some were relatively small – no bigger than the biggest snakes in the reptile house at London Zoo. Which was big enough. But most were bigger. And as the morning wore on they passed four or five snakes as big as the third one in Zigorath's group. All the snakes had different markings. Many had bands or spots and even more that were mostly one colour all over – but there was a distinctive diamond pattern to the trio ferrying them up the mountain, so Penny guessed they were all related.

Every now and then the children heard small calls, little *hoop-hoop* noises. At first they couldn't work out what was making them. Then Penny saw a small blue creature leaping up the slope. It looked a bit like a kangaroo, except it was scaly like a snake. It wasn't an unnaturally bright blue, like a plastic toy, more a kind of smoky blue-grey – almost like a grey squirrel, but with a bit more blue. It had a row of spines down its back and a long, pointed tail. Suddenly it leapt into the air, spread a pair of leathery wings, like bats' wings – and it soared into the air.

"Look, Frank," Penny gasped in amazement, realising what it had to be. "It's a dragon. A real dragon. I thought only the snakes lived here."

"What do you think they eat, human?" chuckled Grimshock.

"Why don't the dragons get rid of the snakes?" asked Frank.

"Get rid of the sssnakesss?" hissed Zanorth, slithering to a stop and rearing up, turning to peer at the humans on his back and regarding them with his scary, expressionless eyes. "And jussst how would the dragonsss do that?"

"Well, don't they breathe fire?" Penny asked. "I mean, the big ones with the hoards of gold and jewels?"

"Gold and jewels?" spluttered Grimshock. The nasty brute was laughing so much Penny thought he might fall off the snake's back. "Forgive me, Lord Zanorth, but the thought of a dragon with a hoard of gold and jewels... let alone challenging you!"

"Sssss... I am ssso pleasssed you find thisss amussssing," hissed Zanorth. "The dragon you jussst sssaw, humansss, wasss a very fine ssspecimen. Normally they are much sssmaller. And the sssmall onesss are the sssweetessst."

With that the snake turned away and started slithering again, quite fast. The monstrous serpent seemed to feel that Frank had somehow insulted him – and the humans were glad about that. They'd both liked the look of the little dragon. Penny wondered if there'd be more of them about, if the snakes didn't eat them.

By now the sun was high in the sky overhead. Penny could see the pass stretching up into the distance, climbing higher and higher all the time. It was dry, dusty and arid – much like the lower valley they'd crossed the day before. By now the children were so tired it was all they could do to breath and concentrate on balancing on the moving snake. Their knees were sore and their back were screaming with cramp. Penny wanted just to lie down and rest, but she had to keep crouched on Zanorth's back.

"Can't we stop for a rest, Grimshock?" she asked.

"We are nearly there, human," he snarled. "Stop complaining. We do not want Lord Zanorth to think you are being ungrateful."

"Where are we going, anyway?" asked Frank.

"Why, to meet the Great Queen," the hobgoblin sneered. "There was a time when you were both only too eager to meet her. I remember. I read the notes you wrote, the ones brought back to us by the worthless traitor Pickatina."

"Don't you be rude about Pickatina," Penny said angrily, but Grimshock laughed. It was a nasty sound, like an engine dying.

"Ignore him, Penny," muttered Frank. "His sort just like it when they make you upset by being mean about your friends."

"His sort? You dirty, cheeky little rat..." roared Grimshock angrily, hauling Frank to his feet by the collar on his neck and raising his fist. But before the hobgoblin could hit the boy, Zanorth gave a great hiss and slowed right down, raising his huge head and turning back to look at the hobgoblin.

"You don't have time for sssuch dissstractionsss, Grimssshock," the terrible snake hissed. "Sssee – the Great Queen hasss ssset herssself up here to wait for you."

Penny looked away from the hobgoblin, gazing around the valley desperately but she couldn't see anything. The mountains towered high on either side, with the narrow valley of the pass climbing steadily between them. Zigorath had stopped ahead...

...And there it was, right beside the biggest snake: a massive, ornate tent like a circus big top, fluttering with flags and streamers. And yet Penny had almost missed it, because it was exactly the same kind of colour as the dusty hills around it.

Grimshock jumped off the side of Zanorth, dragging the children down behind him and catching them roughly before they hit the ground. He bowed to the snake, then dragged his captives towards the tent. Penny saw it was made of cobwebs and it was alive with spiders, creeping and crawling over the surface, spinning more layers of fine webs that trapped the dust.

But there was no time to stop and marvel at it, even as they paused in front of the dark entrance to the tent. It felt as if a whole meadow full of butterflies was flapping around inside Penny's stomach. She knew who was inside. And then they heard the voice, like melting ice running over sharp rocks.

"Bring the children in here, Grimshock. Bring them in right, now!" At last – they were going to meet Ribaldane.

Chapter Forty Seven

The Mistress of Lies

They stepped into the tent. The air was cool and smelt of cinnamon. Penny couldn't see any poles holding the gossamer walls up – the whole huge tent seemed to be floating unsupported in the air. And it was dark inside – so dark they could hardly see anything.

"Come closer, children – I can hardly see you," said Ribaldane. Penny still couldn't see her, but she sounded close.

Frank took his step-sister's hand and gave it a squeeze. "We can't see where you are," he said. "We can't see anything in here."

"Oh, we can't have that, can we?" said Ribaldane – and she laughed. A light, girlish laugh. Then she snapped her fingers. And there was light. Not a sudden light, like switching on a light bulb. A warm, golden light that swelled up and slowly filled the tent.

Penny would have preferred the dark. The first thing she saw was where the light was coming from. Glow-worms. Enormous, curled-up glow worms, hovering in the air. They had tails the size of footballs, giving off the mellow golden light.

Now she could see the inside of the tent was also crawling with spiders. Much bigger spiders than the ones on the outside. No wonder there wasn't any light getting in – fat, black, hairy spiders the size of a child's hand covered every inch of the sides of the tent. As they moved, the canopy seemed to heave and ripple like the surface of a river.

There was furniture in the tent. But it wasn't made of wood. There were chairs that seemed to be made of centipedes – bigger, brighter coloured ones than the chocolate ones they'd been eating. And these ones weren't dead. They seemed to balance in position, upright or lying down depending on whether they were being a leg or a back or a part of the seat. They were almost but not quite perfectly still: while their bodies weren't moving, their legs and antennae were constantly twitching and flexing.

There were insects everywhere. Even the floor was covered in insects, rather than a rug. Looking down to her feet Penny saw a thick covering of millions and millions of tiny red ants, all marching in circles and forming a thick carpet all over the tent.

Penny realised she was doing everything she could to avoid looking at Ribaldane. Part of her was scared of what she'd see. Mayor Sticklebee had described her after they'd broken the enchantment on the Town on the Lake. Warty as a toad, he'd said. As big as Broadwallow, with sharp teeth and nails like knives. She sounded terrifying – the worst kind of child-eating wicked witch.

And Penny felt so betrayed by Ribaldane. The witch had tricked her and Frank, used them to steal from Professor Mitchell. Used them to help her evil plan to overthrow Queen Celestia. It was her fault they were there – her fault that the centaurs had attacked them, that Pickatina and Broadwallow had got hurt. That the town under the lake had been enchanted, that the elves had been terrorised and forced to betray the children. All the pain and discomfort and terror they'd suffered since coming to faerie land. It was her fault. It was all her fault.

Now Penny was ready to face her. Now she was good and cross she didn't feel quite so scared any more. She was ready to give this evil witch a piece of her mind. She gave Frank's hand a squeeze to let him know she was alright.

"Right, Ribaldane..." she began but, looking up, she didn't see her. Penny looked around again, but her enemy wasn't anywhere to be seen. The only other person in the tent was a sweet-looking little blonde boy in scruffy clothes. He was about the same age as Penny and Frank – maybe a bit younger – and he was smiling kindly at them.

Frank squeezed Penny's hand. Really hard. It hurt. She looked at him, then looked back to the little boy... who had vanished. Instead she saw a tall, fair, queenly lady – much like Queen Celestia. Except this queen had a crown of jagged silver set with black stones. She was tall and beautiful, with a long neck and high cheekbones, long black hair cascading down her back. Her skin was pale, her nails were long black talons. Her dress appeared to be the same wispy gossamer as the tent – and it was also crawling with live spiders.

"So you see me as I truly am, Pen," she sighed. "I'm sorry I couldn't be the sweet little boy you thought was writing to you."

"How… how did you do that?" Penny asked, shaken.

"I didn't do anything," she replied. "You did. Your mind. You're so weak-minded, you humans. Your first instinct is always to see what you want to see, what you wish was there. Never what really is there."

"How do we know we're seeing you as you really are now?" asked Frank. "That old goblin in the town under the lake, Mayor Sticklebee, said you were covered in warts."

"Goblins are just as prey to their emotions as you feeble humans," Ribaldane sneered. "The old fool saw what he wanted to see, just as you did until I let you see me as I am. My sister has convinced them all that I am an evil witch, so the goblin saw a wicked witch. I'm surprised he didn't tell you he'd seen me sour milk and ride off on a broomstick."

"Your sister?" Penny asked. "Who's your sister?"

"Why Celestia, of course!" And Ribaldane laughed again, that tinkling, girlish laugh. And it chilled both children to the bone. "Once we had many sisters. There were seven of us once. But now… now it's just the two of us."

"What happened to the others?" asked Frank

"I killed them, of course," Ribaldane said. And she smiled. A mad, haunted smile. Her eyes seemed to go dull – as if she no longer saw the children, just her blood-soaked memories.

"Why? Why would you kill your sisters?" Penny whispered.

"Didn't they tell you?" she laughed. "I'm evil. I'm the wicked witch of the North. I'm the one who will end the world, who will stop time and finally, finally set us free."

"How do you plan to do that, exactly?" asked Frank.

"Ah, brave Frank. Sad Frank. Lonely Frank," Ribaldane

teased. "Think you can get me to tell you all my secrets? Make you look clever in front of your new playmate?"

"Shut up," hissed Frank, blushing furiously. "Shut up."

At this point Grimshock stepped up and cuffed Frank around the head. "Show some respect to the Great Queen, human," he said. But Ribaldane just laughed again.

"They should thank us, these miserable children," she said. "There they were, thrown together by their parents' marriage, each one wanting to be friends with the other but neither having the courage to make the first move, both afraid of being rejected. And yet now look at them – a little adventure has them holding hands like a proper brother and sister."

"You're not like Celestia at all," Penny said. "She's kind and wise and nice. She deserves to be queen."

Ribaldane hissed. "She's not queen, you insolent brat. My weak-willed sister is nothing more than a nursemaid for a nation of lazy wretches, idle dandlers wasting their time herding sheep and eating honey. She knows nothing of what it is to rule."

"And what's that?" asked Frank, shying away from Grimshock in case the hobgoblin hit him again.

"To rule is to conquer!" snapped Ribaldane. "To expand, to harness the power at your fingertips and stamp your authority on the world. To make your mark and say to the universe 'I am here!' To rule is to achieve something."

"And that's going to be invading our human world, is it?" asked Frank. "That's what Grimshock said."

"Grimshock will have to learn to hold his tongue, or I'll rip it out," snarled Ribaldane. "And it's not invading. It's repossessing. Where do you think we came from? Why do you think you have so many stories about faeries and goblins and even dragons and dryads and centaurs? *That* is our world. You wretched humans drove us out of it – but I intend to take it back."

"You've told us your plans," said Frank, smiling.

"Don't think yourself so clever, you vile brat," she hissed. "You'll not live long enough to see it. Grimshock, go and ask

Lord Zigorath to poke his head into the tent. Lunch is ready."

One look at Ribaldane and it was clear that she meant it. Her eyes were wild and there was foam at the corners of her beautiful mouth.

"You won't feed us to the snake, Ribaldane," Penny said. "You've already given me everything we need to leave."

And she reached up, pulled the whistle out from beneath her shirt, put it to her lips – and blew it.

Chapter Forty Eight

Escape!

It was a dreadful risk. Penny knew that. The whistle would transport the children back to the human world – with absolutely no way of knowing where they'd end up. Still, it was true what Ribaldane had written when she first gave the girl the whistle: it was for use in the direst of emergencies. And this definitely counted. Penny couldn't let Ribaldane feed Frank to the snake.

As she blew the whistle, she was aware of Grimshock and Ribaldane both leaping towards her. But they were too late. The children were gone in less than the blink of an eye.

The translation from one world to the next was so abrupt, Penny's head whirled. She shut her eyes and felt sick. For a second she felt weightless. But she concentrated really hard – she was still holding Frank's hand. That meant he had made the jump to the human world with her. That meant they'd escaped.

And they weren't falling. Or drowning. And they hadn't been hit by cars. In fact, wherever they were, it was very quiet.

Penny opened her eyes and looked around. They were on the top of a hill – a high, heather-covered hill. A thin black ribbon that had to be a road running along the valley at the foot of the hill was visible in the distance, but there were no cars on it. All around, wild heathery hills rolled off into the distance, capped with dark green woods in places. The sun was warm and the sky was blue, with white clouds scudding along on a brisk breeze.

"Blimey, Penny," breathed Frank. "Don't do that again without warning me, okay? I think I'm going to be sick."

"You'll be fine, Frank," she said with a nervous laugh. "Just give it a second. Where do you think we are?"

"Dunno. Could be Scotland, I suppose. Canada? Russia? I can't see anyone to ask." Frank smiled. "Bet that made them mad."

"Yes – I don't think they were expecting that," Penny grinned back at him. Then paused. "But we'll have to go back. For one thing, Pickatina, Broadwallow, Paisley and Caro Elora will be looking for us. For another, we still have to get the trumpet back."

Frank looked serious. "I know. Why do you think I haven't moved? We know distance works differently in their world and in ours. So if we want to go back to the same place, we have to stay exactly where we are. The only thing in our favour is that time works differently too. How long do you think we should wait?"

"I don't know. A few minutes. If we wait ten minutes, that should be a couple of days in Faerieland." Penny glanced at her wrist. "I don't have my watch on. Do you?"

"No. I didn't put it on before we went out...this morning." Frank shook his head. "It's crazy to think that, we only left home a little while ago in the human world."

"Yeah." Penny sighed. Then looked up in alarm. "If we're away too long, will we end up too far behind? Will it be too late when we get back there?"

"Relax," Frank said. "We have to wait long enough to be sure that Ribaldane won't still be there when we go back – and we know she's in a hurry to get to the North Pole. But we're not going to be standing here all morning. Just a few minutes will be enough. With a bit of luck, we'll get back there a day or two after she's gone. It'll be fine."

Penny nodded. Neither of them spoke for a minute.

"What Ribaldane said, Frank..." she began cautiously. "Were

you really lonely? I mean before we came here. Or there, rather."

He looked embarrassed. "Well, I was a bit. It seemed like ever since my mum met your dad, she hadn't spent so much time with me. Then they got married and you came to live with us and there was even less time for me. I mean, I really like your dad – he's great and I'm really pleased mum met him and everything. But then he got his job on the oil tanker and we were getting ready to move to the little house and everyone was stressed and... well, I seemed to be on my own all the time, that's all."

Penny nodded. "That's exactly how I felt as well. Why didn't we figure it out and help each other?"

Frank shrugged, but he grinned. "We're kids. How were we supposed to know?"

"What did you see, Frank?" she asked. "When the lights went on in the tent. How did Ribaldane appear to you?"

"Like a kid, I suppose. Like a teenager. Even though I knew Ribaldane was a girl – or a witch, I suppose – I still saw the person I'd imagined was sending me those secret notes," Frank said. "Kind of like a cross between your dad and me – the kind of kid who looked like he'd be my big brother, if I had one. Someone to hang out with, who'd look out for me."

"That must be why the goblins call her the Mistress of Lies," Penny said. "You don't find out who she really is or what she's really like until it's too late."

Frank nodded, but was soon lost in his own thoughts. Silence fell. Penny looked around. Wherever they were, it was beautiful – wild and unspoilt. The only clues that it was the human world were the road and, high above, a fine white line being etched across the sky, the vapour trail from a silent aeroplane like a chalk line drawn across the deep blue heavens. A bird called in the distance, but Penny didn't know what sort it was.

"Has that been long enough?" she asked.

"Give it another couple of minutes," said Frank. "The worst thing that could happen would be to go back there and find they were waiting for us."

"Not quite. The worst thing would be to go back and find the snakes are waiting for us."

"Yeah, you're right." said Frank. But then he laughed. "Old Sticklebee managed to outrun them. I'm sure we could too."

"I wish I had my skipping rope," Penny said wistfully. "I'd sort those snakes out then, that's for sure."

"I wouldn't say no to the secateurs and the metal box," said Frank. "That Grimshock deserves a poke with the death metal if ever anyone did."

"Frank!" Penny was shocked. "How could you?"

"Okay," he sighed. "But I hope that when we meet up with our friends, Broadwallow teaches that bully a lesson. I'd like to be there when Grimshock meets someone his own size."

They stood in silence for a while longer. "Right," Penny said eventually. "That has to be ten minutes. Shall we give it a go?"

"Okay," Frank agreed. "But remember, if they are there waiting for us, just blow the whistle again – straight away."

Penny gripped Frank's hand more tightly, took a deep breath and raised the whistle to her mouth. "Good luck," she whispered, then blew. Again, the translation from into the faerie lands was instant, though it left both children feeling dizzy and slightly sick.

The spider-tent had gone. They were back in the Hydra Pass but there was no sign of Ribaldane or Grimshock. Even better, there didn't seem to be any snakes lurking nearby. It looked like morning, for the sun was only just over the mountains on one side of the valley.

Frank smiled. "So far so good," he said. "Come on, let's get over to the boulders and see if we can get up to the top of the pass before any snakes turn up and try to eat us."

They set off walking as briskly as they could. The pass was very steep and it looked like they still had to walk a couple of miles to get to the top. Mostly they were scrambling up the dusty slopes, feet slipping on the scrubby grass and lose stones. Sometimes they had to clamber over boulders – others were so big they just walked round them.

And still they hadn't seen any snakes. Penny was starting to wonder where they were when she saw a dragon instead. It was about the size of a small cat, though it looked like a scaly kangaroo – with wings, of course. It hopped up onto a rock in front of the children, looked at them with intelligent eyes, said *Hoop-hoop* and hopped off a few paces. Then it stopped, looked over its shoulder and said *Hoop-hoop* again.

"Do you think it wants us to follow it?" Penny asked Frank. She was only joking, but he looked all serious.

"You know, I think it does," he said. "And one thing we do know is that where the dragons go, there won't be any snakes. Let's see where he wants to lead us."

So the children changed direction slightly, following the little dragon as it hopped from rock to rock. It would stop every dozen meters or so, looking back and *hoop-hooping*, as if to check the humans were still coming. Once or twice it spread its little wings, leaping into the air to glide a few meters, but it always waited for Penny and Frank to catch up.

They weren't heading straight for the top of the pass now, though they were still going steadily upwards. The going was tougher and they had to climb more than walk. Penny was weak with tiredness and Frank had to help her up some of the bigger rocks they needed to scale, but the little dragon kept staring and *hoop-hooping* to them, as if to encourage them.

And then, very near the top of the pass, they came to a cave. It wasn't very large – the mouth was a rough oval that Frank could just about stand up in. The dragon stopped just outside and nodded at it, *hoop-hooping* softly. "So this is where you wanted to bring us, was it?" Penny asked. "What's in here?" A warm breath of air blew out of the cave.

And a deep, soft voice came gently out from the darkness: "The last of the great dragons, human girl. Come in. Please. We have lots to talk about."

Chapter Forty Nine

Orobus

Penny reached out her hand and Frank took it. Together they stepped cautiously into the cave, the boy leading the way. Penny expected it to be cool inside, but it wasn't – it was hot and close, like getting into a car that's been parked outside on a sunny day. The floor sloped downwards quite steeply and the cave narrowed as it went back into the mountainside until it was a tunnel, little more than a meter wide and only just high enough for Penny to walk through.

At first she thought they were walking towards a faint light, until it flickered. She had been wondering where a big dragon could be in this tiny cave when she suddenly realised... the light hadn't flickered. It had blinked. Ahead, glowing with a faint light, was the yellow eye of the dragon, looking up the tunnel at the children in the way they would look up a cardboard tube. Frank gasped and Penny knew he'd seen it too.

After a dozen metres the tunnel emerged onto a ledge on the edge of a huge chamber and there, in front of them, many meters below, was the dragon. And it was enormous, glowing with a faint light in the darkness of a truly enormous cave. The cavern was at least as big as a football stadium – probably twice as big. And the dragon filled it.

The great snakes had been big, but even Zigorath – by far the biggest of them – would only have been about the size of the dragon's tail. Maybe not even so big. Its neck was just as long and its red, scaly body was the size of a large house. Its head was as big as a garage. Huge amber wings like the sails of a ship were folded on its back.

The dragon regarded the children with glowing, yellow eyes that were as tall as Frank. Penny was rooted to the spot, amazed by the sheer size of it. She could have lain down across its long, broad snout and not been near the edges. Sharp teeth the size of fence posts could be seen in its partly open mouth and steam curled from nostrils bigger than dustbins.

"Welcome, humans. It has been many years since last I saw any of your kind. I am Orobus, last queen of the dragons. Will you tell me your names?" it said.

"I'm Frank and this is Penny," said Frank. He never seemed to be overawed by anything in Faerieland. Penny thought she'd try to be more like that.

"My children tell me you rode up the mountains on the great snake Zanorth, before entering the witch's tent. Is that true?" the dragon tilted its head quizzically. "How did you then come to reappear in the valley, when they left two days ago?"

"I have a whistle," Penny said, trying not to sound timid. "It's a magic one. I blew it and we returned to our world. Then I blew it again and we came back here."

"Hmmm. Why did you leave the witch and return to your world?" asked the dragon.

"She wanted to feed me to the snake," Frank said.

"So why did you risk returning?" It was hard to tell, but Penny thought Orobus was staring especially hard at them.

"We have to stop Ribaldane somehow," Penny said. "She has a silver trumpet that will give her power over the Black Legion, whatever that is. Then she'll use it to take over this world and then she'll invade ours. So we have to stop her."

"That is a large task for such little humans," said Orobus. More steam puffed out of her nostrils. Penny thought the dragon might be laughing at them. "Why do you have to be the ones to stop her? The witch is ancient, mighty and cunning. Surely there should be someone... bigger... who can stop her."

"There's Broadwallow," said Frank. "He's a hobgoblin. And Pickatina. She's a goblin who does magic. But we were sent because we helped Ribaldane get the trumpet. By mistake – she tricked us. But we have to get the trumpet back."

"Do you know where these goblin friends of yours are?"

asked Orobus. "Why are they not with you?"

"Centaurs attacked us and we got split up," Penny said. "Excuse me, but can we ask you a question?"

"Certainly," said Orobus. "You just did. Though I assume you have another one in mind. What do you want to know?"

"Whose side are you on?" she hesitated. "Are you on our side or on Ribaldane's? Because we need to know."

So much steam came out of Orobus's nostrils that for a second Penny thought she'd made her cross and the dragon was going to cook them alive. It was getting hotter in the cavern all the time and now Penny was sweating.

"That is a very good question, Penny," Orobus said. "I am not on Ribaldane's side – that is certain. Her pet snakes feast on my young. So I am definitely not on her side. Does that mean am I on yours? I suppose I must be, not that it will do you much good."

"Come on," said Frank. "With you on our side, what chance do those snakes have? With you on our side, we should be able to deal with Ribaldane without any trouble."

Steam puffed out of Orobus's nostrils again. Penny was convinced this was how the dragon laughed. "I wish I could do that for you, Frank," she said. "There is one slight problem. You see the tunnel behind you, the one through which you entered my chamber?"

"Yes," both children said.

"It is the only way in or out of here. And as you can see, I am much too big to fit through it." The dragon lowered her head. "I came in as a young dragon, hiding from those wretched serpents, but soon I grew to large to leave again. I have been trapped inside ever since. If I could get out, those snakes would never feast on my offspring. If I could leave here, Faerieland would be a very different place. And I would help you – oh yes, I would help you. But as long as I am trapped here, there is nothing I can do.

"Except, perhaps, I can help you find your friends." The dragon sighed. "My children tell me they crossed the pass this morning. They had travelled all night. There were five of them – two goblins, a pixie, a dryad and an elf. They rushed over the pass, following the trail of the witch and her snakes."

Penny looked at Frank. This was good news: their friends were only a little way ahead. But she could see that Frank was thinking about something else.

"Can you fly, Orobus?" he asked. "I mean, if you were out of this cave would you be able to fly?"

"I think so, Frank. It has been many years, but I'm sure I could." The dragon tilted her head again. "But why? How could you get me out of this cave?"

"I have an idea," he said. "Would you be able to carry us. Without us falling off, I mean."

"Of course. If necessary. Explain." Orobus sounded excited.

"What I'm thinking is this," said Frank. "We sit on your back, then Penny blows the whistle. That'll take us back to the human world. You fly a little way, then Penny blows the whistle again. That'll bring us back here. But hopefully you'll be outside the cave. Then you can fly us to pick up the others, then we'll go and stop Ribaldane."

There was a moment of silence, then Orobus turned her great head and stared directly at the girl. "Can you do this thing, Penny?" she asked. "Can you free me from this cave?"

"I can. But I have to know. If we set you free, can we be sure you'll be good?" Penny hesitated. "In our world we have all kinds of legends about dragons eating maidens and burning down towns and stealing gold – that kind of thing. How do we know you're not trying to trick us?"

"It was Frank's suggestion, not mine," said Orobus. "But it is a fair question. Let me put your mind at ease. For one thing, I am too old now to make flames. All I have is my steam and there's precious little of that left – certainly not enough for a town. I don't even know if there's enough for a snake. And when we leave here, that is what I want: the snakes. I will help you and your friends catch Ribaldane – and then I will get rid of the evil vipers that have for so many years eaten my children."

The children exchanged a glance. "Come on, Penny," Frank said. "What other chance have we got? Grimshock took your bag. We don't have the skipping rope, we don't have the secatuers or the steel box. We have nothing left. But if we have a dragon on our side... well, we might just pull it off."

She took a breath and nodded. "Okay, let's do it," she said.

Orobus lowered her head so her nostrils were level with the ledge on which the children were standing. Carefully, they walked up her broad snout and climbed up behind the ears. She wasn't scaly like the giant snakes – more leathery and knobbly, the way Penny imagined a crocodile would feel if you were to touch it.

"Sit on my neck and hold on to my spine ridges," the dragon said. "I am ready when you are."

Frank put his hands on Penny's shoulders and she blew the whistle... and they were soaring through the air. Orobus was flying high above the moors they'd visited earlier, passing over roads and a small village busy with cars. Quickly, before they were spotted, Penny blew the whistle again... and they were back in faerieland, flying high above the mountains. On a dragon.

Penny laughed. "Look out Ribaldane!" she shouted. "We're coming – we're coming to get you!"

Chapter Fifty

Fresh Fish

The sun was setting – they had returned to fairieland at the end of a day. Whether it was the end of the same day as when they'd left Orobus's cave, none of them knew. Time passed in faerieland so much faster than it did in the human world. Penny just hoped they hadn't been gone for too long – they didn't want Ribaldane getting too far ahead.

The two children clung to the dragon's neck as Orobus

soared through the air on wings as wide as a jumbo jet's. They were so high up they could see the far-off ocean glimmering like a burning mirror as the sun went down. At first the dragon flew high above jagged peaks topped with bright white snow. The mountains marched away left and right, all the way to the sea, their western sides reflected the amber light of the end of the day, but black-shadowed valleys lay between them. Night was coming.

Orobus was flying north, so the land fell away beneath her as she flew, the mountains gradually giving way to broad hills with a thin covering of trees and large areas of open moorland clad in purple heather. It looked pretty similar to the place the whistle had taken the children to, back to in the human world. The difference was that there were no roads in faerieland. There didn't even seem to be any paths or tracks, let alone any villages.

"How are we going to find everyone?" Penny shouted. The noise of the wind rushing past them was deafening – even louder than when they'd flown on the the ducks, leaving Honeypatch.

"I do not have the eyes of an eagle," came back the deep booming voice of the dragon, "But I can ask them to help us. Nothing moves on this land without them seeing it."

"Where are the eagles?" shouted Frank.

"I do not know," said Orobus. "And they will not have seen a flying dragon for many hundreds of years. They may be afraid. But we will find them if we must. However, it grows dark. I shall find a safe place for us to land and then we shall wait together for the morning. And in the morning we shall begin our searches – first for the eagles, then for your friends and lastly for our enemies. Let us hope we will be swiftly successful in all three quests."

The huge dragon landed on an open area of heath, near a small lake. Frank and Penny went to drink the sweet water, while Orobus tramped round and round, flattening a large area of heather. She breathed on it, steaming breath wilting the leaves and softening the woody stems. She settled down, seemingly content, then cocked her head questioningly at the children.

"What do you humans have to eat?" she asked.

"Do you mean," asked Frank cautiously, "What must we eat? Or what do we have with us to eat?"

"Both, I suppose," steam puffed out of the dragon's nostrils. Again, Penny suspected she was laughing at them.

"We need things like meat and vegetables," the girl said. "But we don't have anything to eat with us. We'll have to go hungry, I suppose – at least until we catch up with the others. Pickatina will have something we can eat. Maybe a chocolate centipede."

"You need not go hungry," said Orobus, uncoiling her long neck. She reached out her head until her mouth was dipping into the little lake – then she blew. Two metres from the shore, bubbles came to the surface, bursting with steam. And with the bubbles came fish.

"You will have to wade in and get them, but their flesh should nourish you," Orobus told them. "They will be cooked nicely. Do not worry about getting wet – I shall dry your clothes. I can breathe gently enough to warm without burning."

So that's just what they did – whooping and jumping and splashing through the water. It was cold and clear, the chill cutting through their clothes like a knife. But at least the lake was shallow and they didn't need to swim. They gathered the fish as quickly as they could and came laughing back to the banks, teeth beginning to chatter. Frank got the knife Queen Celestia had given him and carefully cut the heads off them, scraped off the scales and took out their guts. While Orobus gently blew warm air over them, they stood with hunched shoulders and munched carefully on the fish. They were sweet and tender and delicious.

"What do you eat, Orobus?" Penny asked, between mouthfuls.

"A dragon does not eat, Penny," she said. "At least, not to stay alive, the way you do. We are powered by the magnetism of the earth – so as long as the world turns, the dragons can survive. It is a part of our magic. But it is why we must live here, in the faerielands, where the magic is strongest. We can venture into your world but sooner or later, our power leaves us and then we die. It is only here that we can survive. If the snakes don't get us."

"Did many dragons come to the human world?" asked Frank.

"A few," replied Orobus. "Penny said you have heard the tales But the old dragons who dared to enter your lands did not last long. You humans have been as deadly to my race as the terrible snakes – but I suppose the difference is that my ancestors forced your ancestors to kill them."

"You're not cross about that?" Penny asked.

"What would be the point?" asked the dragon sadly. "My people went to your lands, they terrorised villages and stole jewels, ate princesses… did terrible things. They were punished, probably fairly. I cannot change what happened. But now I am free from my cave, I can change what will happen here in the future – if I can stop the terrible snakes."

"Where were the snakes, do you think?" asked Frank. "We didn't see any when we came back – and there had been loads before, when we were riding up the pass on Zanorth's back."

"My little ones told me that Ribaldane led them all over the high pass," said Orobus. "What she plans to do with them, I do not know. The snakes cannot cross the ocean to the North Pole, where the Black Legion rests. They need warmth and cannot survive in the icy wastes of the pole."

"What is the Black Legion?" Penny asked. "Everyone just talks about it as this terrible army, but what makes it so special?"

"I do not know," said Orobus. "To my shame, I know little of the world. I was young when I discovered my cave. I hid there, thinking to avoid the snakes until I was big enough to defend myself from them. But I stayed too long and instead I was trapped in there. The place that had been my refuge became my prison.

"And outside, the years went by. First the Dark Queen Ribaldane arose in her power. Then she was overthrown and the Light Queen Celestia took her place. And all the time, while these great events shook the world, I took no part in them. I was trapped in my cave. So I know nothing of the Black Legion – just the rumours you have already heard. That they sleep, waiting for a true leader, but if they awake and fight they will be unstoppable. Only a true leader will be able to command them."

Frank shook his head. "Better make sure we're the ones who get there with the trumpet, then," he said. "So we can command them to go back to sleep."

"And talking of sleep, you should rest now," said the dragon. "It has been a long, tiring day. I have not spent time with humans before, but even I can see that you are both exhausted. Sleep now, regain your strength – and tomorrow we will resume our quest."

And she held out a massive front paw, with thick black talons the size of JCB scoops. But the palm was raised and the children climbed in. It was surprisingly soft, the leather skin supple. They lay down, wrapping themselves in their cloaks. As they settled down, Orobus breathed gently over them – a warm, sweet current of air – and they both fell instantly asleep.

Penny woke in the morning to the sound of Frank singing. Badly. She peeked over the rim of the dragon's cupped palm and there he was, splashing about in the little lake, washing himself, singing and laughing. She looked away.

A few minutes later, Frank – dry and thankfully fully clothed now – was clambering back into the dragon's paw again. "Your turn," he said cheerfully. "I'll stay here – don't worry, I won't peek. It's great. Orobus heats the water up just right."

Penny jumped down to the ground and said good morning to the dragon, who smiled gently at her with massive, sharp teeth. Then the girl headed to the lake, stripped off and dived into the shallow water. She emerged with a shriek – it was still cold. Steam bursting from her nostrils, Orobus extended her neck to the shore and puffed her warming breath into the water.

It was brilliant to get clean. Penny hadn't realised how dirty and dusty she'd become – but she soon put that right. Once she thought she was clean, she scrubbed her clothes as best she could. When she was done, Orobus blew her dry with warm, gentle breath. It was wonderful.

Even more wonderful was the dragon's news. "While you

two slept, I spotted an owl," she said. "I called to him and he came. He was a wise old bird who remembered the dragons, the lords of the skies. This sage among avians sought out the eagles and told them what we needed. This morning a falcon came to see me. He had found Ribaldane and the snakes – and your friends too – who are near. We will go and see them now."

The children climbed onto her neck again, then the mighty dragon launched herself into the sky. The day was bright, the air clear, they were going to meet their friends again and everything seemed possible. Penny laughed as the wind blew in her hair.

Chapter Fifty One

Throttle

Meeting up with their friends wasn't as easy as they'd anticipated. For one thing, Pickatina and Broadwallow weren't expecting the children to be riding on the back of a gigantic dragon. Quite understandably, the sight of Orobus swooping down towards them seemed to cause a fair amount of panic.

Frank spotted their friends first, even when they were quite high up in the sky – small dots moving slowly across the rumpled brown-and-purple quilt of the moorland. As the dragon swooped down, she passed so low Penny was even able to tell them apart. Orobus flew past just above them, so the children could shout and wave to let them know everything was alright.

This didn't work.

The massive blast of wind created when the dragon flew past was strong enough to tip Paisley from his seat on his badger and send Caro Elora's delicate squirrel rolling across the moorland, the little dryad clinging on for dear life. And of course the noise of the wind was so great that nobody could hear the children shouting.

Orobus banked in the air above the moor but before she

could come back and land beside them, the children's friends were riding off in four different directions: Pickatina was heading north; Broadwallow east; Paisley south; and Caro Elora west. "It seems I shall have to herd them like sheep," sighed the dragon.

Penny banged on her back – she probably barely felt it – and shouted, "Just land by Pickatina. Can you go even more slowly? Try not to scare her dog. Try to fly in really low and gently."

So instead of flapping her wings and flashing down like a jet plane, Orobus settled into a slow, graceful glide and spiralled down from the heights until she was skimming slowly across the heather, less than a metre from the ground.

At first Pickatina ran, 996 galloping and barking as if it was a great game. But the dragon was far faster. As they flew alongside, Penny and Frank were calling and waving to Pickatina. At first the little goblin was crouched in her saddle, head down, concentrating on fleeing and she didn't hear them. But then she must have caught a word floating on the breeze, because she looked over – and almost fell from the saddle with surprise. Her eyes widened and her mouth hung opened. It was all Penny could do not to laugh at her expression.

Orobus wheeled away to one side and landed with a gentle but loud thud. They climbed down as Pickatina rode cautiously up. When the goblin dismounted, 996 went to sniff the dragon, but Orobus puffed hot air and the dog backed away with a yelp.

"Boy Frank? Girl Pen? How can this be?" Pickatina sounded shocked and uncertain. "You are here, not with the mistress. And you are with… with…" Her voice tailed off.

"With the last of the great dragons, little one," said Orobus softly. "Do not be afraid. I will not harm you, or these humans. Indeed, I believe we shall work together. My quarrel is with the terrible snakes that serve the one you call Ribaldane. Penny has freed me so I can help you – and so I can fight the snakes."

"How did you get away?" asked Pickatina. "We were so worried." And she came and gave first Penny and then Frank a hug. She was warm and soft, but did still smell a bit sluggy.

So Penny explained everything that had happened since she'd escaped from the centaurs' village – about rescuing Frank and meeting the elves and getting caught by Grimshock. They told Pickatina about the riding on the giant snakes and going into the spider tent and escaping from Ribaldane.

At that point, Pickatina threw her hands up in horror. "The necklace Girl Pen – the whistle. Where is it?"

Penny reached into the neck of her shirt and pulled it free, holding it up so her friend could see it. Quick as a flash, the tiny goblin jumped up and grabbed it, yanking it hard enough to snap the chain. Before anyone could move, she had thrown it across the moorland heather as hard as she could.

"Pickatina!" both children cried out.

"What did you do that for?" asked Penny.

"We might have needed that whistle again," said Frank.

"The whistle still you may use, Boy Frank," Pickatina said, holding it up shyly. "But the chain – desperate to get rid of it I have been ever since we came here. But I…" She hung her head. "I have been too ashamed to tell you. It was stupid. Forgive me."

Penny thought for a second. "It was a throttle, wasn't it?" The goblin nodded.

"You mean Ribaldane gave it to Penny she could use it to choke her? And you hadn't told us?" Frank sounded furious, but Penny put her hand on his arm.

"It's alright, Pickatina," she told her friend gently. "You've done the right thing now."

As they were talking, the others approached cautiously, one by one. First came Broadwallow, with Buddy Greenleaf sitting on his shoulder. Then Paisley and his badger. Last to arrive was Caro Elora – her squirrel skittering nervously as it approached the dragon. Penny introduced the dryad to Frank and Frank introduced everyone to Orobus. Finally, they were all together. Penny grinned.

"But tell us what happened to you," she said. "I haven't seen you since… well, it seems like ages."

"It has been eight whole days," said Pickatina, "But it feels like much, much more. We have been so worried."

"My cousin has less faith than me," said Broadwallow, smiling. "You saved us from the centaurs. I knew that with your courage and your skipping rope, you would be alright."

"I don't have that any more," Penny admitted. "It's in my bag and Grimshock took that."

"That is bad news," said Paisley with his oddly deep, ringing voice. "Does this mean you no longer have the death metal that was so effective against the harrows and which broke the enchantment on the Town on the Lake?"

"Yup, that's gone as well," said Frank cheerily. "But look, we have a dragon now. Come on! That has to count for something."

"It does indeed, Boy Frank," said Pickatina. "I must say, you have a way of making mighty friends, Girl Pen. That is a talent."

"You were meant to be telling us what had happened to you," she reminded them. "Not asking more questions."

"Of course," said Pickatina, smiling. "My cousin was right. You did save us from the centaurs. As they tried to get to you, the rest of us were able to escape. Several of the dryads had been hurt so we had to take them back to their village."

"Those who could get in," said Broadwallow. "The rocky passage was too narrow for me. I had to wait outside that night."

"But my people looked after you, Captain," said Caro Elora in her tinkling dryad voice.

"They did," he agreed. "And next day we set off to find you stray humans. We still had to be cautious, because the centaurs were out in force and they were angry. Our progress was slow."

"But we knew we were going in the right direction when I met Fairie Oaks, the tree faerie you'd spoken to," said Caro Elora. "She was very excited to have been given a name. And she was even more excited to meet us. She told us all about you."

"It was a relief to know we were heading the right way," continued Pickatina. "We were still travelling slowly, but we thought we were might find you – and then we met Buddy."

"I did what you'd asked, Penny," said the little elf. "As soon as that monster Grimshock had taken you away, I set off to find your friends. Didn't take too long, either – the way they were blundering through the bushes making so much noise. I told them what had happened and which way you were headed."

"Why are you still here?" she asked. "Why didn't you go back to Mrs Bud after you'd told them where to look for me?"

"Well, I thought it was time for an elf to be brave," said Bud. "I volunteered to join the quest. I want to help."

"And a great help our small friend has been already," said Broadwallow. "He has keen eyes and ears, can run faster than any of us – faster even than the dogs – and he has proved to be an excellent scout. It was Bud who led us along the tracks you and Grimshock left as you climbed up the pass. He found where the mistress had camped and showed us where the snakes had passed. He has been leading our pursuit ever since we met."

"But now we're all together again, we can just go and beat the witch," said Bud confidently. "With a dragon on our side, it's just a case of turning up the heat on them, isn't it?"

"It is not so simple," said Pickatina. "I fear even the great Orobus would struggle to overcome the Mistress when she uses her full strength. Mighty and deep, her magic is. And even if it were not, we could not risk a dragon's fire destroying the trumpet. Remember, unless we are taking it and using it, the Black Legion will march anyway – and that is very nearly as dangerous as if it was marching to orders from the Mistress."

"We will still have to defeat the mistress ourselves," said Broadwallow. "But perhaps we can do that before she gets near to the Black Legion. Tell me, great Orobus, can carry all of us?"

"Easily," said the dragon. "Where would you go?"

"To the Last Citadel," said Pickatina. "It is where the Mistress must go to get a boat to the North Pole.?"

"What are we waiting for?" Penny asked, and Orobus laughed, creating huge clouds of steam.

"Climb aboard," said the dragon. "Victory awaits."

Chapter Fifty Two

Augers

Before the children and their friends could all get onto Orobus's back, Pickatina did the magic trick of shrinking all the animals, just the way the Naga had done it back at Honeypatch. She stroked one dog after another, singing softly to them, and they shrank rapidly down to the size of tiny models. Then she did the same for Paisley's badger and Caro Elora's squirrel.

"See how Pickatina grows in power, Girl Pen," said Broadwallow. "Truly she is becoming a power in her own right."

"But not one to challenge the Mistress of Lies," the small goblin said, giving her huge cousin a sharp look. Penny wondered if this was something the cousins had been arguing about.

When all the animals had been shrunk and tucked away in Broadwallow's bag, everyone climbed up onto the dragon's back. Penny sat at the front, with Bud on her lap and Pickatina right behind her. The goblin gave the girl's shoulder a squeeze.

"Is everybody sitting comfortably?" asked Orobus. "Then hold on tight – here we go!" And with that the enormous creature launched herself into the air. Pickatina's grip on Penny's shoulder tightened for a second, then she seemed to relax. With only three beats of her giant wings, Orobus was high above the moorland.

Soon everyone could see the coast, though it was still a long way away in the distance. Pickatina pointed to the right. "Over there is the ocean – which we call the Sea of Dreams," she shouted above the roar of the wind. Then she pointed to the left. "Over there is Great Bay, which is a part of the ocean enclosed by land. And there," she pointed straight ahead, "Is where we must go to catch up with the Mistress. It is the Peninsula of Thorns, where the Last Citadel was built."

Penny could see a long finger of land stretching out all the way to the far horizon. She couldn't see the end of it – it was just a dark mass of land separating the two sheets of water. With the noise of the wind, conversation was impossible and the friends lapsed into silence.

Orobus seemed to fly for a long time. Penny had assumed they'd get to the Last Citadel – wherever it was – in a matter of minutes. Maybe the dragon could have got there that fast if there hadn't been half a dozen passengers clinging onto her broad neck, but the enormous creature had to keep her speed down to stop people being blown from her back.

By early afternoon they were near the sea and starting to fly out along the peninsula. Bud suddenly jumped up from where he'd been sitting on Penny's lap. He trotted fearlessly across the skin of Orobus's neck, holding onto the neck spikes that stood up every so often, leaning out to look over the edge.

"It's the snakes!" he shouted. His high voice could barely be heard above the wind noise. Penny looked quizzically at him and had to beckon him back to her. "It's all the snakes," he repeated as he got closer to the girl. "Down there. They're spread out all across the peninsula like some kind of army."

"I see them too," said Orobus, steam pouring from her nostrils and whipping back like a warm cloud. There were little orange flashes at the corner of her mouth, so Penny could tell that even the sight of the huge snakes made the dragon angry.

Penny looked down but she couldn't see any snakes, not at first. Then she spotted a pale line, like a short river – which had to be one of the huge snakes. Maybe not Zigorath or Zanorth, but one as big as the third snake that had travelled up the mountain with the children and Grimshock. "I see one! There!" she shouted.

"There's another one over there," called Frank, pointing.

"They're everywhere," yelled Bud. "I dunno, you humans are as blind as the goblins. You've spotted a couple of bigger ones but there are loads of snakes down there. I can see at least four more that are as big as those two you've pointed out and dozens that are as fat as the dragon's neck, not to mention all the tiddlers. Well – I call them tiddlers but they'd swallow me whole without blinking. Probably big enough to swallow Paisley, some of them."

"The really huge ones?" Penny asked. "Can you see them?"

"I know the two you mean – the lord of the snakes and his son," Bud shouted, shaking his head. "Can't see 'em. Not down there. But I'll keep my eyes peeled for them."

"Now I understand why there were no snakes in the Hydra's Pass," Pickatina called. "The Mistress took them with her, to guard the road and stop anyone following her to the Last Citadel."

"She didn't count on us having a dragon!" laughed Frank. "Snakes can't stop you when you can fly over the top."

"No, that is true," called Broadwallow slowly. But he sounded worried. "But we could have had ducks with us. Then it would have been easy to fly past the snakes."

"The Mistress would know this," Pickatina shouted over the wind. She sounded scared. She looked around the sky nervously.

"What are you looking for?" shouted Frank.

"I'm not sure," she replied. "But I am afraid. There will be something. Something... terrible. I am sure of it."

"Have no fear, little goblin," said Orobus. "Whatever the dark queen was expecting, it would not have been me. And I am no duck. Whatever she sends, I will protect you."

And no sooner had she spoken than Bud spotted it. At first he was the only one who could see it, but he shouted and pointed. "Over there, look. A black cloud – coming towards us."

"Clouds are nothing to fear, small one," said the dragon. "Even black ones – they are just filled with rain."

"No, this one isn't normal – it's moving against the wind," yelled Buddy. "It's flying towards us."

"I see it too," said Paisley, whose eyes were almost as sharp as the elf's. "It is moving rapidly and it is not a cloud. It looks like a swarm of bees. Except bees are much smaller."

"Oh no..." gasped Pickatina, so softly only Penny heard – and even she could barely hear the goblin over the noise of the wind.

"What is it?" Penny asked, turning to look at her friend, who looked scared.

"I think it is… augers." She held a hand above her eyes and squinted into the distance. Penny turned to face forwards again and did the same, but couldn't see anything.

"Do you see it, Orobus?" the girl shouted.

"I do, Penny. It is still a long way off," said the dragon calmly.

"Can you fly away from it?" called Broadwallow.

"Not if you want me to fly straight to the Last Citadel," Orobus replied. "It flies straight down the peninsula from there."

Then Penny finally saw it for herself – a dark cloud that seemed to be heading straight for the dragon. It seemed to grow and spread, moving constantly, like a flock of starlings at sunset. It wasn't a constant shape, but something ebbing and flowing, getting bigger and lighter, then smaller and darker as it flew towards them. And it was flying fast – the gap between the dragon and the cloud was shrinking rapidly.

"Fly up! Fly up!" shouted Pickatina urgently. "We must get above them. They cannot stand the cold and in the higher air they will move slowly. We may be able to escape them."

"As you wish, lady," said Orobus. "Everyone, hang on." The dragon flapped her wings and climbed steeply. Penny had to grab on to the neck spines in front of her to stop her sliding backwards. She watched the cloud change direction, swinging round to follow them. It seemed to solidify, getting darker and forming a point, like a huge spear. Even at this distance, she could see it was beginning to climb.

But Orobus was climbing faster. The air got colder and Penny realised she was panting. She knew the air gets thinner higher in the sky, so it's harder to breathe. Bud leant back against the girl, wheezing and shivering. But still Orobus climbed higher.

And then the augers were upon them. Penny heard them first, pattering off the wings and belly of the dragon like rain hitting the windscreen of a car. Orobus shuddered, as if they'd hurt when they hit her. Dozens flew up and around her neck and body, buzzing sinfully. And then they turned and flew at them.

The augers were small and black – the size of two playing

cards tied to a pencil. They looked like mechanical butterflies with wings made of some dark filigree metal and a savage point on the front of their long, thin bodies.

They weren't moving very quickly and it was easy to grab them. Penny just stared as the first one flew straight for her face, but luckily Pickatina reached round and grabbed it. It struggled in her hands, but she snapped it. Behind them, Penny heard her friends shouting and crying out. The girl grabbed the next one that came towards her. It flapped weakly but relentlessly. With a grunt, she snapped it in half. It was like breaking a twig.

"These things have… hurt me," cried Orobus. "They burrow into my flesh. What must I do to kill them?"

"Cold – we must get them cold. Or wet," panted Pickatina, snapping another one. "That will stop them."

"Then hold on, friends," said the dragon. "We are going down. Fast." And she began to dive – straight towards the sea.

Chapter Fifty Three

Diving

Augers whizzed around Penny's ears as Orobus dived towards the sea. She realised only the strongest of the metal devices had managed to reach them when the dragon had been at her highest point. That had let the passengers catch and snap them, one by one.

But now the air was black with them as the dragon cut through the heart of the swarm. They bounced off the children and their companions, caught at their clothes and skin, tearing and cutting; they battered them, tattered them and blinded them. Penny heard Bud shriek, but could barely even see the little elf sitting on her lap because the air was thick with augers.

Orobus puffed out a huge cloud of steam – and Penny

thought for a second there was a flash of fire in it. There was a crackling noise like a firework fuse, or milk pouring on Rice Crispies, and the girl guessed Orobus had destroyed some of the augers. A wave of heat and moisture hit her, accompanied by a smell of melting metal, totally hiding what little view she'd had.

And then she felt a sharp stab on her tummy, like an injection. Instantly she reached down and felt an auger. It had stuck its sharp nose point in her and was trying to burrow the rest of its long, pencil-like body into the girl. Furious, Penny ripped it out and snapped it in half, but it really hurt.

Poor Orobus! No wonder the mighty dragon was in pain – she had said the augers had burrowed into her. It was easy to see why she was in a hurry to get to the sea, if that would destroy the nasty things.

Then they were out of the auger-cloud. The sky was clear ahead, though the evil things could be heard buzzing behind them. Penny looked down to see Bud, bleeding but smiling, holding the wings of an auger he had clearly defeated himself.

Penny had to hold on really tight to the dragon's spikes and grip with her knees as hard as she could. The dragon was diving almost straight down. The sea was rushing up at a terrifying rate. The noise of the wind was deafening now. Penny's whole head echoed with the hissing roar of it. Suddenly she felt her fear of heights return and someone was screaming – it took the girl a second to realise it was her. She could faintly hear Pickatina start to sing, her high and sweet voice rising above the windblast.

"Hold tight and take a deep breath," roared Orobus. And then she folded her wings and dived into the sea.

The thing Penny remembered most clearly was the way the sound flipped off in an instant. One second: deafening wind noise. Next second: complete and utter silence. Then she felt the water close around her like an icy hug, the light fading as the dragon dived down into the water, going deeper and deeper. They were well out into Great Bay and the water was dark and deep.

Penny nearly opened my mouth to cry out – then realised

what a bad idea that would be now she was underwater. But she'd just taken a breath – how? She turned in panic to face Pickatina...

And saw a bubble enclosing Pickatina's head, like a diving helmet. Behind her, Frank's and Paisley's and Caro Elora's and Broadwallow's. Penny lifted one of her hands from the dragon's back and felt a bubble surrounding her head too.

She realised it was Pickatina's doing. Penny had heard the goblin singing, which meant she was casting a spell. The girl just hoped her friend would be able to keep it up for as long as they were underwater.

Then it began to rain. Under the sea. Only it wasn't water that was falling past them – it was augers. Shrivelled, twisted augers sinking slowly past them.

Orobus had stopped diving and was turning ever so gradually to head back towards the surface. And all the while, more and more augers were dropping past – as if a truck-load of gravel was being slowly emptied into the water above and sinking down to the dark and distant depths.

They made it back to the air just in time for Pickatina. As soon as Orobus broke the surface of the sea, the bubble of air around Penny's head vanish with a gentle pop. And the little goblin stopped singing, slumped forwards, resting her hand on the girl's shoulder and her head on her back.

"Are you alright, Pickatina?" Penny asked. "Thank you for doing your spell – I think you saved us."

"I will be fine after a night's rest, Girl Pen," she said weakly. "Warding so many is tiring work – especially to keep it up for so long. Myself I can ward for days at a time. One other person, perhaps from dawn til dusk. But six others, of all different sizes as well – I am amazed I kept us all in air for long enough."

"Thank you for protecting my passengers, Lady Pickatina," said Orobus. "And thank you for telling me how to kill the augers. Those infernal things that bit me are no longer burrowing into my body. And it seems all their fellows tried to follow us into the water – so that is the end of them."

"Thank goodness ," Penny cried. "Can we carry on flying now? There won't be any more of them, will there?"

"No, Girl Pen," said Pickatina. "That will have been all the augers the Mistress possessed. It was a great cloud. I confess, I made many of them for her. I suppose I should have expected them – but I am surprised she threw them away so lightly."

"What were they, exactly?" asked Frank.

"Augers are like the harrows and the spite you have seen, Boy Frank," said Pickatina. "They are created by a witch and invested with some of her spirit, or her desires. They can do tasks without the witch having to control their every move."

"How are they made, then?" asked Frank. "And how many did you make? There were hundreds of the things in that cloud."

"There would have been thousands in the swarm," corrected Pickatina. "Witches knit augers the way human ladies knit socks. With practice, a witch can make an auger a day – and remember, I served the mistress for many, many years when she had me fitted with her throttle. What I made for her, she controlled. And I made many augers for the mistress. And she made many more."

"Are you really a witch, Pickatina?" Penny asked.

"Witch is a human word, Girl Pen," she sighed. "We have taken to using it to describe the Mistress, but it is not accurate. We do not have a word for what she is – but I am someone who also uses magic so that means I must be a witch."

"As fascinating as your lesson on language and magic is, Cousin," called Broadwallow, "I think we should be paying attention to where we are and what we are doing."

"What the good Captain Broadwallow means," tinkled Caro Elora, "Is that we'd like to get out of the water before any fish come. Can you do that, Orobus?"

"I must be on land to take off. Though I cannot fly until my wings are dry, lady dryad," said the dragon sadly. "But I am swimming to the shore. We should be there soon."

They sat in silence while Orobus paddled slowly through the water. It was getting towards dark and everyone was damp and shivering by the time they reached a dusty, sandy shore of low dunes topped with scratchy grass. As soon as they landed, everyone climbed down from Orobus – and Pickatina insisted on looking at the damage the augers had done.

Penny was shocked – the underside of the dragon looked like raw mince. She'd had hundreds and hundreds of little holes cut into her by the augers. There were so many holes in her wings that in places they looked like paper doilies and she was still bleeding in places. But she moved around as easily as ever.

"Dragons are tough," Orobus laughed. "I do not feel the pain. And in the morning, I shall be whole again. Do not worry about me." And then she used her warm breath to dry everyone's clothes and stop their teeth chattering. Pickatina produced food – including a fresh chocolate centipede – and they had a meal. Soon they were laughing and joking, all danger forgotten. As the stars came out in the dark sky above, they settled down for the night, all curled up together in one of Orobus's huge paws.

It felt like Penny had only been asleep for moments when she felt someone shaking her shoulder and tugging on her ear. Groggily she sat up.

"What's the matter?" she mumbled, a little grumpily.

It was Bud. In the faint moonlight she could see he looked nervous. "Thank goodness – I can't wake the others, Penny. Or the dragon," he said. "But you've got to help me wake them. Something's coming. And it sounds like a snake. A big one."

Chapter Fifty Four

Thorns

Penny couldn't hear anything. Just the sea hushing gently against the shore behind her. She certainly couldn't hear any snakes – but she knew Bud had much sharper hearing than she did. If he said the snakes were coming, they probably were.

It was inky dark, the middle of the night. Stars twinkled faintly above, a half-moon shone behind faint clouds and Orobus gave off a faint golden glow, but the girl still couldn't see very well. She crawled over to the goblin's messy nest, identifying a lump that had to be Pickatina, curled up beside a slightly larger shape that could only be Broadwallow. Penny poked the smaller bump, which mumbled and tried to turn over, but the girl kept shaking the smaller goblin until she sat up.

"What is it, Girl Pen?" Pickatina asked, rubbing her eyes. "It is still night. Why are you not sleeping?"

"There's a snake coming," Penny explained, trying to sound calm. "Bud says he can hear it. And it's a big one. We need to wake the others."

"It's true, Lady Pickatina," said the little elf. "In fact, now they're getting closer, I can hear two snakes. Both big ones."

"Could it be Zigorath and Zanorth?" Penny asked. "We didn't see them when we flew over the other snakes and those two are the biggest. And the meanest."

"Let us hope it is not," said Pickatina. "I do not think our friend Orobus will be ready to fly. She is still recovering from the damage the augers did to her and her wings may not be dry. But if it is snakes that threaten us, perhaps she will still be ready to fight. You two wake the others. I will wake the dragon."

Penny hurried around waking the others – Paisley sat up, clanging like a bell as he yawned, which woke Caro Elora, who tinkled softly in surprise. Frank mumbled something about butterflies and then jumped up, wide-eyed, looking confused. It took all of them to wake Broadwallow, who lay on his back snoring like a tractor stuck in the mud.

Meanwhile, Pickatina had climbed up the dragon's snout and poked her head and shoulders into one of Orobus's giant ears. The others couldn't hear her shouting, but she must have done something to get the dragon's attention because the huge golden eyes flickered open and the dragon's head lifted from the floor.

As soon as Broadwallow explained the situation, Orobus extended her wings and gave them a careful flap, filling the air with flying sand. She shook her head.

"I am afraid my wings are not entirely dry," she said. "I cannot fly properly like this – I will be able to get above the ground enough to battle the snakes, but I cannot carry you all away from here."

"Cousin, prepare the animals," commanded Broadwallow. "Mighty Orobus, I would ask you to fight the snakes while we ride for the Last Citadel. I know this is something you want to do anyway. All I would ask is that you make sure when fighting one snake that the other is not free to pursue us. Can you do that?"

"I would be honoured, Captain Broadwallow," replied the dragon, with a terrifying tone of determination in her voice. "And have no fear – the serpents shall not pass. Once I have defeated them, I shall come to the Last Citadel. I will help you complete your quest before I deal with the other snakes."

Pickatina was frantically unpacking the dogs, stroking and singing them back to normal size. First Broadwallow's 998, then her 996, Frank's 888 and Penny's 748. Then she got Paisley's badger and returned that to its normal, smelly, snuffling size. She'd just taken Caro Elora's delicate squirrel out when Bud cried and the dragon roared... and the snakes appeared over the dunes.

Orobus leapt into the air, one flap of her vast wings blocking out the stars and moon as she jumped over the top of the children and their friends. The backdraft of wind knocked Paisley and Caro Elora over. Bud would have been blown out to sea if he hadn't grabbed onto Frank's trouser leg as he was flying past it.

The dragon landed on the sand with a huge, damp thud and charged at the snakes. Penny couldn't see much, but she could hear the hissing of the snakes and the snorting of the dragon. There was a great flash of light and a huge cloud of steam, followed by a scream that tailed away into a hiss. Clearly, Orobus was angry enough to produce fire as well as steam.

Then Broadwallow was picking Penny up to set her in the

saddle of 748. The setter tried to lick her as the hobgoblin lifted her. Meanwhile, Pickatina finish reviving Caro Elora's squirrel and Paisley helped the delicate little dryad into the saddle, before climbing aboard his badger.

"This way, friends," shouted Broadwallow. He waved towards up the beach, along the hard sand beside the sea, urging the others ahead of him. As she rode past the hobgoblin, he leaned over and put Bud on Penny's lap.

"You and Bud guide us, Girl Pen," said Broadwallow. "The elf has the best eyes and can pick the best route. And if you lead, you cannot be left behind. I will follow at the rear and make sure we stay together. Let us hope Orobus can contain both snakes."

And so they rode, 748 yelping with delight – the loopy dog was enjoying running along the moonlit beach. Behind them came great echoing crashes and roars, with the occasional bang, but Penny didn't risk looking back. She knew 748 was actually the slowest of the dogs, so she had concentrate on keeping him running to get as far from the snakes as possible before he got tired.

Soon Bud directed Penny away from the sea, up a long gully beside a small river. The land became less sandy and they had to slow down because it was so dark. Eventually they found a place where the river was easy to cross and then climbed up onto a wide, grassy meadow. In the faint moonlight it looked like a field of silver stalks, swaying slightly in the night's gentle breeze.

By now the eastern sky was showing pinks and oranges – soon it would be dawn. Which was good, because then they'd be able to see where they were going better. But it reminded Penny how tired she was. She could hear only faint sounds of the great battle now and the girl was worried for Orobus. She'd imagined nothing could harm the giant dragon until the augers hurt her so. Now Penny was really afraid the two giant snakes might be able to gang up against the colossal creature and damage her as well.

But Penny didn't have much time to spend dwelling on the fate of the dragon. She had to concentrate on riding 748, picking a way across the darkened land. As the sky slowly brightened, she got a better look at the line of hills ahead and, when the sun finally clambered over the eastern horizon, she could make out a tower on the top of the furthest summit.

"Is that the Last Citadel?" she asked Bud. "How far is it?"

"It's probably a full day's ride from here, Penny," he said. "I reckon we should get there before it gets dark tonight. There's no real roads up here, but we should be able to make it easily enough. There's no big trees or woods to get in the way, just this rough grassland between here and there."

So they rode steadily, all day. They did stop for some food at midday and to have a short rest, because the children were both worn. But everyone knew they had to keep going – and with Broadwallow fretting anxiously at the delay all through the meal, nobody was likely to forget the danger they were in. Every now and then they heard the sounds of Orobus fighting the snakes, stray roars and shrieks carried on the wind, which Bud said showed the battle was still slowly heading their way.

Broadwallow said he'd expected this: one of the snakes was trying to fight the dragon, to allow the other snake to chase them. And Orobus was trying to keep both snakes together, to allow them to escape. It just meant they really did have to get to the Last Citadel before the battle caught up with them.

In the afternoon they began climbing up the hills at the tip of the Peninsula of Thorns – and discovered how it got its name. Bud had been right that there were no trees, but there were lots of low bushes on the hills. And the bushes had long, sharp, curved thorns like claws. The dogs all yelped if they got cut and Caro Elora's squirrel screamed in a high, piercing voice like a baby.

Every time one of the animals got hurt, they'd all have to stop so the thorn could be removed from the injured animal's flesh. Pickatina would rub a soothing paste into the cut, then they'd set off again. But as every animal seemed to get cut at least three times, it meant they were travelling far slower than they'd hoped. The sounds of the battle were getting very close indeed.

The sun was setting when they came to the top of the final

hill before the Last Citadel. They could see it clearly, on the other side of one last valley – a vast silhouette against the darkening sky. And then Penny heard the sound she'd be been dreading: a long, evil hiss. One of the snakes had caught up with them.

"I sssmell you, humansss," came the voice of Zanorth. He must have been a hundred meters away. "Firssst I'll ssswallow your friendsss. Then I'm going to ssswallow you…"

Chapter Fifty Five

Fire

They ran. The dogs were exhausted, but the sound and smell of the snake so close seemed to spur them on. The Last Citadel was straight ahead on the other side of a dark, shallow valley – but it was still at least two miles away. Could they outrun Zanorth?

Apparently not. Penny was riding with Paisley and Caro Elora to her left and the others on her right. They were the three slowest – the badger and the squirrel had the shortest legs and 748 had always got more tired more quickly than the other dogs.

It looked like the snake was going to catch them. Glancing to the side, Penny saw it slithering along on the other side of Paisley – still a hundred meters away, but gaining fast, approaching at an angle. Straight away she realised what Zanorth was trying to do – he was racing to split the party up. If he succeeded in getting ahead of them and then looping round, his long, high body would cut Penny, Paisley and Caro Elora from the others, who were gradually leaving them behind. And then they would never be able to get past him – they would never make it to the safety of the Last Citadel.

Even in the fading light, Penny could see that Zanorth had been in a battle. When he'd carried her, Frank and Grimshock up the Hydra's Pass the monstrous serpent had been sleek – but now he looked decidedly tatty, scales sticking up all over his massive body or hanging off in clumps. There were great bleeding cuts on his side where Orobus had obviously swiped him with her claws.

The snake wasn't slithering as smoothly as before, either. In a couple of places his scales seemed to be melted together, stopping his body moving properly. His head seemed raw and one of his eyes was glassy. But even though he was obviously injured, Zanorth was still faster than Penny and her friends.

Then Penny heard a shout. She turned her head in time to see Broadwallow rein in 998. The hobgoblin drew his massive sword with one hand, tugged on his dog's reins with the other to change direction – and galloped straight at the snake's head. Zanorth saw him too and hissed like a kettle on the boil.

As they drew close to each other, Zanorth reared up – Penny could tell he was hurt because he didn't rise straight up, but leaning over to one side. And then he struck.

The snake's head shot straight at Broadwallow and 998. His mouth opened – it was huge, far bigger than a garage door. It looked as though the hobgoblin would ride straight inside, gone in a single bite. Even if he didn't, Broadwallow seemed doomed. A pair of fangs, taller than Christmas trees, stuck out of Zanorth's top jaw. And the terrible snake was moving so fast he was hard to watch – it was like trying to focus on a flying bullet. His jaws snapped shut with a bang like a thousand balloons popping.

Penny screamed and closed her eyes, sure Broadwallow had to be dead. Then head Paisley laughing and cheering.

She opened her eyes to see Broadwallow standing up in the stirrups, riding along the side of the snake. He held his mighty sword in both hands and he had it stuck into Zanorth's side, leaning on it for all he was worth. Mostly his sword skittered across Zanorth's armour-like scales. But in the places where the dragon had already damaged the snake, Broadwallow's blade found exposed, raw patches of skin and sent blood spurting into the air. In the fading light it looked like Broadwallow was being squirted with jets of black ink.

Zanorth made a strange rumbling noise and slewed sideways, away from Broadwallow – though his tail seemed to roll on its side, as if the great snake no longer had perfect control of his massive body. He turned in a great, lazy arc and – ignoring Penny, Paisley and Caro Elora – set off after Broadwallow.

As the hobgoblin turned and rode past, heading back the way the friends had come, he was laughing madly. He waved towards the Last Citadel. "Keep riding," he shouted, digging his heels into 998's flanks to make the dog speed up.

Penny certainly didn't need to be told twice. She was at the bottom of the valley, where the thorn bushes were thickest and most vicious. But her dog was so scared of the snake he didn't slow down – just kept charging through them, oblivious to the cuts he had to be getting. Which was good. Because that's when Penny heard Frank calling. "Go left, Pen – it's Zigorath."

She turned her head and saw the other snake. He was in the bottom of the valley, heading straight for her like a speeding train. As he came, head down, great clumps of bushes were being thrown up on either side of him.

And then Orobus was there. The dim sky went momentarily totally black as she swept overhead, vast wings spread, travelling incredibly fast. The wind almost tipped Penny out of her saddle. Caro Elora's squirrel was blown sideways, bumping into 748 before managing to regain its feet and keep running.

The dragon dipped down as soon as she passed until she was brushing thorn bushes with her claws. As she reached Zigorath, the great snake raised his head, mouth opening to reveal his massive fangs. At the same time Orobus suddenly swept upwards, flicking her tail as the snake struck.

Penny remembered a programme she'd seen once, about how they demolish big buildings. The sound of the dragon's tail hitting the snake's head was just like a tower block being hit by the demolition crew's giant metal ball – but much, much louder.

And watching Zigorath crash down was like watching a building collapse. The whole length of the snake seemed to be lifted into the air and then he tipped sideways, falling like a length of dropped rope. It seemed to happen in slow motion, taking an age for the great serpent to hit the floor.

Orobus had already vanished – she was flying so fast. Zigorath had fallen across Zanorth's tail and the younger snake was struggling underneath its parent's weight. Then Broadwallow was alongside them, dripping with black snake blood but with a wide white smile shining as he grinned. "Quick – we can be reaching the Last Citadel before the snake gets free," he said.

They rode to the top of the hill – aware of the hissing roars of rage behind them. The Last Citadel loomed over them now, huge stone walls as black as night. There was a large gateway nearby, massive thick doors standing open. Frank was already waiting there on 888, beside two hobgoblins in armour like Broadwallow's but Pickatina was standing on the floor at the edge of the thorn patch, arms stretched out and head back.

As the girl and her friends reached the little goblin, she let out a high-pitched shriek that went on and on and on. Penny thought her friend must be in pain and she almost stopped, but Broadwallow grabbed 748's reins and pulled her on. "My cousin summons great power," he said. "Let us be getting inside."

And at that moment, Pickatina stopped screaming and climbed slowly onto 996. Penny could see she was exhausted, but the little goblin managed to ride through the gates of the citadel. A team of hobgoblins closed the doors behind them with a clang.

"To the walls," Pickatina said wearily. "Cousin, lead us."

"Of course, Lady," he said. "Let me carry you – you are weak now." Without waiting for answer, he lifted her from the saddle and laid her over one shoulder.

One of the hobgoblins came over. "Your orders, Captain?"

"Take us to the walls – immediately," said Broadwallow. Everyone else dismounted, leaving the animals with one of the hobgoblin guard, and followed Broadwallow through a door and up ten flights of stairs. Penny's legs were burning with effort by the time they got to the top.

They emerged onto a wide battlement high above the valley. They could see the two snakes still struggling to untangle themselves. "I can't believe that snake's still alive after how hard Orobus hit him," said Frank.

"Let us hope that Orobus can complete the task now," said Pickatina. "Mightily she has fought all day. I hope I have done enough and she has the spark needed to finish the task."

"What have you done, though?" Penny asked.

"Can you not tell, Girl Pen?" she asked. "Smell. Go on."

She sniffed. There was a strange smell in the air. It smelt like… but before Penny could say anything, the dragon was back. She was zooming along low to the ground, flying out of the setting sun. As she reached the valley, Orobus raised her head, flicked it forwards – and a thin stream of fire erupted from her mouth, flicking downwards like a whip.

The whole valley seemed to burst into flame. The snakes, trapped by their own great weight, roared as flames surrounded them. Orobus threw her head back and roared in victory.

"That's what you did," Frank said to Pickatina. "You used magic to soak all those thorn bushes in the valley in oil. That's what the smell was."

"It is the end of the great serpents," she said. "We are safe."

Book Four

The Silent Palace

THE SILENT PALACE

Chapter Fifty Six
Sternbrow

They stayed in the Last Citadel for two days and three nights. That's how long the fires burnt in the valley outside. The thorn bushes, soaked in Pickatina's magical oil, blazed brightly all through that first night and the next day. Through the second night and the second day the flames subsided, but the valley glowed with a shimmering orange-white with heat.

As the flames died down, they could see the two giant skeletons of Zanorth and his father Zigorath, the greatest of the giant snakes. They were still intertwined, where they hadn't been able to separate before the dragon's fire claimed them.

All the while, Orobus circled overhead, unable to land in the burning valley but there was nowhere in the Last Citadel that she could land. It was a strange, sombre place – more of a barracks than a town. All the goblins were soldiers in the queen's guard.

The Citadel was a tall, wide tower surrounded by a cluster of low buildings. Everything was built inside a ring of walls topped with battlements like a castle. It stood on the hill at the very end of the Peninsula of Thorns. It looked over the valley, but on the other three sides there was nothing but the sea. The walls of the citadel blended into the cliffs so the only way down was one wide staircase cut into the rock at the northern-most point.

Frank and Penny went to the very top of the tower only once. There was a big bonfire lit inside a brass cage, with a goblin silently feeding it logs every now and then. The view was impressive, out over the rolling sea all the way to the curved horizon. Penny didn't want to get too close to the edge of the tower and look down – they'd had to climb twenty five flights of stairs to get to up there.

Penny went down to the sea quite a lot, with Frank, Buddy and Caro Elora. Pickatina slept most of the time – the little goblin was worn out by the effort of conjuring the oil Orobus had ignited. Broadwallow and Paisley spent lots of time with Sternbrow, the cheerful hobgoblin who commanded the garrison of the Last Citadel. They were looking at maps and making plans of some sort. So everyone else went down to the sea and sat with their feet hanging over the edge of the broad jetty, singing songs or skimming stones across the gently rolling sea.

They didn't really mix with the other goblins that lived in the Citadel. They all seemed to be busy, moving quietly about their jobs and mostly ignoring the visitors. The guards weren't friendly farmers like the goblins they'd met at Honeypatch or cheerful shopkeepers like the citizens of the Town on the Lake.

But mostly the children and their friends kept themselves to themselves because Broadwallow had told them not to talk about their quest – he didn't actually trust the goblins of the Last Citadel: Grimshock had been the commander of the Last Citadel. Broadwallow didn't know if the garrison was truly loyal to Queen Celestia, or if it served Grimshock and Ribaldane – but he thought he could trust Sternbrow, who was an old friend.

Sternbrow told them about Grimshock's return to the Last Citadel. Two days before they children and their friends arrived, the evil hobgoblin had appeared at the gates with an old lady (who must have been Ribaldane!) and asked if they could borrow the garrison's boat. With no reason to say no, Sternbrow had lent it to them. They'd set sail straight away.

That meant they had a four-day head start – five by the time Orobus was able to land in the ashy waste outside the tall front gate of the Last Citadel. The huge dragon was scared and scratched, one eye half-closed by a bruise from her battle with the snakes. But she seemed to heal quickly. The holes the augers had made in her wings had already vanished and even the dreadful wounds in her underside seemed almost healed.

"Are you alright, Orobus?" the girl asked.

"Penny, I am tired but happy," she said. "Ready to help you further if you wish. Is there something I can do?"

Broadwallow spoke. "Can you be carrying us again, mighty Orobus?" he asked. "Our quarry has escaped – to the north, across the sea. We must follow. Can you take us to the Pole?"

"Of course, captain," she replied. "When do you wish to go?"

"As soon as we can," he said. "I must be checking my cousin is fully recovered before we set out, but time is pressing. How long will it take to reach the frozen lands, do you think?"

"Flying as fast as I can, it would take me half a day," said Orobus, puffing steam through her nostrils. "But carrying a cargo… we could leave at midday today and by midday tomorrow we should be at the edges of the great ice sheet."

Broadwallow nodded. "I shall be making arrangements for Sternbrow to look after our animals here and prepare food for us to take," he said. "Girl Pen, please be telling our companions to be ready to depart as soon as we have eaten the midday meal."

"Yes sir, captain sir," Penny said, saluting. A smile brightened the hobgoblin's usually serious face and he saluted back.

Glad to be busy, the friends gathered their things together quickly and went to the Citadel's giant hall for one last meal – slugs for the goblins, boiled centipede with fluffy rice and carrots for everyone else – then they headed out to where Orobus was waiting. Sternbrow had come to see them off. He and Broadwallow exchanged handshakes and muttered confidences, then everyone climbed onto the dragon.

Nobody said much. As they sat there, Penny realised: this was it. They were about to embark on the final leg of their journey. When they got to the North Pole, they'd have to face Ribaldane and Grimshock – and she had to beat them this time, not blow the whistle and run away. Suddenly she felt butterflies flapping in her stomach – butterflies as big as the dragon.

Then Orobus spoke and Penny felt much better. She realised that at least this time she'd have her friends with her. "Is everybody ready?" the dragon asked. "It will be a long flight, so please try to make yourselves comfortable. Now, let us go…"

And she sprang into the air, beating her wings. The Last Citadel and the still-smouldering valley dropped away as Orobus flew almost straight up into the air.

It was a long flight and incredibly boring. Only Buddy – who was small enough, nimble enough and brave enough to move about on the dragon's back while she was flying – seemed to enjoy it. The rest sat, mostly in silence – though the noise of the wind was so loud it made talking difficult anyway. All they had to look at was mile after mile of empty sea rolling past.

Sunset came and still there was no sign of land, even on the horizon. The air was getting colder – though Penny wasn't sure if it was because they were heading further towards the frozen lands of the north or just because the sun was going down.

As the stars came out, Pickatina passed out the food. Bread rolls filled with a funny runny cheese – Penny didn't like it much, but there wasn't anything else to eat, so she chewed it slowly.

"What was the cheesy stuff in those sandwiches, Pickatina?" asked Frank, who'd already finished eating his. But Penny could tell from his voice that he hadn't liked the taste much either.

"Do you like it, Frank?" she shouted back. "We were lucky Sternbrow is a friend of Broadwallow's or we wouldn't have got it. It is a great delicacy – very hard to find. We call it sputum."

"Spew-tum?" queried Frank. "Where does it come from?"

"There is a kind of insect…" began Pickatina.

"Stop! I don't want to hear," cried Frank, but it was too late.

"…and the female hangs balls of sputum from sticks and lays her eggs inside it," finished Pickatina. "If you find a fresh egg ball, you can harvest the sputum. Delicious, isn't it?"

"Yes…" replied Frank weakly, trying to be polite. When nobody was looking, Penny dropped her sandwich into the sea.

Somehow, Penny slept well that night. She wasn't sure how – she just suddenly jerked upright, realising she'd been asleep. It was a cold morning, the sun just rising in the east.

"How much further is it, Orobus?" she called.

"I do not know exactly, Penny," replied the dragon. "I have never been there before – but I think we have made good time. Look, can you see the edge of the ice sheet ahead?" And, sure enough, on the horizon the girl could see a thin line of white against the sea, misty clouds hanging above it. Somewhere down there, the Black Legion was waiting. And so was Ribaldane.

Chapter Fifty Seven

On the Ice

Gradually Orobus descended. The sea was still below her, like a vast rumpled sheet of blue-black denim with occasional threads of white showing – waves breaking. It was cold now. Icy, bone-achingly cold. Occasional wisps of steam from the dragon's nostrils blew back over her passengers, warm and damp.

Ahead was the edge of the ice sheet. It wasn't what Penny had expected – something picturesque with penguins waddling down to the sea, perhaps. Certainly, she hadn't imagined it would look like this. Towering cliffs of brilliant white ice rose from the water. Waves broke against them, spray flung high into the sky. As they got closer they heard the roar and boom of the ocean beating against the edge of ice sheet.

"Over there, look – do you see?" shouted Bud, who'd come to stand beside the girl. He was pointing to the left. Penny couldn't see anything.

"What do you see, young elf?" asked the dragon.

"Head west – there's a boat there. By the cliffs," Bud yelled.

"So they are here already," said Pickatina sadly. "I had

hoped we would have overtaken them – but I am sure Mistress harnessed some narwhals to tow the boat and make good speed."

Orobus banked to the side and flew even lower – skimming the tops of the waves now. She flew along the line of the ice cliffs so they loomed overhead, at least a hundred meters tall.

And then Penny saw the boat. It wasn't very big – no more than four metres long and very slender. It had a tall mast, though no sail was hoisted. It was bobbing beside a small jetty of clear ice that projected out above the water. As Orobus flew past, the girl saw a flight of stairs cut into the ice.

Orobus soared up again, turning in a wide, slow circle and gliding down to the top of the ice sheet. The friends all leaned out as far over the side of her massive neck as much as they dared, staring down – but naturally it was Bud who shouted first.

"There!" he cried, pointing. "Tracks. To your left, dragon."

Orobus turned, flying as slowly as she could. They were very near the surface of the ice now. Over the noise of the wind Penny heard the others gasp, then she saw it too – a dark hole in the ice, which had to be where the stairs from the boat emerged. Tracks led away from there, into the broad, white expanse of snow.

"I can follow the trail," called Orobus, "But I must warn you – I do not think it is safe for me to land on the ice."

"It's pretty thick, you know," shouted Frank. "I think it's strong enough to take your weight, Orobus."

"You misunderstand me, Frank," replied the dragon. "I am fire, that is ice. If I land on it I would melt into it very rapidly – and at the same time it would quench me. The longer I touched it, the more of it I would melt and the weaker I would become. I think I would be trapped, sinking down into the depths of the ice sheet. And that would be the end of me."

"Okay, so how are we going to get down?" Penny asked.

"We will have to jump," yelled Broadwallow. "But do not fear – the snow will give us a soft landing."

"But what about coming home again?" Frank shouted. "How will Orobus be able to pick us up if she can't land on the ice?"

"I will not be able to do that, Frank," said Orobus sadly. "You will have to use the boat to return. But have no fear – I shall be waiting for you at the Peninsula of Thorns. I have business there with the rest of the great snakes."

"Let's not get too far ahead of ourselves, eh!" shouted Bud. "I can see where these tracks go – and that's dead straight all the way to the horizon. I can't see the end of them. So we're going to be in your company for a good while yet, dragon."

But it scared Penny to think that Orobus wouldn't be there when they caught up with Ribaldane and Grimshock. She had lost the skipping rope, lost the metal box and the secateurs – but that hadn't seemed to matter so much when she had a dragon on her side. But now they were on the ice and Orobus couldn't stay…

They sat in silence as the enormous golden dragon flew across the ice sheet. It wasn't completely flat – in fact, it reminded Penny of the flower plains in some ways. There were small, gently rolling hills and in places there were strange forms apparently carved out of blocks of ice – like snowmen that had melted into odd shapes and then refrozen. Gradually Penny realised they were heading towards something – a tall, straight-edged shape standing clear of the rest of the ice sheet.

"What's that ahead?" she called.

"That will be the Silent Palace," called back Broadwallow. "It is where the Black Legion was banished. It is where the Mistress is headed. Mr Greenleaf, do you see her ahead of us?"

"Sorry Captain," replied Buddy. "All I see is tracks. I think they must have got there already."

"So we're too late?" Penny asked.

"I do not think so," shouted Pickatina. "If the Mistress is already in the Palace, she can only just have got there. Those tracks would not be staying visible for long. They are only just ahead of us. We still have time."

"But once they get in there, surely it's not going to take them very long to do what they have to do and blow the trumpet?" asked Frank.

"The Silent Palace is not an easy place," shouted Broadwallow, who was sitting furthest back on the dragon's neck. "It is a maze. Only in the centre can the trumpet be sounded to wake the Legion. And the Mistress will have to find her way through to the centre before we get there."

"But she has a head start," Penny said.

"Yes, but we have a map," replied Broadwallow. "That is what Sternbrow and Paisley and I were making in the Last Citadel. We pieced together directions around the Silent Palace, from fragments of old books and notes left by the builders. It is said you can wander in there for days if you do not know the way."

"Won't Ribaldane have a map as well?" Frank asked.

"We cannot be certain," replied Broadwallow. "But we can hope. And if we can hope, we can have the courage to continue."

"And now, my friends," called Orobus, "The time has come for you to continue without me. The Silent Palace is here – I will fly round to find the deepest snow banks for you to jump into."

And that's what she did, giving the children a good look at the outside of the Silent Palace. It was huge. Far bigger than Bradley Hall, bigger than the Last Citadel – it was only one building but it was as big as a village. It was laid out in the shape of a massive six-pointed star and seemed to be built entirely of ice, great blocks joined together to make the towering walls and one massive translucent sheet covering it with a gently sloping dome. Just looking at it made Penny shiver. She could only see one entrance – and Ribaldane's tracks led straight to it.

"I don't think it matters where you jump, my friends – the snow is the same all the way round the palace," Orobus said at last. "I will go as low and as slowly as I can – try to jump near the door. I wish you luck – be brave and be careful."

"Alright, everyone," called Broadwallow. "I will be counting to three and let us all jump together. On your feet and ready. One... Two... THREE!"

Maybe Pickatina gave Penny a little push. Otherwise, how could the girl have done it? They weren't very high above the snowy surface of the ice anyway – but Penny still didn't like the thought of jumping. Then, before she could even think about it properly, she was landing in the freezing, fluffy snow. She sank in up to her knees, then rolled forwards, getting covered in it.

She sat up in time to see Orobus soaring up into the sky and waved to her, then turned to her friends. Paisley was helping Caro Elora to her feet, Broadwallow and Frank were laughing as they pulled Pickatina upright. Bud was coughing but also smiling, only his head showing above the snow. Penny smiled to herself and made a snowball to throw at Frank.

And that was when she heard the howl of wolves. They were behind them, but sounded close. Broadwallow issued the order: "Quick, friends – into the palace!"

And they ran.

Chapter Fifty Eight

Wolves

Snow makes running hard. It wasn't all that far from where they'd landed in the snow to the entrance to the Silent Palace. Maybe half as long as the drive that led from the Little House to Bradley Hall. But it felt like miles as Penny tried to run there. The thick snow made it so hard it felt like she wasn't moving – she had to lift each leg up really high then take a step, plunging her foot back down into the snow until it came up to her knee. Then she could take another step.

Bud had climbed up on to the surface of the snow – he was so light he wasn't sinking into it. He ran so fast that soon he was just a dot disappearing towards the distant door. Caro Elora and Paisley also passed the girl, trotting rapidly on the surface of the snow. But Pickatina, Broadwallow, Frank and Penny lumbered along, half-tripping and half-running through the snow.

Paisley and Caro Elora reached the entrance and turned to wave to their friends. Penny heard the wolves howl somewhere behind her, but she didn't slow down or turn to see where they were. But they sounded closer… A lot closer.

And they were. Penny was more than halfway to the entrance when she heard a patter of feet and a grey-white shape flashed past her. Suddenly wolves were all around them, jumping nimbly past. Frank shouted and swung his arms wildly at one as it leapt past him, though he didn't hit it.

But the wolves hadn't tried to hurt anyone. They ran past the friends, forming a line between them and the Silent Palace as they stopped running and drew closer together. There must have been forty wolves in the pack – some were looking towards the huge building, where Paisley, Caro Elora and Bud stood helplessly watching. But most of the wolves turned to face the humans and the goblins. Broadwallow drew his sword.

The wolves weren't as large as the Faerieland dogs, but they were bigger than any wolf Penny had ever seen in a zoo. The largest of them, a grizzled grey animal, stepped forward. His head was at the same height as the girl's and he looked at her with intelligent eyes. He regarded her as if *she* was the dangerous creature. Then the wolf switched his attention to Broadwallow.

"Why do you bring humans here?" he asked, though the words sounded funny. Penny realised his mouth wasn't the best shape for forming words they could understand.

"Our business is not with you, scourge of the ice," said Pickatina. "We are seeking to prevent the Black Legion being awoken. You see the tracks – you know the Silent Palace has already been entered."

"Of course we see the tracks. Of course we know," replied the wolf impatiently. "Why do you think we came? There is nothing for us at the Pole. We would not have come if our watchers had not warned us of travellers heading to the Palace."

"We are not the ones you seek," said Broadwallow. "We have come to stop them. Just as you have come."

"We cannot stop them now they are inside," said the wolf. "We cannot cross the threshold. Enchantments forbid it."

"But we can enter," said Pickatina. "That is why we are here – to go into the Palace and stop the Legion being awoken."

"That is why you have brought humans, is it?" asked the wolf. "How do I know we can trust you? How do I know that you are not the ones trying to wake the Legion and those who preceded you are not actually trying to prevent you doing this?"

"The ones who came first were Ribaldane, Mistress of Lies, with her servant," replied Pickatina. "Do you think she is more likely or less likely to wake the Legion than Queen Celestia's handmaiden and the captain of her guard? We are coming here to stop them – and send the Legion back to sleep if it comes to it."

The wolf stared hard at Pickatina. For a long time, nobody spoke. Eventually the wolf shook his head.

"Yes, the Mistress of Lies could command the Legion," he sighed. "You will need a human if you are to succeed. But you will have to defeat the Mistress – and that will be no small task."

"Excuse me," said Frank. "What do you mean, 'you will need a human'? What are you talking about?"

"Only a human can command the Black Legion," said the wolf. "The mistress is not strictly a human any more, but she and her sisters were, once – long ago. She is human enough that she will be obeyed. But these goblins or faerie folk… the Legion would not obey them. If you win through, one of you humans will have to order the Legion to return to sleep."

"Did you know this, Pickatina?" Penny asked slowly, blood pounding in her ears.

"In truth, Girl Pen, I did. But I did not wish to be worrying you with this knowledge," she said. "And as the mighty wolf says, defeating the Mistress will be our great task. If we can manage that, the giving of the order will be a simple matter."

"You will have to hurry," said the wolf, gesturing with his head. The other wolves separated, clearing a path between them so the children and their friends could walk to the Silent Palace.

"So what will you do?" Frank asked. "And who are you?"

"I am Soren, chief of the ice guard," replied the wolf. "And we will guard your back. Now the Silent Palace has been entered, the bears are sure to come. If you are successful, you do not want to come out of the Palace to find the bears here."

"And if we're unsuccessful?" asked Frank.

"Then you won't be coming out of the Palace," said Soren.

Nobody said anything – there didn't seem to be any more to say. They just walked slowly through the wolves to where Paisley, Caro Elora and Bud were waiting in front of the Silent Palace.

The entrance was a wide arch in a wall as wide as the front of Bradley Hall and twice as tall. And that wall was the tiny point of one arm of the star-shaped structure. From where she stood, Penny could see the arm of the star sloping off for what must have been at least half a mile, to where it joined the massive central part of the Palace.

There was no gate, no door – just the open arch. Yet there was no snow on the other side of it. It was blown in a drift up to the edge of the archway, but then stopped abruptly as if it was up against a piece of glass. But it wasn't glass keeping the snow out of the Palace – Penny realised it had to be magic. The same enchantments that kept the wolves outside.

Together, the children and goblins walked through the arch. Penny's teeth were chattering and her feet were numb with cold, but at least stepping inside got them out of the cold wind that had been blowing. Actually – it was surprisingly warm in the Palace, even stepping a little way over the threshold.

Ahead of lay a choice of two wide passageways. They were as wide as a main road. A cold white light came from above – the icy roof was letting the daylight shine through. The walls of the corridors were made of dirty grey-white ice, carved with strange patterns that extended all the way from the floor to the ceiling.

But the corridors were dominated by the soldiers. There were hundreds of them. They stood as still as statues, in neat niches carved into the walls on each side of both passageways, all the way down the corridors for as far as the eye could see.

They looked almost like those suits of armour you see in museums, but they were bigger – much bigger. Each massive figures was at least three metres tall, with legs like treetrunks and long arms ending in huge fists. Each warrior seemed to have a slightly different outfit, though they mostly favoured horned helmets, spiky armour and massive swords or big, double-headed axes. And all of their armour and equipment was glossy black.

"So this is the Black Legion," said Frank, his voice echoing in the huge corridor. "What kind of creatures are they?"

"They look like… like trolls," said Pickatina. She sounded terrified. "If they wake up and we are here… Trolls eat goblins. That's what our legends say."

Broadwallow grunted, "I would like to be seing them try." Then he chuckled. "Actually, cousin, perhaps I would rather not. I would not go quietly… but neither would I relish facing the Legion. And certainly not on my own."

"Better make sure they don't wake up, then," said Frank. "Come on, which way do we go? I thought you had a map."

"I do, Frank," replied Paisley, his deep voice booming in the frozen corridor. "We start off heading in this direction."

With that, the wiry little pixie led the way into the Silent Palace, Caro Elora at his side, looking confident and happy. But Penny wondered if she was the only one who was worrying: what would they do when they caught up with Ribaldane?

Chapter Fifty Nine

Maritz

"I wish we'd brought the dogs," said Frank, after they'd walked for five minutes along the icy corridor of the Silent Palace.

"Is that because they're nice and warm?" Penny asked, "Or

because you're feeling too lazy to walk?" She smiled to show that she was only teasing and didn't mean it.

"No, Penny, it's neither of those things," Frank replied, a bit stiffly. She thought she might have hurt his feelings.

"I was only joking. Sorry. Didn't mean to upset you."

"Hmmm," said Frank. "Actually, hang on everyone. Before we go any further, this might be important. I said I wished we had the dogs because I thought one of them might be able to track Ribaldane and Grimshock – you know, sniff them out and follow their scent."

"That is a grand plan, Frank," said Paisley, eyes lighting up as he understood what Frank was driving at. "You are thinking the wolves would be able to perform the same service for us."

"You forget, worthy Paisley: they are forbidden from entering the Silent Palace," said Broadwallow.

"They are forbidden from crossing the threshold," corrected Paisley. "I wondered if Lady Pickatina might shrink a wolf, carry it across the threshold, then return it to its normal size. Then the wolf would not have crossed the threshold on its own."

"It has to be worth a try," said Frank. "I know wolves are great hunters. They must be able to follow scent trails."

But when they hurried back to the entrance and looked outside, the wolves were nowhere to be seen. They'd clearly set off to intercept the bears they thought would be coming.

"Mr Greenleaf," said Broadwallow. "Would you be so kind as to run after the wolves and ask Soren if he or one of his kin would return with you. Explain the plan Paisley has proposed."

Buddy bowed and set off at a run, leaving the palace and flashing out across the snow after the wolves. He really did move amazingly quickly – he disappeared from sight in no time.

"That was a good idea, Frank," Penny whispered while they waited. It wasn't long before they saw a grey dot appear from the dazzlingly white snow outside, heading our way. A smaller, darker dot was in front of it: Buddy jogging back casually in front of a wolf, which couldn't run as fast as the elf.

Pickatina and Broadwallow went out to meet them, but everyone else stayed inside, out of the bitingly cold wind. They could see them bowing to the wolf and explaining the plan again, though they couldn't hear what was said. It didn't look as though the wolf liked the idea very much, but he nodded a few times, then lowered his head.

Pickatina began to gently stroking the wolf's head. She must have been singing her spell as well, because the huge animal began to shrink instantly. In no time at all, Pickatina was picking the miniature wolf off the snow and walking back towards the Silent Palace. As she reached the doorway, she hesitated.

"I do not know what kind of enchantments have been placed on the threshold to keep the wolves out," she said. "It may be wise if you all stand back from the entrance. Cousin – you and Mr Greenleaf should be waiting inside, just in case the Palace should try to seal itself when I am trying to enter with the wolf."

Bud and Broadwallow hurried in, then everyone took a few paces down the corridor and turned to watch Pickatina enter. She took a deep breath, smiled bravely and… walked in. With no problems. Paisley laughed, a deep, booming laugh like car doors being slammed. "Magnificent, Lady Pickatina," he said. "You have defeated the enchantments. Frank, your idea could save us hours if the wolf is able to help us track our quarry."

Pickatina walked a little way down the first corridor and set the model-sized wolf on the floor. She soon stroked and crooned it back to full size – which was pretty big. Not as big as Soren, still so large it stood nose to nose with Pickatina.

"That was a very strange feeling," said the wolf, shaking his head. "I am Maritz, son of Soren. I am here to help you – now the lady has done her magic. But for me to do that, I am afraid my nose needs to get to know you a little better."

Pickatina introduced everyone one at a time and Maritz sniffed each member of the party carefully. He had long shaggy grey-and-white hair, with intelligent amber eyes. His mouth was half open in a kind of smile all the time.

"Now I can tell your friendly scents from the scents of the others," he explained. "I smell two of them. They have been here for a little while – maybe an hour. Not more than two. They went in this direction."

Broadwallow nodded. "That is the right direction, according to our calculations. Come, Maritz – you lead the way. Will you be warning us if we are drawing near to them?"

"Certainly, Broadwallow," the wolf replied. "There is one we follow who smells almost like you, but dirty. Him I will smell a long time before we meet him."

So they set off into the Palace again, this time with Maritz leading the way. Broadwallow was next to him, followed by Pickatina and the children. Bud was sitting on Penny's shoulder, with Paisley and Caro Elora walking at the back. The cold seemed to affect the delicate little dryad more than the others and she was moving quite slowly, though she smiled bravely enough.

The Silent Palace closed around them. It was quite a gloomy place, despite the glow coming from the roof. The endless lines of heavily armed, motionless black trolls on either side didn't make it seem any more cheerful. The friends' breath made clouds of steam that hung in the air as they walked. And of course, it wasn't really silent now they were inside. The long, cold corridor echoed with the sound of every footstep, no matter how they tried to tiptoe along. That just made the palace seem spookier – it always sounded as though they were being followed. The walls seemed to be leaning in above them. Soon they were all trying to walk as quietly as possible and hardly anyone spoke.

After turning a few corners, walking down more gloomy passages, when suddenly Maritz stopped. He seemed to get bigger, the hair on his shoulders and back standing up. He looked up at Broadwallow, who was standing next to him.

"Up ahead," Maritz panted. "The one like you is waiting. He is alone. The other one is not there."

Broadwallow nodded, a grim smile of satisfaction spreading slowly across his face. He took two steps forward and unsheathed his sword. "I have been looking forward to this," he muttered.

Slowly, they all walked forwards – Broadwallow a couple of steps ahead of the rest, with Martiz walking at his heels. They turned one more corner and emerged into a huge triangular chamber lined with more of the Legion's soldiers.

And in the middle of it stood Grimshock. He was smiling.

"I had hoped that you would be the one they sent, youngling," he said, drawing his own huge sword and pointing it at Broadwallow. "I'll enjoy teaching you some manners."

"Who could learn manners from a pig?" replied Broadwallow. There was an electric air of tension as the two began to advance slowly towards each other.

Then Frank laughed.

Everyone looked at him. Even Broadwallow half turned.

"Still dragging that offal around, are you?" sneered Grimshock. "I should have fed you to the snake, boy. Maybe I'll still take you back and do that."

"What an idiot," scoffed Frank, pointing at Grimshock. "Look at him, Penny. He's still carrying your bag around and he hasn't even opened it. He's too dumb to use what's inside."

Pickatina and Paisley gasped, Broadwallow snarled and Grimshock laughed. He jumped backwards, dropping his sword and fumbling at where Penny's bag was still hanging round his neck like a trophy. The girl thought the hobgoblin was just going to rip it open, but he didn't. Somehow he managed to open it quite delicately and, even as Broadwallow lunged at him, Grimshock put his hand into the bag.

And then his expression changed. He seemed to go momentarily grey, he staggered to one side, falling to his knees. He fixed Frank with a blood-shot eye and opened his mouth to speak… then Broadwallow was there. He swung his sword and cut Grimshock's head clean off his shoulders. His body fell sideways with an echoing crash and didn't move.

Everyone was shocked. They stood, unmoving, staring at the body. In the silence, Frank calmly walked over to the body. He undid the straps on Penny's bag and took if off Grimshock's hand. He reached inside and held up the metal box. "He touched the death metal," Frank explained. "I said he was an idiot."

Chapter Sixty

Brothers

Only Frank seemed able to move after Grimshock died. The rest just stood there, silent. Frank gave Penny back her bag. There was a tiny speck of blood on one of the straps, but that was it.

Penny didn't know what to think or feel. On the one hand, one of their enemies was dead, defeated. Grimshock had been a monster. Now he could never hurt Penny or Frank or Pickatina again. He would never return to the Elfholme to terrorise Buddy's people. But on the other hand... she'd seen him die. And Penny didn't know how she felt about that. She decided to try not to think about it.

At least she had the skipping rope back – not to mention the metal box and the secateurs. Just touching the death metal had done for Grimshock – or weakened him enough for Broadwallow to behead him easily. And now Penny had the skipping rope again, she felt a little more confident. She reached into the bag and squeezed one of the handles, then put the bag on her back.

They all stood there for a few minutes longer, before Pickatina spoke. "How do you feel, cousin?" she asked.

Broadwallow shook his huge head slowly. When he spoke, his voice sounded raw. Penny realised he was trying not to cry. "It is done," he said simply. "I wish it had not come to this. I wish he had never turned to the Mistress. I wish I had never had to report him, to drive him out, to hunt him down. But I am not sorry that I killed him. He had to die and I am glad I was the one who ended it – even though he was my brother."

Penny gasped. "Grimshock was your brother?"

"Yes, Girl Pen," he said sadly. "My older brother – 200 years older than me. I was just a recruit when I discovered he had been spying for the Mistress of Lies. That he had been betraying Queen Celestia. He was the captain of her guard. I denounced him and my brother fled.

"But he was not always evil. It was the years he spent in the wilderness, the years with the Mistress that turned him so," Broadwallow added. "He used to be kind and wise and brave. But he was wanting fame and honour, a chance to be winning renown. That was when he changed. He began to study our legends. He believed them. Began to yearn for a return to the old times – when we lived in your world and humans were slaves."

"He was corrupted by the Mistress," said Pickatina, sounding bitter. "He believed her lies. He chose to serve her – and he served her well. As I know too well."

"I know you will not miss him, Lady," said Broadwallow. "And I will not be missing the monster he became – but I still remember when he first came home from the guard, as a young goblin. I was little more than a baby. He had his shiny armour on and he was so proud. He swung me up onto his shoulders and told me that if I worked hard and ate my snails, shells and all, one day I could join the guard and be just like him. And I did."

"No you did not, Broadwallow," said Pickatina firmly. "You never became like him. You never became proud or cold or arrogant. You never regarded the rest of creation as lesser beings. You never came to love the darkness, to seek power over others. And you never kidnapped me, forcing me to serve the Mistress."

"Is that what happened, Pickatina?" Frank asked. "It was Grimshock's fault that you had to serve Ribaldane?"

"He came to see me. It was a sunny day and we walked in the gardens of the palace. Everything was normal. And he gave me a present – a beautiful silver necklace. I thought it was the most wonderful thing anyone had ever given me," Pickatina sighed. "Of course, it was the witch's throttle. As soon as I put it on, I was in her power. Grimshock carried me to her – it was the day he fled Queen Celestia's court."

Caro Elora came and hugged Pickatina. "He can never hurt you again," she said, then she looked at Broadwallow. "Or you, captain. Your honour is restored." Broadwallow said nothing.

"Come, friends," said Paisley, clearing his throat with a sound like a scaffolding pipe falling down a well. "Let us leave this chamber. We can do no more here now."

"Yes, we should leave," said Maritz. "The smell of the blood is strong. I may not be able to pick up the scent straight away. The longer I am here, the harder it will be to follow the trail of the Mistress of Lies."

"So which way do we go?" asked Frank.

"I cannot tell," replied the wolf. He seemed to shrug. "There is blood."

"It is this way," said Broadwallow listlessly, nodding to a door. "That is what we calculated, was it not, good Paisley?"

The little Pixie nodded. He walked past Broadwallow, patting him on the leg – he wasn't tall enough to reach to pat the hobgoblin on the back. "I shall lead with Maritz for a while, my friend," he said. "You guard the rear."

So that was how they left the chamber. Grimshock's headless body was still bleeding onto the icy floor, arms thrown wide. They just walked past – first Paisley and Maritz, then Caro Elora and Pickatina, then Penny and Frank, with Bud still on the girl's shoulder. Broadwallow was the last to leave.

The wolf and the pixie led the way down another corridor, shorter than the first ones. It was still lined with the ominous, enormous statue-like soldiers of the Black Legion. They stood silent in the alcoves carved into the ice walls. Penny shivered as she looked at them. Frank must have realised, because he patted her awkwardly on the shoulder.

"Don't worry about them, Penny," he said. "We got your bag back. Now we have the iron stuff and the skipping rope, they won't be able to stop us."

"You're not bothered about what happened back there, are you Frank?" she asked. It suddenly felt really important.

"Well, I wouldn't say that," he said slowly and seriously. "But the way I see it, Grimshock wouldn't have hesitated to cut my head off or feed me to his precious snakes – if he could. It was him or me. I'm just sorry it was Broadwallow who cut his head off, because the big fella seems to be taking it badly."

Penny glanced back and saw Frank was right. Broadwallow looked miserable. Huge silent tears glittered on his cheeks.

"It would have been better for everyone if Grimshock had just cut his finger on the secateurs and gone quietly," the boy said.

Penny slowed down so Broadwallow caught up with her. "Can I do anything to help you, Broadwallow?" she asked.

He shook his head. "There is nothing, Girl Pen," he said. "I had to do a terrible thing. But it had to be done."

"I think you helped him," she said as kindly as she could. "He'd touched the death metal – so he was dying slowly anyway. You just spared him any suffering in the last few moments. Like a vet putting an old dog to sleep."

"What is a vet?" asked Broadwallow. Before Penny could explain, he patted her on the shoulder. "But I thank you for your words, Girl Pen. Maybe you are right. Maybe I did spare my brother some pain and gave him a respectful, warrior's death."

She smiled up at him. "And you know you did the right thing," she told him. "The Queen would have wanted you to stop him. You were just doing your duty."

Broadwallow tried to smile, though he still looked incredibly sad. Penny reached out and squeezed his massive hand.

They'd reached a junction now and stopped. Paisley was talking earnestly to Maritz, though Penny couldn't hear what was being said. The wolf was taller than the pixie, so they looked especially comical, standing having a very serious conference. Eventually, Paisley came back to Broadwallow.

"The wolf cannot pick up the scent," he said. "The smell of blood still fills his nostrils. And I cannot remember the right way at this point. Can you remember, Broadwallow?"

"We go right here, on a short passage, then turn left," said Broadwallow glumly. "The way will be guarded by a centurion."

"What's a centurion?" Penny asked.

"A captain like Broadwallow," explained Pickatina. "One of the mightiest of the Legion's soldiers."

Frank and Caro Elora had already taken a few steps along the corridor and suddenly the boy called to the others. "Wow! come and look at this one!"

Frank normally sounded this excited only when he'd found a new Transformer, an X-Box game or a bar of chocolate. Without waiting to see if anyone was following, he set off along the corridor. The rest hurried to catch up. In fact, Frank had gone only a dozen metres. Another corridor branched off on the left. And standing in a niche carved into the corner where the two passages met was a huge black-armoured figure that had to be the centurion. This one was twice as big as Broadwallow – far bigger than the other soldiers they'd passed.

This had to be the centurion. Penny stood and stared up at it. The creature's face was hidden behind a smooth, flat helmet with a slit where the eyes would have been. His massive arms were bent at the elbows, both hands clasped in front of his chest around the shaft of a tall spear that was planted in the ice at his feet. The head of the spear was leaf-shaped and sharp-edged. Beneath it was a cross-piece from which hung a tattered black flag and a string of yellow-white skulls. Human-looking skulls.

"The centurion guards the way!" said Paisley, his voice booming in the icy corridor. "This is it." And he went to take a step down the corridor. When the centurion moved.

Chapter Sixty One
The Centurion

The speed of the centurion was terrifying. One second it was a statue, icy black but frozen. The next second its spear was blocking the corridor, the blade almost touching Paisley's neck.

It made a rough, grating sound like two stones being rubbed together. Penny assumed it was talking, but she couldn't understand it. She looked at Pickatina, who looked just as confused. And terrified. Penny hadn't seen her so scared before, even when they'd fled from the augers and from the giant snakes. Not even when the little goblin had confronted Grimshock in the cellar when they first met.

Paisley took half a step back, but the centurion didn't move. So Paisley stepped back again and the creature snapped back into its previous position, spear held upright in front of it. As if it had never moved.

The friends looked at each other. Nobody spoke. Frank took a step closer to the centurion, looking up at it in wonder. Slowly, he reached out a hand, hesitated… then knocked on the armour on its leg. Nothing happened, though there was a ringing echo that sounded like Paisley sneezing.

"Why doesn't it do anything now?" Frank asked. "If it wants to talk to us, why not now? Surely if it's guarding the corridor…"

"It may not be truly awake," said Pickatina. "You see how the others are like statues. It could be that this one leaves its magical slumber only if someone steps into its corridor."

"Well how are we going to get past it?" Penny asked.

"How did Ribaldane get past it?" asked Frank.

"Has the Mistress passed this point?" asked Paisley, looking at Maritz.

The wolf shook himself in a way that made Penny think he was shrugging again. "I cannot be sure," he said. "I can detect another scent – a dusty scent like old lavender and spiders and dry, dry wood. That is the smell of the Mistress of Lies, but it is elusive. I know she was here. I cannot tell which way she went."

"I can tell you which way she went," said Pickatina, sounding faintly sick. "She has passed the centurion. I know it. She knew of the building of the Silent Palace. She will know of its guardians – you can be sure, cousin, that if you were able to find out something of the secrets of this place she has penetrated all of them. She will have been learning the ways of the Palace before coming. She will have known how to pass the centurion."

"So what do we do?" asked Penny. "Can you think what kind of magic she would have done to get past it, Pickatina?"

"I cannot, Girl Pen," she said sadly.

"Can we speak to it?" asked Frank. "It made a noise – but only when Paisley tried to pass. Maybe it asked for a password."

"None of us knows what it said," Broadwallow said.

"Actually, I do," said Bud. "That's old troll – very similar to old elvish. He asked on whose orders we came here."

Penny thought Pickatina's eyes would pop from her head as the goblin stared at Bud. "Can you reply to it?" she asked.

"I can try, if you like," said Bud. Without waiting for a reply the little elf took two steps into the corridor.

Instantly the centurion sprang into life again. Suddenly the tip of his spear was pointing at Bud's head – how it got there so fast, was amazing. Penny didn't even see it move. Again, the centurion rasped out its question.

Buddy squeaked an answer, but the troll didn't move. The elf looked at his friends helplessly. "I told it the Queen of the Faeriefolk had sent us, to protect the Legion," he said. "What else can I try?"

"Just tell it to stand aside and let us pass," said Frank.

And the centurion reacted. The featureless helmet swivelled in Frank's direction, then cocked to one side. Frank said, a little nervously, "Can you hear me?"

There was a pause that seemed to last for hours but was

probably not even a minute. Then the centurion rasped another short noise. "He just said one word," said Bud. "He said, 'human'. That's all."

"Go on, Frank," Penny whispered. "Tell it to let us pass."

Frank looked nervous, but nodded. "Centurion," he said. "Return to your post and let us pass. All of us. Humans, goblins, wolf, elf, pixie and dryad. Let us pass."

There was another awful pause, then the enormous troll rasped another word. And then, without seeming to move, it was back in its original position: back straight, head up, spear resting on the floor, held by both hands in front of its chest.

"It just said, 'Accepted'," said Buddy.

So everyone cautiously edged past the centurion, nervously watching it. Penny still half-expected the huge spear to flash out fast enough to cut Pickatina in half as the goblin walked ahead of her – but it didn't come. Once they were safely past the huge creature, they spread out slightly and sped up, hurrying along the corridor until the centurion was far behind.

"Why do you think it did what I told it to do?" asked Frank.

"The Legion needs a human commander," said Pickatina. "If there is more than one human, it follows whoever has been blowing the silver trumpet – but otherwise the legion will be obeying any human who dares to command it."

"That's why Queen Celestia really sent us, wasn't it?" Penny asked. "She wasn't punishing us for having helped Ribaldane get the trumpet but she knew that, at the end, you'd need me or Frank to take charge and tell the Legion what to do."

"Why didn't she tell us?" asked Frank. He sounded angry. "If we have to do this, why didn't she warn us?"

"For the same reasons I was not mentioning it, I believe," said Pickatina. "To avoid scaring you, to avoid putting pressure on you. More than anything, to protect you.

"We have been on a terrible quest – and it is not over yet," she continued. "But can you imagine your fear if you had known the safest thing for Ribaldane to do would be to kill you? Because with Queen Celestia in her palace, the only people in Faerieland besides the Mistress who could command the Legion are you, Boy Frank, and you, Girl Pen. If she had killed you, there would have been no way we could stop her. The only surprise is that Grimshock was not murdering you at the earliest opportunity."

The children looked at each other. Frank saw Penny's eyes light up as the girl understood something.

"She's not sure," Penny said. "Even now, I bet she still had doubts. I bet that's why she left Grimshock out there."

"What do you mean, Girl Pen?" asked Pickatina.

"She means," said Frank, "That even when she'd captured us, Ribaldane was only ever going to feed me to the snake. Not Penny. Just me. Not because I was especially annoying. But because Ribaldane realised she needed to keep one human handy, just in case the Legion wouldn't obey her."

"Grimshock was meant to capture us," Penny said. "Not kill us. Even now, she isn't sure. You heard what Soren said – Ribaldane 'used to be human'. Well, that's not the same as 'is human'. So even now she wants a back-up plan: a soft, stupid little human who'll shut up and do what Ribaldane tells her. Well, I won't be that girl any more."

"But if the Mistress came this way, it means the centurion already obeyed her," said Paisley. "That means she *will* be able to command the Legion."

"Probably," admitted Frank. "Otherwise she'd have been waiting for us back there, with Grimshock. But still, I wonder if she's human enough. I wonder whether the Legion would take her orders over those of a full human – like me or Penny. And I bet she's wondering that too."

"How can we find out?" asked Buddy.

"We do not want to be finding out," said Pickatina. "The only way we could would be for the Mistress to order the Legion to attack us and for Penny or Frank to be ordering it to stop. I do not think facing a giant troll army is the best way to be finding out if the creatures will follow the children or the Mistress."

"If she sounds the trumpet, I do not think the Legion will have a choice," said Paisley. "That is why we must catch her before she reaches the centre of the Palace."

"What Mighty Paisley is trying to say," said Caro Elora sweetly, "Is that we should do a bit less standing around talking and a lot more walking. Because if we stand here much longer while you try to work out who did what and why, then all we're going to catch is a cold."

Of course, she was quite right. So they carried on walking.

Chapter Sixty Two

Webs

The further they went into the Silent Palace, the more confused Penny became. It was a bafflingly complicated maze, not made any easier by the sheer huge scale of it. Paisley seemed to have puzzled out a route through it, but even with Maritz helping sniff their way along, things seemed to get confused sometimes. The little pixie would declare that he was looking for a short passage and everyone would walk a few hundred meters wondering where it was... until reaching a turning, when there would be nervous laughs as everyone decided that for the builders of the maze, a few hundred meters *was* a short passage.

The friends seemed to have been walking for hours. Penny's feet were cold and sore and she was hungry and really, really tired. But they didn't stop. They passed through four more rooms like the one where Grimshock had been waiting for them. Frank realised that these were in the points of the star – so by the time they'd walked through another four of them they realised they had to be almost all of the way round the maze.

The trap was in the sixth chamber. Luckily, Maritz smelled it as he approached, cocking his head to one side and whining.

"What is it?" asked Paisley. The stern little pixie seemed to have taken over leading them since Broadwallow was so upset after killing Grimshock.

"It smells like... spiders up ahead," said the wolf uncertainly. "But not like spiders. It is not a good smell. I do not understand."

"Do you want me to have a look?" volunteered Buddy.

"Be careful, Mr Greenleaf," said Paisley. "Look and come straight back – take no risks."

Buddy nodded and trotted cautiously ahead. He turned a corner and vanished from sight. While they were waiting, Frank and Penny walked up to Maritz. "Is it the same kind of smell as Ribaldane?" the girl asked. "You said she smelled like spiders."

The wolf nodded his shaggy head. "It is a similar smell, but also different," he replied. "This scent is spiders and metal and cinnamon and something else I cannot identify. Something oily or sticky, if you understand? It is hard to explain to you poor-nosed humans how scents seem to us wolves. If you smell anything, it is simply a smell. To us each smell is a building, full of rooms and shadows and meanings We can walk around a smell, explore it."

"But this one you can't identify?" Frank asked.

"It is as if some of the doors in the house are locked," sighed Maritz. "There is something in the room but I cannot get close enough to know for sure what it is. And that worries me."

The friends waited in uncomfortable silence for a few minutes, breath steaming in the chilly corridor. Penny shuffled her feet. Frank's hands drummed on his legs. Paisley hummed, while Caro Elora gave the occasional cough like a bell ringing in a canary's cage. Only the two goblins waited quietly. Nobody could quite meet anyone else's eyes.

Just as Penny was about to ask if they should go and see what had happened to Buddy, the little elf returned, skipping silently down the corridor. He was grinning.

"I am alright, friends," he said. "I am sorry it took so long. Let me tell you what is ahead."

Everyone crowded round to listen. Even Broadwallow,

who went down on one knee so Buddy wouldn't have to shout.

"There is another chamber ahead, just round the next corner," he explained. "Clearly the Mistress of Lies has been there – for it is filled with spiderwebs. I was able to creep beneath and through them to the exits, but you are all too big to do that.

"So I tried to see if the web could be cut. That was when I found the problem.

"The web is full of spiders – as soon as you touch a part of it, they swarm towards you. And the web is sticky... very sticky. I have left my knife stuck to it, even though I tried very hard to pull it away. I wasn't able to cut even one thread of the web."

"So how big are the spiders," asked Frank. Penny said nothing, but she shivered, thinking of the huge spiders that had covered the inside walls of Ribaldane's tent.

"Ah, well... I was coming to that, Frank," said Bud. "Each one has a body the size of a large apple, a head the size of a conker and legs as long as mine. But they aren't real spiders. They seem to be made of brass. And each one has giant metal jaws like two curved knives."

"Like the harrows!" Penny cried.

"Yes," said Pickatina, sounding beaten. "They are favourite toys of the mistress. They are wracks."

"What are wracks?" asked Frank. "Just mechanical spiders?"

"They are much worse than normal spiders," Pickatina replied. "If they bite, their poisoned jaws break off in the wound. They keep chewing. It is almost impossible to get the jaws out."

"Sounds nasty," said Frank. "So how do we get past them?"

"Can we burn them out like the snakes?" Penny suggested.

"I do not have the trick of conjuring fire," said Pickatina. "Besides, in this palace of ice I do not think a fire would take."

"What about the skipping rope?" Penny asked.

"You must not take such a risk, Girl Pen," said Pickatina.

"No, I understand," said Frank. "If Penny can collect the wracks with her invulnerable bubble, I can finish them off with the death metal."

"It is too dangerous," said Paisley flatly. "We cannot allow you to take such a reckless risk."

"Alright then," said Frank. "So tell me what other plans do we have? Because all the time we're standing here, Ribaldane is getting further ahead."

There was a long silence. Paisley and Pickatina looked at Broadwallow, but he was staring at the floor. Eventually Paisley was the one who spoke.

"Are you absolutely sure, Lady Penny?" he sounded worried and uncertain. "I do not like this plan... but I can see no alternative. If you and Frank are willing to risk it, let us hurry."

Walking a little way away from their friends, Penny opened her bag and took the metal box and the secateurs, giving them to Frank. Then she took out the skipping rope, took a deep breath and began to skip.

Penny took great care not to fly up high above the floor – it would have been easy to do because the corridor was so tall. She reached the corner and into the room of wracks and spiderwebs.

For a moment her courage nearly failed. All she saw was a wall of grey – there were strands of web with spaces between them, but there was so much web it looked solid. Like candyfloss without any colour. Dotted within the web were dark spots that had to be the wracks, with their poisonous jaws. But before she could think any more about it or hesitate any longer, she was in.

The skipping rope ploughed serenely into the room as though it was completely empty, or filled with nothing more than a grey smoke. The web brushed up against the front of the bubble, forming a dark solid wall for a fraction of a second – but then it was gone. Penny couldn't really turn her head to see where. She just concentrated on skipping and kept going, heading towards a faintly seen towards the door on the other side of the room.

When she got into the corridor on the other side, she nearly stopped skipping. That could have been an awful mistake.

Luckily, she kept the rhythm going and skipped on the spot, turning around to look at the damage she'd done to the web. What she saw in the room she'd just crossed was a neat hole punched all the way through the wrack-web, with a load of wracks on the floor, scuttling towards her. They didn't look much like spiders – more like small crabs, though the pincers were attached to their heads rather than being waved on a set of arms. They didn't look as big as she'd expected, either. They weren't even as big as a shoe.

Penny rolled back at them, concentrating on keeping the skipping-rope bubble rolling along the floor, to squash the wracks. She rolled over them and in seconds she was back in the corridor where her friends stood.

Chapter Sixty Three

Wracks

"Don't stop, Penny," said Frank, advancing purposefully with the secateurs in one hand and the metal box in the other. He put the box on the floor with the lid open, then reached up towards the skipping-rope bubble with the secateurs.

Penny looked up and nearly screamed. A wrack was clinging – somehow – to the bubble. Maybe its magic allowed it to grip the magic of the bubble. If she'd stopped skipping and the bubble had disappeared, the wrack would have fallen on her.

As she watched, Frank gingerly closed the secateurs around one of its brass legs and flicked it into the open metal box. He flipped the lid shut with his foot.

"Just stay there while I check the rest of the bubble, okay Penny?" he said. She nodded nervously, still skipping. Frank walked slowly all around the bubble before giving a thumb's up.

"You can stop skipping now, if you like," he said. Frank picked up the box and opened it cautiously. Then he tipped it up and poured out some grey dust – all that was left of the wrack.

"That wasn't so bad. How many were in there?" he asked.

Penny shrugged. "Lots. At least twenty. I thought a load of them were chasing me."

"Blimey, Penny – you were right," Frank cried. "Watch out!" And he pushed her back a step, away from the door to the web room. Seven wracks were crawling out into the corridor, following the line of a whisp of web knocked into the passage.

"They cannot see," called Pickatina. "They have to crawl along the web. Stay away from that and you will be safe."

"Right," said Frank, sounding very grown up and business-like. "Penny, you take the box. I'll pick them up with the secateurs. Hold it open and I'll drop each one in, then you shut the lid again – really quick. Okay?"

Penny nodded. She wished Paisley or Broadwallow could have helped, but neither of them would have been able to touch the metal box. Nervously, she took it from Frank and got ready.

Actually, she didn't need to be worried. The wracks were pretty easy to get rid of. As soon as Frank touched them with the secateurs, they went limp and barely even curled their legs as he carefully lowered them towards the box. Penny opened the lid, Frank would let the wrack fall in, then the girl slammed the box shut on top of them. In no time at all, they'd got rid of the horrible mechanisms.

Frank looked at Penny and grinned. "Seven down, only thirteen to go," he said.

"Have you done it already, humans?" called Paisley from further down the corridor. "We do not wish to come too close while you have death metal out."

"We've got rid of seven of them," Penny said triumphantly. "No, eight if you count the one that clung to the bubble!"

But even at that distance, she saw Pickatina's face fall. "So how many will there be?" she asked. "I thought I'd seen about twenty in there."

"Oh, Girl Pen, I cannot say," the little goblin replied. "But surely there will be at least a hundred. Maybe two hundred."

The children looked at each other – they seemed to have the same thought at the same time. Frank held out his hand and Penny handed him the metal box. "Guess I'd better get back in there and smash up all the web," she said.

"That's right," he agreed. "But don't stay in there for too long. Go across the room and back, then stop here so I can check there's none clinging to your bubble before you stop skipping. I don't want one of those things dropping on you."

So the girl set off into the web room again. This time she let the bubble float up slightly, pushing a passage over to the far wall just by the door. She skipped around the edge of the room and then back into the corridor. Frank checked her over, but this time there were no wracks hanging onto the bubble.

But there were plenty coming into the corridor. Penny had barely stopped skipping when she heard a loud bang. Frank had smashed the metal box down on one that had almost crawled over to his foot. He squashed the wrack against the floor and leant on the box for a second. When he lifted it up, there was just a grey smudge on the icy floor.

"Here you go, Pen," he said, handing the box back to her. "We'll do the same lift-and-drop thing as last time, okay?"

It wasn't long before Penny had lost count of how many wracks had crawled into the corridor – but it didn't take long to get rid of them. After that she did two more runs through the web room, each time taking a different route around the walls. And each time the two children got rid of another load of wracks. As Penny went round for the last of these skip-and-smash runs, which she did quite high near the ceiling, a great mess of the web collapsed, landing in a big lump in the middle of the room. They destroyed loads and loads of wracks after that one.

As Penny was getting ready to skip into the room for a fifth time, Caro Elora came up. She stood timidly a little distance from Frank, nervously watching the secateurs.

"I have an idea, Penny," the dryad said. "Can you see more of these evil things?"

Well, she could. The all seemed to be heading in her direction now, more or less. The few tatters of web still hanging near the doorway all seemed to have a wrack or two there – though as Penny had managed to demolishe most of the web, there wasn't much other space for them to hide in. Still, there seemed to be a lot of them left.

"There's lots of them, alright," said Frank. "Most of them crawl out along one of these three or four strands of web. Penny goes back in when they stop crawling out."

"I think they stop crawling because they no longer feel any vibrations in the web – I expect that is how they hunt, just like spiders," said Caro Elora. "So what I suggest is that I hold those webs all together, wrapping the strands to make a rope. And I pull this as far into the corridor as I can. All the while, because I will be making the strands vibrate, the wracks will come. If you two could please pick them off the web before they reach me, then we'll quickly get this done."

It was a brilliant idea. Penny was impressed, though Frank just shook his head – clearly wishing he'd thought of it. Though it didn't matter who came up with it, really. All that mattered was that it worked. The children stood well back while Caro Elora picked up the bits of web and started pulling them. Straight away, they had to rush forwards to intercept the first wrack that scuttled down the web towards the dryad. Penny opened the metal box and Frank flicked it neatly inside.

It didn't take long to get rid of the rest of the wracks. They came rushing out along the web-rope thick and fast, but after five minutes, there were fewere and fewer and finally they stopped coming altogether.

The children went to look cautiously into the room, Frank gripping the secateurs and Penny holding the box raised, ready to bash anything that scuttled. A thin residue of web lay on the floor, like a grey bail of straw that had been kicked open and scattered about. A few straggly wisps of it hung from the corners. Penny was about to walk into it when Caro Elora called out to her.

"Don't walk on it!" the dryad called in her tinkling voice. "I have a problem with the web. If you step on it, you'll have it too."

Penny turned back to look at her. The dryad held up her hands, holding the web rope she'd made. "I cannot put it down," Caro Elora said. "I am stuck to it."

"Can I cut you out of it with the secateurs?" asked Frank.

"No!" Caro Elora and Penny cried.

"Frank, that's the death metal," the girl reminded him. "It mustn't touch her."

"I know," he said grimly. "But the Professor managed to cut the throttle off Pickatina, didn't he? I'd be careful. I promise." He advanced on Caro Elora with the death metal.

Chapter Sixty Four

The Trumpet Sounds

Everyone was a bit panicky. Everyone but Frank, that is, as he walked calmly towards Caro Elora with the deadly secateurs. The others rushed up towards him – but they all stopped and backed away, afraid of getting too close. They knew they couldn't risk accidentally touching the metal. Pickatina spoke, choosing her words carefully.

"If Boy Frank can cut the web right down," she said, "so only the tiniest amount is left binding Caro Elora's hands, then I may be able to unmake it."

"How does that work?" Frank asked, pausing by the frightened-looking dryad.

"The web is a thing of magic, made by the will of the Mistress," the goblin explained. "I cannot undo her concentrated will, but if you can separate a small piece of it from the whole – especially using the death metal – it may be that I can use enough of my own will to unmake that little piece of web."

"You'll magic it away," Penny said.

"That is not strictly what I shall be attempting to do, Girl Pen," smiled Pickatina. "But that will be what you see if I succeed – it will look as though I have simply magicked it away."

So Frank cut the web off near to Caro Elora's hands. It wasn't as simple as it sounds, because the pretty little dryad was so terrified of the secateurs she was shaking like a leaf. In the end, Paisley had to stand behind her, arms around her, holding her wrists to keep them steady. Very carefully, Frank used the blade of the secateurs to saw through the four silver-grey strands of web that were stuck to her palms, leaving less than a centimetre hanging free.

Pickatina put her hands on either side of Carol Elora's, then the goblin began to hum. Quietly at first, but then louder and louder. It wasn't the kind of hum a human could make – it was a strange, fluttering buzz like a swarm of bees. And then, in a sparkle of lights, the web seemed to dissolve and vanish.

"If the Mistress is paying attention," said Pickatina, "I have just told her that I am here. Though I hope she is occupied on other matters and is too busy to notice her former servant destroying a tiny part of her works."

"Actually, I'd prefer it if Ribaldane did notice," said Frank. "That might distract her, because she'd be wondering how we'd got past Grimshock. It might worry her a bit."

"Well, I am worried," said Pickatina. "Usually a witch – as you would call one who uses magic – is aware if one of her creations being undone by the will of another. Even a small part of her works being undone is like having an ant bite at your skin. I fear she will know we are still coming now – and knowing this, she may lay another trap for us."

"I doubt it, Lady," said Paisley, though he too looked worried. "We are in the final straight of the race. The Mistress of Lies will not waste time on diversions now, when victory is so nearly in her grasp. If we do not hurry now then all our efforts thus far will have been wasted. It is not far from here to the final chamber, the heart of the maze in which the trumpet may be sounded to rouse the Legion. We must hurry."

So the friends set off again. There was still quite a lot of the web lying in piles on the floor of the chamber where the wracks had been, like nasty grey straw. There was a clear path across to one door, but there was another door from the chamber that was almost totally blocked by a big heap of broken web.

"I am afraid that's the way we have to go," said Paisley, pointing at the blocked door. Penny shrugged and reached into her backpack, taking out the skipping rope and dumping the bag on the floor.

"Stand back, everyone," she said. Keeping the rope low, she skipped to the big pile of web and pushed it out of the way, skipping straight through the doorway and into the next corridor.

She'd just stopped skipping, which cancelled her invulnerable bubble, when she saw something lying on the floor in front of her. Without thinking, she bent down to see what it was – even though as she leaned forwards, part of her brain was shouting that this was a bad thing to do.

It was. The thing jumped at her. It was a long glove – the kind of thing ladies wear with evening dresses, silky and elegant and slim. And it was trying to kill her.

Penny caught it just as the fingers were spreading to grab her by the throat. The force of it knocked her backwards and she sat down with an 'oof'. The sleeve of the glove had wrapped itself around Penny's arm and was squeezing. Hard. The fingers were trying to claw at the girl's hands, which gripped the glove just below the thumb. All the time it was pushing towards her face.

Penny couldn't even cry out. She was too shocked. And also too focused on just trying to keep the thing at bay. In seconds she could feel her grip beginning to weaken, where it was squeezing her arm. If it managed to get free of her hands...

And then Frank was there. He had the secateurs in but he didn't even try to cut with them – he just rubbed the metal handles on the part of the glove wrapped around Penny's arm.

Straight away it shuddered and began to smoke. It stopped squeezing quite as hard, but it was still squeezing and straining to get at Penny's neck. It wasn't safe for her to let go of it yet, but now it wasn't going to force me let go of it.

Frank adjusted his grip on the secateurs, opening them. He grabbed the thumb of the glove with one hand, pulling it taut, then wedged it into the jaws of the secateurs while it struggled, clamping them shut. When the tip of the thumb was snipped off, a huge gout of black smoke rose from the glove and it shuddered all over, then it went limp.

Frank didn't stop, though. He pulled the glove off Penny's arm and began to methodically cut it into pieces. Each one dissolved into oily black smoke as the secateurs sawed their way through the material.

While Frank was doing that, Caro Elora and Pickatina helped the shaken girl to her feet. She was white faced. "Are you alright, Girl Pen?" asked Pickatina, peering anxiously at her face.

"I'm not hurt," she said. "It just surprised me, that's all. Was it another spite?"

"Yes," said Picaktina. "The Mistress is as cunning as an old fox. Even now she tries to leave nothing to chance. Who else would have thought we could defeat the wracks? Who else would have left another trap waiting, to slow us down?"

"I say we take it as a compliment," said Frank, finishing cutting the spite into pieces. He put the secateurs back in the bag and passed it to Penny. "Even now she's afraid that we'll defeat her if she doesn't do everything possible to slow us down."

"But that's the rub," said Paisley. "The Mistress of Lies knows that she does not need to defeat us to beat us. All she has to do now is slow us down and she will win."

"And soon," Penny said, trying to smile bravely for her friends. "Come on, we must be nearly there. Let's run. Maritz, can you follow the scent and lead the way?"

The wolf nodded and set of at a shambling trot along the corridor. Penny grabbed Frank by the elbow and followed, with Bud and Caro Elora hard on their heels. The others ran after them. Penny thought they'd manage it. They'd come so far, gone through so much – she couldn't imagine failing now. Not now.

On and on they ran, until the cold air that burst from their mouths in warm clouds of steam seemed to burn in their lungs. They turned onto a long curving passage lined not with normal trolls but with the enormous centurions.

"This is the final corridor," shouted Paisley. "Hurry. We are nearly there. Nearly at the heart of the maze."

But of course, Ribaldane had been ahead of them every step of the way, ever since they'd entered the Silent Palace. And she had beaten them to the centre. Penny could just see a doorway looming ahead when she heard it – a long, high, thin note that went on and on. It was the trumpet. Ribaldane was in the centre of the Silent Palace and she was blowing the Silver Trumpet.

And on both side, the enormous centurions began to move. The Black Legion was waking. They were too late.

Chapter Sixty Five

The Traitor

Long spears crossed in front of them. A pair of centurions blocked their path – massive and menacing, crouched as if about to pounce. Behind the friends, giant feet shuffled over ice. Penny didn't need to turn round to know more of the enormous trolls had blocked the corridor. There could be no retreat.

For a long moment, nobody moved. Nobody spoke. Penny hardly dared to breathe. She looked to her left, where Frank was standing. He was staring hard at the centurion right in front of him and trying to look fierce. But she saw his hand frantically clenching and unclenching at his side.

On her right, Pickatina seemed to be shrinking into her

clothes. Her eyes were huge, her mouth a wide O of fear and her hands were drawn up in front of her chest, like a mouse standing on its hind legs. She might have looked almost funny, but instead she looked pitiful – truly terrified. Penny felt so sorry for her friend that she almost forgot to feel scared for herself.

But Penny *was* scared. Of course she was scared. But she was curious too. And the longer the silence went on – the longer they stood there in the corridor with the unmoving centurions surrounding them – the more confident and curious Penny became. She realised that if Ribaldane was really certain of victory, she'd have ordered the Legion to kill them on sight. And she hadn't done that. So what was she actually going to do next?

One of the centurions ground out a noise, like a pebble being crushed beneath a metal roller. They all looked blankly at it for a moment, then Buddy spoke up. "It says we are to follow it to the main audience chamber," the little elf said, sounding scared. "It says that if we resist we will be killed."

The two spears were uncrossed and the centurions straightened, turning their backs on the humans and faeriefolk. They began to walk slowly down the corridor. Penny glanced over her shoulder and saw four more of the huge creatures, swords and axes in their hands, advancing on Broadwallow – who was at the back of the party, his sword drawn.

But then Frank was pulling on the girl's elbow, leading her along the corridor and she had to look forward again. There were no sounds of fighting, so she assumed Broadwallow was following as well. Frantically, Penny tried to think of what she could do.

They'd been so close. So very, *very* close. If they'd managed to go another hundred meters they'd have reached the hall before the Legion woke up. That's how close they were to the door.

It was a big door – and it was the first doorway in the Silent Palace that did actually have a door. All the others had been empty arches, with nothing to stop anyone walking through. But this door was big and solid, a dark wood bound with the same dark glassy material as the trolls' armour.

The centurion leading the way stopped and banged on the door, a deep booming knock echoing through the icy palace. The door creaked open slowly and then the enormous beast led in them into a massive room. It was much bigger than a football stadium – Orobus's cave might have larger, but only because it was deeper and taller. This was the biggest structure imaginable.

It wasn't like the rest of the Silent Palace. For one thing, it was warm – not just less cold than the rest of the Palace. It was really, properly warm. Penny nearly stopped shivering. And it wasn't lit by the same grey-white light filtering through the icy ceiling. It was dark. There were flickering torches around the walls and on stands at regular intervals across the floor, but they weren't bright – their weak light just seemed to fill the room with shadows, making it seem even bigger and more mysterious.

But Penny's attention wasn't on the shadowy corners of the room or the hundreds of tattered flags that hung from the ceiling. All of her attention was on the one brightly lit part of the massive chamber: the raised dais in the exact centre.

And there stood Ribaldane. She looked even more beautiful than the girl remembered, tall and slim in a gown of pure white silk, her crown twinkling in the bright light that shone down from above. As they got closer Penny realised that the dress was more spider silk and it was still crawling with small spiders. Ribaldane watched them approach, a superior smile on her face.

The group of friends stopped in front of the dais. It was made of a dark wood and there were four big steps leading up to it. There was an elaborate device of filigree wires standing on a low table in the centre – a thing like a dream-catcher but half a meter across. The trumpet was on the table beside it. As they came to a halt, Ribaldane walked to the edge of the platform.

"Well done, Captain," she said. "You managed to bring them to me after all. And I see you have disposed of your inconvenient brother. No argument about who will lead my forces now."

Everyone gasped and turned to look at Broadwallow, who marched past them, head held high, not looking at anyone. Penny looked at Pickatina and saw her face crumble, tears bursting from her eyes though the goblin didn't make a sound.

"And you, my former servant," Ribaldane said, switching her attention to Pickatina. "Even in your rebellion you have served me well. If you wish to have my forgiveness, I will give it to you and you can serve me again."

But Pickatina was not looking at Ribaldane. She wasn't even looking at Penny or Frank or the centurions that had formed a menacing semi-circle behind them. She could only stare mutely at Broadwallow, tears of betrayal running down her cheeks.

Ribaldane laughed. It wasn't the kind of laugh anyone would want to join in with. It was a cruel sound. It had knives in it.

"You… you… you filthy traitor!" shouted Frank. And he would have run at Broadwallow, but Paisley grabbed him by both elbows. Again, Penny marvelled at how strong the whip-thin pixie was. Frank was taller than Paisley and much heavier, but there was no way the boy could go anywhere once the pixie was holding him back. He just hung his head.

"Ah yes, brave Frank," said Ribaldane silkily, gloating. "You escaped the snake but here we are again. You really don't learn, do you? I wonder… what shall I feed you to this time?"

One of the centurions husked out a noise. That got Ribaldane's attention. She drew herself up, looking regal and noble and proud. Then she rattled off a reply in a guttural, harsh croak – it was hard to believe such an ugly sound could come from such a lovely face. But then again, thought Penny, knowing what Ribaldane was really like, perhaps it wasn't such a surprise.

The girl looked down at Buddy and mouthed 'what did she say?' But before the elf could answer, Ribaldane was speaking again. This time she was speaking to Penny.

"Still plotting, Penelope," she sneered. "Do you still think keeping secrets makes you special? What did you say to the elf?"

"I asked him what you said to the trolls," she replied.

"That is none of your concern," she replied haughtily.

"I think it is," the girl said. And she looked Ribaldane straight in the eyes and shouted, "Centurions, seize her."

And two huge creatures took two steps towards the dais.

Ribaldane rasped out another command in the nasty troll language. The centurions stopped in their tracks, like robots suddenly switched off. The witch looked at Penny, rage and hatred twisting her beautiful features into an ugly mask.

"Very clever, you motherless brat," she hissed. "My control over the Legion is not complete. But that is why I had Broadwallow bring so many of your friends here with you.

"Captain," she snapped the order. "Bring one of them here. I want you to show Penelope what happens to those who defy me."

Broadwallow slowly turned to look at the girl – his face was a picture of misery. Then he looked up at Ribaldane. "I cannot, Mistress," he said. "I was wrong to bring them. I was wrong to kill my brother. I was wrong to trust in you. I was..."

But the hobgoblin's words were cut off as Ribaldane waved a dismissive hand. Broadwallow sank to his knees, clutching at his neck and gasping for breath. Pickatina shrieked. "He has been fitted with a throttle," she cried. "Why did I not know? Cousin..."

She took a step forwards but Ribaldane thrust out her arm, uttering a short, high, wavering note. A flash of light shot from her fingers, hitting Pickatina and knocking her to the floor.

And then Frank somehow got free of Paisley's grasp. Before Penny realised what was happening he rushed at the steps to the dais and leapt at Ribaldane with the dagger Queen Celestia had given him held in his hands.

Chapter Sixty Six

The Battle

Ribaldane croaked a command in troll as Frank flew towards her and she hopped sideways, out of his way. The centurions were moving towards Frank but straight away Penny shouted at them. "Centurions, protect the humans!" she cried. "Seize Ribaldane. Ignore her orders. She is not a human."

Ribaldane cried out in rage and stabbed her fingers in the girl's direction… but even before her arm was fully extended and her spell had been uttered, a centurion was standing in front of Penny, with a round shield raised. How could such a huge creature move so quickly and quietly? There was a clang as the spell hit its shield, followed by a hiss and a distant bang as it ricocheted off across the vast hall.

Ribaldane croaked another command in troll, but Penny couldn't see what was going on – the centurion was blocking her view completely. Paisley was clanging like a great church bell and Caro Elora tinkling in alarm. Maritz was snarling and Bud was shouting something but Penny couldn't make anything out.

She saw half the centurions behind her turn away from the dais. In case Ribaldane had given them another order to attack her friends, the girl shouted at them again.

"Centurions, seize Ribaldane," she cried. "She is not a human. Repeat, she is not a human." She said it that way because she'd heard men say that in war films. The centurions all grated out a short noise, with a sound like a dozen walls collapsing – they'd repeated what the girl had said. She heard Ribaldane shriek in fury, but still couldn't see anything because of the huge centurion standing in front of her. So she took a decision – and got out the skipping rope.

She skipped up. She went almost straight up into the air. She'd gotten pretty good at this three-dimensional skipping, after using the magic rope so much. She cleared the top of the centurion's head and saw Ribaldane edging backwards across the dais as Paisley, Maritz and Frank advanced cautiously towards her. Pickatina was lying in a heap on the floor, with Caro Elora tending her. Broadwallow was still rolling around, clutching his neck. She couldn't see Buddy anywhere.

The centurions had all halted. Penny decided to try

commanding them again. "Centurions, seize Ribaldane," she shouted. And this time they moved with one purpose, striding rapidly towards the dais. Ribaldane hissed, raised one arm, turned on her heel and...

She grew. She turned faster and faster, twisting and turning and writhing. Getting larger and larger. She span away all the way to the edge of the platform and when she stopped spinning she was nearly as tall as a centurion.

But as soon as she'd realised what was happening, Penny had started to run. She skipped straight at the witch – and got up to a really good speed. Just as Ribaldane turned back, a triumphant grin on her now-massive face, the girl cannoned into her with the bubble, hitting her squarely on her beautiful forehead. There was nothing Ribaldane could do – she was knocked backwards. And as she was right on the edge of the dais, she fell off it, hitting the icy floor of the hall with a resounding thwack.

For a second Penny was exultant – she thought this was going to be simple, that she could defeat Ribaldane without any help from her friends, let alone the centurions of the Black Legion. As if the mighty Mistress of Lies would turn out to be no more dangerous than a centaur. How wrong she was...

As Penny skipped round in a long, steep turn to line up another charge at Ribaldane, a blast of flame shot past her right ear, bending around the bubble. Ribaldane had shot fire at her. None of the flames had got through the bubble – but the heat of the fire had. Penny cried out and almost dropped the skipping rope's handle. Luckily she didn't, because that would have made the bubble vanish for sure and the girl was about four metres up in the air – falling from that high would have really hurt.

Then the centurions surrounded Ribaldane. For a second she was lost to view as the trolls crowded round her. Then there was a terrific flash of light and the centurions were thrown backwards as if they were just dolls. Some hit the floor and didn't move.

"Frank," Penny shouted, "Help Broadwallow – like the Professor. Do it now. I'll take Ribaldane."

And she did, too – she was skipping down as fast as she could, really low to the floor now. The giant Ribaldane was just getting to her feet when the bubble smacked into her again. She didn't get knocked flying this time – but she staggered backwards and Penny was right behind her, hitting her again. The girl bounced the witch across the floor of the hall, banging hard into her two or three times before finally misjudging things and just clipped her with the bubble because she was flying too high.

Penny turned as quickly as she could. Because she was rushing and panicking a little, she nearly messed up. The rope caught on the toes of her left foot and for a dreadful second the child thought she was going to trip and stop skipping and lose the bubble and tumble from the air – she was high above the hall at this point. But somehow she managed to stumble onwards and regain her rhythm again.

But then Ribaldane was on her feet. Six centurions were closing in on her fast, but the witch threw back her head and flung out an arm – a crackling blue light burst from her fingers and zapped to the nearest centurion. Lightning! The huge troll stopped where he was, seemed to shrink in on himself for a second, then he exploded.

Ribaldane tried shouting an order at the other centurions, but they kept advancing on her. Clearly, once Penny had made them repeat that the witch wasn't human, they must believed it. The five remaining centurions were close to Ribaldane, arms reaching to grab her. She turned on her heel again, spinning out of their grasp and growing even larger. Now when she turned back to face them she must have been six metres tall – her head was almost touching the ceiling.

Which was good, because Penny was skipping along just below the ceiling. She hit Ribaldane on the side of her huge head. This time when she fell, she knocked two of the centurions to the floor, squashing them. But the others grabbed her arms and legs.

Penny glanced down and saw Frank and Paisley kneeling next to Broadwallow. The little pixie had his head thrown back, arms out straight, straining every muscle in his body as he pulled at the throttle around the hobgoblin's neck. She couldn't see what Frank was doing as he crouched beside the hobgoblin, but Penny guessed he was sawing away at the evil chain with the secateurs, making sure not to touch Broadwallow with the death metal.

Caro Elora was helping Pickatina to her feet. The goblin looked a funny shade of grey-green. Whatever spell Ribaldane had thrown at her was clearly taking its time to wear off.

There was a muted bang, followed by a series of loud clangs. Penny was still turning to get another run at Ribaldane, but looking over a shoulder saw the witch standing up, the smouldering remains of the centurions scattered around her.

Then the girl heard a roar and, looking back, saw Broadwallow leap to his feet. Frank and Paisley were struggling with the throttle but, now it wasn't choking him, the hobgoblin seemed bent only on getting his revenge on Ribaldane. She was now almost three times his size, but Broadwallow was rushing straight towards his former mistress with his sword held high.

She was more than ready for him. "Enough," Ribaldane shouted in a voice like thunder. She waved a hand and suddenly an icy chill grip Penny. She couldn't move. She'd stopped skipping – but somehow the bubble hadn't disappeared. She'd just stopped going forwards and was hanging in midair. She tried to cry out, but it was impossible. All she could move was her eyes.

Looking down she saw her friends were frozen too. Pickatina had been caught mid-step, so she was stuck in a silly pose. Frank had a rigid grin of triumph in his face and the smoking remains of the throttle in his hand. Broadwallow had been petrified in mid-charge, sword raised above his head.

The giant Ribaldane advanced towards Penny, casually plucking Broadwallow's sword from his grasp as she passed – it looked like a toy knife in her huge hand, even though the blade was actually longer than the girl was tall. Ribaldane reached up her other hand and plucked the bubble from the air, holding it as if it was an apple she was about to bite. Penny noticed that the spiders on the witch's silky gown were now the size of cats. If she could have moved, she would have shuddered.

Ribaldane looked into the bubble and smiled. It was strange, seeing her so large. Her eyes were the size of Penny's head.

"Once again I have you right where I want you – in the palm of my hand, Penelope," she said. And she tightened her grip on the sphere, sinews standing out in her arm as she tried to crush it. A frown flickered across her face as the impervious ball withstood her efforts. "How tedious," she sighed. "Well, I shall have to find another way to burst your bubble."

Chapter Sixty Seven

The Wheel of Destiny

Ribaldane held the bubble beside her head and shook it, like a granny trying to hear the pips rattle in an apple. Penny felt sick, but still she couldn't move – it was as if she'd been turned to stone. The witch peered closely at the bubble again, beautiful face huge and distorted slightly by the forcefield. She looked scary.

Suddenly Penny was falling. Ribaldane had dropped her! The bubble hit the floor and bounced, rolling across the room over and over. And the girl was fixed in one position within it, so she was rolling over and over, feeling sicker and sicker.

She ended up resting against the wall in a dark corner, upside down. Penny was feeling very ill. Ribaldane walked towards her. The witch got close, swung back her foot and kicked the bubble. Penny ricocheted off the wall and bounced away across the hall. Now she knew what a teddy that had been through a washing machine must have felt like. At least when she stopped rolling she was more or less the right way up this time

As she walked across the hall, Ribaldane appeared to steam and shrink, gradually returning to her normal size. She was smiling, but her eyes were deadly. "I do enjoy our little games, Penelope," she said. But then she suddenly stopped smiling. "But the time for playing is past now. I need you to do one more job for me. One more favour, just like when you fetched me the trumpet.

"And you'll have to hurry," she added. "Soon the soldiers of the Legion will begin to arrive to muster in this hall. You don't have to worry – they won't hurt you or Frank. But your little goblin friends now... The Legion won't like them. At all."

Her voice dropped to a lethal whisper. "And you do not want to make the mistake of testing my patience further with the skipping sphere. Understand? I see you have removed the throttle, but that just means I will kill you outright, then use Frank to do my bidding."

Ribaldane moved her hands and hissed strangely, like whispering a poem while breathing in. A warm tingling spread through Penny's body. She realised she was going to be able move again any second.

Ribaldane looked at her. "Don't risk it, Penelope," she said. "My patience is almost exhausted. I meant it when I said I would kill you – I still have Frank, if I have to use him." Her blank expression was terrifying. Penny knew she was serious.

So as the tingling turned to pins and needles, and Penny realised she could move again, she didn't try to keep skipping. The bubble wavered, then flickered and vanished. The girl didn't try to bring it back – didn't try to knock Ribaldane over. Just stood, staring resentfully as a hateful smile of triumph slowly crossed the witch's beautiful face again.

"Good girl," she said, leaning on Broadwallow's sword. "Now, we need to hurry. Get over to the wheel on the platform."

Meekly, Penny went to do as she was told. But it wasn't enough for Ribaldane. "Leave the skipping rope there, Pen," she said, her voice flat and menacing. Sighing, the girl let the rope fall to the floor, stepped over it and walked past Ribaldane.

She was followed to the platform by the threatening skirsh of the tip of Broadwallow's sword being dragged along the floor by Ribaldane. She must have been incredibly strong even when she was normal sized to carry the huge weapon.

Penny climbed the steps and went over to the low table in the middle of the dais. It was higher than it had looked – nearly the height of the kitchen table in the Little House. The silver trumpet stood on the edge, but in the middle of the table was the strange wheel-like device. It was quite big: perhaps half a metre across. The outside rim of the circle was a fairly wide, flat band of dull grey metal, but inside it was a complex pattern made of forty-two fine strands of the same grey metal, stretched between hooks inside of the outer circle. It looked a bit like a dreamcatcher.

Ribaldane hadn't climbed up onto the dais. She was standing beside Frank, holding the hilt of Broadwallow's sword in two hands, with the wide blade resting casually on her shoulder. When she saw that she had the girl's attention, she smiled.

"Let's understand each other, Penelope," she said. "I give the orders and you follow them. You follow them exactly or bad things happen."

"You're bluffing," Penny said, her throat dry. "You won't hurt Frank in case I don't co-operate and you have to kill me. You'll keep him alive. You want a spare."

"Frank?" laughed Ribaldane. "My dear child, of course I wouldn't do anything to hurt Frank. Yet. But this common little pixie standing beside him... Believe me, Penelope, I won't hesitate to chop him into dog-meat unless you do exactly what I tell you to do. Understand?"

The girl nodded, chilled to the bone. "What is that?" she asked, nodding at the funny dreamcatcher thing.

"It is the Wheel of Destiny," Ribaldane replied. "It what truly gives control over the Legion. Or rather, that controls the limits to their behaviour. Since you have stopped them heeding me, even though I blew the trumpet, you must re-configure the wheel to give control to me."

"But how?" Penny wailed. "I've never seen it before. You can't hurt Paisley just because I don't know how to work it."

"Calm down," said the witch. "I know how it works. If you do exactly as I say you have nothing to fear. Your friend will be fine if you follow my instructions."

Ribaldane was smiling sweetly. But Penny didn't think she could believe her – she was afraid that, even if she did exactly what she was told, there was no way Paisley would be fine. She didn't think any of her friends would be fine once Ribaldane got her way. The problem was, if she didn't do as she was told, then Paisley would definitely suffer – there was no doubt about that.

Suddenly there was a banging from the back of the hall. Someone or something was trying to open the door. Ribaldane's head whipped round to look at it. And something scuttled across the floor by the dais. Before Penny could turn to get a look at it, the witch was shouting at her again.

"That is the Legion," she said. "I have sealed the door and it will stay shut... for a while. But it will not stay shut forever. You must hurry now, Penny. I am no longer the greatest threat to your friends – the trolls outside that door are. Will you do what I say?"

Reluctantly, Penny nodded. She had no choice. "You'll have to explain it carefully. Don't rush me or confuse me."

"I have to rush you, Penny," said Ribaldane. "We don't have much time. But we will do this one step at a time. Now, you will need to move the wires within the wheel. You need to reconfigure them into a different shape, using the hooks on the inside – do you see that some of them currently hold no wires?"

Penny peered at the wheel. She could see that. "Why didn't you do this yourself?" she asked.

"Because it is made of the death metal, of course," snapped Ribaldane. "Concentrate, child. We don't have time to chatter. Do you see the two wires that cross in the middle?"

Penny nodded, but really had to force herself to listen to the instructions. Her mind was racing. Ribaldane couldn't touch the wheel because it was made of death metal – and suddenly Penny dared to hope that there would still be a way to defeat her.

"The wires, Penny," Ribaldane snapped. "Do you see them?"

"Yes, I see them," she replied. "Crossed in the middle of the wheel. Right there. What do you want me to do with them?"

"Nothing!" Ribaldane sounded panicky. "Whatever else you do, you must never, ever move either of those wires – understand? Move those and the Legion will be truly free – free to ignore the call of the trumpet, free to ignore the restraints of the wheel. Free to kill humans if they want, as they did before the wheel was created."

"I thought you were going to use the Legion to invade our world and kill humans," I said.

Ribaldane hissed. "There is a difference between trolls being ordered to kill something and trolls being *free* to kill anything and everything, child. The Legion is a weapon only as long as it is disciplined and bound by wheel and trumpet. But move those central strings and the trolls will be free. They will kill every living thing they meet and when nothing else is left alive, they kill each other. So Penny, never, EVER touch those central wires."

"Okay, I get it," Penny said. "Never move the crossed wires in the middle. So which ones do you want me to move, then?"

Chapter Sixty Eight

The Survivor

"Alright, let's go to work," said Ribaldane testily. "You need to look at the wheel and find the patterns. There are three triangles within this pattern that have sides of equal lengths – do you see them?"

Penny stared at the wires. Most seemed to form triangles of some sort. But she couldn't see patterns – it was just a jumble of lines of grey metal. She felt sweat break out on her brow.

"Concentrate, Penny," shouted Ribaldane. "Look through the wheel, not directly at it. Let the patterns come to you. All three of the triangles point downward, though not one of them touches the very base of the circle. Can you see them yet?"

"No," she wailed. "I can't see them at all. I..."

Something had moved, down on the floor of the hall. Something small had disturbed the shadows by the remains of one of the centurions. Penny's eyes snapped there, trying to see what it was. She stared there, but whatever it was didn't move again.

But because she was looking through the wheel, suddenly she could see the triangles. All three of them rested on points to the left of the lowest part of the circle. She kept looking through the wheel, afraid that if she tried to look at them directly, she'd lose sight of them. Slowly, cautiously, she reached out a trembling hand towards them.

"Good," whispered Ribaldane. "You see them, child – I can tell. You must move them. One string at a time. They must move to the other side of the base point. The one that is closest must become the furthest away. That is the one to move first. Start with the lowest point and unhook it. Can you do that Penny?"

Silently, Penny nodded. She didn't want to do it, but couldn't see what else she could do – not while Ribaldane was standing beside Paisley with Broadwallow's sword. But she was afraid that if she moved too much or too quickly, or even if she spoke, she would lose sight of the triangles completely.

Her hand was on the bottom hook where the triangle was connected. She tried to budge it but it was taut as a bowstring. There was no way she could move it. "It's stuck," she said to Ribaldane – and she could hear the terror in her own voice.

"No it is not," the witch hissed angrily. "It cannot be."

"It must have rusted in place," Penny said desperately. "All the water and ice and snow at the North Pole – it's not a place you want to keep anything iron. It must have rusted in place."

"Just pull it you pathetic, moaning, weak human," shouted Ribaldane furiously. "It will move. Just pull it or so help me this pixie is going to lose an arm, right now!"

Sobbing with fear, fuelled by terror, but still not daring to look directly at the wheel, Penny stared into the dark shadows on the far side of the hall and yanked the string as hard as she could. And it moved – not much, but it moved. She grunted and pulled again, the fine wire cutting into her fingers. She pulled again and it came free. Before she could stop herself, she looked at it.

Then there was a renewed pounding on the door, louder and heavier than before. "Hurry up, Penny," said Ribaldane. She was trying not to sound angry or threatening, just encouraging – though the girl could sense the anger simmering beneath her cheerful tone. "Hurry up now. There's not much time left."

Penny looked back at the wheel – but couldn't see the triangles now. The pattern had vanished. A small moan escaped her lips. Ribaldane must have realised what had happened.

"Don't look at it, Penny," she called, her voice oily and sweet. "Look past it – look to the torches on the far wall. If you stare at the wheel, you'll never see it. Look through the wheel and look at the wall. Just let the patterns come to you."

Fighting back tears of pain and terror, the girl tried to do it. She looked through the wheel... and again saw something move on the floor. Something small. And this time she recognised it and she almost gasped. The small shape was Bud.

As Penny watched, amazed, the little elf crept stealthily across the floor. And suddenly the patterns in the wheel snapped back into place in the corner of the girl's eye. Still focusing on Bud, she moved the wire. At least, she tried to. She could see the hook it needed to go, but just couldn't make it stretch all the way to get there. She grunted and tugged harder at it, the wire cutting into her fingers again. It hurt a lot. But just as she was about to give up, she felt it catch on the hook. Gasping with pain, she gave it one final tug and hooked it over.

"Very good, Penny," said Ribaldane. "Now quickly, move the other two points of that triangle. Follow the wires and move them round – bring it back into balance as fast as you can."

A roar came from somewhere outside the hall, a terrible multi-throated cry of rage and there was a hammering on the door. An elephant stampede would sound something like that, Penny thought. She tried to shut it out of her mind and concentrate on the wires. And all the time she watched Bud creeping across the hall. As she unhooked the second point of the triangle, he reached the far side of the hall. The girl couldn't see what he was doing there, but as she strained and whimpered to hook the wire on to its second new point, the elf bent down and was lost from view in the darkest shadows at the foot of the wall.

Penny kept scanning the far side of the hall, trying to get another sign of the little elf. But she'd puffed and cried her way through the agony of moving the third and final point of the first triangle before she saw him again. As she eased it on to its new hook, she cried out in pain and caught sight of the little man.

"Well done, Penelope," said Ribaldane, sounding smug and insincere. "You're doing really well. Now, just two more to do."

Penny looked at her, holding up my hands. "I can't do any more – the wires are cutting into my hands."

But Ribaldane just smiled at her, looking radiant and young and lovely. "But this sword will be cutting into your little pixie friend if you don't, Penny," she said cheerfully. "We don't want that, now, do we? Come on – just a little more. You shouldn't worry about a few little scratches from the wires. Those will heal easily enough. I promise you that a sword-blow to Paisley's head will not heal so easily."

As she said that, there was another huge pounding on the door of the hall. "Hurry, Penny, or we will all be dead," Ribaldane hissed, suddenly sounding scared. "That first triangle was the one protecting humans from the Legion. Unless you realign the rest of the controls, there will be nothing – nothing – to restrain the trolls and we shall all be doomed when they break in here."

Shuddering with fear and pain, Penny returned her gaze to the wheel. Or rather, to looking through the wheel and trying to spot Buddy. He was sneaking slowly back towards the middle of the hall. The girl still had no idea what the elf could have been up to. As she watched him creeping from shadow to shadow, the triangles in the pattern sprang into focus again. Wincing and trembling, Penny extended her bleeding hands towards the wires.

"Stop!" cried Ribaldane. "This time you must move middle triangle, starting with the upper-left point first."

Nodding but trying to watch Bud – without giving Ribaldane any clue that he was there – she gripped the wire. He could the little man move when everyone else was still frozen?

Penny's hand stung as soon as it closed around the wire. She cried out, but didn't want to show weakness in front of Ribaldane. So she gritted her teeth and pulled as hard as she could. As Buddy crept past Broadwallow, she unhooked the first point of the triangle.

This second triangle moved more quickly than the first one. It wasn't any easier or less painful, but Penny had mastered the technique – and fear helped her overcome the pain. The pounding and roaring at the door was getting louder and more insistent all the time.

Also, Penny wanted Ribaldane to concentrate on her. Bud was crawling slowly across the icy floor towards Pickatina… but if the witch saw him, she'd kill him. "Very good, Penelope," she said. "Not much more to do."

"My hands," the girl said. "I don't think I can do any more."

"You have to," hissed Ribaldane. "Show me your hands."

Penny glanced at her hands. Six raw lines had been cut into the flesh of the fingers of each hand and they were bleeding freely. She held them up to show the witch.

"Well done, Penelope," said Ribaldane. "I bet you never knew you could do this. See how I've helped you become stronger? Even so, I believe you may struggle with this last one without more assistance. Very well."

And she took a deep breath and then puffed it out in a pale blue cloud. The warmth of it closed around Penny's hands like gloves. When the girl looked at them again, the cuts made by the wire had been healed.

Chapter Sixty Nine
The Black Legion

The pounding on the door was more ferocious, but it had taken on a different quality. It was rhythmic rather than random. Penny heard vague roaring sounds like a sledgehammer smashing on stones. Someone on the other side of the door was giving orders – shouting something like "one, two, three... *hit!*" And then the door would shudder beneath a huge blow.

"A centurion has arrived," Ribaldane told her. "The trolls at the door will be organised now. You have to hurry – that door will not hold much longer. You must reset the final triangle or I will be powerless to protect us once they break through the door. They are ready to fight for themselves."

Penny nodded. She turned back to the wheel and tried to look through it, to let the patterns emerge when she unfocused her eyes and looked beyond the muddle of wires... but they didn't appear. Penny was really scared now. More scared than she'd ever been.

"Come on, Pen," said Ribaldane. Except she didn't seem to be Ribaldane any more. The girl glanced away from the wheel and saw... her dad, standing there. "Come on, Pen," he seemed to say. "You can do this. You know what to do."

"Yes," she said. And she did know what to do. Because now she was sure. Ribaldane had tried to trick her, disguising herself as Penny's dad. And she was convinced that there was some bigger trick going on, somehow. She was the Mistress of Lies – and though she hadn't worked out what it was, the girl was convinced the witch was lying to her about something.

She looked back through the wheel. Took a deep breath, breathed out. And looked through it.

And saw Bud. The little elf was creeping up towards Ribaldane. He was just by Frank's legs, edging forwards and dragging something. It was the skipping rope!

Penny couldn't just stand there staring at the elf, or Ribaldane would get suspicious. She let her gaze lift slightly, so she could no longer see Bud – and this brought the triangles into view. Hurrying, she reached out and grabbed one and pulled one of the wires. Ribaldane let out a roar.

"What are you doing, child?" she demanded, looking like her old self again but with an ugly frown contorting her beautiful face.

"Sorry, sorry," she cried. "I got confused. I took the wrong one. I'll just put it back. It's... It's a bit stiff. Hold on..."

"You're trying to hook it on the wrong place, Penny," hissed Ribaldane and the girl could tell the witch was really trying not to sound cross. "Come on – just take a deep breath and slow down. We need to hurry but rushing is just making things take longer. Stay calm and you'll be fine. Now when you're ready, hook that wire back where it came from – one hook over to the left. That's right... on that one. Come on now, you can do it."

Penny was confident that Ribaldane thought she was close to getting what she wanted. That's why she was being nice. Penny took as long as she could to hook the wire back where in place.

Slowly she began to look for the next strand that Ribaldane wanted her to remove. Really, she was looking through the wheel, trying to see Bud. There he was – lurking in the shadows behind Frank's leg, peeping nervously at Ribaldane. Penny still didn't know what he was up to, but she realised she had to distract the witch, or there was a good chance she'd spot the elf next time he moved.

So she took the strand in her hand and then turned to look at Ribaldane. "How do I know you're not lying to me?" she asked. "How do I know you won't just hurt us all anyway when I've done what you want?"

Ribaldane started as if she'd been poked with a pin. Penny hadn't sounded scared or even polite. She looked at the child and narrowed her eyes. There was a long pause before she spoke again.

"You don't know, Penelope. You have no guarantees at all. And I'm afraid I can give you none," she smiled. "Only the guarantee that if you don't do as I tell you, your friends will very soon regret it. Your stepbrother will regret it and, before I cut your head off, you too will regret it. So while you have no guarantee that I won't harm you when you're finished, I can guarantee pain now if you don't do as you're told. But when you've done what I want, I would have no need to hurt you."

Penny looked into her eyes and saw, lurking behind the innocent smile, a twist of cruelty. She knew that when this was done Ribaldane would hurt them all – just because she could. Just because she'd enjoy hurting them. But Penny had to pretended to go along with her for a moment longer. She looked through the wheel but couldn't see Bud.

Penny took a deep breath and reached for the wire. Suddenly she realised what Bud must have done – because she could see the skipping rope. He must have tied one end to Frank's ankle and snuck past in front of Ribaldane, trailing the rope behind him.

The door creaked as it was hit again and something cracked and flew across the room. Penny's eyes snapped to the door and saw it was sagging in one corner, shuddering as it was hit again.

"Hurry, child," snapped Ribaldane, sounding close to panic. "You must do it now. Right now. Or your friend dies."

Straining, gritting her teeth at the pain, Penny pulled the wire out and quickly hooked it in its new position. She wasn't looking at Ribaldane. She was watching the door twist on its hinges. She had the second wire in her hand, whimpering with pain as she pulled it free, when the door to the hall finally flew open. Penny tried desperately to ignore the trolls striding into the room while she hooked the wire onto its new place.

As she did, Ribaldane took a half-step forward.

And Buddy stood up in the shadows on the other side of the witch and pulled the skipping rope tight, lifting it off the floor just enough to catch Ribaldane's elegant foot. The witch staggered towards the dais, off balance and weighed down by Broadwallow's massive sword, which was still over her shoulder.

She half-turned, shrieking in fury at the elf, who had dropped the skipping rope and was running as fast as he could. Ribaldane dropped the huge sword and began to raise her arm to fire some sort of spell at Buddy.

Which was when Penny hit her over the head with the Wheel of Destiny.

She'd started to prepare herself from the moment she'd seen what Bud had done with the skipping rope. As soon as she'd seen the witch stumble, the girl had picked the heavy metal device from the table and rushed to the steps that led up to the dais. As Ribaldane turned to curse Bud, Penny smashed the wheel down onto the witch's beautiful head, ramming it down with both hands and forcing her head between the wires until she was wearing it like a collar.

Ribaldane shrieked and raised her hands to try to tear at the wheel, but it was no good. Smoke was rising from her hair and neck and she was shrinking before Penny's eyes. It was almost like watching the water drain from a bath, the way she wavered and diminished. She sank into a pile at the foot of the steps, a foetid stink filling the air as she was worn away by the death metal. In minutes there was nothing left.

It was only when Ribaldane was finally reduced to a small pile of spiderweb in a pool of smoking green liquid that Penny realised the hall was now full of gigantic black-armoured trolls. They stood in silent ranks, just staring at her. They seemed to absorb the light from all the torches hung on the walls, making the hall seem dark and crowded, menacing and very, very scary.

There was a patter of feet and Bud rushed up from the shadows on the far side of the hall. "Penny! Penny!" he cried. "Is that it? Is the witch dead? Hooray! Hooray!"

"Bud, what... how... why..." She had too many questions to know where to start. "How come she didn't manage to freeze you like all the others?"

"Oh, her feeble magic can't touch an elf – you should know that, Penny," he said. "We're small but we're ancient. We might not be strong but at least we're magic-proof. I didn't think I could do anything to stop her – especially when she was huge – but she couldn't do anything to hurt me either. Well, not unless she trod on me by mistake or hit me with that sword. So I hid. But when you dropped the rope I had an idea."

The girl looked around the hall nervously. The trolls were just standing there, watching her silently. They weren't moving at all. It was as if they were robots that had been switched off.

"Bud, what's going to happen now?" she asked. "Why aren't the trolls doing anything? And what's going to happen to Frank and the rest of our friends?"

"We will be fine in a moment, Girl Pen," said Pickatina, sounding sleepy. "The Mistress's spell will wear of directly."

"Hey! Who tied this to my leg?" shouted Frank, tugging at the skipping rope. Penny laughed.

"Why are the trolls standing here?" asked Broadwallow. "Where did they come from? Where is Ribaldane?"

"Ribaldane's dead," Penny said. "I hit her with the wheel – it's made of death metal and it finished her off."

Their jaws all dropped. Penny smiled modestly. "I couldn't have done it without Bud," she said. "He's the real hero."

"The trolls are awaiting your orders, Penny," said Pickatina, patting her on the arm. "Ribaldane may have been the one who sounded the trumpet to rouse them, but you killed her – you are their commander by right of conquest."

"But Ribaldane said the wheel was what really commanded the Legion and she was making me rewire it so she could have control of them," Penny said. "Will they do what I say?"

"Let's find out. It has to be worth a try," said Frank. "Tell them to return to their posts."

Penny cleared her throat. "Black Legion, do you hear me?"

"WE HEAR YOU PENELOPE OAKS," they roared, deafeningly loud. And they were speaking English, not troll.

"Am I your new commander?"

"YES, PENELOPE OAKS."

"All troops return to your stations. Centurions remain in the hall," she said.

"WE HEAR AND OBEY, PENELOPE OAKS," they roared.

And the trolls marched out – so quickly and silently it was like magic. One second the hall was full of the giant warriors, three seconds later there were about twenty five centurions left, standing around the outside walls. There were spread out with uneven gaps between them – but Penny guessed the spaces would have been occupied by the centurions Ribaldane had destroyed.

"Centurions, come closer," she ordered.

"WE HEAR AND OBEY, PENELOPE OAKS," they said. A second later they were all stood neatly in front of the dais. They'd barely seemed to move – they just crossed the distance from the walls to the centre of the hall in the blink of an eye.

"Centurions, provide instructions. How do I return the Black Legion to sleep?" she asked.

"THE WHEEL MUST BE SET AS IT WAS BEFORE, PENELOPE OAKS," they said, all together.

"Is that all I have to do?"

"IT IS ENOUGH. IT WILL CONFINE US TO THE PALACE. WE WILL SLEEP UNTIL WE ARE SUMMONED AND RELEASED AGAIN, PENELOPE OAKS."

"And you don't mind?" Penny asked. She suddenly felt almost sorry for them.

"WE HEAR AND WE OBEY. WE EXIST TO SERVE. WE WILL WAIT UNTIL WE ARE NEEDED, PENELOPE OAKS."

"Thank you, centurions," she said. "Return to your posts."

"WE HEAR AND OBEY, PENELOPE OAKS," they said. And seconds later they had all left the hall.

And then, finally, all her friends were crowding round her, hugging her and clapping her on the back. Paisley began to sing a song in his deep, bell-like voice and Caro Elora joined in with the high notes in her clear, tinkling voice.

"Come on, Penny," said Frank. "Let's sort this wheel thing out. Then we can go."

For a second she hesitated. "Do you think we should just leave them here? I mean, wouldn't it be cool to take a troll back with us? Or at least set them free?"

"No, Penny," said Pickatina gently. "You have seen what they are like. They need orders, all of the time, or they just rest silently. Even one troll would be a burden if you took it with you.

"And if you set them free – well, that was the fear that drove us here. If there were no constraints, they would seek out someone willing to lead them – and they would find someone willing to lead them to war. Worse, they would come to your world to find a human to lead them if you will not do it. The destruction could be terrible. The Legion must be returned to sleep. It is why we are here."

So Frank and Penny set the wheel back on its table on the dais. The girl stared through the wheel until she spotted the patterns again. With Frank helping her pull on the wires, she was able to reset the triangles to their original positions quite quickly. And though it was still hard, with the two of them pulling on the wires, neither actually cut their fingers.

Their friends were standing around at the bottom of the steps to the dais, smiling and looking relaxed. Even Broadwallow finally looked happy. Frank smiled, picking up the Silver Trumpet. "Let's get this back to where it belongs," he said.

"Are we all ready to go home?" Penny asked.

Pickatina looked at her and grinned. "Of course, Penny. You are the hero of the hour. Of course we're ready to go home."

So they did.

Epilogue
The Long Way Home

Of course, "going home" wasn't quite so simple as it sounds. It took the friends three days to get out of the Silent Palace, across the ice sheet escourted by Soren's wolves and down the stairs to the boat Ribaldane had taken from the Last Citadel. Pickatina could only charm a single narwhel to pull the boat, so it took them almost a week to sail to the Peninsula of Thorns.

The great dragon Orobus was waiting for them in the valley of ash outside the Last Citadel, looking healthy and glowing bright with renewed fire. The dragon took three days to reach Queen Celestia's palace, stopping on the way so Buddy, Paisley and Caro Elora could return to the Wild Wood and Broadwallow could stay with the Naga in Honeypatch. He had decided to leave the Queen's guard and take up farming.

As they flew south, the children began to worry about how long they'd been away. Even though time in Faerieland moved so differently to time in the human world, Frank began to worry that his mother was bound to notice they'd been gone too long.

He needn't have worried. They were welcomed as heroes when they reached the Faerie palace – but what cheered the children most was that when they were ushered into the throne room, Professor Mitchell was waiting with Queen Celestia.

"You've been gone for about two hours," he reassured them. "But now it's time to go back before Maggie does smell a rat." The professor took the Silver Trumpet, to return it to its secret storage place – along with Penny's skipping rope…

After the professor had left the room, The Queen made the children promise to leave their faerie capes in her palace and swear to keep their adventure secret. Just before she said goodbye, she told them they were free to visit Faerieland any time they pleased. Normal humans were still not allowed to cross from one world to the other, but heroes were always welcome.

Pickatina led the children to the Professor's personal door – a secret passage from the landing that led to a panel in one of his upstairs work rooms. They stood for a long moment in the darkness of the narrow corridor, then Frank coughed and hugged the little goblin.

"Goodbye, Pickatina," he said, slightly awkwardly. "Thank you for looking after us and helping us find our way around." He hurried out into the human world before she could reply.

The goblin took Penny's hands. "Girl Pen, I must be thanking you. For saving me, for saving my cousin, for saving the queen, my father… all of us."

The girl blushed. "I have to thank you, Pickatina. For believing in me, for being my friend."

They looked at each other for a long moment. Penny was on the verge of tears. Then they hugged, quite spontaneously. "Remember," whispered Pickatina. "You can come back. But nobody can know."

"Nobody can know," agreed Penny.

She turned and hurried through the door to Bradley Hall, to find Frank waiting for her. They rushed downstairs together, laughing and joking. Maggie raised an eyebrow as they tumbled into the kitchen, still chattering – but if it seemed unusual to her to see them together, she didn't say anything.

And that's when they really went home…

Printed in Great Britain
by Amazon.co.uk, Ltd.,
Marston Gate.